WAKE UP
AND
SMELL THE BEES

DONALD DEWEY

MILFORD
HOUSE

an imprint of Sunbury Press, Inc.
Mechanicsburg, PA USA

MILFORD
HOUSE

an imprint of Sunbury Press, Inc.
Mechanicsburg, PA USA

For information about special discounts for bulk purchases, please contact Sunbury Press Orders Dept. at (855) 338-8359 or orders@sunburypress.com.

To request one of our authors for speaking engagements or book signings, please contact Sunbury Press Publicity Dept. at publicity@sunburypress.com.

ISBN: 978-1-62006-252-4 (Trade paperback)

Library of Congress Control Number: 2018940785

FIRST MILFRED HOUSE PRESS EDITION: April 2018

Product of the United States of America
0 1 1 2 3 5 8 13 21 34 55

Set in Bookman Old Style
Designed by Crystal Devine
Cover by Lawrence Knorr
Edited by Lawrence Knorr

Continue the Enlightenment!

For David and Eileen

RS: *Last time you mentioned "imagining" the accident.*

PF: *Just before you threw me out.*

RS: *We were running out of time. I didn't want to cut you off in the middle.*

PF: *Right.*

RS: *So, tell me. What have you imagined?*

PF: *What I said. The accident comes into my mind. The last seconds or so before it happened.*

RS: *Are we talking about nightmares or when you're awake?*

PF: *When I'm awake. I'm reading the paper and suddenly lose sight of the print. I start thinking about it. Takes forever to get through* **Dilbert**.

RS: *And these details you imagine, are they what you learned from witnesses or what you thought had to have happened?*

PF: *I told you, I imagine it!*

RS: *From what point?*

PF: *Jennifer was already on the road in the Villager. Susan was in the back. She refused to drive alone with Susan up front.*

RS: *Did you agree with that?*

PF: *Sure, I did. When you have a driver who's splitting her attention between the road and a child next to her …*

RS: **Driver**? **Child**?

PF: *You know what I mean.*

RS: *Then say it and we'll both know.*

PF: *Funny.*

RS: *I didn't intend it to be.*

PF: *Okay, okay. Jennifer was a better driver when she didn't have anything else to think about. We all are, aren't we?*

RS: *So, you never had reservations about your wife's driving.*

PF: *Did I say I did?*

RS: *It seems a point worth clarifying.*

PF: *I'm not blaming her for what happened!*

RS: *Go on with what you imagine.*

PF: *She's on the road. She's still pissed off at me for drinking too much and collapsing in her father's guest room. She's pissed off at the old man, too. If he hadn't been so thick-headed about making his Christmas turkey without her help, we would've eaten a couple of hours earlier and I wouldn't have gotten so sloshed.*

RS: *So, Jennifer blames her father for you drinking too much, too?*

PF: *It's my fantasy. Let me have it.*

RS: *Go ahead.*

PF: *Susan's in the back. She keeps asking why they couldn't have gotten me up so everyone could go home together. Jennifer's tired of the question.*

RS: *So, Jennifer's a little frazzled.*

PF: ***I'm*** *saying she was.* ***I'm*** *the one imagining that.*

RS: *In this picture you have.*

PF: *How could she not be?*

RS: *Stands to reason.*

PF: *Which means what? It's irrational to think so?*

RS: *Jennifer is on the road.*

PF: *Yeah. The damn snow finally stopped, but the highway is like an ice rink.*

RS: *Jennifer is driving cautiously?*

PF: *She always did, with or without Susan in the car. It took her five minutes to go from the garage down to the corner.*

RS: *But she's still steaming about you and her father.*

PF: *Sure as hell acted like it … I mean …*

RS: *Go ahead. How you see it.*

PF: *She comes to the intersection with Delaware. There's nothing coming either way, but she stops to give it that extra second. You know, like that strong premonition you get sometimes that there* ***might*** *be something speeding up to the corner just out of her sight. She stops, sees nothing, then accelerates too much. The front-wheel drive is good for traction, but it sways some- times when you gun it like that. She must have panicked, and the ice underneath did the rest.*

RS: *This what you imagined or what you're theorizing now?*

PF: *What I see! Her goddamn brown boots never know how to do anything halfway. She loses control—just a little, but enough* to slam down on the brake with those boots. Now she's spinning. Susan starts yelling in the back. Jennifer shouts, tells her not to worry, to squeeze herself into a corner and duck her head. I'm thinking, What the hell kind of advice is **that**? She's not going down in a plane, for Christ sake! Like Susan's supposed to wait for the oxygen mask to drop down to her? Jennifer wasn't thinking. She had no right to say that.

RS: **Right**?

PF: I mean she was panicked, she wasn't thinking clearly. And what are we talking about anyway? Nanoseconds? Who thinks that clearly in so little time? I wouldn't. Would you?

RS: But you have.

PF: Why?

RS: You're a cop. I would suppose you've been in more than one situation like you're describing. Chasing somebody, for instance.

PF: Jennifer wasn't a cop.

RS: That's right. Go on.

PF: She can't stop the skid. She's cursing a blue streak, and that just scares Susan more. Susan is screaming in the back—that yowl of hers when she cuts her knee and wants us to stop the bleeding. Jennifer tells her to be quiet, let her think. But she's already rolling over and then she's thinking she's still alive. But the thump against the back of her seat is Susan bouncing on the floor. Even if Jennifer comes out of it ...

RS: What, Paul?

PF: She knows it's too late for Susan.

RS: She's so sure?

PF: She doesn't want to be, but she is.

RS: And what?

PF: By the time the Villager stops rolling, she wants to be dead, too.

RS: And she is?

PF: What's that supposed to mean?

RS: I'm just listening to you.

PF: We should have taken the Subaru.

RS: Another car?

PF: My car. It's all-wheel traction.

RS: *And that's what you regret most—not taking the Subaru in-*
stead of the Villager to your father-in-law's?

PF: *Fuck you.*

RS: *I'm asking. The thing you take out of all these moments of*
playing it back to yourself is the car?

PF: *The Subaru would've handled the ice.*

RS: *Because you would have been driving it?*

PF: *I didn't say that.*

RS: *But it's your car. Jennifer drove the Villager and you drove*
the Subaru. So, if you had the Subaru, you would have been
behind the wheel. The accident wouldn't have happened at all.

PF: *You're not going to get me to say I blame her.*

RS: ***Her.***

PF: *It wasn't Jennifer, it was the goddamn car!*

RS: *So, sue.*

PF: *Yeah. Will do.*

RS: *We hear about flimsier lawsuits every day.*

PF: *That's not the point.*

RS: *What is the point?*

PF: *You're supposed to tell me, aren't you?*

RS: *If we work at it successfully, you'll tell yourself.*

PF: *I don't want to work at it.*

RS: *Then we have a handicap.*

PF: *I can deal with it.*

RS: *With what? The accident? The loss of your wife and daughter?*
Or the feeling that maybe your wife was responsible for it?

PF: *Whatever you like.*

RS: *Susan dies first, so Jennifer's at fault. When she dies after-*
ward, it might even be her sentence.

PF: *You've got a nasty mind, Doc.*

RS: *But at bottom not even Jennifer was responsible, right?*

PF: *I didn't say she was.*

RS: *No, it was those "goddamn brown boots," not her.*

PF: *Whatever that means.*

RS: *I'm just asking. In this picture you have, Jennifer's respon-*
sible, but not really. You don't want to go that far. You drink
yourself to sleep, but it's your father-in-law's fault for taking

forever to put your Christmas dinner on the table. If you'd had the Subaru instead of the Villager, none of it would have happened. Jennifer crashes, but it's her boots. See what I'm saying? We're always kind of stopping at third base.

PF: *I'll take it. Maybe that's how I deal with it all.*

RS: *What is it exactly you can deal with, Paul?*

PF: *All of it. I've dealt with ...*

RS: *What?*

PF: *Never mind.*

RS: *Worse? Is that what you were going to say?*

PF: *Whatever.*

RS: *I don't think so. What could be worse?*

PF: *Like you say, I'm a cop.*

RS: *Or not.*

PF: *That a threat?*

RS: *I'd prefer not to make it a recommendation.*

CHAPTER 1

Don't get shot. Anywhere. It hurts. The doctor who treated my arm mistook me for John Wayne and actually called it "only a flesh wound." I wanted to shove his gauze roll down his throat. *Only a flesh wound.* As opposed to what? A spirit wound? Maybe 25-year-old interns in Emergency Rooms should have just gone and fucked themselves. But as earnest Michael Forte, M.D., went about covering up the numb blood-smeared design of Florida down from my left elbow I didn't say that any more than I attacked him with his gauze. Instead, I remembered what my grandmother always said when confronted with dimwits like Michael Forte, M.D. God bless, she had said, meaning she didn't want God spending a second thinking about blessing them. This was no small thing for somebody from Limerick, where it was second nature for everyone to be blessing the mailman for delivering postcards and the landlord for walking away with the monthly rent. "*God bless now, and have a good day.*" Vice versa, not being genuine about extending a blessing to nitwits in the old country was a very grave thing. My grandmother didn't want them dropped down to Hell necessarily, she just wanted them to be the opposite of blessed when she said God bless. How could you tell when the wish was genuine or not? You had to be there. In any case, it was from my grandmother that I inherited the Finley family trait of using the same words to say both what I meant and what I didn't mean. So God Bless, Michael Forte, M.D.

But all things considered, getting "only a flesh wound" for weeks of trouble—and for years of not recognizing I'd set myself up for it—was a small enough price to pay for my inheritance from Jerry Christman. It wasn't as good as the guess-what attitude my grandmother had left me, but who had time to measure with so many bodies strewn around? As any number of people could have attested (some of them through gnashed teeth), I had come out of it all in relatively good shape. Better than good. A first bout with a bad conscience is bad enough, but at least you can tell yourself it's dues for living on the planet, want to be a member or not? When the second bout comes along more than five years later, and for the same reason, you spend a lot of time wondering why you have been picked out for so much torment. You were supposed to have dealt with all that mess the first time. There had been shrinks, a change of profession, a new home address—what else were you supposed to have done to get straightened out? Didn't the New Testament I read in parochial school say something about sowing this to reap that? Old New Testament promises die hard.

What you must know is that, before Jerry Christman came back into my life, I didn't see myself as especially fragile, especially buttoned up, or especially anything else. I had good points and bad points, and with some luck the good covered over the bad. Some people thought I was kind and sensitive, others thought I defined the crass and the selfish. I was bright, tall, and pretty fit without anyone mistaking me for Einstein, a circus freak, or an Olympic champion. I was a big sport—open-minded about things I wasn't closed-minded about. I was a Nice Guy in that vaguely boring Harrison Ford way, but without his looks. I had willy-nilly developed a philosophy of life that came down to a belief that the small, the petty, and the sniveling—as a one-time event or as a personal characteristic—rolled more boulders down mountains than dynamite did. I drank when I thought it was a natural part of being sociable—sometimes too much, but hardly with crippling regularity. And just to be sure, I sometimes declared dry months, an exercise in self-discipline that never really felt like all that much self-denial. There was ginger ale instead of scotch, and Johnny Walker just had to apologize for me to its stockholders.

It was my version of a 12-step program, and without the need to knock on the super's door to ask forgiveness for leaving the Chinese menus out in my hall. The same thing with smoking: If I found myself buying more than a pack a month, I skipped a month and invested in Juicy Fruit for those trying oral moments. My love life? Moving right along. Naming names would embarrass too many people.

All by way of saying that a few weeks ago, I didn't see Paul Finley, commander-in-chief of Finley Investigations, as doomed to losing any battles except those against Visa. When I woke up in the morning, I had hopes—and for more than having clean socks and underwear in my dresser. When my phone rang, I assumed it was the pope inviting me to Rome all expenses paid to investigate one of his devious cardinals. Okay, that had never happened, but on a good day I won the second prize of an insurance company wanting me to look into a medical malpractice suit, the third prize of a tenant group asking for help in gathering evidence against a slumlord, or the old standby of a suspicious husband or wife demanding more details about those late-night business meetings that have ruined so many supper roasts. When the caller one morning turned out to be Jerry Christman, though, I was too surprised to think of it as any prize at all.

Christman had been part of my former life as a Nassau County cop. Because a tumble off a Long Island Railroad station ramp had chewed up his hip and leg and tied him to a cane, he had been desk-bound at Major Cases over the tail end of my time there. Once off the street he had really been only a glorified clerk, but one with a weapon, a shield, and a bark for anyone who cracked that was all he had become. The truth was he had gone from being a mobile pain in the ass to a sedentary pain in the ass, but he also liked the Mets and had shared my opinions of some of the other people in the bullpen, so we had forged whatever that wink-wink bond in the gap between friends and colleagues is called. He had also been the only person at Major Cases to phone after I had collaborated with Dr. Renata Stallworth to kick myself off the job, warning me against letting the fuckers get me down. That had been giving the creeps too much credit, but it had still been nice to have even a one-man rooting section in those gloomy days. It had made for reassuring—modest but reassuring—contrast to the mobs screaming for me to be dumped into the Long Island Sound.

Anyway, here was Christman on the phone more than five years later, sounding a little raspy in the throat and asking how I was doing. I was tempted to tell him I had become flush as a private investigator, then to tell him the only marks in my bank account had been made by a computer printer leaking ink. In the end I settled for the snicker meaning we were all God's creatures crawling around on the forest floor until the carnivorous plants found us. He worked it out without needing footnotes and immediately went into a ramble about how the office had missed me (lie), how the predictable people had risen to the top (truth), and how he had been on leave with a lung tumor (yikes). But he was recuperating now, he said, and he counted on returning to duty as soon as he worked out how much more that would net him than taking early retirement. His wife still didn't understand why, if he had to get cancer, he couldn't have gotten it from some drug dealer in the line of duty to qualify for full disability.

I clucked when I was supposed to cluck, laughed when I was supposed to laugh, and couldn't have agreed more that we had to get together for a coffee or whatever. All the while, of course, I was waiting for him to get to the purpose of his call. I was still waiting after I'd hung up. I gazed around at the Bay Ridge living room that doubled as the headquarters of Finley Investigations for a revelation, but none came. The drab seascape over my couch looked offended I should expect more from it than covering up flaking plaster. My first thought was that I had missed something during our conversation, brief as it was. Had there been a word or phrase between the lines that should have tipped me off to the real reason Christman had reached out to me after so long? If there had been, it would have been nice if he had given me a copy of the code book he was using.

Since I didn't have a clue about why the man had reappeared in my life so abruptly, I had little choice then and there but to chalk it up as the latest daily adventure of Finley Investigations.

Sometimes I ran out of breath just counting the thrills. There were days when *both* the telephone and doorbell rang. Mind you, I wasn't about to file a complaint with the Better Business Bureau. The few times things had gotten hectic, to the point of needing the weapon I kept in my sock drawer, had done little for me, the people I had tangled with, or the forces of law and order that should have made my energies unnecessary. Thrills not only didn't buy groceries, they made for more enemies among both the living and the dead. After a hard day's tail of Jane who was doing Johnny on the sly, I was more than content to return home and write up my report for Mr. Jane while some TV autopsy show played in the background of my living room/office. My "only a flesh wound" has confirmed that enlightened outlook.

As for the sources of my trade, I'd like to say it was mainly word-of-mouth—one satisfied client in a muddle recommending me to somebody in a worse muddle. After a couple of years that might have even been true. But initially, at least, I owed most of my nickels and dimes to my very ethnic name in the telephone book. I wasn't Acme Inquiries or Young, Smith, and Jones Private Research, I was Finley Investigations, and this already told the prospective client that I knew about the perils of sin, especially the sex kind. With a name like mine, I had to be Irish and most likely raised as a Catholic, so I had some knowledge of the bonds of the confessional when they came to unload their dreary tales. I mention this now because the Pandora's Box opened by Jerry Christman's call dragged me right back into that ambience with a vengeance. And here I had spent years on the illusion that I had moved on to wider, more secular horizons.

It wasn't that I stopped thinking about Christman's call while I went about what passed for my daily business. When you're waiting for a crabby civil servant to dig out some record allegedly available to the public, you wander down all kinds of other entertaining byways to pass the hours. My favorite theory was that Christman had my idle habit of surfing the Internet for the names of one-time acquaintances to see how much they had prospered or rotted in his absence from their lives. Granted I'd never gone so far as to track down a name and then call it up, but when you have lung cancer and spend your day shuffling around in slippers and a bathrobe, you were ripe for taking the surfing one step further, right?

Wrong.

I wouldn't have known how wrong if not for my routine of reading *Newsday* every morning over breakfast—a sentimental carryover from when my old man had brought the paper home from the factory at the end of his overnight shift, daring me and my mother to find a page that wasn't wrinkled into an origami or a story that wasn't half-blotted out with machine grease. The deaths of Long Island detectives weren't big items for city papers like the *Times* or the *News*, but they still merited paragraphs in *Newsday*. One second I was chewing on an English muffin at the counter of Sal's Fourth Avenue luncheonette and scanning an obituary for an old actor born in Amityville, the next my muffin was sticking in my throat as I took in the details of Jerry Christman's fatal lung cancer after going to this and that school, joining the police force, and ending up on Major Cases. There was a line about the wife who had made the joke about full-disability cancer and something about two sons who probably wouldn't have liked the joke if they had heard it. It was then that I finally made out the message between the lines of Christman's call: He hadn't called after so much time to say hello, but to say goodbye!

And I still didn't understand it.

If I knew I had only hours left on the clock, would I have called Jerry Christman? I couldn't see it. The solidarity among fellow Mets sufferers went just so far. Before pushing on to the next world, had he wanted to collect a thank-you for his chin-up message five years ago? I thought I'd given him his thanks back then. Where would law enforcement be if cops didn't understand each other's grunts? No, I told myself, whatever reason he had called after so long had nothing to do with the bad old days.

Leaving what? Between us there were no bad *new* days. The truth was, I had been taking it as a barometer of my mental health that I had been giving less thought with every passing month to the Major Cases era, Christman very included. Skip the odd nightmare and I indulged that period only when the TV news showed some perp walk in Mineola. Golden memories were still golden memories. Who could ever forget the tingling excitement of keeping the cameras and furious family members away from some child molester? But those jogs down memory lane had evaporated as soon as the news had moved on to a Ford commercial. I was sorry for Jerry Christman, but I hadn't even known he was sick.

Which made it doubly annoying that I straddled Sal's counter stool with the weight of having to make a choice. To the left there was the obit notice spelling out the funeral home address in Lynbrook and the visiting hours; to the right my morning drill of returning to the apartment after breakfast and writing out the questions I intended asking my latest Doctor Shaky Hands in the afternoon. I had fallen into this schedule because of a butcher named Lenhoff who had insisted he could see me only in the morning. I hadn't realized until walking into his office that he had suckered me by during his prime visiting hours, knowing that all the old men and old women with curved spines in Brooklyn would be stomping their walkers in the waiting room for him to get rid of me and get back to serious work. I had given Lenhoff his points for cunning, reported to the insurance company that the prick had invented medical malpractice, and had never again seen a doctor in the morning. But with *Newsday*'s obit page staring up at me, that shaped up as a past triumph. I really had no decision to make at all. My morning preparation for my afternoon interview was hardly like having to memorize *O Captain! My Captain!*. I had worked up a comprehensive questionnaire I could have recited from in my sleep, case specifics slid in as needed. Meanwhile, I had plenty of time to drive out to the wake in Lynbrook and maybe find out from the widow or sons why Christman had telephoned me. I had never been ashamed of my curiosity gene.

CHAPTER 2

By the time I hit the Sunrise Highway, the sun was working itself up
to a good June boil. Usually I would have taken a week of summer
sweat for an hour of winter cold, but on this particular morning
the heat threatened that one aggravation too many. Ahead of me
were old faces from Major Cases best left for those TV news perp
walks. Who did I want to see least? Herb Levine came to mind.
Unless he'd had a personality transplant, I was in for a hefty
catalog of sneers from Levine. We had reported for duty at Major
Cases the same day, the lieutenant in charge at the time, Harold
Lincoln, had blithely waved toward two desks, I had gotten to the
window desk first, and my relations with Levine had deteriorated
from that point on. Coolness had ripened into hostility a couple of
years along when Lincoln had assigned me a woman as a partner
and the Department had done everything in its power to show it
was an equal-opportunity employer by giving us the most prominent assignments. That had killed my last shot at being on Herb
Levine's Hit Parade. I had never been an icon for Ray Black or
Connie Marchese, either. Neither one of them, ten years younger
and on the make, had ever warmed up to my notion of public relations, afraid my occasional flights into fact for the media would
reflect on them. That wasn't why they had toiled to get the highest
marks in Communication Studies at the Academy. If they had
taken the trouble to learn how to sound like robots in front of
microphones, why couldn't everyone? Black and Marchese had

probably competed with Herb Levine to host the celebration after I'd taken my hike.

But thoughts of Levine, Black, and Marchese were just a decoy, and I was disappointed I had still resorted to it after so much time. The one person I really didn't want to see was my ex-partner Ellen Miles, now a lieutenant and the head of Major Cases, according to Christman. Count the reasons. We had started out together in the *pre*-days—*pre*-my marriage and *pre*-her fascination with the politics of the job. Back then we had liked each other, had taught each other, had covered for each other. We had even kept our hands off one another until my marriage had ended in a car wreck and before her flirtations with politics had led her to marry an assistant district attorney big on capital punishment and other issues that made him sound tough, masculine, and American. Our history was so twisted we hadn't even broken cleanly. Months after I had been off the job and had stuck my toe in the private investigation waters, she had gritted her teeth and taken in a teenager for homicide because I had loaded up her desk with too much evidence for her to do otherwise. She had despised me for that because her husband and the other movers and shakers on the Island had wanted to point the finger elsewhere, to a politically more profitable target, but she had listened to her conscience. Maybe what she had most despised me for was having counted on her to do exactly that.

I had been to the Lynbrook funeral home before. I had been to a lot of funeral homes in eastern Long Island and hadn't missed them with my move into Brooklyn. I took it as a good sign that there were only four cars in the rear parking lot; at least two of them figured to belong to employees. An even better sign was seeing the widow talking to a white-haired man who looked like the funeral director at the desk in the vestibule: She obviously didn't feel any urgent need to be in her husband's viewing room with visitors. *Newsday* had called her Sarah, and I remembered she had dropped by the office a few times to pick up Christman. She was a small spidery woman in a black dress a size too big and with red hair that had lost its flame and been put up in a prim bun. She looked up as I came in the front door, thought she recognized me, thought again, then looked totally confused as I went up to her. "Paul Finley. I worked with Jerry a few years back. I'm sorry for your loss."

It was a ritual expression I'd first heard as a kid from my Uncle Jack and I hadn't heard anything better since for getting over the awkward first seconds. "Of course," she said. "Forgive me for not being sure . . ."

"It's been a long time."

She nodded, maybe picturing me from the bullpen, maybe recalling scuttlebutt from Christman about my end at Major Cases, maybe confusing me with a moron from a TV reality show. The white-haired man took advantage of her hesitation to point me toward the first viewing room along the hall off the vestibule. Whatever they were talking about, his gesture said, was too important to be interrupted by the arrival of a mere mourner, and she gave me a flat smile that said she agreed with him. As I left them, I wondered if they had been discussing the money shorts Christman had hinted at on the phone. The basics were always the basics.

The viewing room was a small stadium with a good hundred folding chairs divided into neat rows that stretched from one wall settee to another. I knew it wasn't planning overkill: Nobody attracted more mourners than a dead cop. It was one of the fringe benefits every Academy cadet ultimately got to cash in. The Emerald Society bagpipers alone were crowd pleasers. At the moment, though, only one of the chairs was taken, and it wasn't by anyone from Major Cases. He was a wide-shouldered black guy somewhere in his 40s or early 50s with a melon of a head, a broad nose to match, and, to judge by his tan Nehru jacket, a taste for unfashionable fashions. He turned around, nodded to me, then swiveled back to the casket at the front. I would have bet African rather than African-American, but then again, I had once bet George W. Bush could never be elected President.

I went up to the bier hearing every squeak of my loafers. The closer I got to the florist shop of wreaths and arrangements across the front wall, the thinner the smell of flowers. Had Whitey outside sweetened the back of the room with aerosols? What was in between gilding the lily literally and still just gilding it figuratively? I promised myself to ask the Professor: He was the expert on all those profound metaphorical questions.

No doubt it was Jerry Christman in the casket, or at least the Christman from the old photo that had inspired the embalmer. Who knew what he had come out really looking like after surgery, chemotherapy, and radiation? But at least he was close to my five-year-old memory: a beaky face with a big nose, a few strands of brown hair still reaching his forehead, noticeably small hands crossed over his abdomen. The only thing wrong was that his glasses were missing. Hovered over his forms all day, he had worn his gold-rimmed specs from the moment he sat down in the morning to the end of his tour. And the funny thing was, although they had been bifocals, he had never worn them while on his feet, not even to get up from his desk to hobble out to the hall coffee machine. So if he was so confident of his long-range vision, why hadn't he invested in simple reading glasses? Seeing his corpse without the bifocals, I wondered if somebody—Sarah, maybe Christman himself in his will—was trying to remind people he had once been on the street full-time like all the other 20-20s at Major Cases. Okay, that wasn't the most generous thought to have, but the truth was I had been as guilty as everyone else in the bullpen of thinking a little less of him for breaking his bones and turning into a processing clerk. There had always been something a little flippant—the flippancy of an outsider—about how he had greeted us back at the house after a bad shoot or sloppy arrest with his calls to get our paperwork done. Too bad he hadn't known I had shared that peeve toward him with everyone else. He could have saved himself two calls to me five years apart and I could have saved myself the drive out to look at his corpse.

Uncle Jack had given me a useful line for greeting a widow at a funeral home, but he hadn't been much help for the second most awkward moment at a wake—in front of the casket. Was a 10-second stare enough respect? What about 20 seconds? Or was it just any length of time at all that gave the impression of being devoted to a prayer or a sympathetic thought? I opted for the just any length of time at all for a prayer or a sympathetic thought and turned back to see the Nehru jacket waiting for me with a wide smile. "Jesus will take it from here," he said with an accent that definitely came from one of those old English colonial movies set in Africa. "He was a good man."

He seemed to be waiting for me to agree, so I gave him the grunt Christman would have understood and looked around at the theater of empty chairs. I didn't have any intention of waiting around until they were filled, which was suddenly the same thing as saying I hadn't had any clear intention in coming out to Lynbrook in the first place. "Take care."

He nodded with another unnerving smile, and I headed back to the door. There had probably been quicker in-and-outs to funeral parlors, but I was ready to leave that to the Guinness record researchers. The visitors book was open to a page with the single name of Samuel Chil-something. I saw no reason not to add my name; in fact, I liked the idea of Miles or Levine coming in later and seeing it.

Neither the widow nor Whitey was anywhere to be seen when I returned to the vestibule. I made a note not to get myself waked in the place, not unless I wanted my corpse easily whisked off for some ransom demand, and went back out to the lot for my car. In no more than 10 minutes the sun had risen to Thermal Catastrophe. Too bad the air conditioner back in my apartment had whimsical ideas about when to be useful.

"Mister Finley?"

Samuel Whatever didn't look at all hot as he stood at the entrance of the parking lot in his Nehru jacket; he was holding a brown schoolbag I hadn't seen before. "You are Paul Finley who used to work with Jerry, yes?"

So he had followed me up to the visitors book. "That's right."

Another big beam as he nodded and stepped onto the gravel; he wasn't particularly heavy, but he lumbered like somebody carrying too many pounds between his wide shoulders and squat legs. "You have saved me the morning," he said, speaking softly and precisely, accent on every word. "I thought I would be here until I had to report to work."

"For me?"

"Exactly that," he said, stopping behind my car and laying his bag on the back fender to snap it open. "Not that I mean disrespect to Jerry, but it is good you came so early. I am sure Jerry appreciates it, too. Don't you see him smiling down at us with our Savior at this very moment?"

What could I say? I didn't know who he was, why he was opening his schoolbag, or why he had apparently been ready to wait for me all day. The bliss of a Jesus freak was the least of it.

"Maybe you do not," he smiled again, coming out with a bulging manila envelope. "But believe me, he is in the embrace of the Creator right now and he is very happy matters have turned out this way."

"Look . . . Samuel, right?"

"Samuel Chilumu, that is correct. We seem to have stolen each other's habits—reading the visitors book. You know what they say about that? Steal one another's habits, steal one another's concerns."

I told myself to shut up, just stand there.

"Jerry insisted you have this," he said, extending the envelope. "It was one of his last wishes. 'Only to Paul Finley,' he said. 'If anybody knows what to do with it, Paul Finley will be that person.'"

"What is it?"

Samuel Chilumu buckled his bag closed again with a shrug. "I did not look too closely, but they appear to be police reports of some kind. That was what Jerry worked at, yes? . . . Oh, I am sorry. I did not identify myself. I was Jerry's nurse. He was a very weak man near the end, and Sarah thought it best he have somebody with him at all times. I would like to think we became fast friends."

"So you were with him when he called me?"

"Yes, he had me look up your number in Brooklyn."

"And the reason he called . . ."

"What is in your hand, I believe. He never went into specifics with me. But he thought it was important to give you that."

The contents of the envelope certainly felt like paper. "You didn't know I was coming here. *I* didn't know it until an hour ago. Why didn't you just mail it to me?"

There was slightly more tolerance in his smile. "I work at the hospital only three blocks away. It was also an opportunity to pay my respects to Jerry. The way he spoke of you, you sounded like somebody who would also be sure to pay his respects."

I heard the ping of cheap tin; there was nothing I'd ever said or done that would have given Christman that kind of an impression. In fact, the more I thought about it, the more I realized I had never particularly liked the guy, the Mets or not. "I didn't see him in five years. Something doesn't scan."

"Doesn't . . .?"

"Make sense. He didn't mention this envelope or you on the phone."

"Jerry was not always serene in his final days," he nodded. "That envelope he handed me days before he called you and told me to put it aside. It is possible that when he was speaking with you, he did not recall giving it to me. The ravages of his disease can be quite disturbing, Mr. Finley. Sometimes he was fine, other times the injections had their effect on him. The day he spoke with you on the telephone was one of his more lucid days. We can only be thankful he is reunited with his Creator."

There was so much wrong with the pitch I wondered if the guy's name was even Samuel Chilumu. One way or the other, it seemed smart to open the envelope while I still had him in front of me. But just as I squeezed the metal clip together, a gray Corolla came bumping into the lot. It was Connie Marchese, and he gaped at me through his windshield the way you were supposed to when Publishers Clearing House rang your doorbell. I changed my mind about opening the envelope. Maybe the nurse hadn't heard right, but anything involving "police reports" had an outside chance of also involving Connie Marchese and that might have complicated my morning more than my idiot drive had already done.

"Jesus, is it you, Finley?"

The mustached pencil took enough time parking to compose himself for a civil greeting. He even wanted to shake hands. "I saw the obit in *Newsday*," I said to be equally friendly. "Sounded like Jerry had it tough."

That already felt like too much information, especially with the way Marchese slid his eyes over to Samuel, then pretended he wasn't there. "Thought you were a big city boy now," he recovered. "Didn't know you still read our Island papers."

"Some habits are hard to break. How's life, Connie?"

"Same old same old. And the private eye business?"

I said something hoping Samuel would take it as a shield for moving on. I didn't know the man or why I was worried about it, but I had a gut feeling he might blurt out another hosanna to the Creator covering what was in the envelope. Call it ESP, but he seemed to pick up my vibe and thrust his mitt of a hand out to me. "You know where to find me if there is anything else I can help you with. My name is on the envelope there."

I hadn't noticed the name and phone number before. I hadn't been noticing much of anything. "Thanks a lot, Samuel."

Marchese didn't take his eyes off the nurse all the way out of the lot. "Friend of Jerry's?"

"Mine," I said.

He nodded as though that explained everything. I remembered one of the things I didn't like about Connie Marchese: The next black guy he trusted to be anywhere but in a lineup would be the first. "Well, I guess I better get in there," he said. "Sarah here?"

"Yeah. Nobody else. You beat the rush."

He seemed to have learned Herb Levine's sneer. "But I didn't beat you. Always one step ahead, huh?"

"We try, Connie. We try."

CHAPTER 3

I was close enough to Garden City to feel a guilt attack coming on if I didn't drop in on the Professor. I'd been trying to see him once a week or so, especially since they had put balloons in his heart, and by now that had become so much of a routine he managed to get in a grumble or two when I didn't live up to it. If it was a ploy on his part, it worked because driving him to the supermarket for stuff he wouldn't have otherwise admitted wanting felt even more virtuous when it kept his gripes at bay.

To put it nicely, there was a lot of baggage between me and the old man, starting with the death of my wife (and his daughter) Jennifer and my daughter (and his granddaughter) Susan. Driving over to his place, I could think the worst of that was over even if that five-year-old Christmas sent a greeting card every so often so I wouldn't get to thinking the past was content living in the past. Lighter deliveries sometimes tabled the philosophical question of when a father-in-law stopped being a father-in-law. I'd never found an answer to that one, though the subject had come up one night for profound discussion at the Green Fox, my neighborhood saloon. The consensus then had been that fathers-in-law remained fathers-in-law the same way wives remained wives: A new wife meant the old father-in-law vanished, too. I'd come around to not caring what the answer was. The bottom line was that Joe Carroll, retired chairman of Adelphi's History Department and fellow conspirator in the deaths of Jennifer Finley and Susan Finley, was the nearest to family I still had. The rest of it was my lookout.

At a traffic light on the way over, I glanced at the papers Samuel Chilumu had given me. He had been right about the police reports. There were exactly eight copies of processing forms. From what I could tell from the dates at the top, they went from the present back five years or so. Jerry Christman's This Was My Life? And why did he have them in the first place? Better, why had he been *collecting* them in the first place? From what Chilumu had said, he hadn't sounded in condition to drop by the office recently to print them out. And all that was aside from the minor detail that he had been breaking who-knew-how-many statutes in putting together his collection. I felt new admiration for Jerry Christman. I couldn't recall that kind of nerve in him when he had been stapling his papers in the back corner of the bullpen. If anything, he had been the grammar school ass-kisser in adult life. But having the envelope on my lap gave new definition to hot sheets.

The Professor's house always hit me as needing a plastic windmill and cartoon characters on the stamp-sized lawn. From the outside at least, it was more than small, it was miniature—the kind of place Disney would have built if it wanted to exhibit Donald Duck's one-family middle-class Long Island home. The green shingles winked they also came in cherry and chocolate flavors, the windows seemed more for peering in than looking out, Little Bo Peep figured to be herding her sheep in the living room. In other words, I had just never gotten over the colonial Tara a few blocks away where I had first known Jennifer. Again, my problem. Why should the old man have gone on roaming that minimansion and encountering the ghosts of his dead wife, daughter, and granddaughter wherever he turned? No reason. But neither did I have to be reasonable about my prejudices.

My attitude toward his new house made for another topic Joe Carroll had become touchy about. He was touchy about a lot of things—the years that had forced him into retirement, the ugly fish facial features that had kept him out of beauty contests, the ignorance to be encountered on every public thoroughfare about

the true causes of the Crusades. Whether it concerned the present or the Middle Ages, earthlings had no other purpose than to
come up with new ways to irritate him. Given the years between
us, it was a wonder there were any subjects at all I could still
raise without him turning scarlet. And the tradeoff? Every so often, he had been good for Finley Investigations. Sometimes he
had steered clients to me, sometimes he had given me a hand in
surveillance. Or, to put it another way, he was the closest to a
family I still had. But I already said that, didn't I?

I let myself in with his spare key. He had given it to me with
the crack that "*some*body has to find the body," and every time
I stepped into the overly pine-scented vestibule I wondered how
far he was ready to go with his little witticism. I found him at the
living room mirror fixing his tie. He was wearing the green sports
jacket he always did in summer for what he deemed serious dates.
"You didn't tell me you were coming. Lose my number?"

"I was in the neighborhood. Where you going?"

"A lunch at the university. Another idiot's written a book on
the great Theodore Roosevelt. Nobody seems ready to accept the
man was a gasbag. Only thing you could trust about his so-called
war on the trusts was they'd still be there the next day trusting
away."

"And you'll be sure to tell that to this author."

"Damn right I will." He turned around for my inspection. He
seemed a little closer to busting the buttons of the jacket since
the last time I had seen it on him. "Fit for the public?"

"You don't have any other jacket but that PGA thing? You
belong on TV handing a check to Tiger Woods."

"Screw you. Why you out here anyway?"

"I thought that heart guy told you to go easy on the cakes and
buns."

"Oh, now you're my dietician."

"More profitable being your tailor."

He reminded himself to save his energy for the Roosevelt
admirer as he gathered up his billfold and keys from amidst a
mountain of books on the coffee table. I hadn't imagined the
weight gain: His gut practically ran up to meet his chin as he bent

down for his stuff. "Wait till you hear what I found here," he said, grabbing one of the tomes about Sumerians, Babylonians, and Assyrians he had been committing to memory since the Great Adventure in Iraq. "A Sumerian dining tip. Ready? 'For the last day of the next to last month of the year, no nectar compares to tripe from a mule's ass stuffed with fly shit.' I dare you to tell me that doesn't make your mouth water."

"It makes my mouth water. What's that got to do with Roosevelt?"

He scowled and slammed the book back closed to the bookmark. "Everything, but I haven't got time to educate you right now. And you're still avoiding my question. What're you doing out here?"

"Wake over in Lynbrook. One of the Major Cases people."

"Didn't know you were still in contact with them. Who was it?"

"Guy named Jerry Christman."

"Broke his leg or something?"

It was one of those jabbing moments—a reach from the days when he had unquestionably been a father-in-law and had known all about the minor things his daughter's husband did for a living. "So your memory will be the last thing to go. Want me to drive you over to this lunch?"

He saw something on my face he didn't like, then pretended he hadn't seen it. "Great idea. Then I'll have to pay for a cab home."

"Maybe somebody at the lunch will take pity on you and drive you."

"I'll drive myself right now and save all you martyrs the trouble."

I didn't want to drive him to Adelphi anyway. What I really wanted was just to sit down for a few minutes. My English muffin and *Newsday* at Sal's felt like a hundred quiets ago. "Mind if I get myself a coffee before heading back to Brooklyn?"

"There's some in the kitchen. Anything else?"

"What anything else?"

"I don't know. You're the one who looks like a train's about to hit you. Make sure you lock up."

I looked shaky? The penny didn't drop until I heard him pulling away from the front of the house. Then, finally, I saw how hard I'd been gripping Samuel Chilumu's manila envelope; the edge of it was a solid patch of perspiration. It hadn't been just the Professor's recall of Christman that had scalded. The date on the oldest accident report I'd flipped through at the traffic light had once been branded into my brain. How could it not have been? December 25ths were like that, with or without losing a wife and a daughter on them.

CHAPTER 4

I skipped the coffee but took the kitchen. A yellow Formica table under a sun funnel coming through the curtained window felt more demanding than a couch for seeing what else I didn't want to see in Christman's envelope.

The form I had glimpsed in the car was at the bottom of the pile, and looked to be the oldest of the eight. It was clipped to two others under a cover sheet listing road accidents the same Christmas. All three reports from that day had been signed off on by Walter Rigas. Rigas was a misanthrope who preferred the hysterics of operas to the everyday manias of those who walked the streets and who, at least back in my day, had filled in on the paperwork when Jerry Christman had been off. He had never liked the duty. Pagliacci hadn't done it, so why should he? It was a woman's job. Give it to Ellen Miles or Doreen Lawlor. He hadn't shut up about it until one day he had come in to find his latest embarrassing target range score nailed to the wall. I'd had to put up the price for two bottles of Johnny Walker to the range sergeant to get the damn thing. Ellen had said it served me right for coming up with the idea.

But Walter Rigas had gotten even. If he hadn't signed off on the accident report at Delaware Avenue, I dared the sun funnel to contradict me, Jennifer and Susan might still be alive. It had been Christmas. Who would have noticed if he had forgotten to check off all the appropriate boxes and sign everything with his florid **WR**? Jerry Christman wouldn't have been that much of a bastard about it all. I didn't know why I hadn't thought to call Jerry at home and have him interrupt his holiday to relay instructions to Rigas to tear up the report. If I had, I wouldn't have had to be brought to the accident scene to see Jennifer and Susan sitting in the car like test dummies that had failed the test. Not calling Christman and getting him to override Rigas was one more thing I should have done that day but hadn't.

I sat back to calm myself. The reason I hadn't called Christman was that I had been passed out in the Professor's guest room while Jennifer and Susan had been dying. I shouldn't have glossed over little details like that. It made me open to attacks of self-pity. Dr. Renata Stallworth wouldn't have been happy with me.

I thanked the sun funnel for its timely scolding and flexed the sheaf of papers in my hands. Rigas signing off on the accident reports was hardly normal business for Major Cases. Jennifer and Susan, okay; that was a 301 that touched on one of the office's own. Ellen Miles, just as a friend, would have wanted to know as much as possible about the ice skid and would have doubled up on whatever Auto had done. Rigas would have had to second that for the files under any circumstance. But why the other two reports? Same Christmas, but nothing to do with Major Cases people. A collision in Freeport with people named Cassidy and Lewin killed and a pileup on the Sunrise Highway with no casualties. Even if some overeager-to-please Auto clerk had sent the other things upstairs with the report on Jennifer and Susan, that didn't explain why Major Cases had kept them. What the hell had so intrigued Jerry Christman about Christmas revelers who had sipped too much eggnog before getting behind the wheel? Forget his solidarity call five years ago. When I really needed the bastard, he was stretched out in a casket.

I almost missed it. Christman *was* there, in the report of the Sunrise Highway pileup. He had used a yellow Magic Marker to highlight a statement from one Felipe Morante that the accident had happened "after I had to get over on the lane because these two guys were chasing one another . . . If I didn't get over, they would have killed us all." What two guys? Morante hadn't known. Make of the cars? Morante hadn't been able to say. But one of the drivers he had smashed into had backed up his story. Sort of. "I don't know if they were chasing each other, but yeah, there were two idiots speeding along a second before," said one Richard McCoy.

I didn't have the slightest idea what any of it meant—to me or to Jerry Christman. There were no Magic Marker highlights in the other reports to help me, either. In fact, Christman himself was barely present. Almost all the reports had been signed off on by Rigas, with Christman putting in merely a token appearance here and there. In one case I would have sworn Christman's initials had been erased under those of Rigas. Had the guy been reaching out to me to even old administrative scores about who had totaled the most reports? Was there an extra bonus in it for his widow if I proved he had filed three more reports than he had been given credit for? Or had he just been sneaking more meds than his special messenger Samuel Chilumu had noticed?

I changed my mind about the coffee. I needed to stand up from the table, to get away from Jennifer and Susan's names. I had managed to avoid seeing them as part of bureaucratic business for five years and I should have quit while I was ahead. The officially impersonal was always a step beyond the dead. The officially impersonal had *never* existed, had *never* called me husband or father. The Jennifer and Susan of the officially impersonal consisted of nothing more than a call from Major Cases over to Auto with a request for a copy of the report. Paper here, paper there, in the end initialed by Walter Rigas because it had been a holiday and he had been filling in for Jerry Christman. Jennifer and Susan were no more real than a holiday tour schedule five years ago.

I was working up a nice snit against everything, starting with Jerry Christman and Samuel Chilumu and including the watery coffee the Professor had left in the percolator. Had the old man offered me his insipid coffee the day everything had changed? Probably not: He had been too busy proving he could roast a holiday turkey as well as Jennifer could. That Christmas had been his big coming out. After three morose holidays, he had come to accept the death of his wife Helen and had even brought down his artificial tree and decorations from the attic so Susan would feel better about having to spend the afternoon away from her own real fir at home. For the first two hours of his slamming around in the kitchen, Jennifer had said nothing but to protest being exiled to the living room to watch Laurel and Hardy with Susan. I hadn't said anything because I had been too busy drinking up the old man's bar and regretting we hadn't insisted on hosting as usual. No, he didn't want anybody in the kitchen with him. He had everything under control. How many times had he had to say it? By the time dinner had finally been served, I hadn't been able to taste the food. There had been a close call trip to the bathroom, the bed in the old man's guest room, and blessed unconsciousness. I had missed all the squabbling between Jennifer and her father that had led to her taking Susan home without me. What had their argument been about? His stubbornness about being the cook for the day? Some old Carroll family sore he hadn't liked his daughter reopening? Once upon a time Joe had told me, but I didn't remember anymore. There was only the state cop with the Smokey the Bear hat waking me up with a report on icy roads and other crap I hadn't wanted to hear.

None of that belonged on Walter Rigas's desk and none of that belonged in Jerry Christman's private collection of official papers.

So why was it all sitting on the Professor's kitchen table anyway? Had Christman been more of a dipshit than I remembered? Had he stuck the report on Jennifer and Susan into the pile just to get me interested in whatever else had been obsessing him? How could I put it past him? It wasn't like the guy had ever been a close friend. But suddenly I was the only one he could trust with his little puzzle. What was the Groucho Marx line about refusing membership in any club that would accept people like him?

In case I hadn't noticed, Jerry Christman's little envelope wasn't doing much for my ego.

I sat down to look again. The most recent report was only a couple of months ago, probably from just before Christman had taken leave for his operation and signed off on by him, not Rigas. It papered the arrest of an arms dealer named Aaron Garrett. Herb Levine had made the bust. Much of the report was a grocery list of the weapons Levine had seized in Garrett's car—Raven MP-25s,

Street Sweepers, Tec-9s, on through the arsenal. Another chunk was a nutshell of Garrett's priors and reference numbers to his sheet. Aaron Garrett seemed to have the personality of Godzilla: What he hadn't tried to shoot, knife, or swing his way out of had been lost to history. What wasn't there, on the other hand, were details on how Levine had been alerted to the cache found in Garrett's car or why he had made the bust without a partner or backup. None of that sounded like Herb Levine, let alone the best way to approach somebody with Aaron Garrett's recorded reactions to stress. In my time Levine had written encyclopedias for a traffic summons. And do something on his own? The thought of him taking on a Garrett by himself was ludicrous. And what about Christman? On a good day he would have never accepted such a sketchy 49, but would have endeared himself even more to the bullpen by throwing the paper back for a do-over. Had he been already feeling so rotten he hadn't cared one way or the other?

I flipped to the 49 under Aaron Garrett, then stopped. The sun funnel hadn't been satisfied pouring light into the kitchen, now it wanted me to feel the heat, too. Or maybe it was the coffee planting its anxiety grounds in my stomach. One way or the other, I didn't want to look at any more of my inheritance from Jerry Christman. It felt like ill-gotten gains of some kind.

And maybe not just because they had come from Jerry Christman.

CHAPTER 5

Doctors are as much on the take with medical supply houses as with drug companies. That's why if you ever need a bandage for what the trade calls a flesh wound, they wrap you up in enough Johnson and Johnson to make a mummy jealous. I can't blame Michael Forte, M.D., for playing the game. I try hard to blame him every time I lift my arm and every hair on it gets yanked to its root, but I'm a mature individual who knows how to keep things in proportion. In firepower, for instance, I didn't go blasting at some of my least favorite cops like some extra in an old Italian spaghetti western, but tried to keep to my economical ways. It wasn't my fault I tried to do it with somebody else's Glock instead of my Smith &Wesson, and ended up with a spaghetti western, anyway.

Taking down cops is no fun. I don't mean to make that sound like a bulletin. Anyone who thinks it *is* fun is one of those demented assholes who calls 911 with a false report so they can open up from a rooftop on an arriving patrol. I mean it was especially no fun for me because it wasn't so long ago that I was wearing blue. That fact probably cost me an extra second or two of hesitation when the push came to the shove. Maybe by the time I get the bandage on my arm down to a couple of yards, it'll really sink in that my one-time brothers in uniform really tried to kill me.

CHAPTER 6

For two or three days after my first run through the Christman papers in the Professor's kitchen, I tried to focus on living, paying clients. One was St. John's Realty, which deigned to concede me a per diem for sitting in my car in Prospect Heights to stake out how many Haitians marched into a scarred brownstone where the tenant had cut up his second-floor apartment into nine cubicles. After a couple of days, I gave St. John's Realty a number; it was almost the same one on the check it gave me back for my services. Then there was Kim Dolittle, M.D., who didn't talk to animals and certainly didn't want to talk to me. On the other hand, she had left a gabby paper trail of police complaints and malpractice lawsuits through three states up to her Windsor Terrace office. Unlike St. John's Realty, the lawyers who had hired me to look into Dr. Dolittle were ecstatic with my background findings on behalf of their own client and sent me a check for $150 more than I had been counting on. My favorite distraction, though, was Bobby Sprowl, a sore loser in civil court who had been getting back at his ex-partners in a restaurant chain by slipping cockroaches into table napkins and ice water pitchers from Brooklyn Heights to Bensonhurst. When I caught him at it roach-handed at the Buona Italia outlet in Carroll Gardens, he took a swing at me that I ducked with relief not so much because of the punch he intended but because of what he might have still had clenched under his fingers. I was golden twice over when I shoved him over his table and he hit the floor with no more wildlife streaming away from him. Only two seconds later was I sorry I hadn't actually connected with his jaw.

Through all these diversions I sometimes went a whole half-hour without thinking about the Christman collection in the top drawer of my desk. They were the only stretches during the day I could convince myself I wasn't dragging deformed shadows after me. For the first time in years, sleep wasn't always an escape, either. An old nightmare—of Jennifer swerving on the ice and yelling for Susan to scrunch over in the back seat—returned like a horror movie revival. I could almost make out Jennifer's reedy voice, almost hear Susan screaming. Even as it was unfolding, I yelled at the nightmare to stop. Both times I wasn't sure when I woke up if it had stopped because I had ordered it to or just because it had run out of footage, had nothing else to show me. Either way, I was working up a real hatred for the projectionist who insisted I look at the screen. It didn't help that I couldn't blame it on my old police shrink, Renata Stallworth. Was that another sign of maturity, or of just having run out of credible fall guys?

The Professor didn't help disperse the shadows. As threatened, he called—not the day after I'd dropped in on him since that would have made him seem too eager, but two days later. Once finished recounting how he had put the Teddy Roosevelt scholar in his place, he got around to the curiosity that had prompted his call. "You had something on your mind the other day. Have to do with this dead cop?"

I held back. I told him about Christman and the envelope, but I didn't see any reason for including the report on Jennifer and Susan. Misery had had enough of that company.

"If he was so sick, why give a damn about this gun runner?"

"I don't know, Joe."

"Know what it sounds like to me?"

"The plot to kill Kennedy."

"Want to know what I think or not?"

"I'm listening, I'm listening."

"Sounds to me like Christman thought these reports were bullshit. He was compiling evidence of some kind."

He didn't have the best reason (the 301 on Jennifer and Su-san) to know that couldn't be true, but I didn't mind having him prattle away for a few minutes; not even Samuel Chilumu had been in a position to play devil's advocate with me. "Evidence of what?"

"How the hell should I know? I didn't work with him."

"Either did I for a long time. But one thing I remember: Jerry Christman might've been a ball breaker around the office when it came to his little reports, but he never shied away from polishing apples when it might do him some good. He had a substitute named Rigas who was just like him. The two of them could have set up a Contempt Club—as long as the bosses never got the feeling it was aimed at them."

"But this same Christman couldn't go off to the Happy Hunting Ground without saying goodbye to you. What does that tell you?"

Nothing I wanted to think about, to tell the truth.

"Anyway," the old man said, "people faced with little things like cancer operations have been known to change their worldview. Something to do with seeing the bigger picture, they tell me. Besides, he's not upsetting any apple carts, big or small. He seems to want *you* to do that."

I had wanted something to chew on, but I hadn't asked for Key Food's inventory. There was something too uncomfortably plausible about what the old man said to get my concentration back fully on the Doctor Dolittle who didn't speak to chickens and rhinos. So Christman had not only spent his last days in physical agony, but also totally self-deluded? There had been good days and bad days, Samuel Chilumu had said, implying that the bad ones had been the norm. The trouble was, the norm hadn't been in operation when Christman had called me. *That* Christman had sounded exactly like what the Professor had said—the coy guy renewing his street cred with somebody from whom he wanted a really big favor.

Well, too bad for him. On the one-in-a-thousand chance he hadn't been hallucinating, I was still the last person in New York State able to give him that favor. Paul Francis Finley, son of

Hempstead's Edward and Rose Finley, poking around in Nassau County's Major Cases business? No way. Been there, done that, and been advised (even by myself) not to do it again. So better for both Jerry Christman and me that he *had* been hallucinating.

CHAPTER 7

Cynthia didn't think much of my sense of commitment. In fact, she didn't applaud much of anything I said once I tired of another *NCIS* rerun and took my battle against the heat and my restlessness down to the Green Fox on the corner. She was so disapproving from the second I walked into her fumes shop that a passerby might think she preferred the company of Johnny Yeager, Blanche Walsh, and the other regular Green Fox skels clustered around the short arm. The local con man who went around collecting for a liver transplant got a warmer reception. I wanted a gin and tonic instead of a ginger ale against the heat? What about my unsolicited pledge in front of her about no booze in June? Hadn't I been serious about going on the wagon for the month? (I detected relationship issues beneath this indictment.) I liked the way she had done her hair in blonde ringlets? Meaning what—I didn't like the down-the-center Puritan part she had been sporting before? (No, I had hated it.) If somebody was reaching out from the grave for my help, didn't I feel just a teensy-weensy bit responsible about giving it to him? (No, not when he had probably been under the influence of his meds when he had been asking for it.) My penance? A gin and tonic in a glass so tall scuba divers had to go down to search for the gin.

A bald Asian halfway down the bar gave me a solidarity shrug as Cynthia put his Bud in front of him. I could have done without it for two reasons: I didn't like solidarity shrugs that seemed to come out of the Dagwood Bumstead school of "Oh, these women!"

and I didn't like people who had better hearing than your average sonar detector.

"Maybe I'm just superstitious," Cynthia said, coming back to me and trying to make it sound like she was relenting some. "When somebody dead asks you for something, you do it. Otherwise, you get ghosts rattling chains in the middle of the night."

"He didn't know what he was asking me for."

"You don't know that, Finley."

"No, I don't know that."

"Well, do you?"

"The guy who took care of him around the clock knows it. A moment's clear thought knows it. But me, no, I don't know it."

"I think Finley's getting a little defensive!"

What else was new? *Compos mentis* or not, Jerry Christman had opened walls I had spent more than five years sealing over. It was okay for me to notice that the plaster covering up the Great Hurt was bumpy here and there, but that didn't make it okay for others to notice. Suppose Christman had stuck in the report on Jennifer and Susan not to attract my attention toward something else, but, just the opposite, to raise suspicions about how the accident on the ice had happened? Crazy, I knew. There was nothing like that in the 301. But I had been a cop too long not to indulge for a second every whim that torched a brain cell.

I could have sulked all that out to Cynthia, and with half a shot at persuading her I was in a confessional enough mood to stick around until she had closed for the night. I could have, I could have, yes, I could have. I knew her well enough by now to tell the difference between Cynthia as nails and Cynthia wanting to be nails, and to tell I was seeing number two. For reasons I preferred not knowing, she had wanted to argue with somebody, and I had made myself available. And her ringlets *were* seductive, set off her wide, vaguely clownish face at the same time that they streamlined her chunky body. I could have undressed her right there behind the bar. But I also had the clammiest sensation that would have been a lie and that I was already surrounded by too many lies.

What lies? Aside from not mentioning the report on Jennifer or Susan to the Professor, I had no idea what they were. But I also knew before Cynthia's waiting stare and the faint odor of onions on her breath that I would have told more of whatever they were if I didn't take a detour thanks to the newscast on behind the bar. It was video of some Keep America Godly group waving signs and placards in front of an abortion clinic somewhere on the Island. Two of the placards identified the demonstrators as belonging to something called the Faith Renewal Movement. "Doing good work!" Johnny Yeager piped up from the short arm, immediately winning approval from Blanche Walsh and the rest of his boozer pals.

Cynthia looked at me to make the first crack. I looked at her to do the same. Neither of us said a thing, but we were both relieved to be talking—or not talking—about something besides me and Jerry Christman!

He was inscrutable, but I think the Asian guy approved of our decision.

CHAPTER 8

Back from the Green Fox and condemned to the tribulations of ascetic monks, there was no way to go to bed without taking another look at what Chilumu had given me. I was still the guardian of the seal, wasn't I? Since I had already launched Sin Night with my *Eau de Gin* down at the bar, I dug a Marlboro Light out of a jacket pocket in the closet to have company while I saw what had been gathered under Aaron Garrett and his gun hobbies. The cigarette—my first in two weeks—was as much staleness concentrate as it was tobacco, but it let me feel cannier about what I was doing as I flopped down on the couch to read about Jimmy Fantone.

I knew Jimmy Fantone. Every cop in Nassau and Suffolk counties did because at one time or another every cop in Nassau and Suffolk counties had been forced to deal with a Jimmy bent on showing how he had inherited the earth by being the son of Marcello (Mike) Fantone. According to the 49 filed by Connie Marchese and Ray Black and initialed by Christman, Jimmy Fantone was picked up this time for knifing a hooker outside a night club in West Hempstead; she had apparently made the mistake of not knowing the royalty she was coming on to. I remembered the case—or at least the *Newsday* photo of a very wild-eyed, scruffy Fantone being cuffed in front of the club. I hadn't noticed then that the plainclothes in the rear of the picture were Marchese and Black. I also didn't remember how the case had come out. Maybe that had never reached the papers or maybe that had been the morning my newsstand had sold out *Newsday* before I had gotten there. Given Fantone's gutter celebrity, though, it was strange there hadn't been more about his little adventures.

I had a personal basis for thinking it odd. I'd had a run-in with Jimmy and one of his right-hand retards when they had been seen hanging around outside a high school selling false IDs. This alert of the century had fallen into our laps because a school security guy knew how much the Major Cases hierarchy liked Fantone family events and the headlines that went with them. So one afternoon there had been Jimmy behind the wheel of his rose Corvair down the block from John Q. Adams High. As Ellen Miles and I had come up from the rear, he had been meditating on his windshield while his crony had been negotiating driver's licenses with two kids through the side window.

"Got one for me too, Jimmy?"

He hadn't liked my question, and followed orders to get out of the car with a pissy smile that promised me a long afternoon for intruding on his business affairs. I had really been close to smacking him, but that would have set a bad example for the crony and the kids Ellen had herded together on the other side of the car. It wouldn't have played too well, either, for the reporter and the photographer from *Newsday* just then driving up. Gee, I had wondered, who could have tipped them off?

The next three hours had been booking, reporter questions, the arrival of the Fantone lawyers, more reporter questions, denials by the school kids they had been doing anything but answering a request for directions, and more reporter questions. The hierarchy couldn't have been happier the next day when Ellen and I were all over Page 5, at least until the day after that when the same picture had been published to accompany the news that Jimmy had pleaded out to a minor package of trespass and disturbing the peace. Some might have said that was your tax money in action, and my bosses at the time wouldn't have found that the least bit cynical. The Fantones had come through for them again with prominent mention of Major Cases. Publicists on the payroll couldn't have done a better job.

Which made me wonder again why there had been no follow-up, at least that I could remember, to the hooker slashing. There was certainly no clue in the 49 Christman had included in his collection. Unlike Levine's write-up on Aaron Garrett, it seemed to include everything. There was no special reason at all for Christman to have copied and held on to it. If there was anything at all curious, it was why Marchese and Black had been involved. There was nothing about a sidewalk slashing that fell under the heading of Major Cases. A coincidence they had been in the vicinity when the knifing had gone down?

An old sergeant of mine had told me never to rest my head on a coincidence if I didn't want lice in my hair. Okay, no coincidence. And from a wider angle Marchese and Black bagging someone the West Hempstead cops should have handled did fall into line as another anomaly in Christman's collection. Levine going solo on Aaron Garrett. All the accident reports from the same Christmas Day. Was *that* what had tantalized Christman? How there was something off-center about every report? That seemed easy enough to check by looking at the others. I didn't know what that would prove, but it felt like the first trail I'd had since Chilumu had given me the envelope.

I was so grateful for the remotest sense of direction that I felt a beat behind the phone ringing on my desk. Welcome back to present reality where—what? Cynthia had changed her mind about going to bed alone after closing? A hospital was calling up to say the Professor had collapsed with another heart attack? I called it even at one good and one bad possibility as I picked up the receiver. I had been half-right about the hospital part.

"I thought I might see you at the funeral," Samuel Chilumu said. "The ceremony was fortifying. I believe it gave strength to everyone present."

I didn't need his advice for deciding what funerals to attend. But there was something a little shakier in his voice than in the Lynbrook parking lot. "Glad to hear it, Samuel."

"Yes, Jerry has completed his journey and found peace. It is one we will all have to make one day."

"Never doubted it."

"I am glad to hear you say that. Are you a religious man, Mr. Finley?"

"That's between me and my false idols, Samuel."

"I am not sure I understand."

"It's not important. What's going on?"

"Oh. Yes. What I wanted to tell you was that your friend from the funeral home was at the Mass and the cemetery and he acted quite interested in knowing our relationship."

I subsided in my desk chair. I hadn't needed the rancid Marlboro to feel the roof of my mouth caking. "Marchese?"

"Yes. When I told him I was doing a service for Jerry, he had many questions. He was a policeman . . ."

"So you told him about the reports?"

There was too much silence; he hadn't really counted on his misgivings about Marchese to be confirmed. "He is a policeman who worked with you and Jerry, yes?" he finally asked.

I pictured those colonial movies again, those British policemen in Africa who strutted around in their short uniform pants and riding crops and the Africans who were far too impressed by them. Then I thought of Africans like Samuel Chilumu booting them the hell off their continent a lot more easily than they had driven them out of their nervous systems. "What are you saying, Samuel? He acted like he was on some kind of police business?"

"No, not exactly . . ."

"Be exact."

Too aggressive. The voice that came back was a little confused and a little irritated, but most of all it was intimidated. I could have fitted myself out for a pair of those uniform shorts. "I told him what I knew—that they seemed to be processing forms. More than that I could not help him."

"Nothing else?"

He was supposed to have answered no, that he had told Marchese to go fuck himself. Instead, he said: "He just wanted my name and address. Was there any reason not to give it to him?"

I could think of several even without Christman's forms in the middle. If there were any crosses to be burned on Long Island lawns, Marchese was certain to have a supply of them for sale. "No, of course not."

"He made it sound like what Jerry had was not legal."

"He said that?"

"Not expressly. But it was my feeling."

I thought of my grammar school friend Slinky Malone. When the two of us had found a victim in the schoolyard, we had stuck him in the middle between us and told him he had to reach one of us before he was hit with the Spaldeen we took turns firing at him. If he managed it, we had promised, his prize would be becoming one of the throwers. None of our marks had ever made it, of course. I had a bad feeling Jerry Christman and Connie Marchese had gotten Samuel Chilumu to stand in the middle between them. "You have nothing to worry about, Samuel," I said anyway. "If there's anything wrong about Jerry having those forms, Marchese will get in touch with me."

"Yes?"

"You told him I have them, right?"

"Maybe I should not have."

"Forget it. It's not important."

I didn't leave him time to debate the point. He went back to emptying his bedpans and I went back to whatever the Aaron Garretts and the Jimmy Fantones were telling me I should have been taking care of. I didn't like Marchese being so interested in either the reports or Samuel Chilumu. I didn't know why I didn't like it. I probably wouldn't have liked Marchese being interested in the latest wheat crop estimates from Nebraska. I just didn't like it. There was a sour stink to the man that weighed down the air, like someone who had been wearing the same socks for a week and expected you not to notice. He was everybody's friend but not really anybody's friend. I'd even overheard him once pretending to be interested in Walter Rigas's operas—this from somebody who kept his car radio stuck on a heavy metal station. If Christman had been secretive about his little collection of Major Cases files, Connie Marchese would have figured to be somewhere on the list why.

Fifteen minutes more of going through the reports, and my main achievement was not losing my temper. The thread of something being off-center about each of the reports turned out to be a non-starter. Some of them could have been included in textbooks as regulation form work. Did Christman want me to decipher what he had been after, or didn't he? I sat back and took a deep breath. Jennifer had said I could be like one of those Indy 500 racers who went from ignition to rage in three seconds when I wasn't in control. She had been right—back then. But she hadn't known the more mature Finley. I stayed calm, reminded myself I didn't have to solve all the world's ills, even those handed on by Jerry Christman. So I did what any mature, shrewd person would do—I removed the Christman file from my sight, burying it in the bottom drawer of my desk. Who could lose his temper about something dumped on top of a broken stapler?

CHAPTER 9

I was feeling pretty decisive about things until I was about to take a shower before going to bed. I'd just gotten the cold and hot water to the right mix when I had a bad flashback about people with hearing that was too acute by half. From the Asian down at the Green Fox it was simplicity itself to connect what Samuel Chilumu had said about Marchese at the Christman funeral. Had one been keeping an eye on me at the bar while the other had been up to naughty work in my apartment?

I ruined my good water mix by turning off the shower and going back outside for a look at my front door lock. There might have been unnatural rifling, there might not have been. I had never paid enough attention in Forensics class. Maybe I should have rung the bell of my neighbor Mrs. Chalian and asked her straight out if she had interrupted somebody trying to pay me a surprise call for my birthday. But I didn't. Knowing Mrs. Chalian, she would have corrected me that my birthday wasn't due for another three months. That was the problem with telling astrology maniacs what your sign was: You couldn't invent another one for the paranoid occasion.

I went back to the bathroom reassuring myself that, whatever the Asian and Marchese had been up to, I still had Christman's papers. That seemed better than dwelling on the possibility that I was losing it altogether.

CHAPTER 10

The rest of Finley Investigations business hardly sent me pirouetting through Prospect Park, but at least it related to the exciting present. There was my cockroach buddy Bobby Sprowl, for instance, who decided to go for seconds in a courtroom by suing me and his ex-partners at Buona Italia for wrenching his back and neck in our little Carroll Gardens set-to. The lawyer filing the claim, a creep named Martin Nesbitt, had been chasing covered wagons before ambulances, a fact the surviving restaurant partners reminded me of. It was nice to hear them laugh off the suit, guaranteeing there were plenty of Buona Italia customers ready to swear I had caught Sprowl doing his insect number and that he had swung at me first. I didn't remember seeing anyone taking down the names of the customers at the time, but I was at an age where memory lapses were regarded as instinctive.

I also blamed age for my awkward scene with Jeffrey Chalian, the 20ish son of the astrology widow next door. There had apparently been street sightings of Jeffrey back and forth from school when he had been younger, but these had stopped once he had fulfilled the city's education requirements and he had graduated into his bedroom to zap aliens and super villains on play stations 24 hours a day. It was my hard luck that the dork's bedroom shared a wall with mine and that the aliens seemed to hatch most of their invasion plans after midnight. None of this was new; I had been listening to Jeffrey's echoing laser guns since moving in to my apartment. But around the same time I was trying not to think about Christman's file, I felt myself turning into the kind of neighbor Slinky Malone and I had dealt with in Hempstead—the crotchety kind who didn't want kids to have fun, ever, on this planet or any other in the cosmos. Finally, after one whoop too many one night after one o'clock, I got up out of bed and went marching out in my T-shirt and Bermudas to Mrs. Chalian's bell. I hated myself every second of the wait as a door opened inside and somebody scraped over to the peephole. How could it have been worse? The frightened "Mr. Finley!" from Mrs. Chalian as she took me in—that was how. By the time she finished dismantling the Fort Knox of locks on her door, I didn't know why I was standing in the hall in my shorts upsetting widows with idiot sons. What could I say when the bulldog-faced woman stared out at me with a cringing sympathy ready to offer me protection against any disaster I wanted to relate? What else but "Hi, Mrs. Chalian. Did you just ring my bell for something?"

Over the next few days I couldn't mistake Mrs. Chalian's suspicion that I had been drinking before ringing her bell. Big faces like hers weren't made for subtle reflections. And if I were half the man I wanted to think I was, I *should* have been drinking. There were too few good excuses in life for being an asshole not to be able to use them when the occasion arose. It certainly would have been better than giving her an enthusiastic greeting whenever we crossed paths in the hallway or in front of the house. Naturally, that only made things worse—convincing her I was hitting the bottle as regularly during the day as at night. I wouldn't have trusted me, either. When you were losing it, you were losing it.

Then, a few days later, when another body popped up, I had more to worry about than my public relations with Mrs. Chalian.

CHAPTER 11

I had just seen the Mets take the Marlins and had switched to the local news Cynthia watched on her late shifts because the guy at the anchor desk, unlike her Green Fox regulars, still had a waistline and a nose smaller than W.C. Fields's. He seemed to have been waiting for me to tune in. "A tragedy on Long Island," he announced with appropriate gravity. "Senior Detective Ralph Marchese, assigned to Nassau County's Major Cases Bureau, was found dead in his apartment this evening, apparently the victim of a self-inflicted gunshot." And suddenly there was Lieutenant Ellen Miles in my living room, standing in front of a picket line of microphones and saying the same thing the anchor had just said. She looked more flustered than grave. As far as she was concerned, it was "too soon to draw conclusions. Our investigation into this sad incident has just begun."

Where did I start? Ellen looked good; a little out of season and too much like one of Santa's elves in her red suit, but with a bob that flattered her black deer eyes and with chained glasses hanging down over her chest to make her the epitome of office (any office) efficiency. Her habitual silver bracelets seemed to have been sacrificed for her promotion, but I didn't notice any other big changes.

Had I known Marchese's real name had been Ralph? I might have, he had received as many wall plaques and citations as anybody else, but who would have given them more than a second's glance anyway?

And aside from Shelton of Internal Affairs, how come I didn't recognize any of the brass standing around Ellen as she answered media questions by not answering them?

More than five years of being away, that was how come.

Then what the anchor and Ellen had been going on about sank in: Connie Marchese had passed on to wherever dead Connie Marcheses passed on! What about those seconds spent after Samuel Chilumu's call wondering if Marchese was going to drop around sniffing out more information about Christman's manila envelope? And what about the seconds before my shower when I had imagined good old Connie breaking into my place for the envelope? The bald Asian in the Green Fox? He'd just had very good hearing! As I should have known by now, that was the trouble with paranoia: You could never really count on it turning into reality.

But what also caught me off guard was that I had so many distinct memories of Marchese. Between not particularly liking one another and him a relative junior on the squad, I should have remembered a lot fewer one-on-ones with him than I did with, say, Jerry Christman. But the opposite was the case. Christman, for instance, had never stepped foot in my house, nor I in his, but I remembered Jennifer giving Marchese a can of Sprite one afternoon in our kitchen and on another day dropping by his place to pick him up for a court appearance. It was one of those pocket apartment buildings that had gained its own theme over the years—in this case, the divorced and the separated who had given up hope of returning to their split-levels but needed to stay in the area for kids or jobs. Had it struck me as depressing then or just in recalling it after hearing about the suicide? Who knew? What I was sure about was that we had talked that afternoon about the weird prints on his living room walls. They were rubbings from Pompeii a cousin had sent him, he had told me while closing his Venetian blinds so I could see them better; they were supposed to be erotic, but he'd had trouble enough making out the body parts let alone get turned on by them, so had decided just to frame them and hang them on his wall. And the strangest thing? The longer they had hung on the wall, the more he had felt close to them in some generational way. They had absolutely nothing in common with the photographs he had seen of Italy as a kid in his grandparents' house. His grandparents would have been the first to throw them out as either obscene or meaningless. But he had begun to warm up to them as his connection to places he would never see. More than once he had caught himself looking at the things as though they would have told him unknown stories about his ancestors if he stared long enough. Minus the cancer crack from his wife, had I ever heard anything personal like that from Jerry Christman? He didn't like the look of the Mets starting rotation? Who the hell did like it?

And so what? Connie Marchese had now blown his brains out. It was a good thing I hadn't been in an office suicide pool because of all the cops in the Major Cases squad I had known, he (after Ellen) would have been my last pick to eat his gun. What was the word? There was something too *un-introverted* about him. It wasn't that he was a flamboyant good-time-Charlie; it was like he had said about his Pompeii rubbings—people who knew better than he did said they were erotic, he didn't see it, but what the hell, he wasn't going to get into an argument about it, he would just buy some frames and stick them on his walls, maybe brighten up the place. What you saw was what you got from the beanpole and what you saw was a foot soldier, an ear to whatever the next guy said (no matter how dumb it was), and never too many second thoughts about being a racist or just a bonehead. The few times I'd seen him try to break out of that mold—talking to Rigas about opera, for instance—he had been awkward and unconvincing. Somebody with a desk near his had been passionate about Italian and German singing, so he had given it a shot at understanding why. One shot only, though, before another soup can top glittered in the garbage to give him pause. Connie Marchese just went along because everybody else seemed to be going along. Nobody had cringed more when we had to do a perp walk in front of the newspaper and TV pack. Maybe it wouldn't have been his first social choice, but he could have survived easily enough in anonymity.

Except that he now had a TV spot all to himself. And as I had tried to tell Samuel Chilumu in the funeral home parking lot about something else, why he had it simply didn't scan.

CHAPTER 12

My movie came back that night. This time Connie Marchese, dressed in a heavy gray overcoat and wearing brown leather gloves but without a hat, was in it. He was just standing by the culvert at Delaware Avenue nodding for me to go over to the upturned Corolla for a better look at Jennifer and Susan inside. But that didn't make sense. The Corolla was his car, not ours. We had taken the Villager that day because Jennifer had said it was roomier, as if she had been expecting the Professor to laden us down with a department store of Christmas presents. Marchese told me not to worry, that I would still find Jennifer and Susan inside, upside-down, and dead.

He was right. Jennifer was tied upside-down inside her belt. A trickle of blood had invaded her hair but left her face untouched before falling into the car's endless space under her. The tiny stud of her silver earring was safe, could be removed and resold without any fatal accident stories attached to it. I had given her new jade earrings as a Christmas gift, and why she hadn't worn them was beyond me. Which made it a theme for the movie because absolutely everything was beyond me, starting with her. I had never been so far from her small ear or the side of her face. Corolla or Villager, her stillness said she had surrendered completely to the car. I was the one who was making the melodramatic scene by standing outside in the cold night and demanding she confirm what car it was. Why was that detail so important, she wanted to know; she was dead, wasn't she? Why did I have to push even now like a cop for particulars that might have impressed Ellen Miles and my bosses at Major Cases but did nothing at all for her?

I appealed to Susan. She seemed to have her eyes closed, but I couldn't tell because they were on the far side of her twisted neck. It wasn't true what they said about dead children looking like dolls when their heads were distorted: The dolls in Susan's room were slicker, rubbery, nowhere near as white in the skin. And they didn't have the fresh mouths Susan did when she told me she agreed with her mother, that the make of the car wasn't important. I was on the verge of grounding her for her tone. I turned back to get Marchese to back me up, to make her understand that we were talking about adult things and adult things demanded adult attitudes. But Marchese was gone. Everyone was. The movie was over.

CHAPTER 13

The papers I saw the next morning at Sal's didn't say much more than what the TV guy had said except to pinpoint the death around dinner hour, before Marchese had been due to report to work. Par for the course, *Newsday* gave it more space than the *Times* and *News*, but mainly with padding about Marchese being divorced and having a high school-age daughter who lived with her mother. (I might or might not have known that.) The one item that gave me pause was a quote from Roger Ware, known in my circle of one as Mr. Ellen Miles. According to the assistant prosecutor, his office "shared the loss of Detective Marchese with the Nassau County Police Department." I didn't know why it did, at least for public consumption. Getting a reaction to Marchese's suicide from an assistant prosecutor was about as enlightening as getting one from a counter kid at McDonald's. Why bother asking? On the off-chance Ware would say great, good riddance to Connie Marchese?

Then I saw the byline attached to the reactions story and I heard the *Twilight Zone* theme. Nobody knew in what direction the backroom smoke was blowing on the Island better than Alan Crosby. A former student of the Professor's and a steady presence in a rotisserie league the old man and his son-in-law had organized in our past lives, Alan Crosby loved swimming with the sharks around the Sound, then telling his readers how many teeth he had counted. The most personable Alan Crosby was the annoying one; after that, it was a quick drop through grating, infuriating, and whatever had driven Samson to pull down those pillars. Which might have been why I tolerated the guy more than most: He was as pure as anyone I'd ever met in his ability to aggravate the powers and semi-powers (including me and Major Cases back when). When I hadn't been involved, I'd always found his single-mindedness entertaining. He seldom did anything without an agenda and he was a beaver about keeping the agenda up to date. If he had thought it relevant to get a quote on Marchese from Assistant Prosecutor Roger Ware, he'd had some specific connection in mind—one he couldn't resist signaling the Who's Who crowd he had recorded in his notebook.

What did that have to do with me? Absolutely nothing. As the good devil on my left shoulder whispered, Connie Marchese could have had a dozen reasons for taking his life; some of them might have even been tasty (gambling debts, compromising meetings with Al-Qaeda terrorists, feared exposure as the head of an illegal tattoo racket). But that still had nothing to do with me. A connection to Jerry Christman and the magic envelope? Why? Because he had interrupted me and Samuel Chilumu in the funeral parlor parking lot and then had quizzed the African about our conversation? That was too tenuous even for my fantasies.

The bad devil on my right shoulder couldn't have agreed more. He was tired of how easily I was distracted from the meat and potatoes of the business, the Bobby Sprowls and Kim Dolittles who kept me eating, how I always seemed to be trying to make it up to some grade school teacher who had predicted a sterling future for me. Sorry, Mrs. McGinnity. I was the PI I was. I wasn't a Noble Prize winner or even a Good Housekeeping winner. I was the commander-in-chief of Finley Investigations. I was what I was. This was how the cards had been dealt. I was even pretty good at what I did.

But then the bad devil made the mistake of showing me something I shouldn't have seen: the calendar behind Sal's counter. The calendar said it was Wednesday. Serendipity. I knew exactly where Alan Crosby would be that evening—at the Professor's house. Where he was most Wednesdays when he wasn't working.

CHAPTER 14

I'm speaking from unwanted experience when I say you don't want to walk back to your apartment house and see a motorcade of patrol cars out front and all the tenants of the building corralled behind a police line across the street. You especially don't want to see a Bomb Squad van in the middle of all the patrol cars. Maybe if I'd watched more poker tournaments on ESPN, I would have been reassured by the fact that there were dozens of apartments in the building's two wings, making the odds against me being the source of all the disturbance pretty high. And what about Jeffrey Chalian? Couldn't some of his play station aliens have gotten tired of being zapped and sent a punitive mission down to earth against him?

No, they couldn't have. A local 68 Precinct sergeant named Silva, a drop-in at the Green Fox who liked Stoli O on the rocks, confirmed the worst as soon as he spotted me. "Who you been pissing off, Finley?"

He was being gracious. It felt more like who *wasn't* I pissing off. Every housewife and pensioner who hadn't gone off to an office for the day seemed to be boring holes into me from across the street. Right in the middle of them was Mrs. Chalian, in her pink housecoat and slippers and undoubtedly filled with tales for those around her on how I had been behaving lately. I didn't see Jeffrey. He must have been down at the video games store spending more of the mysterious funds he never seemed to run out of.

Silva told me more than he asked, which made wonder how he had risen to sergeant. Not that there was that much to tell. An anonymous call to the station house. Male voice. Very precise about the apartment that was going tick-tick-tick. So far, though, the experts and their sensors upstairs hadn't found anything. Did I have any idea who might want to make me the butt of a practical joke like that?

He should have stuck to not asking questions because the one he did ask only made me grumpier. Since the caller hadn't specified a time for the explosion, why was Silva so quick to believe in a practical joke? The whole building could have gone up while we were standing there on the sidewalk yakking away, couldn't it? But I forgot to ask that and, instead, killed another few minutes reciting the names of all the practical jokers on my official client list. We had barely started when we were joined by a chirpy redheaded detective named Carrington who looked more earnest than Silva about recording the list. Silva didn't want the help, he all but held his nose against the redhead's intrusion, but he plowed on so I couldn't use the intramural relations down at the 68 command as an excuse for not doing the same thing. Did they want just the males or also the women who might have had hot-headed husbands, brothers, or second cousins? Whatever I thought might be helpful. I knew the drill, right? And on we went, Silva and Carrington pretending we weren't playing charades and me coming up with song titles further and further afield. What choice did I have? No, I didn't want them tramping through the Bobby Sprowls and Kim Dolittles from my files. But what I wanted less was them hearing about Jerry Christman and Connie Marchese and pointing out that Marchese was being drained by an embalmer even as we were speaking. Or maybe I should have thrown in the bald Asian for a pinch of Shanghai intrigue? The best any of that would have led to was a cot in the Kings County mental ward.

When the Bomb Squad finally came down to give the All Clear, the bubbly Carrington insisted on accompanying me upstairs for a last go-around. He tried to make it sound like he wanted to check nothing had been removed or destroyed in the apartment, but in his place, I would have looked forward to a more candid moment without Silva around, too. And at least his added bulk in the smelly elevator car gave me an alibi for pressing the button quickly before Mrs. Chalian and the rest of the unhappy masses streamed back across the street to return to their apartments. Say this for Carrington ("Call me Billy"): He thought it was hilarious when the elevator doors closed impolitely on the old crab who lived down the hall on my floor. "This isn't your day for winning friends and influencing people, is it?"

"That horse is out of the barn."

"So I hear!"

I didn't see why that was funny, but he didn't need my vote to laugh. I figured the guy knew his job; he was too casual not to. But I also had the feeling that back in the day I would have volunteered for the canine corps before having him as a partner. He just swayed a little too much for somebody walking on an even floor.

The Bomb people had done their standard Mister Clean job on the apartment. Whoosh, whoosh, whoosh—whatever could be knocked down or over in the interests of public safety had been knocked down and over. Some of it I understood; all the drawers of my desk had been opened, the back of the TV set had been screwed off and examined, every shoe from my bedroom closet was out in the middle of the floor looking for its mate. What were pillows and book shelves good for besides being tossed? But my seascape above the couch? How could anybody have planted a bomb behind that thing without Mister Magoo seeing it the second he came through the front door? And the linoleum-covered kitchen chairs? Why did they have to be overturned? I could see under every one of them without entering the kitchen.

"They have a hard job." Carrington's eyes were on the kitchen chairs, but he was mostly giving me another chance to laugh with him. "Goof-offs would just inspect the place, then put things back. Our boys take pride in their thoroughness. They want you to see it and admire them for it."

I gave him his snicker. It was useful for covering up my look at the bottom desk drawer to make sure Christman's file was still where I'd left it.

Carrington's blue eyes were waiting for me when I looked up again; he had stopped laughing. "So which of those useless names you gave us downstairs do you think might be the least useless?"

"You asked me to speculate. I speculated."

For some reason he looked taller when he sat down on the couch; maybe it was because he had long legs and was sitting down without my invitation. "But I get the feeling there's another candidate not in my notebook. Who we talking about? The client who gave you those stolen emeralds you put in your bottom drawer there? The new boyfriend of your old girl friend? The old boyfriend of your new girlfriend?"

"You have a touch, Carrington."

"Just curiosity. Soon as the call came in, we had a full-court press. I'm not saying there wouldn't have been due diligence anyway. We live to serve. But this one came with something more. Like maybe somebody wasn't all that surprised your name would come up in an anonymous bomb threat."

"You're creeping me out." And he was. I had to remind myself Connie Marchese was still on an embalming table.

He counted to three, then shrugged. The smile was back. "Well, if you don't know, how can Billy Carrington know? I guess I'll just have to spend the day running down all this speculation of yours."

"Sorry for that."

He was up on his feet as quickly as he had gotten off them. Thanks to a full display of freckles, I had given him fewer years than he probably had. Now I guessed closer to 40 than to 30. "Anybody else occurs to you," he said, handing me his card. "How long were you with Major Cases?"

He didn't show anything, so I hoped I didn't. "I say twelve. The pension board said a little less."

He nodded with another glance around the living room. "Fuck them."

"What I say."

"Mind a personal question?"

"What have they been so far?"

"Right. But you a big religious guy?"

"What the hell's that got to do with anything?"

"You know what I mean. One of these anti-evolutionists, anti-gays, anti-abortion people?"

"That what you call religion?"

"You know what I mean."

Actually, I didn't have a clue to what he meant, but if it got him out the door faster, why not answer him? "On the front lines. Every time I see *Inherit the Wind* and Spencer Tracy wins, I figure it's a lesbian plot."

He smiled reflectively. "Yeah, that's what I thought."

I should have left it at that. I almost did. But then as he was walking through the door into the hallway, I said: "Thank whoever it is in your command who was so worried about me."

He liked another idea more. "Tell you what. When some other name occurs to you, we'll have a beer and exchange the names."

He didn't wait for an answer, just walked down the hall to the elevator. I might have added something else if the elevator door hadn't opened and Mrs. Chalian hadn't walked out looking for a fight. I got my door closed before she readjusted her eyes from Carrington's chest down to me.

* * *

Bomb threats, the false alarm kind or not, don't do much for your *joie de vivre*. You can't even claim much importance as a target. If somebody really doesn't like you and wants you to stop taking up space on his planet, the least you should be able to expect is some one-on-one attention—a gun, a knife, maybe a piece of piano wire. But a bomb has none of that respect. It wants you dead, all right, but if others go with you, if the walls come down around you ruining the dinette table, if generations of water bugs get blown out of the kitchen and bathroom pipes in the bargain, that's fine, too. The original target becomes just another piece of the rubble.

I was thinking of that just now as I was changing the dressing on my flesh wound. At least the Keenan crowd was dedicated to killing me, not the Chalians, the crab down the hall, and any delivery boys who happened to be in my building when an explosion went off. I'd like to think of that as the last statement of principle by Captain Patrick Keenan; makes me think of him as the next best thing to being honorable. It's much better to keep that positive frame of mind as I yank some more hairs off my arm than to wish I could raise the fuck from the dead so I could shoot him all over again.

CHAPTER 15

Even before retiring from Adelphi, the Professor had been hosting fixed Wednesday evening gab fests. The only change over the years had been in moving the weekly salons from his big house to his cartoon box. The talk itself could be about news events, movies, or how Charlemagne hadn't accomplished as much as he should have; what came up came up. The people sitting around the living room (sometimes more than a dozen, other times only three or four) had as many opinions on what was discussed as the old man did, and some could match him in pontificating. A few were good for only occasional rounds, but most didn't stay away too long. Either was all right with Joe Carroll because there or not there added to the randomness he liked from week to week. More important than an individual bruised ego was that if you were connected to Adelphi or any Garden City store where he shopped, you knew where the lights would be on at seven o'clock every Wednesday. Ballgames could be rained out, but the Carroll house was as reliable as anything printed in *TV Guide,* just the specific teams TBA. One week there might be fine wines and specialty deli sandwiches waiting, the next Bud and Kraft cheddar. Nobody was discouraged from contributing to the bar and snack table; in fact, if you showed up empty-handed too many weeks in a row, *that* might be the first topic of discussion.

I was a regular irregular, dropping by about once a month. If the Wednesday fell the day after I had already been out to drive the old man down to the mall, I let it slide to the following week.

Then again, I sometimes put off my good deed until late Wednesday afternoon so I could hang around to get the latest scoop on the French and Indian War. Rarely did Alan Crosby miss a gathering when he was in town.

All this made for second, third, fourth, and fifth thoughts on the drive out to Garden City. I couldn't say I was content to make it up as I went along because there were thick brown wisps somewhere in my soul warning that whatever I made up would prove costly. Having the Bomb Squad in my apartment was good for reinforcing that premonition. How far was I ready to go just because there might have been, could have been, in my dreams *was*, some flimsy link between Jennifer's accident and the reports Christman had left for me? So far, I could measure the distance only in gas and anonymous phone threats, but my eagerness for the ride to see Alan Crosby was a little spooky. If there had been a Dial-a-Shrink, I might have doubled Verizon's profits all by myself.

As I drove down North Franklin toward Union, I was sure there was a difference between obsession and mania and it was only for me to figure out what it was. It was a philosophical conundrum that left me about three yards shy of joining Jerry Christman and Connie Marchese in the Netherworld. The lights were on my side, I wasn't talking on a cellphone, and my aftershave lotion was still working. But for all that, the gray Datsun shot out across me from Union giddy its target had finally arrived in its sights. I managed to keep my lungs below my throat as I hit the brake, but I might not have if I had glanced right to see the blue Toyota erupting from the same cannon. I made out a couple of goofball teens laughing in the front, but nothing else. Then they too were whizzing by me in hot pursuit of their friends in the Datsun.

I counted to three in Aramaic before hitting the gas again. I didn't hate teenagers. I only thought I did. I just wanted them to crawl around covered with acne for the rest of their lives. And then I wanted them to *really* suffer.

Failing their suffering, there was mine.

I was already around in my U on the way back to Union when I questioned what I was doing. I was ready to chase the bastards into the Sound if that was what it took. But how could I have caught them at their speeds without going just as fast and probably getting myself killed? The first answer was I couldn't have and the second answer was I should have cared more about the first answer.

It was only back at the corner of Union that the numbness began to slide off my body. Was it some kind of moral victory that the teenage apes had scared me less than I had scared myself?

CHAPTER 16

"You look like hell!" the Professor, already presiding in his leather chair, greeted me across his living room. "An improvement, I'd say."

He got his chuckles from the seven or eight people there ahead of me. At least that was what I could count through the thick glaze laying over the room. Daylight was still glaring through the windows, but every lamp had been turned on. And thanks to the lamps, the room was stifling. One of those pretending not to notice the matted sweat on his forehead was Alan Crosby. "I have some taleggio."

"Whatever that answers."

A young couple in matching paleness, skinny arms, and university T-shirts—the inevitable Joe Carroll Disciples—gave him another eager laugh from the floor. But on the couch a political science teacher I had come to know as Furry Brows had had enough of my jovial interruption and got back to cases on the sacking of Baghdad museums. Furry Brows always unnerved me. While even the Professor had surrendered to short sleeves, FB looked totally immune to the heat in his plaid flannel shirt and the undershirt peering up at the neck under it. He wasn't the kind of teacher you begged to raise your C+ to a B- for a better grade average.

"You okay?" the old man asked, liking the idea of keeping Furry Brows at bay for another second as much as inquiring after me.

"Yeah, sure."

The lingering worry in his eyes said he wasn't convinced, but he turned back to the talk business at hand. Since there was already an awaiting platter on the bar table against the living room wall, I couldn't disappear for a few seconds into the kitchen to sew my nerves back together. It had been a longer day than I had been ready to admit. Call it Delayed Shock, Part II, The Serious Part, but my legs were suddenly grainier than my nerves had been watching the Datsun and Toyota disappear down Union. Add my arms. Some of my malpractice surgeons couldn't have been shakier about getting the cheese out of its paper onto the plate. What had the report in Christman's pile said about that crash on Sunrise Highway? Cars chasing one another? How old would those teenagers have been back then?

"You *do* look a little discombobulated," Crosby, suddenly alongside me, murmured. "Rough day?"

He asked like someone who recalled a rough day of his own back in 1987. It was part of the charm that made me wonder how he had managed to stay in one piece for so long. It was bad enough he had been compiling black books on the Island notables and liked alluding to entries when his latest assignment gave him the chance, but physically he was also from that section of the zoo—weasels, jackals, hyenas—that screamed out for medium game hunting. Gnomish, more scalp than hair and too much jaw (the better for crunching, grandma!), in need of a shave five minutes after his last one. How was it in anybody's interest to put up with him? And why was he always running back to the Professor? Instead of reminding everyone how he had once been a student, shouldn't he have been smoking cigars in some political club and compiling more insider gossip? When I was feeling particularly uncharitable (most of the time), I decided he still hungered for the old man's approval that he was writing modern history for his paper.

"A couple of idiots just did their best to sideswipe me," I said, giving him room to cut at the cheese I had finally laid out. "You never realize how much you want to stay alive until you're almost not."

"Know what you mean."

He might or he might not have; even I wasn't sure where that epiphany had come from. It certainly hadn't come from the half-wit impulse to go chasing after the teenage bastards. But much sooner than I had counted on, he had given me an opening. "I saw that suicide story today about Marchese."

"That's right! You worked with him!"

"Give seniority its privileges. He worked with me."

Bopping right along, but he didn't act anxious to get back to the conversation behind us about Mesopotamian bracelets. "As somebody who once worked for you," he asked, not quite as sardonic as he wanted to sound, "did you peg him as a suicide?"

"Never."

He took it in with the cheese. He endorsed both. "That's what I get, too. And there's no trace of any illness, mental *or* physical. So why does a cop do something like that, Finley?"

"Ask a cop."

"No, seriously."

There was no denying the beggar's bleat in his eyes, but that still didn't explain why he had gotten as many people as he apparently had to open up to him. Or was it the opposite? Was he so transparent about being on the make you couldn't resist telling him how you were one up on him? "I have no idea, Alan. But in these things, there's no such thing as *a cop*. This one was Connie Marchese and he had Connie Marchese problems."

He had considered that possibility—and not thought too much of it. "Think it has anything to do with this other old colleague of yours who died. What was his name? Christman?"

There shouldn't have been a mirror on the wall behind the table. I didn't need it there to know my expression had failed his little test. "Jerry Christman? What's that got to do with it? Christman didn't kill himself."

Crosby smiled as some sweet perfume came up behind me. "No, I didn't say he did," he said, starting back to the conversational circle. "I think you've got a run on your cheese."

The run was Belinda Massey, the most regular of the regulars. A heavy brunette around 45 with seriously hooded eyes and apple

cheeks, she was wearing black jeans and a lime silk shirt that
didn't mind advertising her rose bra. I didn't mind it, either. She
had one of those moles on her right breast that belonged on a fan-
waving countess in a French court. The real Belinda, on the other
hand, looked like she had followed her usual salon routine of
being the first to arrive, downing two quick wines and then nursing the third when she realized she was getting tipsy. It was as if
she never saw any food on the table until she was into her third
glass exactly. The old man wasn't as impressed as I was. To hear
him, all she did was *hover*—first over the wine bottles, then over
her sobriety, and, most important, over his widowhood, bachelor-
hood, or whatever his state of life was. One of his last hires in the
History Department, Belinda Massey was tireless about finding
ways for somebody to come up with a new honor for the old man.
His crankiness that all the scrolls and plaques were mainly for
her to have an excuse to have dinner with him might have been
justified. But then again, I hadn't heard of him saying no to any
of the tributes she had engineered.

"You always bring this delicious cheese, Paul. Why can't I get
it at my supermarket? You have to ask your store the name of the
supplier."

What I actually had to do was get back to Crosby with my
question about Mr. Ellen Miles. But now he was folding his legs
under him on the carpet and trying to pick up the thread between
the Professor and Furry Brows, apparently in for the duration on
what had been looted in Baghdad. I wondered if he already had a
lead on some of the museum swag being fenced by an assembly-
man from the Hamptons.

"Could I ask you something, Paul?" Her voice had dropped to
a near-whisper and she was making sure she kept her back to
the room. "Do you think Joe's been putting on too much weight
lately?"

"I don't think it. I know it."

There was something Harpo Marx about it—the two of us talking while we stood shoulder to shoulder staring at the wall mirror.
I felt like extending my arms to see if the Paul Finley in the mirror
would do the same thing. Belinda wouldn't have noticed: She was

busy profiling her good-sized ass. "I guess we all let ourselves go once in a while," she ventured reluctantly. "But I just think after his heart problems . . ."

"I've already mentioned it to him. And will again."

"Could you? It's really not my place."

I poured myself a ginger ale. It was good to know I wasn't the only one being disingenuous about wanting what I wanted.

CHAPTER 17

I got what I wanted—sort of—two ginger ales later. The living room lights finally began to take effect, but that came at the cost of even more heat, so I gave up struggling to pay attention to the Disciples going at Furry Brows about classical music and slipped out to the backyard for a little air. A little was exactly how much there was, too; even the stars seemed to have wilted off to sleep. The turgid rise and fall of the voices in the distant living room was about as energetic as it got.

The old man had been trying to plant a vegetable garden, but from the look of the withered leaves and a handful of exploded tomatoes on the vines, the effort was beyond him. I had a picture of him getting exhausted from bending over, and I didn't like it. I wasn't in the mood for another funeral. But it was like he had deliberately set about filling up his new heart balloons with every starch and pastry for sale.

"I don't believe that. Do you?"

Crosby came out the back door of the kitchen, trying not to look furtive about lighting a Winston. "What don't you believe?"

"The Fifth Symphony stuff they're talking about. Okay, Beethoven, Mahler, Sibelius, Tchaikovsky, whoever, their fifth symphonies are popular. But that doesn't mean there's some magic in a fifth symphony. Most of those guys have had pretty popular fourth and sixth symphonies, too. Right?"

"Right." He didn't offer me a cigarette from the pack in his shirt pocket. Once that would have been bad manners, now it was supposed to mean the smoker cared about your health. I still thought it was bad manners.

"Nice ankles on that one in there, though, huh?"

I owed him for his bad manners, so I pretended not to understand. He looked disappointed I hadn't matched his ogling of the skinny Disciple named Jill and the way she had taken off her sandals and been wiggling her toes on the thighs of her boyfriend for the last half-hour. He would have been more disappointed if he knew I'd done twice as much heavy breathing as he had watching her. But I was supposed to have bigger fish to fry. "One funny thing about your story on Marchese," I said. "That quote from Roger Ware, the prosecutor. You just filling up space?"

Crosby restrained himself from smiling too proudly. He also looked high from his first drag. "What's so funny? You get a public servant going out like Marchese, you get a reaction from another one."

It was his lead, so I had to be as coy as he was. "The only time I ever heard somebody from the prosecutor's office eulogize a dead cop was years ago when Carl Schenley died taking a bullet for somebody over there."

He moved over to the wicker chair where the Professor probably supervised his plants rather than worked on them. "Is it all this Fifth Symphony stuff clouding my brain or are you asking me something?"

"I thought it was funny seeing Ware in there, that's all."

"Ware! That's right! You were partners with his wife!"

"Gee, funny how that slipped your mind!"

He made a stab at looking shamefaced, but didn't come close. "Sorry. Bad habit. You ever wonder about Ware?"

"Wonder what?"

"Well, I mean here's this fresh-faced assistant prosecutor with ambition coming out of every pore. All that Faith Revival Movement behind him. The priests and Charismatics and pro-lifers can't get enough of him. Who's going to go after him without being accused of hating God and Country? But he was a lot fresher-faced a few years ago. Why not go for the biggest seat in his office? What's been holding him back?"

I remembered the demonstration crowd from the TV news at the Green Fox, but otherwise drew a blank. "I should know? That's your turf."

"I just thought you might . . ."

"No."

"Okay, okay. But what I was about to say was that from what I hear, he was working with Marchese on a case."

"Cops and prosecutors work on cases every day."

"Yeah. But this seemed to be . . . I don't know. A friend of a friend told me they had a scene in George's the other day. Marchese went up to Ware's table, they huddled a few minutes, and Ware exploded at him."

"Know how many times a cop can't tell a prosecutor what he wants to hear for a trial and the Yalie throws a fit? It comes with the territory."

He nodded—and once again discarded the thought. "I looked into it a little. Marchese hasn't been in a courtroom in weeks and wasn't scheduled to be. This was something else."

"Yeah?"

Crosby smiled up at me with more control over the tobacco fumes swimming inside him. "So I get slow days like everybody else and I start looking into things. You know the feeling, right?" I gave a kick to one of the rotten tomatoes. It figured that Ware would belong to something like a Faith Revival Movement; for some reason that had been part of his charm for Ellen. "Marchese wasn't working on anything somebody else in Major Cases wasn't working on. But—and this I found curious—he'd been nosing around at Immigration."

"One of his cousins from Naples wants to come over?"

"No Italians. Ghanians."

I saw a Nehru jacket and a brown schoolbag. It seemed like a point of honor—and the best defense—to blank out the name of the guy wearing the jacket and carrying the bag.

"Which is why I found the suicide curious coming so soon after the death of your other old friend at Major Cases. There was a Ghanian who was taking care of Christman his last weeks."

I didn't know why Samuel Chilumu insisted on reminding me of his name. "And this means what? Ware and Marchese were investigating a new drug connection in Ghana? And Ware wanted faster results than Marchese was giving him? You need to move on to a blog, Alan. Your paper's not keeping you busy enough."

I had crossed a line. He wasn't so satisfied with his deviousness when he was being accused of inventing stories. Glancing at the kitchen to make sure nobody else was coming out to the back after us, he leaned over with his cigarette with a hungrier look on his face. "I'm good at what I do, Finley, because I don't stop at second base."

"And home plate here is . . .?"

He had to remind himself again I didn't work for a rival paper. "I still don't know. What I do know is that the Ghanian who worked with Christman was the subject of a series of phone calls between Marchese and Immigration. What I also know is that the calls stopped after Ware had his little snit at George's restaurant. And I guess now, with Marchese dead, they're stopped for good, right?"

"Jesus Christ, a kangaroo doesn't leap like that!"

He leaned back for another puff; the smugness had returned. "So I just got Ware's reaction to the suicide because of what happened at George's. He didn't have to read anything more into it than that. Here he has a public spat with somebody who kills himself a little later. Must make him feel shitty, right? Answer your question?"

I went back to looking for rotten tomatoes to kick. None of them had Crosby's face on them.

"Good. Then you can answer one of mine."

"What's that, Alan?"

"I'm not into blogs. Gives away too much of your good stuff for free. So I stick to first principles and take a very long lunch hour for working them. We have Marchese looking into Immigration about Ghanians. We have Ware blowing up at him. We have Marchese eating his gun. We have that as the second death of a Major Cases detective in a few days. We have the first one with a Ghanian nurse. So I wander over to this funeral home to cross my

t's and dot my *i*'s that Marchese knew about Christman's Ghanian nurse. And the nice old guy there lets me see the visitors'
book to confirm that Marchese brought his condolences to Mrs.
Christman. And whose name do we see there the same day he
dropped by? First, we see the male nurse's, then right under that
we see yours. How's that for closing a circle?"

He didn't need his nicotine high to be smiling this time.

"So what I'm asking myself, Finley, is what connects all these
dots. You have any idea what that might be?"

I shook my head. If I kept my mind a blank, I told myself, he
wouldn't be able to see into desk drawers with old staplers. He
didn't have a chance to press, anyway. Out came Belinda Massey
waving a magazine in front of her face for some air. I wouldn't
have minded seeing the Professor's expression when he discovered she was using one of the pricey journals he had subscribed to
for learning more about the Babylonians. Maybe I wouldn't have
been so smug about that or anything else if I'd known then there
was already a third body connected to the Christman papers.

CHAPTER 18

I hung out at the house until only the Disciples and Belinda Massey were left, drove home without running into more teenagers, resisted the idea of a nightcap with Cynthia, and checked that Christman's file was where I had left it. Only then, with my admiration for my self-restraint waning, did I see that my sweat had smudged where Samuel Chilumu had written his number on the envelope and call Information for Lynbrook Hospital.

"Samuel Chilumu?" the operator asked. "Let me connect you to Nursing. They can tell you if he's on duty."

Somewhere along the line I had misplaced the character who insisted on believing good things were in the offing. I was so geared for hearing that Samuel Chilumu had been packed off back to Ghana that I felt a letdown when he himself answered the phone. "It is good to speak to you, too, Mr. Finley," he said, making it clear where all my natural cheer had been transferred. "I trust all things go well with you?"

"Couldn't be better. I'm sorry to bother you at this hour, Samuel . . ."

"People need assistance at all hours, Mr. Finley. And sometimes, sad to say, they are beyond assistance. At this time, for instance, I am attending a patient who has gone from too much alcohol to his automobile to the final moments of his earthly life. Another illustration of the moral of the Garden of Eden, I'm afraid to say."

The last thing I needed to hear about was drunk drivers, but I also wanted to lead up to my question as casually as I could. "I don't see the connection between a DWI and the Garden of Eden."

He couldn't have been happier to explain. "Because you accept the common version that Adam and Eve were brought low by an apple. It wasn't an apple, Mr. Finley. It was a grape."

"Right."

"And of course, we know what you make from grapes."

That seemed like enough of a lead up. "Never thought of it that way. But listen, I was curious to know if you've been bothered lately by anybody at Immigration. You know, about your residency?"

"My residency at the hospital?"

"No, in the United States."

His bafflement rose toward stiffness. "That is not in question. I have my green card. All is in perfect order."

Not all, I thought: The commander-in-chief of Finley Investigations was in perfect disorder. "So nobody from Immigration has been bothering you lately. Asking about your status."

"You are making me worry, Mr. Finley. What is the problem?"

"No problem. I've just been trying to get a line on this new chief they put over there. One of my clients says he's been spending a lot of his time reviewing legal green cards."

It wasn't even good as a scramble-lie, and he heard it. "As I know, the person in charge over there is a woman, and she has been there for some time. Is there a new district chief?"

Some minutes passed slower than others. By the time I hung up, I had chalked up about two weeks. Only with a spasm of positive thinking did that seem like a cheap price for knowing that whatever Marchese had been doing at Immigration, it hadn't affected Chilumu. With some luck, the African would have also gotten over my call by the end of his shift and gone back to thinking about the grape vines in the Garden of Eden.

And that should have been the end of it right there. That should have been the exact minute I stopped thinking of Samuel Chilumu, old Major Cases colleagues, and, God help me, even Jennifer and Susan dying near Delaware Avenue. Yes, I liked to think of myself as thorough, but that didn't mean being a fanatic about tying a bow on everything. Some things just didn't have full and tidy explanations.

I pulled the Christman reports up from the drawer for a last look. I wasn't sure if I was going to put them in the Miscellaneous file in my cabinet (Abandon Hope All Ye Who Enter Here) or toss them out altogether. I was leaning toward the first more than the second (Cynthia wasn't the only one superstitious about disappointing the dead) as I riffled through the forms to make sure I hadn't overlooked some clearer message from Christman. They were as mute as they had been the other dozen times I had gone through them. The only yellow-marked passage was still the one about the accident on the Sunrise Highway. There were no other, more subtle markings.

Maybe it was the immediate frustration of again finding nothing, maybe it was the five years bursting out of my walls, but the tears hit me like a hammer. One second I was dispensing paper, the next I was clinging to the blurred scrawling of Jerry Christman and Walter Rigas like they were more of those greeting cards that showed up every once in a while to remind me how the Professor and I had connived to kill Jennifer and Susan. The difference this time was I wasn't the sender; these cards came from the Nassau County Police Department, making public what the old man and I had wanted to believe for years was our dirty little secret. How had I preserved that self-delusion for so long? By being me, how else? As long as I had pulled rank to have to identify Jennifer and Susan only at the accident site, to let the neighbors dig burial clothes out of closets for them, to have Ellen Miles relay my instructions to the undertaker to have closed caskets for the wake before the cremations, and to sit next to Joe in the church like two pals catching a play with the two star actors invisible, I had hung on to the chance that they hadn't really been killed. But five years later Walter Rigas and Jerry Christman had disabused me of that idea once and for all. They had put their names to it, making it as official as arresting a Jimmy Fantone for knifing a whore on the street. Who the hell had I been kidding?

I had to laugh at the sloppiness of it all. I had been caught unawares. What was I to blame it on—the ginger ales at the Professor's house? Jennifer had seen it coming for years, long before she had skidded and turned over on the ice across Delaware Avenue. I remembered every single word of what we had said the night after her mother's funeral. We had been in bed, and she had been wearing the silk cream nightgown with the spaghetti straps that had made her seem whiter, taller, and bonier from her shoulders to her feet. Out of habit she had opened one of those massive English novels about India, but then had immediately folded it face down on her stomach bump to gaze off at the photos of her parents on her bureau. She had been worried about the old man's reaction to her mother's death and she hadn't understood how somebody supposedly so intelligent could be torn up about his failure to cry. "It's like he expected to cry right away, and if he didn't, he was less than human. I told him, I said, 'Daddy, you're not a machine. Mom was sick for a long time. You've been preparing for this for months. You battened down the hatches. They don't suddenly spring back up because the calendar says it's time. Five, ten years from now, you could be talking about one of your European queens, and just like that you'll think of Mom and really, really understand she's gone.'"

I had nodded along in gratitude to have such fundamental good sense in bed next to me. She had called the old man intelligent, but the fact was that he was merely an intellectual and she was the intelligent one. It would have been total serenity listening to her that night—if I hadn't also known she was talking about herself as much as her father. I should have said as much, not for the sake of argument but to help her feel freer about herself. But I hadn't, not in words. I had let the silence of the bedroom say it. I had let her think it for herself, maybe confuse her with the doubt that I hadn't noticed. And if I hadn't noticed something so basic, what kind of a husband could I have been? How could she ever have counted on me for anything important?

Sitting at my desk with Christman's damn reports in front of me, I didn't know who I was crying for or even exactly who had died. There were suddenly too many candidates.

CHAPTER 19

If the first rule is don't get shot, the second is be a ballplayer. By that I mean that when you're the one who's done the shooting, avoid big highs and big lows over it. Keep within yourself, take it one day at a time, and all the rest of those ballplayer clichés. I came out on the winning side with Patrick Keenan and his goons? Great. I had to shoot cops? I'm really sorry about that, and it's no use pretending it was the same as getting past a gang of grocers. You belonged to the league you belonged to. I hadn't graduated from an academy of grocers. Major Cases hadn't meant the cereal cartons in the store basement. But hey, new game tomorrow. You can't psych yourself out of that one before it even starts. Let's just turn the page. Tomorrow is another day. There's always a dawn after the night. You can't live on yesterday's wins and losses. Life is a marathon, not a sprint.

And if you're lucky, you can come up with enough of those bromides to last the entire length of the marathon.

CHAPTER 20

Chirpy Carrington hadn't wasted much time working out which of the names I had given him was the least useless. One pass through his computer had turned up a four-year-old charge against Bobby Sprowl for threatening to blow up some food supplier back in the days when he had still been a partner in good standing at Buona Italia. From there it had been the ABCs of confirming the phone from where the threat on me had come, a comparative voice test with the 911 call, and Bobby's defiant one-note defense to the 68 Precinct cops that he didn't like being knocked around in restaurants by private investigators. Why had he called the precinct instead of me directly about his nonexistent bomb? Because he liked official people to know he was pissed off. Why hadn't he left things at the civil suit? Because four-star morons like Bobby Sprowl never left things at civil suits.

"You'll have to drop down to the house to make a statement," Carrington said. "But what's a half-hour out of your busy schedule when you have a double win? You get a bomber out of your life, *and* he'll never be able to go through with that lawsuit now."

I had already figured that, and could have heard the rest of the arrest details on the phone. But I hadn't forgotten Carrington's promise to swap names the next time we met, so had suggested we have a coffee at a Third Avenue cafeteria a couple of blocks away from the 68 Precinct. It was one of those places with a plane hangar sprawl of tables and booths, mountains of devil's food cake under plastic, and a menu bigger than the telephone directory. Carrington knew the place well. "My mother ate in here at least once a week," he smiled. "She couldn't get over all the choices she had—Greek food, Italian food, Chinese food. I tried telling her when you have three thousand things listed and only four short-order cooks in the kitchen, it's all going from a can to the microwave. But she didn't want to hear it. I was being too negative, she said."

"Mothers know best." I didn't want to talk about Bobby Sprowl or cafeteria menus. For all my good intentions in sticking the Christman reports in my Miscellaneous file, I was still curious about the NYPD command people Carrington had said had me on their radar. And at least he didn't dick around on his trade promise. Without any segue from his mother's view of him, he looked across the booth and said, "Patrick Keenan."

"Who's that?"

"Doesn't ring any bell?"

"No."

He was disappointed; he had had something invested in my answer. "Captain in the office of the Chief of Detectives. He's the one who called the precinct about you. You must've crossed trails somewhere."

"What's he look like?"

"Like all the people you saw in church as a kid. Gray Irish, rimless glasses, pushing 60. To the NYPD straight from the Marines. He honors the Corps with his brush cut and lifeless stare."

I knew a dozen cops who fit the description. Some were named Patrick and one Keenan, but none were named Patrick Keenan. And all of them were out in Nassau or Suffolk, not in the NYPD. "Says nothing. And I thought this was a 911 call. How did he get involved so fast from Manhattan?"

He was back to chirpiness. I was beginning to think it was part of a go-to therapy he had been given for his down moments. "9/11. Any bomb threats must be relayed right away to the office of the Chief of Detectives as well as to the precinct commander. Depending on the moon, you get five to ten a day. Mostly loonies and none of them bringing calls from Patrick Keenan. Must be nice having a special guardian angel like that."

"So why doesn't it feel nice?"

He directed his grin at the coffee he was rippling with his spoon; he had deeper thoughts. "Okay, Sprowl for Keenan," he said after a second. "We're both honorable guys. We live up to our word. But there's still another name out there. The one you didn't put on your list at all . . . C'mon, spare me, Finley. You know how it goes. The vic lists all the trinkets the burglar's taken from him. But there's that little break in his voice when he comes to Object X. Better not declare that because that could lead to trouble down the road if the loot is ever recovered. You had that kind of break in your voice when you were listing your bomber candidates. Like somebody you *really* didn't want us messing with."

I wasn't so sure I would have chosen the canine corps over him as a partner, so it was just as well the choice wasn't there for me to make. "Who cares now? You got Sprowl."

"Clearing up the bomb threat problem. But Sprowl wasn't what made Keenan so interested in you. For an imbecile like that he doesn't make sure we mobilize like we're being airlifted to the Middle East."

"Tell me more about Keenan."

"No, you tell me more about those bad thoughts about Object X."

"On the assumption it's any of your business."

"On the assumption you seem to have more serious enemies than this Sprowl and I'm Officer Billy Carrington always here to help."

"It's not an NYPD problem."

"Okay, it's a job for the Mounties. So entertain me with wild Canadian tales while we have our coffee. Tell me about Object X."

I surprised myself: That was exactly what I did, starting off with Jerry Christman's goodbye call and right through to my little chat with Alan Crosby. Why did I? Then and there I told myself I wanted to talk about Christman's reports to somebody who wasn't the Professor, somebody who didn't make me censor the part about Jennifer and Susan. And maybe I also wanted someone to applaud me for sticking the manila envelope in my

Miscellaneous file and moving on with my life. I had never been applauded before for moving on with my life.

Except Carrington was slow to do any applauding. "And this dead guy Christman was your average anal retentive in the squad room?" he asked, finally sipping his coffee.

"He invented the type."

"So it took special nerve for him to go outside the lines and make these copies of the reports."

"He had a death sentence hanging over him," I said, parroting the Professor. "Probably made him less uptight."

He thought I was being funny. "And you turn off the lights and close the door, Good Night to all that? Jesus, Finley! I don't care if this Christman had every fatal disease known to mankind. He jeopardizes whatever he still has left to jeopardize by copying these reports, he has this nurse look you up so he can call you years after you had anything to say to one another, the nurse is on the scene to give you this treasure trove, and the one cop who shows interest in all this traffic eats his gun a few days later. What do you do for a living up in that apartment of yours? Watch soaps?"

"In between fielding bomb threats."

"I'm making a point."

"Or something."

He looked stymied for a moment, but then brightened at the sight of the waitress holding the encyclopedia-sized menus as she led an old couple to the booth behind us. "Know what I always ordered when I met my mother here? A burger or an omelet. The basics for a joint like this, the reason it went into business in the first place. General Tso's frozen sesame chicken and the Birdseye lasagna came later. What are the basics in Christman's reports? Sounds to me like it's that report on your wife and daughter."

I'd had toothaches flare up less abruptly. "They were killed in an accident. Five years ago. Christman was . . ."

"What? Just trying to get your attention?"

"I said it before: You have a real way about you, Carrington."

"So let me look at these reports of yours."

He couldn't have been more serious—and shouldn't have been. "Brooklyn that slow these days? You want to help out Nassau County?"

He sniffled over his cup and took another deep swallow. He was making up his mind about laughing off his eagerness or repeating his request. He decided not to laugh. "Want to know about Captain Patrick Keenan, Finley? He's a fucking toy, that's what. Put AAA batteries in him and you'll make a fortune next Christmas. Works over in Police Plaza every day, goes home to the Island every night, and you can time his arrivals within three minutes both ways. The kind of guy who thinks he's taking a chance moving his jaw every couple of weeks. His neighbors admire him for tying down his garbage cans and keeping his lawn mowed. They like him more since his kids grew up and moved out of the house away from him because now they don't have to hear him shouting his daughter's a tramp because she has a boyfriend and his son's a fag because he carries a shoulder bag. The one reason he might be late home every so often is bowling. He's a big bowler—maybe because it's the only thing he ever did with his father, maybe because it's what he used to retreat to doing when the other kids in class were feeling up their girlfriends in the backs of cars. He marches in the local holiday parades. He goes to the cemetery on the anniversaries of the deaths of his mother, father, and another son. Seems to like dropping down on his knees in the dirt, reassuring God he still knows he's a humble creature. Then there's the occasional Sunday communion breakfast where he mingles with gentry like assistant prosecutor Roger Ware. Right, the same one who seems to know a lot of the same people in this you do. Keenan and Ware and their friends, they're solid citizens who get dirt smudges on their foreheads Ash Wednesday, think the Republicans are too left-wing, and warn nurses in abortion clinics and same sex marriage partners they're headed to Hell. They'll provide the transportation if they must. Most of this they do in the name of this little club of theirs they call the Faith Renewal Movement. Why I asked you the other day about religion. If you want a flight to Lourdes or Fatima, miracles included, the Movement's the place to go. Discount rates and some side touring of the countryside. They're very big with nuns, priests, and Evangelicals who are tolerant of Catholics who have cut out awkward passages of the Bible. In case you haven't picked up on it, I don't like Captain Patrick Keenan, Finley. Call it one of my unresolved issues from my parochial school days."

For a second I could believe his freckles had been left over from the last rant that had turned his face red. "Or maybe from some promotion he put the kibosh on?"

Chirp, chirp, chirp: He was calm again. "Or maybe that. You're right. Never trust people more sanctimonious than the people they want to nail. But let me tell you that unless Keenan's thinking of recruiting you to head up some new chapter of the Renewal Movement in Bay Ridge, you could really do without the attention he showed you the other day. His attention isn't just *his* attention, if you follow me."

"I don't."

"Which is why you should show me those reports."

"I told you what they were."

"No, what you told me was you can't make head or tail of them. Maybe I'll do better."

"Because you've got this Irish Catholic bug up your ass."

"Because Patrick Keenan doesn't put himself out for anybody unless it's in his political interest," he said evenly. "And I just find it funny as hell he thinks you're in his political interest. Tell me you don't."

What I really wanted to tell him was that he was too high on all the holy water he had blessed himself with as a kid. But I had already told him that, and it hadn't rippled him in the least. And the truth was I hadn't had a rabbi—or a priest—who had worried about me like Captain Patrick Keenan even when I had been back on Major Cases. Whatever Carrington wasn't telling me about his jones for Keenan, that *did* stink to the skies.

"All I'm getting from this is that you don't like Patrick Keenan." He nodded. "That's fair."

"But since when does that make a case for bagging him? Or has Billy Carrington's dislikes become a new felony?"

"Who said anything about Keenan and felonies?"

"Okay. You just like thinking about people you don't like."

"Could be. But what the hell? Even if I was on to something with Keenan, I'd hardly pass it on to one of his Bay Ridge henchmen, would I? Where you going to set up for the Renewal Movement? There's a garage over on Fort Hamilton Parkway that's been empty."

I was supposed to smile. I preferred my watery coffee.

"C'mon, Finley. Show me these police reports you have. What have you got to lose besides all this wallowing around in the past you've probably been doing lately?"

That answer I knew. "Maybe some skin on my knuckles."

He smiled and waved down the passing waitress. Just like that he wasn't so interested in seeing Christman's forms, had to report in for work. I didn't delude myself I had threatened him off. I'd only met the guy twice, but both times I had the feeling of having taken an exam with him and of having done only well enough to be given another one next time around.

CHAPTER 21

It took me a couple of more days to see where I had been going wrong since Christman's call. The vision came from a fishwife reverberating through the courtyard about how *sensitive* her husband had been about something—an attitude that clearly annoyed her. She had a point: I too had been devoting a lot of time to being *sensitive*. Jerry Christman had died so I had been sympathetic and gone to his wake. Connie Marchese had splattered himself all over his walls and I had kept my tactful distance on that curiosity by pussyfooting around secondary sources of information like Alan Crosby. I had been a walking condolences card and in the true Hallmark spirit: Here's my preprinted sorrow, don't ask for anything more because I haven't got any thoughts of my own. In short, whatever it might have looked like, I had mainly been demonstrating I didn't want to know what Christman and Marchese had been up to. None of it had anything to do with Jennifer and Susan. That ground had been covered years ago. The priority was the pieties over two former colleagues, God rest their souls. Who could have objected my attitude was out of line?

Just my grandmother, of course. She would have heard one syllable of "God rest their souls" from me and known I had wanted them at anything but rest. And as for me, if I'd taken the tack with my regular cases that I had taken with Christman and Marchese, Buona Italia's outlets would have already been under new cockroach management.

CHAPTER 22

Sarah Christman lived in Malverne, a 10-minute walk from the Lynbrook funeral home that had buried her husband. What could she have told me Christman hadn't? Ask my new insensitivity. Being torn to death by cancer hinted at hope. It wasn't out of the question that someone coming out of surgery or down from chemo, or just having a panic attack before submitting to either, ran his mouth more than normal as he clung to his wife's hand. And at least to judge from the crack about being eligible for full disability because of the cancer, the lady seemed to have her tart moments. Granted that wasn't much on which to base a hope the widow would be helpful, but nobody was handing out alternatives. For a start, Sarah Christman had to do.

The address from the Internet was for a two-story red brick affair at the end of a *cul-de-sac.* Age seemed to have crept over the block. There were as many flags as cars outside the homes, but not a single tricycle, plastic toy, or sign of the school kids who had started their summer vacations. Aside from the jays chirping in the trees, the only life on the block was an old-timer hosing down his lawn.

The Sarah Christman who came to the screen door looked older than the one I'd seen at the funeral home. It was almost one in the afternoon, but without her mourning black and with dark red curls straggling over her ears, she might have just rolled out of bed and into her blue housedress. She screwed up her eyes as I reintroduced myself, vaguely remembered the Major Cases

connection I had made for her last time, and nodded as if I had
just come by again to pay my respects before going directly back to
my car. She came alert only when I asked to step in for a minute.
She took a long time processing the idea, then decided she didn't
care one way or the other and opened the screen door. I followed
her through the vestibule to a front room. She had what Jennifer
had called piano legs, and there was a big red blotch on the back
of her left calf from a chair rung she had been pressing against.
The vestibule had the same heavy pine odor as the Professor's.

Except for the discolored white doilies on the couch and chairs,
the furniture in the front room might have just been delivered
from a department store. Nothing looked sat on or lived in, and
the wide spaces between the pieces on the uncarpeted wooden
floor might have been for exhibition purposes. There wasn't even
dust on the television screen in the corner. I wasn't the only one
Christman had never invited home for a beer.

"It's been a very disorienting time, Mr. Finley," she said, waving me to the tan couch and perching on the edge of a tall stuffed
chair. "There's always another practical detail. My sons try to
help, but there's just so much you can leave to others."

I let her roll on. Her whole face, not just her eyes, seemed
bloodshot, and I had the eerie feeling she was carrying on with a
conversation she had been having with Christman's ghost before
I had rung the bell. There was a *People* magazine next to a cup of
clotted pink and green mints on the coffee table, but nothing else.
I thought again of the day Marchese had shown me his Pompeii
erotica and how that still gave me more of a personal recollection
of him than anything Jerry Christman had ever said or done.

"I hope you're not here to collect some debt."

The canny smile had appeared from nowhere. Christman
might have been the record keeper at Major Cases, but there was
no doubt about who had been keeping the bank books at home.
"Not money, no."

She was relieved and not so relieved. "I'm not sure that answers my question. What other kind of debt are you suggesting?"

I had already decided to leave Samuel Chilumu out of it; who
knew what oaths private nurses took to do and not do? "Before

he died, Jerry sent me an envelope with some old cases from the office. I haven't really figured out why or what they're telling me."

"Police business? I thought you left there years ago."

"Exactly. And why Jerry reaching out like this is so odd."

She was ready to give me dumbfounded agreement, but then came up with something from the knee she was cropping at nervously. "You're the one who lost his family in that horrible accident, aren't you?"

It had the sound of an accusation—one I hadn't heard in a long time. Jennifer Aniston gave me a perky, reassuring smile from the cover of *People*. She had absolutely no resemblance to my Jennifer and shouldn't have been in the room. "Five years ago. That's right."

"Somebody mentioned that at the wake."

"Oh?"

"They saw your name in the book or something. I'm sorry. It didn't register with me at the funeral home."

What should have been an innocuous remark sneaked up to miff me. One of the Green Fox skels, Johnny Yeager, had told me about his sister-in-law being killed in a plane crash more than four years ago, and I remembered that every time I saw him. And Sarah Christman couldn't remember what had happened to one of her husband's colleagues? "Of course not," I said anyway. "But Jerry mentioned the accident recently?"

She was supposed to have said no, I was supposed to have apologized for disturbing her, and she was supposed to have accompanied me to the door and wished me a good drive back to Brooklyn. Instead, she nodded into the sun filtered through the Venetian blinds behind me. "Yes, he was spending a lot of time with those papers," she said. "Arrest forms or something, he told me they were. I found it strange, but it kept him occupied. He really didn't have much of an attention span the last couple of months. Whatever distracted him I thought was good."

"But did he ever say why they interested him?"

Again, she had her cue and flubbed it. Instead of giving me a simple no, she said: "He told me they weren't right, that people at Major Cases had falsified them in some way."

I waited for her to reconsider what she had said, but she just stared blankly, expecting another question she had made up her mind not to evade and maybe hurt someone in the bargain. "That's a serious charge," I managed, sounding like a bureaucratic oaf. "Did he have any proof of that?"

"I guess he thought those forms were the proof. But it wasn't something I gave much thought to."

"But if there . . ."

"I understand, Mr. Finley" she said, impatience peeking out. "You think you know all there is to know when somebody close dies, then suddenly you have to face new facts. Nobody understands that more than I do."

I didn't know what she was talking about, but I had a feeling it was a continuation from the conversation—the *angry* conversation—she had been having with Christman before I had come by. "My wife and daughter died in an accident on a Christmas evening, Mrs. Christman," I tried again. "The cause was an icy road. Everybody signed off on that. *I* signed off on that. Why should anyone file a false report about it?"

"I really have no idea."

The ferrets in my nerves were far past being awake; they were already sizing up where they should start biting. "Are we saying the same thing here, Mrs. Christman? Because Jerry didn't like what he read in five-year-old reports, I should start having second thoughts about how my wife and daughter were killed?"

"You asked me what Jerry was doing. From what he said, yes, I suppose your wife's accident was one of the reports he thought was phony."

"But how? He must have hinted at something."

I didn't know if it was weariness or coldness, but I was in front of the eyes that had wanted to see lung cancer covered by full disability. "I really can't remember, Mr. Finley. I can imagine how it's important to you, but what I was more concerned about was Jerry having something to do during the day besides worrying about blood counts. If looking into those reports filled his time, I was glad. I didn't listen to all the details. Do you understand that?" Sure, I did—and didn't care about her feelings any more than she cared about mine. If I'd ever been interested in looking for my perfect equal, on the other hand, I'd found her. Whatever secrets Christman had taken to his grave, he had left the two of us holding hands around the pit. "Okay, I understand. But let me try this. Did he leave any notes while he was working on those reports? I don't know. Maybe not even written notes, just lists or some doodles while he was thinking about what he had. Something that might not mean anything to you."

More wall. "I haven't touched his stuff yet," she said, making a point of looking at her watch. "And I don't remember anything like that. But I'll be sure to keep an eye out."

It erupted in a blurt, and why not? I was already being shown the door. There was nothing more to lose. "I don't mean to intrude. You have to believe that. The big things and the small things after something like you've gone through, they're enough to fill anybody's plate, and you don't need me piling them higher. What you should have done or said, what Jerry should have done or said— you get bitter over idiotic things and then you hate yourself for being bitter. The calendar can't go fast enough until . . . well, until it has. One morning the worst of it is *back there* and that turns out to be another kind of weight. But that's the way it has to be. It's what keeps you going. If I've managed to keep going after what happened to my wife and daughter, Sarah, some of it is because I was sure about what happened to them. *That* cause, *that* place, *that* time. It's not much—next to nothing—but it's what I've accepted. But now Jerry's telling me I shouldn't be accepting it, I've been kidding myself all these years about what happened. And that's why I need your help. Now. This afternoon."

What was I expecting? The way she'd been acting, she had discovered Christman had been screwing a neighbor, had thrown the IRAs away on sure things at Belmont, or had redone his will and left everything to Tom Cruise and the Church of Scientology. Where did my little problem rate next to any of that? And like Cynthia had said, you were also supposed to tread lightly when dead people were in the middle. What I wasn't expecting was that Sarah Christman would keep staring at me until she found something she seemed to approve of. "You talk to me like I'm just another *lead*. I didn't realize I could still be so useful."

"I didn't mean . . ."

"Yes, you did. Wait here."

As she got up and pushed out of the room, I tried thinking of nothing but how the red impression on her calf had all but faded. I didn't know what I wanted her to bring back. Stick figures drawn by somebody drugged out of his mind? Scribbling that explained why Christman had been so suspicious of the arrest reports? I broke a green mint off its partner and turned over the cover of *People*. The last thing I needed to see was a perky Jennifer talking about her latest career move in Hollywood.

Sarah Christman came back in with a yellow legal pad. She took a final glance at it, to reassure herself she wasn't giving away the store, then handed it to me. "He walked around everywhere with this, even down to the hospital when he had to do the chemo. I didn't mind that so much, but he always put his pen in his shirt pocket or pajama pocket and he never seemed to close it. I never really got those ink marks out."

The first two pages were columns of numbers—dates and times. The third page was filled with initials and what looked to be phone numbers. The different pens and pencils said they had been written down at various times.

"Does that tell you anything?"

"It might."

"Maybe it's something you don't want to know."

She hadn't sat down again, but stood behind the back of the tall chair seeming to dare me to give her back the pad. "You're right. I'd like to leave this with you right now. But . . ."

She didn't want to hear the rest. "Then take it."

"I could find a copy place and . . ."

"Just take the goddamn thing! Please!"

It was plea and anger, get out and disappear with the rest of the cops and ex-cops in her life. And if I got hurt, so much the worse for me. I knew exactly what she meant. I wanted me gone, too.

CHAPTER 23

I began with the initials and phone numbers. Except for one number that rang and rang without an answer or a message machine, I had pretty much covered Christman's jottings within a half-hour. The sociology was extra. For instance, the thug Jimmy Fantone had an affected wife or girlfriend who said Hello like the Queen of England greeting a commoner. Richard McCoy, the aggrieved party in the Sunrise Highway bang-up, owned a garage that was doing loud business. Felipe Morante, the other one in that crash, liked to drink his lunch. A housekeeper at a Catholic church in Rockville Centre couldn't help me if I didn't know the person I wanted specifically and probably wouldn't have helped me even if I did. A Claudia Troy named in a domestic beef apparently ran a travel agency close to where I lived. And on through all the names mentioned in the reports. Whatever Christman had sniffed in the reports had led him through felonies, misdemeanors, and just plain accidents (I hoped). He might not have been pursuing anything real, but *he* didn't know that.

I didn't identify myself to anyone; just used the usual wrong number ploy. There was time enough for more ambitious conversations if I had to have them. I considered myself already ahead in going down the list not to come across my initials or the Professor's. Whatever Christman had convinced himself of didn't include our role in the Delaware Avenue part of the plot. Or were we missing because Jennifer's accident had never been part of the suspect exhibits, because he had indeed included it just as a tactical move to get me interested in the other reports? One way or the other, thank you very much, Jerry Christman. Now go screw yourself.

The one number that didn't answer belonged to Aaron Garrett, the gun runner busted by Herb Levine. That suggested three possibilities: Garrett was dead, Garrett was behind bars, or Garrett was typical of his trade in moving from cellphone to cellphone one step ahead of United Way solicitors. Since he was the most immediate mystery, I returned the favor, calling Jimmy Heyer as soon as the idea occurred to me. Anybody who had ever made the mistake of having his name printed on more than a clothing label was Jimmy Heyer's prey. Reaching out to him had cost me a few times, including one mess of trailing his son's teacher who might or might not have been conducting extra-curricular activities with students in her bedroom. But in for a pence, in for a pound, as Jimmy Fantone's affected lady friend might have said.

I didn't like the eagerness in Heyer's voice to help; it smelled like another big return favor in the offing. Just to be sure it wouldn't be for merely finding out Aaron Garrett was on the kitchen staff at Attica, I threw in Billy Carrington to even up the eventual trade. I could have just as easily thrown in the Professor's name for testing Heyer's thoroughness, but it seemed like the perfect opportunity for finding out why I might have trusted "Call me Billy" more if he hadn't been so chirpy.

For once, Heyer was back to me within the hour. "You want the good news or the bad news first?"

"They're usually the same thing."

"Aaron Garrett is free as a bird somewhere. Last time he ran into the law was back . . ."

"Four years ago."

"Seven, actually."

"No, that's not right. He was picked up four years ago . . ."

"I'm telling you seven. He was picked up at a pawn shop in St. Albans for trying to fence some rare collection of knives and those other blades the Filipinos use to whack at the jungle. They were on a stolen goods list."

"Your computer's falling down on the job, Jimmy." I scrambled to find the report Christman had copied and read off the arrest date. "By my math that's four years ago, not seven. The arresting officer was a Herb Levine and we're talking about guns, not machetes."

"Nope. The arresting officers were Ben Fleishman and Miguel Perez and there's nothing about guns. Garrett walked because the pawnbroker wouldn't finger him for trying to sell the stuff."

"I've got the gun report right in front of me!"

"What can I tell you, Finley? Not a trace of any guns four years ago. I'm not saying the computer's god . . ."

But of course, it was god. Everybody, including Jerry Christman, knew that. The dead bastard *had* been on to something. "You better give me the good news before I go strangle a corpse."

"*That* was the good news. You asked, I found. Or are you just taking all this hard research of mine for granted these days?"

"Carrington?"

"What did he tell you he was?"

Heyer would have been disappointed if I didn't sound like a building was coming down on my head. "Tell me he doesn't exist."

He laughed; humorlessly. 'There's a lot of people who wish he didn't. He's Internal Affairs, Finley. One of their all-stars."

I told myself that made sense, a lot more than an ex-altar boy trying to nail Captain Patrick Keenan because they didn't have the same take on the papal encyclicals. That also explained why Sergeant Silva hadn't been so grateful for Carrington's help standing on the sidewalk in front of my apartment building. It explained so many things I should have been euphoric as Heyer went on with his information. So why wasn't I euphoric?

". . . Carrington's father was on the job for the full twenty. Rose to Lieutenant. So what do you think? Little Willie doesn't have the guts to tell Pop he doesn't want to be a cop, so he does the next best thing? Join up and then go IAB to turn in every cop he can?"

"Reading those paperback psychology books again, Jimmy?"

"Like I should wait for your phone calls, instead?"

The fact was, I enjoyed Heyer's little analysis: It felt both plausible and mean-spirited, and where could you find a better combination than that? Then he spoiled his brilliance by taking his turn at the favors. It felt like a win when he was interrupted for another call and I was able to hang up with nothing more than his threat to call me in a day or two "about something."

The relief lasted about a second and a half. If Carrington was IAB and he was after Patrick Keenan for something, what did that have to do with me or Jerry Christman or Connie Marchese or any of the other things that had happened out of his jurisdiction on Long Island? Whatever it was, Chirpy Billy, son of an NYPD lieutenant, seemed to have decided I was the connecting door. When had I signed up for *that*?

CHAPTER 24

My old man was no scholar. He liked cracking that the only reason he got out of high school was that the building had been condemned and no one wanted to be responsible for blowing up the place with him still sitting at his desk. But he also gave me savvy test-taking advice when I whined to him one time about not doing well on an exam because I couldn't get past the fourth and fifth true-and-false questions and ended up leaving a slew of later ones unanswered. "You know the expression doing it by the numbers?" he said to me. "That's what it means. They number all those questions so you won't get lost. You don't know number three, you move on to number four, then five, six, to the end. You can't get lost going back to number three when you're at the end. The numbers don't come in invisible ink. They'll still be there, and you just go backwards. That's what they mean by playing it by the numbers."

Okay, so that wasn't what they had meant, my old man wasn't Plato, and nobody had ever been a hero to his team by skipping second base on his way around from first to third. But that piece of advice had always impressed me as being as much of a wise saying as all those proverbs they used to post around the classroom because Benjamin Franklin had said them. So with Christman's reports I played it by the numbers (the Finley family version), jumping past the questions I had no immediate answer for and taking care of what seemed like the easy ones first. Needless to say, I also glossed over why I was taking the test in the first place. Jerry Christman had laid it on my desk, I had a pencil in my hand, and I was supposed to know what to do next. Absolute silence. No peeking at your neighbor. Get the damn thing over with once and for all. One way or another, I'd feel stronger for the experience.

CHAPTER 25

Claudia Troy shaped up as the easiest True-False question of all. She ran a travel agency within walking distance of my apartment, and Christman's report made her troubles sound as routine as a domestic disturbance call ever got. Three years ago, the cops had been called to the Wantagh home of one Arthur Featherstone to break up a fight between Featherstone and Troy, the parties had been separated, and no further action had been required. Troy was identified in the usual bureaucratese as Featherstone's "common law wife."

The travel agency was pretty common, too—a sterile box of a storefront slathered with posters for the three I's of Ireland, Italy, and Israel. If you wanted a special deal for a trip to Sierra Leone, you were probably better off going elsewhere. Claudia Troy herself was a petite, pony-tailed brunette with green eyes, heavy nasal speech, and noticeably big hands. She wore tiny purple dots for earrings, but there was no way of missing them with her hair pulled back. Her single-shoulder silk dress with wide swaths of blue and green stripes might have been imported from Calcutta. She didn't seem to know whether she wanted to be picked out of a crowd or not.

She was disappointed I didn't want to go to Dublin, Rome, or Tel Aviv, and the desks behind the counter said she might have had extra reason to be. Hers looked pretty clear of pending business. The dorky-looking guy sitting at the other one might have been scanning recent bookings or just a list of his favorite Hollywood westerns. Then there was the local gossip that the agency's whole block was facing the old one-two of abruptly tripled rents and evictions before a wrecking ball cleared the way for a new building complex. On the other hand, what I had expected to be the main area of resistance—talking to me about three-year-old family tiffs—only perked her up. At first, I thought it was because she saw through my line about working for a hotline that was checking on the practical follow-ups to domestic disturbance complaints. She might well have, but she was mainly surprised that there was any file at all about her problems with Arthur Featherstone. I thanked my father for his instincts as she ushered me around the counter to her desk. "Roy, why don't you take an early lunch today?" she said to the dork. "There's nothing I can't handle by myself for now."

Roy paused only to long enough to cover up *Shane* and *High Noon* with a file folder before skipping out.

"Why're you surprised there's a record? The cops were called. They have to keep a record."

She had sat me down, but wasn't in a hurry to take her own chair. Either she wanted to watch Roy from the window or she didn't mind me studying how tightly her dress shaped her little ass, especially on her extra high heels. "Then you don't know Arthur or his friends," she said. "My lawyer told me there was no record of those cops coming to the house. Where did you get this information?"

"The public record," I said, maybe stretching a point.

She nodded: something else she might or might not have believed. "Well, if what you want to know is what follow-up there was, you coming in here today, that's it."

"You didn't have much of a lawyer."

"You think? What I didn't find out until too late was that he belonged to the same religious gang as Arthur did. Always do a background check on your lawyers, Mr. Finley."

"*Religious gang*? You mean these . . .?"

"The Faith Renewal Movement out on the Island. They're not big on sin. They weren't too big on me, either." She finally took her desk chair and grabbed for a Bic to keep her big hands busy.

"That's how it all started. Arthur was listening to too many of them telling him he had to marry me or get rid of me. I thought he was kidding. With all the little boy scandals the Catholic Church has, these saints are still worried about who's walked down the aisle and who hasn't? Like *hellooo!*"

"But Arthur didn't see it that way."

"No. He said I didn't take his beliefs seriously and that was a bad sign. About that he was right. The real sign was he had already made his choice, and it wasn't to marry me."

I was beginning to warm up to Claudia Troy. Who knew? If she kept talking, I might have gone to Dublin or Tel Aviv just to get her a commission. "Did you want to marry him?"

"No, not really. I mean, I could see myself doing it out of inertia after a few years, but it wasn't something I thought about all the time. You know, 'let tomorrow come and I'll deal with tomorrow until the next day.' I'm not proud of it, but that was about as far as I was thinking."

"So why the fracas?"

She hesitated. Then the pen gave her permission to go on. "He was a goddamn hypocrite, why else?" she said, poking her palms back and forth with the Bic. "Is there anything worse than people pretending to give you a choice but knowing already what they've decided? Maybe some fatal disease is worse, but that's about the only thing I can think of. So I sold his letters and he blew up."

"Arthur wrote epistles to the multitudes?"

"Not those kinds of letters. His athletic letters from high school. He'd been a star on the basketball and football teams. Half the wall in the living room was covered with these big ugly green G's. When he wasn't talking about the Holy Ghost and the stock market, he was going on about the big game with these friends of his who came by. I mean, they were all in their thirties, but they could've played these games yesterday!"

"Saturday's Heroes."

"I would've settled for just hearing about it on Saturday. But those damn G's were in front of me seven days a week. So when he gave me this ultimatum that wasn't supposed to be an ultimatum about getting out of the house, I went on E-Bay and sold all his letters. You'd be surprised how many sad people are out there waiting to lie about what *they* did in high school. I have to admit they're even more pathetic than Arthur and his friends."

"And I guess Arthur didn't like seeing this wall blank."

She tried to fight the memory of her satisfaction, but it still brought a whisper of a smile. "No, he didn't. He came home one night all bursting with news about some stock that had done what stocks do when it's good news. He sees the wall, and before I knew it, he was choking me. I thought he was going to kill me, I really did. Thank god, we knocked over enough things that the noise got one of the neighbors to call the police. They came, took down what we had to say, then insisted on waiting until I packed a few things and left to go to my sister's."

"No summons of any kind?"

"Sure. We even had a date for a desk appearance. But by then nobody seemed to remember anything. I went back to the house to ask Arthur about it. He just waved his hand at me and said nothing ever happened, and if I tried to say something had, he'd sue me or kill me or something. That's when I went to the lawyer. Plenty of stuff in that house belonged to me, not to mention the little detail about choking me."

I told myself that could have been it: Once choking got mentioned in a domestic disturbance complaint, the law started getting vague about what was and what wasn't assault. But of course, that couldn't have been it. I was sitting where I was because Jerry Christman had sent me proof that the cops *had* established some kind of assault. I didn't know what to ask her next.

"It's confusing to you?" she laughed. "Think how confused I was. Then to top it off, a couple of weeks later, I get a call at my sister's from Arthur telling me if I'm still interested in some things at the house, I can drop by at such-and-such hours to pick them up."

"At least that."

She was disappointed in me again. "No, Mr. Finley. I wanted the stuff because it was mine and I wanted the law to say it was. He wanted me just to get the stuff because he didn't want any more evidence of his sinful ways around. There's a big difference."

I had second thoughts about going to the Wailing Wall just so she could have a commission. "But you did get the stuff in the end."

"Hell, yeah. With these two old maids sitting around to make sure I didn't steal his BVDs or something. Two of his religious friends. You know the kind. They smile at you like they're offering you apple pie or eternity in Hell, either one is okay with them."

"So you blame this Faith Movement for your troubles with Arthur?"

She rolled her eyes to the ceiling; she was having second thoughts about selling me a ticket even if I did want to go somewhere. "I'm not that naïve, Mr. Finley. I blame my troubles with Arthur on Arthur and my stupidity thinking I could have lived in Wantagh hearing about the big games from the Clearasil days. I've moved on from that, thank God. But what I am blaming those little saints for is pressuring the cops not to do anything about Arthur assaulting me. That's still against the law, isn't it?"

"But you don't have any proof of this pressure."

She had heard that objection before, maybe a hundred times; it didn't surprise her, but it didn't rack up imagination points for me, either. "What do they say about the duck? If it looks like a duck and quacks like a duck . . .?"

They say quack, quack, I thought. They didn't say I had the answer to what was common about the reports Jerry Christman had sent me. Carrington and Claudia Troy had both mentioned the Faith Renewal Movement, but the Widow Christman hadn't, and the closest her husband's notes had come to it had been the telephone number for the Catholic church.

No doubt about it: Quack, quack.

CHAPTER 26

Jeffrey Chalian would have been proud of me. I went directly home from the travel agency to the Internet. There were enough entries on the Faith Renewal Movement to entertain me for the afternoon if I wanted to be that entertained. I didn't. I was more than content just to get a rundown of the players and of some of the louder games they had played.

The logical place to start was with the group's website. It unfolded on my screen in blue and gold from a dove's wings. Claudia Troy's allusion to the Holy Ghost probably hadn't been accidental. Once all the banners and curlicues were in place, there was the usual menu of HOME, ABOUT US, CONTACT, and LINKS. ABOUT US didn't mince words: Everything was going to hell, immorality and unAmericanism bestrode the land, and God had to be restored to our personal and national lives. It wasn't enough to pray for this development, it had to be the consequence of daily church militancy. Oh, and by the way, something had to be done about all the immigrants, too.

The rant wasn't anything that couldn't have been heard on a half-dozen radio and cable TV stations every day. What singled it out was the imprimatur of a couple of bishops and Long Island town officials, their names prominent under the dove's flapping wings. If Claudia Troy had been right about the pressure on the cops to keep her Arthur away from station house summons desks, its source was apparent.

And so what? Welcome to the world of knowing somebody when you needed somebody. Unlucky for Claudia, Arthur Featherstone knew people. The more serious issue was that there was no correspondence between the website names and those mentioned in Christman's reports. The closest connection I could see on the letterhead was the Reverend Bernard Tully from St. Brendan's in Rockville Centre and the call I had made to the unhelpful housekeeper: The numbers on the letterhead and Christman's legal pad were very close. Still, a DWI for a whiskey priest didn't seem like much of a payoff for the conspiracies Christman had apparently wanted me to see.

When I keyed in Arthur Featherstone, I arrived at a two-year-old *Newsday* story about a protest demonstration in Syosset. Arthur was only one of several people quoted as explaining that the march on a local Triple XXX video store was "in the name of our children and our children's children." I didn't push that one even in my thoughts as I followed another Arthur Featherstone link to Facebook. I could see what Claudia had meant. There were three photos in Arthur's inner circle: a stock broker, a skin-headed wrestler described as "a high school buddy," and Jesus Christ. Arthur himself was barely distinguishable through the darkness of his lousy picture, but I didn't make out anybody resembling George Clooney. I also didn't make out anything that would have interested Jerry Christman.

I looked for two more names—Patrick Keenan because Carrington had made me curious about him and Roger Ware because Ellen Miles's marriage to him had all but burned the curiosity gene out of me. Keenan appeared nowhere, not even as a face in the march in newspaper stories about demos. Ware had had a lot to say, but, as Alan Crosby had hinted, only years ago, when he could have still been described as "one of the Young Turks in the Prosecutor's Office with an eye on the top job."

I shut off the computer before I summoned up any more dead ends. It was more productive to think about Claudia Troy in her tight Indian dress.

CHAPTER 27

Richard McCoy's garage was in Hicksville, on a gravel road not far from the LIRR station. It wasn't what people had in mind when they referred to a high-class neighborhood. Across the street was a razor-wire-enclosed compound of abandoned sheds sprawled over acres of dead grass; it looked like a place that had once manufactured something military for some war. The fact that the real estate crowd had left the land to rot instead of buying it up for a new mall told you there must have been enough toxins under the sheds to make for a gargantuan sledging and disposal bill. Or maybe I was just imagining the thick sulfur stench in the air.

MCCOY'S MOTOR WORKS, as it was called, was doing a pretty good business. Four mechanics were busy wrenching apart or banging away at three sedans and a panel truck, and the schedule board on the wall outside the glass box of an office had most of the calendar squares filled up with jobs and pickup times. McCoy himself was a beefy blond in tortoise-shelled glasses who hadn't missed too many meals since being hit by Felipe Morante. As my mother might have said, his nose was big enough to fit enough quarters for a nice bank account. On the other hand, he wasn't charmed by my business card. Dropping down behind his desk with the grace of an elephant, he was in no mood to talk about ancient accidents. I took it as a particularly bad sign that he didn't tell me to get rid of the grease rag covering the only other chair and to sit down.

"Let me guess. You represent Aetna and you want to reimburse me for the higher rates you've been chargin' me since that damn night."

"Sorry. I'm just trying to catch up on some old reports."

"Yeah? For who?"

"It's not your insurance company."

"Yeah, right. I can guess for who. But don't you have enough paper already? The cops. My insurance company. Morante's insurance company. Even the EMS must have somethin' tucked away somewhere."

I tried thinking of when I had filled out a report without mentioning an EMS presence. It had to have happened, but then and there I couldn't remember when. "What's official is bad enough when it's just official. Now it's official *and* old."

McCoy thought that over, then reached into his jumpsuit pocket for a half-smoked cigar. Just in case he counted on his smelly smoke to drive me back out of his life, I got rid of the grease rag and sat down. He thought I was funny. "Look," he said, getting his cigar going. "Morante's taken this long to call in the lawyers, tell him from somebody who knows he don't have a prayer. I wait a month to go after some of the deadbeats who come in here and I'm still scratchin' my ass five years later for a simple brake linin' bill. And tell him not to count on me. The description I gave of those cars that night is as good as it gets."

Not only hadn't there been any mention of the EMS in Christman's report, but McCoy, not Morante, had come out of it as the more aggrieved party. "From what I read, you were the one who took the broadside."

"Remind me. You're makin' my day. But you haven't read all the official paper very close, have you? See me? Here, look! Hands and legs workin' fine. You won't find that with Morante. Least from what I hear."

One plus one made two: Morante had been hurt, and that was why the EMS had been on the scene. And it still added up to three. "I won't bullshit you, McCoy," I had to say. "They threw me in the water here and I'm just splashing around. You mind giving me two minutes just going back over exactly what happened?"

He considered that a reasonable request—either that or he had just lighted his cigar and didn't want me to leave until he had taken a few draws. "What happened was what happened," he said through a sudden pause in the banging outside. "I'm comin' home from my mother's house for Christmas. Cold, lousy night. No angels singin' in the sky. This Impala ahead of me, it's movin' along, no problem. That's Morante. Then suddenly this bat comes flyin' out of hell at Glendon, just ahead of another one. The first one—blue Acura, which already tells you all you need to know about the driver. Every time somebody says to me they're off V8 engines and into Acuras, I'm thinkin' to myself, 'okay, here's another customer in a few months.' You can build *two* V8s for the price of one Acura, for Christ sake! Anyway, this genius veers around Morante in front of me and keeps goin'. The second one's a black Mustang. More smarts down at the lot, but no more sense away from it. He has a second of hesitation about gettin' around Morante. One second too many for Morante because the idiot decides to swerve right. I guess he figured he used up his luck with the Acura. Anyway, here he goes hittin' the ice and spinnin' off the road. But he don't stop there, son of a bitch! He's goin' to regain control *against* his skid! So like that I'm suddenly lookin' at his nose as he's comin' straight for me! Boom! Too bad for Morante and too bad for my premiums. And a Merry Christmas to one and all!"

I was so far behind him that any reach at all seemed better than nothing. "Your description of the two cars back then was pretty vague. Now you know for sure it was a blue Acura and black Mustang?"

It was either me or the cigar that rushed the blood to his head. I didn't think it was the cigar. "Hey! Finley Investigation Services or whoever the hell you are! Look around you! What do you think I do for a livin'? I wasn't no fuckin' *vague* about nothin'.".

The banging outside resumed. I could have done without my old man's test-taking wisdom. McCoy wasn't among the easiest questions at all. "From what I read, those two cars chasing one another were just background noise."

"Fuck you and your background noise! They *caused* Morante to go skiddin'! Without them he don't come near me!"

"A blue Acura and black Mustang."

"New York plates, both of them. The Acura was 96X and I didn't get the rest. The Mustang was two zeroes at the end. That's all I remember." He took counsel with his cigar to calm down. "They really did just throw you in the water, didn't they? Who? Morante's sister? She was a real hot pepper. Wanted to sue everybody, startin' with me. I guess I owe at least that much to the DA's office."

"What's that?"

He shrugged. "That she had no case. That I was the one who was hit, not her brother. They made that pretty clear to her."

Suddenly I was back in the game. I just *knew* what he was going to answer. "Somebody specific in the DA's office?"

He had enough of his cigar, squashed it into the tray on his desk, and made a face like somebody who had been warned he would regret taking a few tokes. "Yeah," he said, slapping the desk with his two hams and hefting himself up. "Guy named Ware. He was handlin' all the questions for them. Got a broomstick up his ass when you see him on the tube, but he saved me a headache with the Latina back then."

I didn't know why he was in such a hurry to get rid of me. I was getting comfortable with the hammer blows from outside.

"One more thing."

"What?"

"You belong to this Faith Renewal Movement?"

He needed to squint to see me clearly. "That Born-Again crowd over in Rockville Centre? Why the hell would I belong to that?"

"And they've never contacted you for any reason?"

He was *definitely* getting tired of my company. "Why? The Popemobile need a tune-up? Tell them to go somewhere else. They make my wife nervous marching around with all their fetuses in jars, and when she's nervous I get nervous. We finished here, Finley Investigations?"

"Finished."

CHAPTER 28

Calling up Cynthia on her day off seemed like a good idea. Ordering in egg rolls and steamed dumplings was a better one. The best one of all was talking about everything except people named Christman and Marchese while we ate and split four beers. I almost carried the evening off.

Until we went into the bedroom.

"Who's here with us, Finley?"

"I don't know. Let me get up and check."

"I'm asking a question. And I know you want to answer me."

Cynthia in GRAVE MODE behind her bar was bad enough: Natural barriers were what they were. But Cynthia in GRAVE MODE on my bed in nothing but her black silk panties made the barriers mine, and they were the opposite of natural.

"This is about that dead guy again, isn't it?"

"You say that like you mean the *other* dead guy."

"This isn't foreplay. What's going on?"

I could have done without the genuine concern and the light rub up and down my arm. It was more effective than the dumplings as extortion. "I've talked to two of the interested parties about those reports I mentioned. About the only thing tying them together is they agree the reports are as fishy as Christman said. What are the odds against the others being crap, too?"

She had wanted to hear something else, but it was too late. "And I imagine you don't care about the others except for one."

"That may just be a joker in the pack. To draw me in."

"But you're not sure."

"Pretty."

"A hundred percent?"

"No. And there's this thing about two cars drag racing around the time of an accident. I don't know why, but I have this itchy feeling they might be the stars of this show. There was no other reason for certain people to act the way they did. It's like VIP 1 was in this blue Acura and VIP 2 in a black Mustang. There was a lot of sweating to keep them out of the picture."

"So find out. That's what you do for a living, isn't it?"

A dozen cracks occurred to me, starting with the benefits of having a living client to pick up the incidentals. But I wasn't feeling smart about anything. "I thought it might all go back to these pious Peters out on the Island. But one guy says no. Then there's this captain of detectives that's stirred up the hornets in Internal Affairs. He's one of the pious Peters, but he isn't making himself conspicuous about it. I don't know, Cyn. I don't see the curtain, let alone the wizard behind the curtain."

She shifted her head on the pillow. If I didn't know she could already see what there was to see, I might have thought she needed a clearer look at me. "So what? You're not up for it?"

"Hilarious."

She needed a second to realize how witty she had been. "God, I'm funny even when I'm not trying to be. But that's not what I mean. I'm saying I can relate, I really can."

"Thank you."

"I'm serious. I stand behind that bar six days a week. 'What's it going to be, ladies, gentlemen?' That's the best part—when I don't know what they want. I have to wait for them to tell me. The *best* part, Finley!"

"Your point being?" Her poke in my chest almost went through my right lung. "Ow!"

"I told you: I can relate. You're always giving me another version of my job when you talk about this romantic business of yours. 'What's it going to be, ladies, gentlemen?' You wait for the phone to ring, for some e-mail. You don't even leave this castle of yours unless somebody has told you where to go. '*Ready to serve, sir!*' It's a wonder you don't have your food parachuted in. But now you must put a shirt on and go after something without waiting for an order. And Paul's a little scared of that. He's supposed to have all those street smarts and experience, but at bottom he'd really prefer waiting for another phone call telling him what to do next."

"I sure as hell would."

"I'm not talking about your wife and daughter, I'm talking about what this Christman has been forcing you into. You should thank the man. He's gotten you to think on your own. Me, I could almost envy it."

"I don't think so."

"Don't tell me what I can envy and what I can't."

"All right, I won't tell you."

The idea had been to lie back and stare up at the bedroom ceiling, to figure out what size seascape I could get to cover over all the plaster that would come down one night while I was sleeping and shard me to death. But she insisted on rolling over on me and blocking my view of the work to be done. "I look at you sometimes," she said, breathing right through me. "I look and I think to myself, 'maybe if this was a little different or that was black instead of white. I wouldn't have to overhaul him completely to be acceptable, just a little tweak here and there.' It's fun. It lets me imagine an unreal Finley, and how could that *not* be fun compared to the original? But the longer I look and imagine all these tiny changes, there's this other question that starts creeping into my head. 'Why am I looking at him at all,' it asks. 'Why don't I use my time to find someone who already has the changes I want to make? Why am I wasting my time thinking of him, trying to convince myself that it's only for me to stare better to see what I want to see?'"

"And what's the answer?"

She didn't blink. She had known the answer for a long time. "Inertia. I'm still waiting for the ladies and gentlemen to tell me what they want to drink so I can hop to it."

Claudia Troy had said the same thing. Did that make me another Arthur Featherstone? What letters would *I* have put on my wall?

"Doesn't say much about me, does it, Finley?"

What could I say? Sometimes humiliation worked as an aphrodisiac. Especially when it worked in both directions.

CHAPTER 29

Felipe Morante lived with his sister Mireya in Carroll Gardens around the corner from the Buona Italia where I had decked Bobby Sprowl. I kept my nostalgia pangs under control. Thanks to what McCoy had told me, driving over to the pockmarked brownstone had the sluggish feel of running out the groundball. The muscular 30-year-old in a wheelchair who came to the gate of the areaway apartment under the stoop was being called out at first. In another life, the one he had before becoming a cripple, Morante might have been a T-shirt model, a Marine, or a middleweight prize fighter. The thick Old Spice aroma and the military crease on his khakis said he had once fancied himself entering rooms. Now, though, he was a fixed scowl for being marooned at home for the afternoon while Sis was off at work. At least he was sober, not the drunk I'd heard on the telephone. I didn't look like his idea of a burglar, so he let me in. I was as good as anybody else for helping him kill a few minutes until his sister came home.

"You want something to drink, I can't help you," he said, rolling through the dark vestibule to a front room where a portable black-and-white TV and a loud fan were sharing a coffee table. "I've used up my quota for the week in coffee, beer, wine, scotch, and whatever else I can't give you. I go over the limit and I get told what a burden I am."

I was tempted to ask for something anyway. But as he went over to kill the sound on one of those TV judge shows and then spun back to me, he looked as humorless as he was agile on his wheels. I couldn't fault him: Even within the dim low-ceilinged room he looked dwarfed. "Some questions have come up related to your accident. We're trying to clear them up."

He was thrilled. "Who's *we*?"

I couldn't say an insurance company; that might have led to awkward phone calls. The same for the police or Roger Ware's office. That seemed to leave only one candidate. "A woman and her daughter were killed in another accident near where you had yours around the same time that evening. A witness has just now come forward talking about the same two cars chasing one another as you and Richard McCoy did."

"And what? You represent the family?"

Sometimes the truth sounded more like a lie than a lie did. "Right."

He should have said something to double my shame, but didn't. The fan next to him was roaring in his ear more than the TV he had lowered, but he just fidgeted with the black leather sweatband on his wrist. He had gotten used to shutting out what might have bothered the rest of the world. "So this is about them, not about me."

"Can you deal with that?"

He thought about being insulted, then made the sacrifice not to be. "They were killed, you say?"

I assumed the collection of small, single-flower ceramic vases on the wall shelf behind him were the sister's and that she was either big on senseless objects or devoted to the nephew or niece who had made them. "This witness says they were forced off the road by two cars having a drag race. Sounds like what you and McCoy told the police after your accident."

"Fuck that McCoy! He's why I'm in this chair today! You know that?"

He might have believed it or just gotten used to the story he and his sister had been telling for years. Then again, McCoy's version might have been bullshit. I didn't really care. "I can't help you there. All I want to know about is those two cars."

"Bastards almost killed me. What else is there to know?"

"That's what I'm hoping you can tell me."

His look said some people didn't have use of their legs, others of their brains, and he should have been charitable to the less fortunate. "Where'd this other thing happen?"

I told him, wishing I could have been shouting it through his barred street window and then running down the block. I wanted him to say there couldn't have been a connection. But he didn't say that. "Yeah," he nodded. "If they kept going where they were headed, they could've hit Delaware. I didn't get a chance to ask them."

"Anything you can tell me about those cars?"

"Like what?"

"I don't know. Color. Make."

His laugh came out as a burp. "Black and blue. But not as black and blue as me when it was over."

"One was an Acura, the other a Mustang?"

"You know more than me."

"What about the drivers?"

"First guy was my age," he shrugged. "What I was then. We're not talking about yesterday, you know. That was the blue car. I was too busy to make out the second guy."

"So nothing stood out about them."

"Yeah, they were the motherfuckers who ruined my life, that's what stood out about them. Them and that . . . Never mind. We finished?"

We should have been. The guy couldn't even get it straight who had dropped him into his self-pity—McCoy or the drag racers. He was as helpful as Christman's reports. But then the rattling of keys outside the front door told me sister Mireya didn't have a nine-to-five job. What the beefy young woman in a green blouse, white skirt, and white heels did have was an armful of files and folders. I would have said some kind of school teacher. She didn't appreciate seeing me standing in the middle of the room and guessing. I got out my cover story before Morante had to. She wasn't impressed, but it was enough for her to drop the files on the sofa and assume a more authoritative pose. "And this has nothing to do with Felipe's tragedy?"

He groaned, she kept a straight face. "Not directly, no."

"Then how could he help you?"

Morante let go with a machinegun spray of Spanish at her. She never dropped her skeptical eyes from me as the words ricocheted off her and she threw in a syllable here and there to shut him up. I changed my mind: not a school teacher, but somebody from a city agency counter used to waiting out irate taxpayers until they gave up out of exhaustion. But Morante wasn't shut up so easily. Maybe he didn't like being referred to as a *tragedy*, maybe he especially didn't like it when it seemed to come so automatically to her talking about him, or maybe he just needed to vent in front of somebody who wasn't counting the coffee beans and cans of beer he could have, but the more she deflected his anger, the irater he became. If I had been working for them, I probably would have missed not speaking Spanish. Since I wasn't working for them, I didn't miss it.

When Morante finally ran out of wind, she came close to smiling at her fortitude and wanting me to applaud it. "So there's nothing you've talked about over the years about those two guys," I said instead. "I don't know. Something that came out just once after a long time."

She was taking a deeper measure of me, and didn't mind me noticing. I stared back with my own message: STOP BLAMING YOUR BROTHER FOR YOUR LOUSY LIFE. "I wasn't there," she reminded me.

He rolled closer. "You sound like you already know who it is and just want us to help you nail the pricks. That what you're playing at? Well, what would be in it for us? We got bills here. Tell him, Mireya."

The Morante kids were back on the same team, and I was the opposition. I had wasted my time worrying about phone calls to the wrong people. They were going to be made as soon as I walked out the door anyway. Slugging Bobby Sprowl around the corner before he had let loose his roaches felt like my last act of finesse. "From what I understand," I said, trying one last time, "you blame McCoy for the accident. But you also say it was these guys in the blue and black cars."

Every once in a while, you won two bucks on a scratch-off ticket. I didn't have to turn back to Morante to know he was matching her suddenly nervous look over at him. "How do we know you're not here representing this Richard McCoy?" she asked, more accusation than question.

"You don't. But I don't give a damn what you two and McCoy are accusing each other of. I'm interested in this woman and her daughter. You're all sitting around with your bitter memories and the money you could have, should have, might have gotten, but they're dead."

She had another objection at the tip of her tongue, but Morante cut her off. "It was the cops," he said, sounding reluctant to me but vindictive toward her. "They told us we'd never get anywhere with the description we had of the two cars, that if we expected any damages, we'd be better off blaming McCoy. At least he was there."

"They actually said that?"

"Not the Highway cops the first night. They just took down everything the way they're supposed to. But the next day there was another guy, and he's the one who said to stick to McCoy. Not in so many words, maybe. But the message was there."

Mireya dared me to make something of it. When I didn't, she threw up her head in a resigned laugh and collapsed down on the couch. "They had it all worked out, and we fell for it. We blamed McCoy, and then a week later, when it was too late to blame anybody else, they told us we would get nowhere accusing McCoy. The District Attorney's office itself told us that. We were supposed to be intimidated, and we were."

"Not us," Morante corrected, a touch of sympathy in his voice for her. "That goddamn lawyer we had."

"Same thing, Felipe."

I knew who had done the intimidating from the DA's office. But that was only half the answer. "This cop who came by the next day with the advice about suing McCoy, who was he?"

"A detective," Morante said. "Thin guy named Marchese. Didn't look like he had the muscle to open a door. Mister Friendly. Just wanted to help us out with all the red tape."

"Ralph Marchese," Mireya said more emphatically.

Everybody but me seemed to have known his real first name.

CHAPTER 30

I let business get in the way the next day. Jimmy Heyer cashed in his IOU for the information on Garrett and Carrington by sending me a Mrs. Gwendolyn Cutter, a frantic mother who didn't like the relationship between her 19-year-old daughter and a middle-aged community college track coach. Considering the last job I'd done for Heyer about his son and the kid's high school teacher, I was beginning to wonder if Jimmy had opened a Predators 'Re Us franchise in his spare time. But there was also the small difference that a 19-year-old wasn't a 15-year-old; so what if Gwendolyn Cutter didn't like the girl's taste in after-school companions? On the other hand (and I had a lot of hands listening to her), aside from the auburn dye that stopped well short of her black roots, the mother didn't hit me as having an overripe fantasy life, especially when she started talking about out-of-town track meets in Connecticut and Pennsylvania that had to be cancelled because of electric power problems in the arenas, but only after the coach and her daughter had checked into local hotels.

What could I say to the woman? College sports venues weren't what they had been? Her daughter was old enough to choose her own reprobates? What I did tell her was not to expect much—and before those words got across my desk, that I would look into things just to put her mind at ease. She reacted by looking grateful. I might have been grateful for her gratitude if she didn't immediately stand up with her bag and walk out of my apartment.

Apparently, Heyer had told her not to worry about opening her
checkbook.

I told myself I needed the break anyway, to figure out my next
move with what Christman had left me. Time wasn't a factor anymore. Even if I had been operating under the radar before, the
Morantes were sure to have put an end to that with phone calls
far and wide as soon as I had said goodbye to them. So why not go
out to Randall's Island and see leggy teenagers blowing out their
lungs to be the first across the finish line?

The theory was good. What wasn't good was having to go to
the three-watt stadium on Randall's Island, where the mosquitoes
not only outnumbered the track addicts in the stands but seemed
to have been bred by eagles. It was between swats in the air that
I squinted hard enough to zero in on the coach and his special
protégé. Either they had brought along their electricity problems
from Connecticut and Pennsylvania or I had a date coming with
an eye doctor. I finally had to give up my approximate idea of
sight to stroll down to a seat behind the team bench. The guy
was somewhere between 40 and 50 with that queasy flicker in
his eyes that said he wanted one more shot at reliving whatever
heroic thing he had done on a college athletic field. The girl was
recognizable from the photo her mother had given me, but only
because she was white and the other members of her team were
black. Otherwise, the runners all looked like they were ruining
their spindly legs in their scruffy track shoes and couldn't wait
for the coach to finish his instructions so they could drop their
hands from their almost-hips and get on with it. Whatever he told
them—or they ignored—worked: One member of the team won
both races I saw, with three of them placing one-two-three in the
longer relay. My client's daughter wasn't great at handing off the
baton, but she could pick them up and lay them down.

It bothered me that the coach was apparently good at his job.
Dirty old men were supposed to be dirty old men, and nothing
else. Whatever the connection, my disappointment got me back to
thinking about my next move with Christman's reports. The most
obvious way of proceeding was more of the same—looking up the
Fantones, Garretts, and others for getting a better idea of why

they had all interested Christman. But I had a feeling I'd already gotten the best of happy cooperation I was going to get operating that way, and McCoy and the Morantes themselves hadn't exactly been models in that department. A Jimmy Fantone and an Aaron Garrett threatened to be in another league of balkiness altogether. Then there was the alternative: Just jump to the front of the line and see what fell out.

"You a friend of Mrs. Cutter's?"

There was no excuse for not having seen the coach until he was in my face. He had been yards away, going back to the sidelines bench to consult with one of his assistants when I had last been paying attention. A wise guy answer didn't seem to cover it, either. "That's right."

He hadn't been expecting the truth, but he rolled with it. "Well, you might just remind her that Nina is 19, of legal age."

If he hadn't been expecting the truth, I had been watching it from another planet. "You're saying . . ."

"I'm saying that I don't like being snooped on for something that isn't wrong. And I don't think Nina's going to like it, either."

I was staring into the face of either True Love or Balls. I thought I should have been able to distinguish them, but then and there I might as well have still been running around a lane for a race that was already over. "Kind of a big age difference, wouldn't you say?"

He heard my wild grasp, and thought I was funny. He had a point. His assistant coach on the bench thought so, too. And Nina and the other spent runners were wandering across the lanes back toward us to make it unanimous. Then the guy unbuttoned his blazer and spread his arms wide as if to give a blessing to me and whoever was sitting behind me. "Tell Mrs. Cutter to wake up and smell the bees," he said solemnly.

Wake up and smell the bees: It was the first time I'd ever received that advice. All the way home I tried to think of some sage counsel even close, but no luck. I might have meditated on it for the rest of my life if there hadn't been a message waiting for me on my machine when I walked in the door. I hadn't even jumped to the front of the line yet, but something had already fallen out. And for a bonus she would throw in the third body.

CHAPTER 31

Ellen Miles sounded more nasal on my machine than she had on television talking about Marchese, but she was just as cryptic as she had been with the media. She would be unavailable for a call-back, so instead of wasting time that way (hint: don't try to reach her in case of having to go through a third party), why didn't we just meet at ten o'clock the following morning where we had once debated the virtues of dropping the second A-bomb on Nagasaki? She wasn't joking, and I needed a few seconds to remember where that had been and why that particular conversation should have stuck out in her mind after so many years. Then that cold gray day came back full force. She had driven me to Gibson in Valley Stream so I could talk to a realty agent friend of hers about putting my house up for sale. It had been weeks after Jennifer's accident, and I had spent most of it being adamant about getting rid of the house. According to Ellen, her friend wouldn't screw me over. I hadn't really cared one way or the other. The main thing was just to unload all the voices in a place that had become the one thing worse than a stranger's house—a house that was mine and only mine.

There was nothing good about the message on the machine. It wasn't good Ellen was being so secretive about meeting. It wasn't good she had apparently tied me into her investigation of Marchese's suicide. It wasn't good her suspicions about my involvement were so serious she had broken the long silence between us. And there was certainly nothing good about the jump in my chest at the prospect of seeing her again. It thumped out like the drumbeat when she had told me about her marriage plans with Roger Ware.

CHAPTER 32

The morning took forever to come, and it brought a drizzle that made everything hotter instead of cooler. The small commercial area around the Gibson LIRR station hadn't changed much since the last time: the realty office, a Burger King, and a handful of mom-and-pop stores. I saw no sign of Ellen in the station parking lot, so walked through the nagging rain over to the deli for a second morning coffee. Great minds thought alike.

She still had her perky bob and startled eyes, but had swapped her Santa Claus suit from the TV press conference for a simple blue skirt and white blouse. She might have been heavier around the hips, but not to the point of having to come in with me on the truck scales I had been thinking of installing in my bathroom. What hadn't changed in the least was an expression expecting to hear the worst but that she could also somehow switch to a smile without making it look artificial. I had missed that flexibility more than I had realized.

The woman ordering potato salad on line in front of her helped with our awkwardness: The deli wasn't the place to do more than to nod to each other and say hello. There was no need for either the other customer or the counterman to hear how we had been doing over the last five years or so. That we saved until we had collected our coffees and went back out to the lot. The wait hadn't been worth it, and not only because of the steadier rain or because, with the help of the clumsy shoulder bag she concentrated on maneuvering, she almost poked my eye out opening her umbrella. The amenities were lame even as amenities. No, her friend no longer worked in the realty office. Yes, her father was still suffering from arthritis and still living in Boca Raton. When she recognized my car as an old habit I hadn't conquered, I took the suggestion she preferred sitting there rather than in her own blue Honda a few parking spaces away. She thought it was sharp of me to pick up on that.

"So what's going on, Paul?"

The fresh smell of her umbrella closed next to her legs against the front seat caught me off guard with a rush. It had been raining the night we had broken our agreement to be only partners; that time it had been my umbrella between us. I slowed things down by telling myself the coffee tasted the same as it had the day we had gone to see her friend in the realty office. "With me? The crisis in Pakistan? What?"

She couldn't open the hole on the lid of her coffee; she had never been good at it. "Could we skip the fox hunt and just get to it? Your name has been all over two men I've lost lately. What should I be looking at you for? Bad luck in reunions?"

Her perfume was orangier than the one from our partner days. I didn't like the picture of her dabbing it on in a bathroom she shared with Ware, but at least it was a timely reminder we *weren't* partners anymore. "Why be looking at anybody for cancer and suicide?"

She finally gave up with the lid and pulled it off the top of the container altogether. I could have poked the hole for her, but I didn't feel like it. I hadn't missed the officiousness of the last few times we had seen each other and that she seemed to have no trouble slipping back into. Then, in the same tone: "Marchese didn't kill himself. First, he'd have to have a self to kill. You know that as well as I do."

She wasn't conceding anything. Her tone said that investigating the suicide had convinced her Marchese's death was the least of her problems. "That's schoolroom psychology. Any police work to back it up?"

"Like what? Getting jackets out of the tailor's an hour before?"

"He didn't want the tailor holding the bill into eternity."

"Thoughtful. I'm sure the tailor appreciates it."

"What else?"

"Too many things to list."

"Meaning nothing?"

"Almost. There's a security camera in the lobby of the building. We ran it back to after four o'clock, when Marchese went out to the tailor's and wherever else he went. Nobody after that entered the building who didn't belong. Unless you think the bad guy's another tenant."

"Why not? There are people in my building who'd be good for putting me out of my misery."

"We've talked to all of them. Half of them didn't even know Connie."

"What about a delivery entrance?"

"That door hasn't been opened since they invented rust."

"Ray Black agree with you? The schoolroom part?"

"He's been walking around in a fog since it happened. The only coherent words he says are that his partner was no suicide. Who would know better than he would?"

"He knows, you know, I know. We're all geniuses."

"Connie Marchese didn't kill himself."

"*Some*thing is bothering you about what you found."

"Idiot thing."

"Pretend you've got an idiot audience."

Not even a smile. "We found the jackets he brought home from the tailor on the bed. They didn't have the usual plastic wrapping. But the lobby surveillance camera shows they did."

"So he threw it out."

"There was nothing in any of his trash cans."

"So he must've gotten rid of it between walking into the lobby and reaching his apartment."

"Yeah, right. Like everybody does."

I felt better. Not for Connie Marchese's family, but for my take on mankind. I hadn't needed a piece of plastic from a tailor to know Connie Marchese hadn't killed himself. "Okay, you've got an open case. But you're not telling me why we're sitting in this goddamn parking lot."

"To give you a heads-up."

"For what?"

She finally found me more interesting than her coffee; in a melancholy way. "You really find that so hard to believe?"

"If I knew what you were talking about, maybe I wouldn't."

"Right."

"So I'm wrong. And I'm probably also wrong that what's personal here has more to do with you than me."

"Damn right it's personal. They were my people."

"So grieve for them. Be pissed off. But why call me?"

"What's this—the third Finley phase? Finley All Self-Esteem, Finley No Self-Esteem, and now Finley All Self-Esteem Again?"

We both felt better. And she couldn't have been more right about the fox hunting: Neither of us was going to have anything to show for the morning except deli coffee if we didn't stop saying non-things. "Jerry Christman called me out of the blue. Took me a couple of days to figure out I was on his list of goodbye calls. I thought that deserved a little drive out to the wake. Wouldn't you in my place?"

"And you merited being on this list, but I didn't?"

"I don't know what your relations were."

"But I know what yours were—nonexistent."

Somewhere behind her glare she really was disappointed she hadn't made Christman's last-call list. "Don't ask why he had to share with me after so long, but he seemed to think your office has been papering over jobs."

"What jobs?"

"Starting with Jennifer and Susan."

"That's ridiculous!"

"What I thought. But then strange things started happening. Marchese got interested. An NYPD cop named Keenan got interested . . ." Her jaw tightened, and she was a second too late returning to her coffee. "So what can I tell you? It's got me wondering about a lot of things."

She consulted with the scraggly bushes in front of my fender before asking: "You didn't take all this just on the word of a dying man on the phone. You've seen this so-called papering?"

Instinct told me to give her a final exam, just to be sure. "Yeah, I have it. Old processing forms Christman copied and ripped off."

She passed. "Then you better hand them over. In case you've forgotten, they're not public property."

"You're not picking up the theme here, Ellen. You shepherded all the accident stuff on Jennifer. Was there anything at all that made you think twice? Just a feeling that it wasn't as . . . simple as it seemed?"

"And you really think I wouldn't have told you before now?"

"I'm asking. It's not about you or me. It's about what Christman saw as a little off about that accident. You're right about the guy being in bad shape. So why would he worry about this shit with his last breaths?"

She almost said a reasonable thing: that Christman had been gaga toward the end. But she held back. And that gave me a little chill. "That Christmas night? For god sake, I would've been the first one over it!"

I didn't doubt that; couldn't have doubted it. But I had known that before leaving Brooklyn. And the only reason I had left Brooklyn was because she had asked me to meet her. "You didn't want me calling you back on your office phone. That much I understand. But you still have a cell, don't you? Why wasn't that number safe?"

"I didn't call you on my cell, I . . ."

"Right. Pay phone. But why wasn't it safe to call you back on the cell you have in your bag?"

She went back to the bushes, and I knew the only difference between us was that she hadn't put a manila envelope in her file cabinet. "I'm not sure," she said more unsteadily.

I didn't even know it had been a hope until it jumped in all its sleazy misery to the front of my head. "I gather we're talking about Roger."

"You are."

"Okay. I am."

She stared out through the windshield until an express train finished screaming through the station. "If anybody's been fiddling around with the files lately, it wasn't Christman," she finally announced to the bushes. "It was Walter Rigas. I was about to question him about it."

I told myself to stay quiet. Babbling that I'd discovered how Jerry Christman had found the balls to break every rule he'd lived by didn't seem like much of a breakthrough.

"But just as I was working up the nerve to call him in, he had a heart attack. Spent his last week in an oxygen tent. I haven't lost two people lately, I've lost three."

The tumblers fell into place. Christman had visited Rigas in the hospital and had somehow come away with the unwanted gift of the police forms. He had pored over them through his own medical problems, probably trying to persuade himself that Rigas had been crazy. When that hadn't worked out, he had unloaded his treasure on somebody as far removed from him and his family as he could think of—me. *That* was the hollowness I'd heard in the funeral parlor parking lot with Samuel Chilumu: Christman had bullshitted the nurse, too, about how I was somebody to count on. All the better to make sure his unwanted burden would be delivered.

"I don't care how many laws Rigas or Christman broke," I said, sounding like somebody defending the way he had been spending his time lately. "The reports I've looked into are definitely off. And Rigas seems to have thought the problem started that Christmas night."

"What reports are we talking about specifically?"

I told her about Claudia Troy and McCoy and the Morantes, then about Fantone, Garrett, and the others I hadn't checked up on yet. I didn't expect her to yell *Aha!*, and she didn't. "And no common arresting officer?"

"Give me *some* credit. I've been through them sideways and ass backwards. We have Marchese and Black, we have Levine, we have a name or two I don't recognize. I thought for a while they might all have to do with those Catholic zealots in Rockville Centre, but that hasn't panned out, either."

"That must have been a comedown."

"Moving right along. The only thing common about them is that they all ended up in the same packet Christman sent to me."

"What about Rigas and Christman?"

"I guess there's more Rigas than Christman, but who remembers the details of 6-5 games?" There was a perverse satisfaction in seeing her look as stumped as I had been. Then I realized why I hadn't exactly been supplying her with fresh information. "How did you get on to Rigas in the first place?"

She stared off past the bushes to a clothesline in a backyard behind the parking lot. Somebody in the house wore a lot of green polo shirts. Only after a second did she register the question. "What?"

"Rigas and these files."

"Levine," she said. "He went downstairs to look up something on an old case he couldn't find on the computer. Just as he walked in, Rigas was shoving a couple of things into a file drawer. He laughed at Levine, made a joke about the dust, and hurried out. Just Rigas trying to act friendly was reason enough to be suspicious."

"And it never occurred to good old Herb to ask Rigas what he was doing? I mean, instead of marching up to you and telling you what he'd just seen Rigas doing?"

She gave me the classic Miles expression, ready to go either way. "Not everybody's graduated from kindergarten like you have. Herb is Herb."

"And what about Ellen? Why didn't she just ask Rigas?"

"You've been out of the loop lately. If I'd done that, it wouldn't have been a colleague-to-colleague question. I have my own flag stand in an office now. That means my questions are supposed to have ramifications. I checked it out myself before doing anything."

"And?"

"I went to the drawer Levine described. There were no missing file numbers. I went back upstairs to check with the computer. Everything corresponded. Then Rigas had his heart attack and there were the thousand daily crises we're supposed to be eager to deal with, so everything got pushed to the back of the stove. But one thing I do know absolutely: Jennifer's file was nowhere near that drawer."

That seemed to leave only my pet theory. "While Christman was going through the chemo stuff, he ever drop by the office?"

"Once or twice. Why?"

"Rigas may have been the one to take the others, but I'd bet Christman took the report on Jennifer and Susan. To guarantee my interest in the rest of the things he was sending me. I'm sorry if I implied anything else."

She—and I—needed more than an apology. I clenched her hand on the seat. She exhaled more thankfully than I deserved and left her hand there until I lifted mine again. "So how far have you gotten with your deep thoughts about it all?" she asked, re-settling her bag on her lap.

"I've talked to a couple of people who don't recognize themselves in the reports Christman sent me. There's also a woman who was mainly surprised there was any kind of record at all."

"And that's why you're saying they're false?"

"No, I'm saying they're false because at least two of the people named don't like each other but come down on the same side of saying the reports are crap. I'm saying they're false because, unless he's developed a new personality in the last few years, Herb Levine doesn't go up against a gun runner alone. Or maybe he's been crowing about a daring adventure?"

"I have no idea what you're talking about. Levine going up against a gun runner by himself? You've got to be kidding."

"Rigas or Christman, not me."

"That's crazy, Paul. Why invent something like that?"

"I don't know. But then it's not my job to know, is it?"

It lasted only a second or two, but for some reason reminding her we weren't partners anymore made me feel as though we were again.

CHAPTER 33

I wouldn't have minded sitting in the lot for, say, another week. That should have been time enough to cover the hundred things we hadn't yet touched on, starting with why mention of Captain Patrick Keenan had put her on edge and why she hadn't been more forceful about denying hubby Roger had anything to do with her uneasiness. Then there was the minor detail of how the Marchese investigation was going. But all those professional issues laying there for professional people like us to be professional about, I just wanted to stay nestled inside all the rain, drifting away on another storm five years old. With some luck I could have turned on the radio and found the same old wheezy recording of a bossa nova version of *Chances Are*.

Then the phone inside her bag beeped, and one of us *did* have to act professionally. "I've got to go," she said, after listening a minute and tuning out.

"We should go over those forms."

"You mean I should go over them when you send them to me."

"No, I mean I can backstop you unofficially. That'll give you more time to decide when it should go official."

The stranger came back into her eyes. "In another world," she said, "I might even be flattered. But in this one . . ."

"Three reasons why I'm your best option right now. One, there's an IAB guy from the city named Carrington who's sniffing around Keenan and all his Island friends and who seems to think it's all somehow connected to god knows what lately. Two, there's our old friend Alan Crosby who *knows* there's some kind of connection between Roger and your dead cops. Three, there's Jennifer and Susan in the middle of all this. Maybe they're just there as a fake-out to me, almost for sure. But until I know with absolute certainty, I have a personal interest with or without your help. You want to play it by the book, go ahead. The worst that happens, I'll be out on bail and still be bothering you, while Carrington and Crosby will have more grist for their little mills. You're this far from being taken off this case altogether, Ellen. Maybe it'll be a phone call from Carrington to Shelton and your local IAB rats. Maybe it'll be tomorrow's edition of *Newsday* with a new Crosby scoop. Bottom line: You're on borrowed time before you're sidelined for conflict of interest. But in the meantime, I can help you. I can go places you can't."

If she had thought it through, she should have seen she was even closer to having Marchese taken away from her than I had said. But she also had a lousy domestic conversation with Mr. Ware coming up, and she didn't need two bad scenes on the day. "I want to see those forms," she decided, reaching for her door handle. "I'll call you about when and where. Meantime, please don't make yourself conspicuous."

She almost forgot her umbrella, but then reached back into the car for it. She missed it with her first grab, but then got to it before I could hand it to her. She got away before she had to make any more eye contact.

CHAPTER 34

I spotted my friend at the second stoplight after leaving Ellen. But after my fantasies about the bald Asian at the Green Fox, it wasn't until we got to the third stoplight that I let myself be sure. It was a gray Elantra, and the driver was too insecure about tails to tolerate more than two cars between us. He also didn't seem to know why I would be heading for Bay Ridge. Ergo? Ergo, he hadn't followed me to the LIRR parking lot, he had followed Ellen and decided to find out who her friend was.

By the time the Verrazano Bridge loomed up, the rain had slackened back to a drizzle. It was also pretty clear my friend intended following me all the way to my apartment building. And if he wasn't a four-carat dimwit, he had to have my plate already, so there was nothing I would gain by driving down to Borough Hall and pretending to be the Borough President. But it still felt like a punting call, so I took the Fourth Avenue exit not to my building, but to the 68 Precinct. He was still behind me when I drove into the precinct lot, and slowly enough that I could return the favor by getting his plate. For what? Maybe to rebalance the scales with Jimmy Heyer on who was doing more favors for whom. Or maybe just to give Ellen's shadows some pause that Lieutenant Miles was consulting with a Paul Finley close to the NYPD. Maybe by the time whoever they were had made all the requisite phone calls for greater illumination, she would have accumulated another few days on Marchese. Not everything was baseball; sometimes the game was soccer and a tie was as good as a win.

The uniform copping a smoke in the lot didn't like me using NYPD property for driving maneuvers, and didn't look all that satisfied when I gave him a happy wave while I was backing out into the street again. So much for trying to please all the people all the time.

CHAPTER 35

There's being witty and wily, then there's being smashed in the face.

For 24 hours I did my best to honor Ellen's request not to make myself conspicuous. I did nothing related to Christman's reports except to pass along the Elantra's license plate to Jimmy Heyer and to keep warning myself I would become extremely conspicuous if I gave into a hovering temptation to drop by Jimmy Fantone's well-known hangout in Franklin Square. I felt so virtuous attending to distracting matters that I piled them on—doing the laundry, getting a haircut, separating my bottles from the rest of the garbage, paying the older halves of my double telephone and electricity bills, buying toner for my computer printer. I knew it was a good sign when I couldn't tell my diversions from my obligations.

Then Heyer started rolling the boulder back downhill. First, he didn't like me saying his latest reference, Gwendolyn Cutter, the mother of the track star, had assumed my services were part of Medicaid. What that got was a pout that he couldn't look up the information I wanted until the next day. When somebody holds the key to the cyber universe, attention must be paid, even to sulking. Then, when he finally did call and tell me the driver of the Elantra was Connie Marchese's partner Ray Black, I felt that watery weakness in the intestines you get after chomping down on that bruised peach you knew you shouldn't have touched. Ray Black figured all too well. He and Marchese had practically been wearing each other's clothes since they had joined Major Cases together.

Forget about what Ellen had said about him being so broken up about Marchese. How else would he have been expected to act? The bottom line was that if one of them was into any extracurricular activity, the other was pretty sure to be involved, too.

But *what* extracurricular activity? Falsifying police reports that went back years? I had read the damn things until my eyes had blurred, but I hadn't seen any career making opportunities in them. Squashing a domestic abuse call? Talking somebody out of an accident liability case? Even at the level of a favor for a well-placed friend, they didn't make much sense. Why should Marchese and Black have been doing that kind of favor? I didn't have an answer to that any more than I did to Carrington's interest in Patrick Keenan.

Being an optimistic soul who never drank from a glass less than half full, though, I latched on to the consolation of having something to tell Ellen the next time I saw her—that one of her minions wasn't being such a minion, that he liked sneaking around after her. I knew that would charm her. But then the mailman spoiled satisfaction with that prize, too, with an envelope that looked like it had been addressed to me from some Kindergarten Penmanship class. The postmark was Mineola, and the two stamps were of those Claymation movie creatures nobody had told me had become a national symbol. Since I didn't have a lab in my building lobby for fingerprint testing, I slit the thing open right there in front of my mailbox. Inside was a single sheet of paper with more block letters asking YOU LIKE ICE CREAM? THERES A GOOD PLACE. THURSDAY AFTERNOON.

I knew right away where the "good place" was. It was no secret on the Island that the Fantones had adopted a Franklin Square ice cream parlor called Giolitti's as their unofficial headquarters. Goons long swallowed up in the federal witness protection program had repeatedly cited it as where the old man Marcello had met with this one and that one. The place had originally attracted the family by being directly across the street from what had once been the headquarters of the Franklin National Bank, the international money hive that had fallen off the tree in the 1970s after somebody had discovered the place had more chits than money

on deposit, a lot of it from the Vatican and the mob in Italy. According to the stories, old Marcello had sat in the window of the
ice cream parlor for years keeping an eye on who went in and out
of the bank, lifting his bulk every so often to go to the pay phone
in the back to alert his betters that another cop of some kind had
just gone in for a sniff. The Franklin National Bank wasn't around
anymore, and I hadn't heard of a Marcello Fantone sighting in a
long time, but with Franklin Square thin on social clubs, Jimmy
Fantone had followed family tradition by using Giolitti's as his
stage for receiving public tribute.

I didn't mind thinking about rattling Jimmy Fantone's cage,
but him rattling mine was another story. The prospect of meeting
the woman with the affected British accent who had answered
his phone didn't seem like much of a tradeoff. How did he even
know his name was part of the Rigas-Christman package? And
then there was the small consideration that if I had a list of people
I didn't want to know my home address, Fantone would have
ranked at the top with Burial Plots Now and Jews for Jesus. Another consequence of meeting with Ellen in Gibson? I didn't see it.
The Claymation crap aside, the envelope's stamps were normal—
double the postage needed, but not enough to inspire Mineola's
P.O. sorters to work overtime to make sure I got my invitation
within 24 hours. Ergo, Jimmy Fantone had decided to shoot the
breeze with me before Gibson.

I saw no reason to consult my conscience about going out to
Franklin Square. Ellen had asked me not to compromise what
she was doing by being conspicuous, but as far as Jimmy Fantone was concerned, I was already doing a striptease in Times
Square. What bothered me more was the feeling I'd not only had
Big Brother watching me for a while, but Big Brother's sisters and
cousins. Add Fantone to the list (Crosby, Keenan, Carrington) of
people who had been too aware of what I'd been up to lately. And
that was without counting Ellen's official investigation. By com-
parison, Bobby Sprowl with his cockroaches and bomb threats
felt like mild headaches in simpler times.

CHAPTER 36

Giolitti's would have been one of those retro ice cream parlors for the Yuppies except for the fact that it had already been making strawberry frappes and banana splits before anyone knew what retro meant. When you walked in the door, you looked instinctively toward the ceiling fans, to make sure they weren't about to spin down on you. The white-and-blue tile floor extended from a long black marble counter with wooden high chairs at the front to a good dozen booths in the back. Along a side wall was a three-tiered showcase of chocolate in bars, boxes, and red bows. Most of all, though, there was the aroma—Sweet Everything with an edge of burnt toast. If there wasn't a guy named Giolitti down in the basement churning out the pistachio and the maple walnut in huge vats, I would have been stunned.

Instead, I was just surprised. From a back-booth Jimmy Fantone aimed an unpleasant smile at me. He'd gained about 30 pounds, a gray mop on his head, and camel bags under his eyes since I'd hauled him in outside John Q. Adams High. But I could barely make out those changes over the mountainous back planted between us. I hadn't counted on being the one to record a sighting of old Marcello.

"Finley!"

Jimmy's oily glee was par for the course—and not. When I reached the booth, I saw that he had mainly been announcing my arrival to his father, who not only had his hippo back to the door but wore the thick sunglasses of a blind man.

"Here he is, pop! Told you he'd come."

The old man grunted and raised his massive jowls in my general direction, but without sloshing any water. He didn't look like he cared all that much anymore about shaving or keeping his shirt collar flaps under control. "Give him room. Don't sprawl out like you always do."

Jimmy could have done without the paternal command in front of me, but did what he was told. I wouldn't have minded sitting by myself at the adjoining booth, either, but we were all Marcello's children for the day. What was a little squeeze in the gut from the edge of the table as a comfort tax?

"Thanks for comin'," the old man said, targeting me too much off to the right. "You like ice cream? The special today is pineapple. Get it. They put big chunks of fruit in it."

It was tempting, but why look like a party reveler for the FBI camera across the street in the real estate office I was sure still had the Fantone traffic in its sights? "Just ate, thanks."

"What, you on a diet, Finley?" Jimmy cackled. "Or you just gotta keep those food expenses down?"

The one advantage of being bundled together with Mensa Junior was that if I wanted, I could reach his gut with my elbow. The old man wasn't there for sideshows, though. "Shut up, Jimmy. Man don't want ice cream, he don't want ice cream. How about a coffee?"

"No, no, I'm fine, really. So what have we got to talk about?"

With a start I recognized the look of disappointment: It had been Susan's expression after she had failed to talk me into something she had mainly wanted for herself. There were no plates of any kind on the table, and I could see Marcello talking up the ice cream as a chance for glomming some off me. "I guess you noticed I'm blind as a bat," he said. "Diabetes."

"Sorry to hear that."

"Not as sorry as me. Especially sittin' in a place like this."

"No reason you can't have a Tab, pop."

"Just one reason," came the snort. "I don't want no fuckin' Tab." He moved closer to my eyes. "Okay, Finley? We were talkin' about Tab and coffee and pineapple ice cream when they ask."

"Fine. And what are we actually talking about?"

He nodded in approval. Aside from diabetes, he seemed to have trouble moving his bulging neck. "All these guys you used to work with are dyin' off like flies. In your place maybe I'd be interested, too."

Junior was making another mistake by strumming his pudgy fingers on the table, but it worked for me. I hadn't expected the old man to get to the point so directly. Any distraction at all was useful for thinking twice before blurting back something stupid. "Couldn't make any of the funerals. Been a long time now."

"Yeah, but . . ."

"Shut up, Jimmy. And stop with that racket on the table." The finger strumming stopped immediately. "Let's do this simple, Finley. No bullshit from me, no bullshit from you."

"Okay with me. Let's start off with how I don't like you keeping tabs on my movements."

"Information that came my way. If it's wrong, tell me right now. If it's right, let's move on."

"After you tell me how you got this information?"

He had hideous dentures; not that a smile with good ones would have been any more reassuring. "I don't think so. Ready to move on?"

"Whatever."

He hesitated; only for a second, but it was there. For somebody who had spent most of his life used to getting his way, he seemed taken aback by agreement that came so easily. It also sank in that there were none of the wrestlers usually photographed with the old man in the nearby booths—not unless they had morphed into ladies at lunch or mothers with kids. Apparently, we were there for very intimate Fantone family business. "Good. So here's where we help one another."

"Always an idea."

"You're nosin' around things that would've been too big for you back when you were in the middle of all that blue. Now you don't even have that protection. You're what they call vulnerable."

"Bad start, Mike. That sounds like a threat."

"Advice."

"From you or somebody else?"

It could have gone either way, and I hadn't even gotten a pine-apple ice cream out of it. But then his George Washington teeth came out again, and I had passed. "You think these cheese balls out here tell *me* what to do? I'm old and blind, Finley, not dead."

"He don't get it, pop."

"If you'd shut up, maybe he would."

"I'm just saying . . ."

"Here's where I think you are, Finley. You got these dead . . . what do you call 'em? . . . ex-colleagues. And because one of them has sent you all these phony reports, you figure you got an obliga-tion to them."

I counted instead of gagging. I counted Ellen, Sarah Christ-man, and Carrington as knowing about the reports. Then Cyn-thia, the Professor, Samuel Chilumu, and the dead Marchese, of course. Come to think of it, who the hell *didn't* know I had them? "You have good sources of information."

"I better have."

"And the reason these reports bother you is because one of them is about your heir here?" He wasn't impressed; a second later I realized why. "No, what really annoys you is that even as phonies, these reports insist on traveling down memory lane to Jimmy's romantic adventures with Westport hookers. Somebody's sense of humor?"

He released his smile in pieces, and this time it didn't look so hideous. "You got a brain, Finley. No wonder Jimmy says so many nice things about you." There was a belch from the other side of my elbow. "Yeah, you're right. Somebody thought they were bein' funny by keepin' that crap on file. Supposed to be a cloud over Jimmy's head. *And mine.* But guess what? I don't see clouds no better than any other fuckin' thing. So that part of it don't bother me no more."

"And this concerns me because . . .?"

The dry hide around his ears turned wine red. "You're no-body's favorite dish," he snapped. "They say you got a big foot, like to trample over things. I don't need that style comin' back to . . . Westport."

"I see."

"What do you see?"

"Don't trust him, pop."

"You shut your mouth. Let your little pilot fish pat you on the back for cuttin' that whore. For me, your Princess Diana lets you outta the house with a blade in your pocket, you both deserve what you get."

Jimmy said something else about my integrity, but I was too busy beating through the jungle to take it in. Who would have been more familiar with the statute of limitations on assaults than the Fantones? And especially if the victim was a hooker probably long since paid off, scared off, or beyond caring in some more permanent way?

The old man was waiting for me to get it. And I finally did. "It's not the slashing in itself that bugs you."

He gave me my gold star. "That's right. But if somebody goes trampin' through old news and we get a whole lot of noise about it . . ."

"Conspiracy investigation."

"Who knows where somethin' like that could end up? I don't need that, Finley. My son's mother don't need that. The whore was paid off years ago. History should stay history. Not come back as current events."

"So I just drop Jimmy's card from the deck?"

"I told you, pop: He's a smartass."

For once Marcello didn't disagree with Junior. "That would be nice, and who gives a damn about the rest of these bullshit papers? But we both know it don't work that way. What you got are copies. Any nosin' around in the file drawers they got still turns up the original on Jimmy."

"So talk to these friends of yours with the big sense of humor and get them to destroy the original, too. Then nobody will be the wiser about Jimmy's love life and I can get on with the rest of it."

He had considered that possibility before. "I appreciate the offer. But it's gotta be all of them. In other words, forget all about what Christman sent you and stick to your other clients."

The *Christman* detail was dropped in for effect, and it had one. I had a lousy picture of Junior and some of his goons driving down a sleepy Malverne street to visit Sarah Christman. But why own up to the obvious? "And in exchange for this you'll be grateful to me."

"And you'll still have your head on your shoulders!"

Marcello indulged a smile at Junior's idea, but then remembered he wouldn't have been able to see me decapitated anyway. "I'm the genie," he said, widening his arms. "You do me a little favor and I do a little one for you. A couple of new clients, maybe? Let's see if I can accommodate you."

Why not believe it? Marcello Fantone was the genie offering me three shots for getting to the bottom of the McCoys, the Morantes, and all the rest of the garbage collected by Rigas and Christman. But down to it, I didn't give a damn about those things any more than he did. "One of these reports is about the accident that killed my wife and daughter. Why is it in there?"

Junior's bafflement answered for both: They didn't have a clue. "Your wife and daughter?" the father asked. "Sorry for your loss, but what's that got to do with anythin'?"

It was my Uncle Jack's *pro forma* condolences, and had never sounded so bloodless. "The genie's leaving the building," Jimmy recovered to needle.

I felt like an idiot for wasting my first wish on what I'd already known about Jennifer and Susan, then like a double idiot for scrambling for whatever favor was still on the table. I had a hunch *Goodfellas* wouldn't seem so funny the next time it was on TV. "Okay, you can't help me there. But what I'm getting since I sat down is you coming to me because you're near the end of an understanding with somebody. And knowing what the Fantones are good at, I'd guess that understanding was some kind of mutual blackmail."

"Watch your mouth . . .!"

"Shut up, Jimmy." The old man was amused. "Go ahead."

"You want to tell me who *they* are, I'd go dancing through the fields. But you're not going to give me that, so I'd settle for knowing what your part of the understanding has been."

"For what? Happy thoughts between innings at Yankee Stadium?"

"Wrong ballpark. Just for my own satisfaction. Knowing I haven't been wasting my time on minor league crap. I have personal standards."

"I told you, pop: He's a wiseass."

"You don't expect me to believe that, do you? I tell you anything like that, I'm givin' you more reason to bother me, not less."

"Then you'll have to take my word for it."

"His word!"

Maybe the old man had never done a crossword puzzle in his life and so didn't miss them. But his glasses were suddenly trained on me like they had seen as good a substitute as they were ever likely to find for an old mental game. "And you swear on your mother's grave that wouldn't keep you interested in things none of your business? Cross your heart and hope to die?"

I wanted to laugh, and knew he wanted me to laugh. But why push Junior over the edge altogether? "Cross my heart."

"Pop, don't . . ."

"One thing I always liked, Finley, was people tellin' me they weren't fuckin' me over while they were fuckin' me over. What do you call that?"

"On their part, stupidity. On yours, a lot of self-confidence."

"Exactly! You don't have that, you don't get nowhere, right?"

"Right."

He made a move that was supposed to hunch him closer to the table, but didn't budge him an inch. "Just for your own satisfaction."

"Just that."

"He wants to play you, pop."

He put his wedge of an index finger to his lips. Only when he was sure Junior wasn't going to lean in too did he all but whisper: "There was this big commotion one night a few years back."

Did I dare hope for some piece of truth? "Christmas."

"Christmas. Cars goin' left and right. Bodies here and there. One asshole chasin' after another. And what happens when they catch up to one another? Bing, bang, boom! The cars had to be pulled apart by a fuckin' crane! Both drivers—no more worries about payin' their taxes. But they made such a mess of bleedin' and their friends doubled down on that in tryin' to cover it all up that any entrepreneur with half a brain could see the possibilities for the future. So everybody got naked in the woods and sacrificed themselves to the god of hush, hush, hush. You don't talk about this, I don't talk about that. Be good for everythin'. The economy, politics, raisin' your kids according to the Golden Rule. And everybody lived happy ever after." He leaned back, and again without seeming to disturb any air currents. 'How's that for while you watch your Mets lose again?"

I knew he could have only meant the accident in Freeport—the report that had been stuck between Jennifer and Susan and the McCoy-Morante business. And naturally, that was the one I had paid the least attention to. "I guess it'll have to do."

"Yeah, it will. So we have an understanding now?"

I didn't see how. The Marcello Fantones of the world didn't volunteer the kind of information he had to the Paul Finleys. Junior had been right about somebody being played, but it wasn't his father. "I'll stay out of your way."

"No, no, no," he corrected. "You'll stay out of the way of anybody this entrepreneur's had dealin's with. They may have a bad sense of humor sometimes, but that's for me to settle, and without interference from you."

"You let him walk out of here, pop, and you got trouble."

The wine was back in his ears, but this time for Junior. "Gee, I wonder when you became an expert in that? Been takin' night classes in these schools where you do your penny-ante shit?"

It was good to hear Junior was still playing his high school ID games. I hadn't missed *that* much by moving to Brooklyn. And I had nothing to regret, either, about never having come up against the old man in his prime. Whatever he was up to had nothing to do with the stay-away threats he had repeated in front of Junior. When did no mean yes?

I didn't like admitting it, but walking out of Giolitti's, I felt the budding of a thrill that the old man had included me in his web. I was so rapt up in his favor that I walked around to the side street

where I had left the car in a haze. Even when I heard Junior behind me, my first thought was that he was going to scream at me
for not showing enough respect to his father. I didn't think that
was too smart of him. Whether or not the side street was away
from the FBI camera in the realty office, there would have been
plenty of footage of him running out of Giolitti's after me.

I would have told him how much of an imbecile he was being
if he had given me a second. Instead, he just charged up to me
and fired a pudgy fist with a blue-and-gold ring into my face. It
was hard thinking he was the imbecile as I slid down the door of
my car into the street. I couldn't even have sworn there was an
insignia on the ring.

CHAPTER 37

Here's the next rule: Never assume you deserve what you get if you don't like what you get. Nothing says weakness of character more than that attitude. I'm not immune to it, either. In between running to my bathroom mirror to check on the swelling around my right eye and dripping melted ice all over my desk that afternoon, I wondered if I'd asked for Jimmy Fantone's sucker punch. I'd been too slick with the old man and hadn't minded showing it off in front of Junior. And at least Junior had his filial stake in his sleazy notions of family honor. Who was to say that the ring that had left a dent under my eye didn't contain some Roman symbol attesting to a centuries-old tradition of a loyal son just looking out for his corrupt old dad, a kind of family version of Freemasonry? Me, on the other hand? Any idea of a personal involvement in the Christman package had died with the reactions of both Big Fantone and Little Fantone to the accident form on Jennifer and Susan. My second, fourth, and forty-fourth suspicions had been right: Christman had thrown in that report just to keep me interested in what he had been too yellow to follow up on. I didn't have the slightest doubt that, radiation, chemo, or nuclear zapping notwithstanding, Christman had hobbled into the file room during the visits Ellen had mentioned between the time he had taken on Rigas's burden and had asked Chilumu to look me up. And so? So anybody stupid enough to fall for that come-on deserved the black eye that would commemorate his trip out to Franklin Square.

Does that make me the most or least authoritative person for offering the rule about not blaming yourself for what you get? On second thought they seem like the same thing. Maybe we should be satisfied with a life lesson: to wit, if you find yourself at Giolitti's, make sure you order the pineapple ice cream, pay your bill, and get the hell out of the place without being the smartass Jimmy Fantone had rightly taken me for. The alternative is running out of ice cubes and having to refill the tray all day.

CHAPTER 38

Naturally, I looked for consolations. But what should have been the most obvious one—the Freeport smashup—just threw a spotlight on how much I had missed. How about something as basic as the names of the victims? The Garretts, Fantones, McCoys, and Morantes—I had drilled their names into my head so deeply they could have been high school classmates. But somewhere in my dedication to digging more hurt out of the Delaware Avenue accident, I had glossed over Robert E. Lewin, as the report had been identifying him from the first time I had read it. It was a blind spot that mortified me. "Pay Back" Lewin, as anyone who had ever graduated from the Academy on the Island should have recalled, had been a free-lance collector for every bookie in Nassau and Suffolk counties, sometimes moonlighting in Brooklyn and Queens. When the talk had cited Pay Back as a "leg man," it hadn't meant he drooled over women's thighs in skin magazines. If Robert E. Lewin had been chasing after somebody, it had been to take a crack at knees with a baseball bat.

Which still left the big question: Why had Lewin and his quarry been worth all the after-the-fact sweat Marcello Fantone had insinuated? The other victim's name was Edward Cassidy. That might have meant something to Mr. and Mrs. Cassidy, but not to me. To the Internet it meant too much. There was Edward Cassidy the priest, Edward Cassidy the actor, Edward Cassidy the drummer, and Edward Cassidy the rancher in Montana, but they all shared the disease of still being alive. I might have continued to Google screen #123 for other Edward Cassidys if Christman's report hadn't reminded me it contained a specific date when the collector Lewin had made the fatal mistake of catching up to the deadbeat Cassidy. That starting point worked faster. What eventually came out was the *Newsday* story of the accident. For starters, there was the small fact that the cars in the crackup were a blue Acura and black Mustang. Full points to Richard Mc-Coy. I didn't deserve Fantone's sucker punch? That might have still been debatable, but what came next, I didn't deserve. As the skimpy newspaper lines put it without being asked: ". . . Cassidy, son of Eileen Cassidy Keenan . . ."

Chirpy Carrington had left out a tiny particular: that the dead son Keenan liked kneeling in the cemetery dirt for had actually been a stepson. There might not have been a Paul Finley involvement in the phony reports Rigas and Christman had willed to me, but there was definitely a Patrick Keenan involvement in them.

CHAPTER 39

Some called Sal Rini, the owner of the luncheonette where I had breakfast in the morning, "colorful." What they meant was that he was
a bitter bastard who liked telling tales of how he had never found
anybody in his 60-odd years who hadn't pissed him off for one
reason or another. Being a listener to this bile didn't exempt you
from Sal's bobo list. If you made the mistake of thinking so, you
were setting yourself up for twice as much phlegm being hawked
in your direction once your back was turned.

But Sal had his soft spots. One was the occupational di-
lemma of all bookies that too many people—but also not enough
of them—knew about their book. The only thing Sal did more
than advertise that he was ready to take bets on everything from
Belmont to the Red Bulls was not advertise it. He wanted more
bettors, but he didn't want them knowing he did. Sometimes this
got comical. When a luncheonette customer sometimes had an
egg sandwich, walked up to Sal at the register, and was given a
few fifties as his change for a twenty, it wasn't because he had
promised to recommend the egg sandwiches. For these payoffs
Rini's snarl was something that belonged on a gargoyle, and he
couldn't wait for the winner to grab a toothpick and move along.
He didn't like anyone cluttering up his view of the counter and
potential eyewitnesses to the payoff.

Sal's other vulnerability was his Parliament habit. Once
an hour he left his cashier's post to his wife to go outside for a
cigarette. This took more out of him than a winning horse with

long odds since it meant having to say hello to passersby, not to mention having to hear casual cracks about his smoking. The cigarettes might or might not have given him cancer, but they definitely gave him more reason for despising humankind.

I went prepared, old Marlboros in my pocket. There was no way Sal wasn't going to be suspicious of my sudden need for nicotine in front of his bistro, but it was too late to worry about that. He knew I'd been a cop, and at first that had gotten me fewer words and longer stares than his other regulars. The next phase had been testing me with leading questions about races, fights, and whatever bowling tournaments he was covering to see if I qualified as a man's man. When he had finally accepted that I hadn't been patronizing his joint just for a client bent on putting him out of business, I had been consigned to the vat of bobos who had never made his life easier. As long as I had the money to pay for my English muffins and French toast, I was entitled to exist on the margins of his world. He had even thrown in coffee refills without being asked.

What I was hoping was that he would also throw in some information on Pay Back Lewin and Edward Cassidy.

I got a break when I arrived at the luncheonette just as he was coming out with a Parliament and a Bic in hand. He gave me a light with the joy of turning over the day's receipts. But then there was something almost like a smile as he asked about my black eye, nodded indifferently to the usual door whack story, and muttered about the heat. Any passerby from another planet might have seen him as a relatively pleasant guy—an impression reinforced by his neatly combed white hair and mustache. Sal Rini hadn't aged so much as just let his hairs gradually change color over the years. I would have picked out his layer cake head and square jaw in his high school yearbook.

I figured my Marlboros and shiner were enough of an ice breaker. "I was wondering if you could help me on something."

"Yeah, me too." He kept his eyes on the supermarket delivery van across the street in case I got the idea he was being funny.

"Pay Back Lewin."

"What's that?"

What had I been expecting—a simple yes? "A collector. Got killed in a car crash on the Island a few years ago."

"Sorry to hear it. Ever notice how they take forever to set up those unloading runners from the back of the truck? You can pull out the goddamn boxes by hand in half the time."

"It's an old case I'm working on. I could use an arrow."

That he didn't mind showing he found funny. "You don't say."

"I'm guessing you had lots of thoughts when you read the bad news about Pay Back. Maybe the grapevine had others. The guy he cracked up with was named Edward Cassidy."

"You got more info than the *News* this morning. Should I give a shit about any of it?"

I knew he was curious: He wasn't using my name or—worse than that—going through the charade of asking me what it was. At least I was something of a given in his bookmaking universe. "Anything you can tell me about what Lewin was up to. Who he was collecting for. Maybe others this Cassidy left holding the bag."

"You're really serious!"

"Has nothing to do with you, Sal. Now or then."

He stared at my shiner a long time. Level one was that I sounded like I meant what I said; level two that I had to be conning him; level three that I wasn't stupid enough to think I could con him. Then he turned back to where the runner coming out of the van had stopped cold with the cartons on it. "You hear things," he conceded, spraying smoke too close to a woman going by with a grocery cart. "There was a Cassidy years back who couldn't get action anywhere without putting up his arms and legs as collateral. Stiffed every book outside Manhattan. A lot of people got very tired of him."

"To the point of sending Lewin on an Indy 500 race across most of the Island after him?"

"That what happened?"

"That's what happened."

"So if you know that much . . ."

"What I know just tells me what I don't know. Somebody had to make good for Cassidy getting killed that night. His stepfather was a cop."

He wanted to be distracted by the argument boiling up between the two van unloaders about who was responsible for what, but he was remembering too much. "Possible," he finally nodded, "I was doing okay for a few weeks there. Lots of people on the Island walking softly. I saw customers I'd never seen before and haven't seen since."

"I hear the Fantones."

"I never did." This time the smoke was sprayed in my direction. "The Fantones never needed outside enforcers like a Lewin."

That part of it scanned: Marcello and his clan wouldn't have had much extortion leverage, especially with cops, if they had been directly involved with Lewin and Cassidy. "Any theories?"

In retrospect I probably owed his answer to the explosion of Urdu or Bengali across the street. A third East Indian in a supermarket smock came along to break up the argument between the first two, and it took only seconds for all three of them to be going at it and for Rini to be laughing as if he was watching the Three Stooges. "I can tell you from here what the trouble is," he said. "They got to fold those runner tracks higher, like the plunge of the Cyclone down in Coney Island. The way they got it, the damn boxes have to go bump and up and bump again. When they move at all, they go over the side. Who the hell hired those guys?"

"Theories? Wild stabs?"

"Sure," he said, his mood lightened by the scene around the van. "Some Mom and Pop operation."

"Lewin wasn't cheap."

He couldn't resist. "You mean could I afford him? Not worth the trouble. That's why I have a strict no-arrears policy and don't carry any Cassidys. They cost more than just what they owe."

He pinched away his cigarette sooner than he wanted to and took a step back toward the luncheonette. The bang of a box on the opposite sidewalk and still louder arguing stalled him with a grin. If he believed in omens, he had a good day coming. "I once had a shot at a place out in Hempstead," he said, not looking at me. "One of those silver chrome arenas. You sat at the counter, you thought you were in a space ship. The trade was all lawyers and cops and professional hotshots. Could've charged an extra dollar for Diet Cokes. Then one night the place burned down. What do they say? Sometimes the best trades are the ones you don't make?"

I didn't remember any fire, but I didn't remember too much from that period. As I watched him go back inside, though, I knew Sal Rini remembered it clearly enough for both of us.

CHAPTER 40

For about a block on my way back home, I was satisfied by what Sal Rini had sort of told me. I'd discovered something I hadn't known before, hadn't I? But two blocks away, I was back to showing off what Renata Stallworth had called my "mood swings." Maybe it was the sight of a one-eared calico cat diving under a parked car before it lost more than the other ear to a panel truck shooting by. Once again, I was feeling like somebody still running out the groundball after being called out at first.

I wasn't alone. When I walked into my apartment, I found a message on my machine from one of the Buona Italia partners informing me that, so sorry, Bobby Sprowl was going on with his lawsuit against me. By the time I got back to the partner with my sputtering, he had obviously consulted with his own attorneys on the best way to keep me calm. *Of course,* it was ridiculous that somebody out on bail for threatening to bomb me into the next life was carrying on personal injury litigation. *Of course,* Sprowl had provoked the scene in the restaurant by unleashing the roaches and then taking a swing at me. *Of course,* he was probably pursuing the suit only at the instigation of the ambulance chaser Martin Nesbitt. The one thing that wasn't *of course,* unfortunately, was that I would need witnesses to attest to Sprowl's initial swing and, ah, well, nobody had the names of those diners. But hadn't they assured me they did? Yes, and that turned out to have been baseless optimism. The head waiter assigned that task had gotten distracted with his usual seating duties. But—and of course this was another *of course*—don't forget the partners themselves were also cited in the suit so they stood ready to testify on my behalf.

I hung up before I dared ask *what* they stood ready to testify. There might have been bigger losing propositions than being a co-defendant with a corporation in a lawsuit, but none occurred to me right away. Working for nothing on the Rigas-Christman Follies and on Gwendolyn Cutter and her track star daughter suddenly felt like big paydays.

I killed the time waiting for more *pro bono* work by Googling up Hempstead fires in the weeks after the Lewin-Cassidy crash. It took only a few minutes to ferret out the Columbia Diner, which had been leveled to the ground by what a fire inspector called "suspected arson." The suspicions didn't have any follow-ups on the Internet, though, and the owner, Max Katz, had nothing more to say than that he was relieved there had been no human casualties. That also turned out to be the only entry for Max himself, which was too bad for me and the Jerry Christman list. I was beginning to think Jerry had a malicious sense of humor, that the only thing the eight reports had in common was that they had nothing in common.

When the phone rang, I grabbed it before the second ring with every intention of going to the Gobi Desert if that was what a new client needed.

"We need to talk. Same place?"

Maybe I just wanted to hear my agitation in somebody else's voice, but Ellen sounded like an echo. In all likelihood a squalid fact or two had tumbled out onto the kitchen table from her heart-to-heart with hubby. But that didn't make it the moment to tell her why going back to the Gibson station parking lot wasn't such a hot idea. "No, not there. The Professor's been asking about you. How about his house?"

"I don't want . . ."

"How about his house?" I repeated.

She got it. "Four o'clock. And bring that stuff with you."

She didn't wait for an argument. Which was too bad since only with the click in my ear did it dawn on me that the Professor had moved to his smaller place since she had dropped in on his salons with me a couple of times. Calico street cats without ears didn't have it *that* bad.

I considered calling her back to give her the right address, but knew how much she would appreciate that. Then I thought about trusting her to forget where the old man had lived five years ago and to look it up in the phone book to refresh her memory. But how did you start counting on other people's forgetfulness? You didn't, especially when the other person was Ellen Miles, she of the steel trap for a mind. Then the commander-in-chief of Finley Investigations recalled that just because the Professor had moved didn't mean his old house had. So why not wait there for a reasonable time and if she didn't show up, go over to the new place and walk in on the old man lecturing her on the ins and outs of the Tigris and the Euphrates? Rather than being pissed at me, she would have been grateful for my rescue.

And I would have had another triumph on the day!

CHAPTER 41

I got out to Tara with a quarter-hour to spare and parked three houses down the block. The closest thing to activity was a squirrel hopping across a plastic garbage can at the curb. The colonial mini-mansion looked like it had been sanded and repainted since I'd seen it last, and there was a basketball hoop above the garage. I'd always thought of the place more in terms of croquet. I tried to imagine Joe Carroll at any age shooting baskets, and couldn't make it. Jennifer had had long legs, but not the manic focus that would have helped her pile up points. It had never struck me so starkly before how she hadn't been happy if she hadn't been, as they say, multitasking. When she hadn't been running her library branch, she had been running the house, and when she hadn't been running the house, she had been running language programs for immigrants and endless one-shot things that didn't last as long as the posters advertising them. In the circus, she would have been walking a high wire while juggling batons and firing knives at some target on the platform where she was heading. And all the while she would have insisted that she wasn't busy, that she still had time for helping me with my clown act down in the sawdust.

I didn't like thinking about that in the suffocating heat. It came with too much of an old resentment bill that had never been completely paid. I owed that spineless prick Christman for lots of things I hadn't wanted to remember. What was it Jennifer had said about how her old man would feel the loss of his wife on some indefinite day when he was yakking about his European queens? She could have said it about me, too, except that instead of European queens, the occasion was disabled cops whose broken heads had just caught up to their broken bones. Never underestimate the snivelers like Christman and Rigas: They always sent the biggest boulders down the mountainside. They were guilty about something they had done or not done while they had still been alive doing their official records, and who better to pass their guilt along to than yours truly?

I didn't know why I was suddenly so convinced of that scenario. Maybe it was just being in front of the old house again. Maybe it was because, the Mets aside, Christman had always sensed that I didn't like him very much and had gone the extra mile to wallow in his self-contempt. It would have been nice if at least the squirrel objected no, no, I was wrong, but it too had disappeared down inside the garbage can.

Ellen came cruising down the block in her blue Honda. I gave her a minus-one for not seeing me. She seemed to recognize the house, then continued to the corner and turned in search of a parking space. There was no Elantra behind her. Maybe Ray Black was off doing serious police work. Stranger things were known to happen. I was sitting in front of the house where I had once gone to pick up my girl, wasn't I? And who should have just driven by but my ex-partner from another life? I should have just accepted the *déjà vu* wonder of it all.

I had underestimated the lieutenant. When she came back around the corner in her cork-heeled sandals (evidently not anticipating any street work for the day), she walked directly past Tara and down to me. This time she wore a mustard skirt instead of blue, but the white blouse might have been the one from Gibson. She surveyed the homes along the way like a real estate scout checking out locations. "What happened to your eye?" she asked without ceremony as she got in. "Another satisfied customer?"

"We call them clients."

"And that's why you're out here instead of in the house?"

"Joe doesn't live here anymore. You hung up before I could tell you."

She wasn't impressed, and five years of people changing their lives by moving here and there instantly vanished into insignificance. I couldn't have agreed with her more. "Well, we can't sit here," she said. "There's private security in this neighborhood, and I don't feel like having to explain myself to some Rent-a-Cop."

"I'd like to hear that."

"Drive, Finley."

I drove. And waited for her to ask for the Christman reports in my glove compartment. But she didn't. She was wound too tight. The last thing she should have been wearing was a tiny locket around her throat. As I moved along to nowhere, she stared ahead at corners and traffic lights, at houses and hydrants, seeing none of them. Her only move was to reach into her shoulder bag for sunglasses against the late afternoon glare. I could have opened my mouth, too, but I knew better. Back in the day we had been able to go 20 minutes without a sound except the radio reporting a push-in miles away. There had never been any rush to admit to one another that we were confused or depressed by something. Smelling each other's deodorants had covered most of it.

A Verizon truck broke the spell. I didn't see any wires, cables, or pulleys over the middle of the residential street, but the truck apparently had. Why else be parked there for repair work, making it impossible to get past in either direction? By the time I had finished pleasantries with a goofus in a yellow plastic helmet and orange flak jacket and he had moved his wagon, the silence in the car was gone. "It's a mess," she said.

"You talked to Ware?"

"You mean did I talk to my husband Roger?"

"Yeah, that's what I mean."

She gave the correction another few seconds to settle, then: "He said the same thing you did—this won't be my case much longer."

"His perspective may be different than mine."

"Completely. He'll be happy if I'm taken off it."

"Because?"

She needed another reminder of who she was before answering that one, so pointed to a parking space just shy of the Seventh

Street commercial strip. Orders from the brass were orders from the brass: I followed her finger to the spot wondering why she had raspberry toenail polish but nothing on her fingernails. "Because it might come back to bite me," she said as I killed the engine in front of a blank side wall from a store up on Seventh. "I told him it was decent of him to worry about that."

I hadn't missed much by not being a third party to their conversation at home; she had brought a ton of leftover ice with her into the car to catch me up. "What is it that's supposed to come back to bite you?"

"Both of you could be wrong," she said, ignoring the question. "Why shout fire if there isn't any?"

She didn't believe it, not after whatever Ware had admitted to her, but why not an audience of at least one for trying out the rationalizations she had been trading with herself for 24 hours? An old nicotine pang came back, and I wanted to kick myself for my cigarette with Sal Rini. I was over too many things I really wasn't over. "Let me go first," I said, sounding noble even to my own ears. "It seems to have all started with a bookie collector named Pay Back Lewin. He got too zealous about his job and killed . . ."

"Edward Cassidy." She took off her glasses and put them back in her bag; maybe because she didn't need them in the shade of where we were parked or maybe because it gave her something to fidget about instead of looking at me.

"Stepson of."

"Check."

"Ally of Roger in so many worthy causes. What do they call their little clubhouse? The Faith Renewal Movement?"

I wanted her to snap at my snideness, at a minimum to tell me again we were talking about her husband. But she just came out of her bag with a tube of Life Savers and tore some of the top paper off. "Roger has a lot of associates I don't like," she said. "I have a lot he doesn't like. It's supposed to add flavor to a marriage. What it mainly does is give you an excuse to catch up on another *Law and Order* rerun and then ask him the next morning if he had a pleasant evening. Life Saver?"

It wasn't a cigarette, but it was better than nothing; certainly better than the airy tone she was daring me to challenge. "But I'm guessing the mess, as you call it," I said in my best obliviousness, "wasn't just the accident. There was this Lewin's employer, the one who sent him to collect from Cassidy."

"A fire."

"The Columbia Diner. Roger told you this?"

"What Roger told me, Finley, was a lurid story filled with names, none of which were Mr. and Mrs. Ware. There was a Mr. Ware here and there, but the Mrs., she didn't make the cut. Nothing at all to make me think of two married people who shared what worried them. What *had been* worrying them for a long time. How's that for slow-on-the-uptake detective work?"

When she finally did brave looking at me, I didn't want to look at her. I hated the butter scotch Life Saver in my mouth. There were a hundred better flavors. Why the hell buy butter scotch?

"Or does it matter as long as you're brought up to speed eventually?"

My bad angel had an urge. "You've got two problems here, Ellen. One is for a marriage counselor. The other is about Connie Marchese and a lot of files that have been altered and what that might have to do with his death. The only one who can connect them right now is you. *Are* they connected?"

"Roger's had nothing to do with Marchese or those files."

"And you believe this because he's a forthright guy."

"Don't push it."

"Then why?"

"Because he explained some things. Choices he's made over the last couple of years."

I remembered again what Alan Crosby had asked me in the Professor's garden. "Mister Ambitious turning out to be not so ambitious? Maybe getting antsy about where the Faith Revival Movement was taking him? Their politics all-American and all-God, but not their leaders?"

I liked thinking of her surprise as admiration. "How did you know?"

"I didn't until just now."

She tried to look like a good sport. "He had a good shot at the DA's office a couple of years ago," she said. "They were all after him to run. The parties, the diocese, even his boss. So many phone calls from strangers with rosary beads in their hands we had to change to an unlisted number. And you could see he wanted nothing more. But he wouldn't go for it."

"And you never asked why before this week?"

"I thought I knew why. I thought it was . . . ideological, political. That he was falling out of love with the Movement's rhetoric, with the crazier and crazier people who seemed to be joining it. God knows Roger can be to the right of Genghis Khan on some things, but he's never been a marching moron like so many of these people. Some of them go around showing you the stigmata in their hands."

"And that's why you thought he got queasy about things."

"Yes."

I wasn't even sure I *wanted* to believe her. Why make Roger Ware look better—even minimally—than I had decided he was? "And instead it was just because of all these potholes dug out there by Keenan." Sticking her Life Saver out to the front of her tongue seemed to be the same thing as nodding. "But Roger never came right out and said that."

Her sigh might have been for either of us. "Never get to a place where the obvious is humiliating if you come right out and acknowledge it? Maybe you've lived more of a sheltered life than I thought."

"Boom, boom."

She all but spat out her candy. "You can't begin to understand it! Everyone on the Island would've been poking Roger in the ribs for a little consideration if he went into an election campaign! Me, I wanted to think that was the normal parasite thing around a candidate."

"Even when some of the pokers were the Fantone kind he spent most of his work week prosecuting?"

"He's my husband, Finley. And I just told you: I thought he was putting distance between himself and those people for political reasons, for deciding who he was and not seeing himself in Patrick Keenan and his gang."

"But nothing so ambitious. Not Roger having a life-changing epiphany, but Roger just not liking his chances for an electoral one."

"If it makes you happy to think that," she said, subsiding in her seat.

"What doesn't make me happy is the idea fairies sprinkled you with sleep dust. C'mon, Ellen. Pretend I still have a brain."

"Misgivings aren't evidence."

"You weren't booking Roger, you were sleeping with him."

"That can't still excite your fantasies."

I needed a Time Out. We both did. We weren't back to our days as partners, but to the later days, when Mrs. Ware and Lieutenant Ware hadn't liked the private investigator Finley poking into official Major Cases business. She wasn't the only one who needed a counselor.

A refreshing wave of muggy air seemed like the next best thing. I had no idea what I was doing getting out of the car. The getting out part, yes: that fit under the heading of Decision, Action, Run Away. Firm, heroic things. But meandering down to Seventh Street had less direction than the hot coals rising from my stomach to my lungs. Mood swings Stallworth had called them, and she hadn't meant some golden oldie by Glen Miller and the Big Band.

"Paul!"

She had to do better. I wasn't necessarily *Paul* because we were friends. I could have been *Paul* for her because she didn't want any passerby hearing my surname and turning that into evidence against her down the road. Her calculating mind had been invaluable as a partner; off the job it had always been a pain in the ass. "Just some air!"

I was pretty calculating myself. I was supposed to be winging it, but I still glimpsed her out of the corner of my eye to see what she would do. She looked up and down the block for eavesdroppers before slamming the car door and coming after me. I didn't mind the company for the dreary array of fast food franchises and electronic stores that waited along Seventh. In the middle of them—and how perfect was *that*! —was a bridal gown store. Moral: Whatever the retail, it always meant rental.

"Paul?"

That Paul I accepted. It wasn't for the grandstand, it was just for me. Her mouth looked shaped by it. There was even a tiny light back in her black eyes; she was in. "None of it's personal. Do you get that? What's over is over, and it has nothing to do with the breakfast we had this morning or five years ago. Wake up, Lieutenant Miles. It's about your job. Not mine or ours, only yours. Want to be ambitious about something, be ambitious about that."

"Who are you to . . .?"

"Me, that's who. You've got bums all around you, and I'm not even talking about the home fires and that extended family. A couple of them are dead, and they wouldn't have done much for you if they'd gone on living. Another one followed me from Gibson the other day. He followed me because he'd been following you. Ray Black."

She looked ready to chew her jaw. "Son of a bitch."

"Who else but Black? He was joined at the hip with Marchese. But unless they got a windfall of brains since I knew them, neither one of them could've been behind all this crap. They're foot soldiers."

She wanted to disagree, wanted to run back to her office and have the showdown with Black that she hadn't had with Rigas. But trucks went past on Seventh Street, and she knew there would be others coming along after them. "Leaving what?"

"Leaving Roger's confessions about being bigger than his political ambitions half the story. Unless you're not telling me something he said."

She shook her head once, but was standing back in her living room or kitchen or wherever else they had screamed at one another. By all odds it shouldn't have been, but the light was still on in her eyes.

"Do what we used to do. Go back to the beginning." She didn't understand. "*Your* beginning. The day Levine told you he saw

Rigas acting sneaky in the file room. You checked those files and you were about to call Rigas in for an explanation."

"I told you that."

"You wanted to be thorough. You wanted all your ducks lined up before you accused him of anything."

"Yes."

"And just that? Rigas had no more associations for you? Maybe he'd bought you lunch or something and you didn't want to come down on him?"

"That's not funny."

But I could smell it. She didn't know what it was she was missing, but she was good enough to know there was a something in the big bag she resettled more comfortably over her shoulder. "What did you think to yourself right off the bat? 'Walter Rigas up to hanky-panky? The Walter Rigas I always took for granted? The one who just sits out there and does his forms and drones on about the operas he's always going to? How could that same Walter Rigas be up to something down in the file room?'"

She got it. "He was a big marcher at first."

"For this Movement thing?"

"Yes."

"At first."

"I hadn't heard his name in that connection from Roger for a long time. And I was glad. When I first took over the command, it was a little awkward seeing him out at his desk, then running into him at the house with Roger and Keenan and Marchese."

"Marchese? He was one of these marchers, too?"

She shrugged off the idea as serious. "The way he was anything. He always looked like he was along for the ride. You know that. But I still didn't like seeing him at work and then in my living room."

"All right. Go back to Rigas."

"He was a real true believer. Then . . ."

"What?"

She had all the pieces of the timeline, she just couldn't figure out their order. Why that deserved another butter scotch Life Saver I had no idea. "He'd been sick for a while," she said, sounding as if she were grabbing for any piece at all. "Before he had the heart attack he'd sit there at his desk some days like he needed an ambulance to get him home. He missed a few days, too. I was on the verge of ordering him to Medical. I didn't expect a heart attack, but when I heard he was in the hospital, I wasn't shocked."

"And this was around when Levine caught him in the file room."

She didn't bother nodding. On the other hand, she was looking across the street at the Arby's and the bridal gown store, and I didn't think she wanted a roast beef sandwich or a lace veil. My grandmother would have complimented her for her misdirection. I wasn't sure what I wanted to compliment her for, but I knew it had something to do with getting around to clear thinking. "Make a stab, Finley," she finally ordered.

I remembered what the Professor had said about Christman getting a new worldview after he had found out he was dying. Right analysis, wrong Major Cases cop?

She didn't find it so hard to believe. "So Rigas changed those forms for Keenan or whoever, then found out he was in bad shape and got contrite, wanted to make amends before he went to Hell?"

"Maybe not that exactly, but something like that."

She shook her head as much at a mob of ghosts behind me as at me. "Jesus, Finley, these people can't be that deep into the Dark Ages!"

She saw the answer on my face, and looked away before I was tempted to say it. Who knew better than she did about consorting with the Dark Ages? "Give me something better," I said instead.

She was too flustered to try. "None of this helps me with Marchese," she said, her impatience turning official again. "Whatever Keenan might or might not have been mixed up in five years ago doesn't explain Marchese. Help me on that and you'll be helping me. Otherwise . . ."

"Otherwise what? It's ancient history?"

We both knew that wasn't likely.

CHAPTER 42

I recognized Connie Marchese's living room even in the small Polaroid squares. The chairs and lamps were from one of those warehouse department stores, but the artwork on the walls could have only been rubbings from a cousin in Pompeii. The best shot of Marchese himself might have been another rubbing—the close-up of the jagged bullet wound through the chin and throat as abstract as anything in the wall frames. From one angle it could have been a stalagmite of flesh, from another a torn piece of linoleum. As Marchese had said, there was nothing erotic about it.

The Arby's busboy threw us another look to finish off our coffees so he could collect the paper cups with the rest of his garbage and have more of an excuse to go out back for one of the cigarettes in his shirt pocket.

"He was sitting at his dining room table. Single shot to the temple. Downward angle. The weapon was on the floor next to his chair. Guck on the table. Not too much of it, but where it should have been and who wants to make jokes about Marchese's brain matter? The chair may have ricocheted against the wall with the spasm, but the wear line was too old to be sure." She swept the photos up from the table for a new deal. "Forensics says there's nothing to contradict suicide."

"Maybe that's what it was."

She was so dismissive of the idea I was beginning to warm up to it—and to the certainty that there was some tiny detail she had forgotten to pass along. "It went down around five or six o'clock, before he was due to report in for the night tour," she said briskly, putting the pictures back in an envelope and the envelope back in her bag. "The neighbors didn't hear anybody ringing the bell or moving around inside the apartment except who they assumed was Marchese. Just the TV set."

"Self-defense in that building."

"What do you mean?"

"It's just not the place where I'd hold my eighteenth birthday party. Lots of shooting on the TV, I bet."

"It was on a channel that was doing a marathon of Hollywood westerns around the time the ME said he died."

"Who found the body?"

"When he didn't report in, we called. Nothing."

"And who found the body?" I asked again, knowing the answer.

"Ray Black. He went around. The super let him in."

"Black didn't have a key of his own?"

She tried not to look annoyed. "Why should he?"

"No special reason. But they were close . . ."

"The super let him in."

That seemed to answer something, but I wasn't sure what. "This TV marathon—did Marchese like westerns?"

"According to Black, yes."

"According to Black."

"He'd know Marchese's tastes, wouldn't he?"

"Sure."

"What's that mean?"

"Nothing."

"You said it yourself. One never went anywhere without the other. Can you really see Ray Black killing him?"

"No. But I also wouldn't have bet on him covering up for somebody else who did."

"Who said he was? I told you, he's been walking around in a trance. And there's also the little item of the lobby camera. Unless you've got Black down as Dracula, he figured to show up there, didn't he?"

"Right. And you ran that back to . . ."

"When Marchese went out on his afternoon errands. Of course, there could've been somebody already hiding in the lobby before then . . ."

"Unlikely."

"Occasionally, I get off a joke."

"Hardy-har. And the camera picked up nobody but tenants?"

"Two of them he even said hello to as he was going out. Maybe one of them didn't think he meant it."

"What Black said about Marchese's taste for westerns—did you find a DVD collection in the apartment?"

"Don't take flight on me, Finley. I'm running out of people, and I don't need to start games with one of the few I've got left."

"Who follows you around."

"Who probably doesn't trust me at this point because he's just lost his best friend and doesn't want to hear any suicide theories."

There were too many ricochets in that for me to follow, but they still seemed to come down to finding it a walk in the park to rationalize for Ray Black compared to doing it for her husband. "The DVDs? Westerns?"

She shrugged. "And what? If there're none, it's because he liked seeing them on television. If there're two, it's because they were his favorites. If there're twenty-two, it's because he was an addict, the ideal audience for this marathon. Take your choice, take your baggage."

"But it'd be nice to know which baggage."

"If we're just trying to impress bookkeepers."

She was right, of course, and the fact that she would look into the DVD collection as soon as we said goodbye didn't make her less so. But that didn't make the elephant sitting with us at the table any smaller, either. "What aren't you telling me, Ellen?"

"I mentioned him picking up jackets at the tailor's."

"Yes, you did. And it bugs you there was no plastic over them. But I don't mean just Marchese. What aren't you telling me?"

She didn't blink. "What I'm not telling you."

Sometimes that old Indy acceleration came back—I could be at fury speed in two seconds. It had happened with Carrington's crack about Jennifer and Susan in the diner and now it happened again. Maybe I should have just stayed out of fast food joints. "Enough. I've got plenty of my own problems with assholes suing me from their jail cells. Either give me all the information that might, just might, help me be useful to you or go back home to Roger and wring your hands about what he knew and when he knew it."

She just sat staring for a moment. I heard all the phrases clicking over the table. *I knew it was a mistake talking to you. Who the hell are you to talk to me that way? I must be out of mind sharing confidences with you.* But none of them reached her tongue, and that calmed me down a little. "Here's how fast the clock's running," I tried again. "According to Alan Crosby, Roger and Marchese had a scene in George's restaurant just before Marchese turned up dead. That one of the things you're not telling me?" What was icier than ice? "Fine. So think of yourself as ahead of the game if he at least told you about that little set-to."

"It was nothing."

"Right. It was about an earthquake in Indonesia."

"It was nothing relevant," she said again.

"Great. So we're finished here. I'll drive you back to your car, give you what Christman gave me, and *adios.*"

I didn't know myself if I was bluffing. What was I going to do without her and Christman's papers—meditate on Bobby Sprowl? But I didn't have to go so far as to make a theatrical move to get up. "Marchese told him about Christman passing on those reports to you," she relented.

"Nothing relevant?"

She didn't need objections. "Roger didn't know what he was talking about at first, but Marchese's tone said he should have. Obviously, somebody had given Marchese the impression Roger knew all about the reports. When Roger understood, he told Marchese to go away, it was none of his affair. Connie wouldn't let it go. Something about how Roger had to call Immigration for him about an African nurse who'd worked for Christman. Roger didn't know what he was talking about half the time, but he knew Marchese was desperate. And yes, about something he didn't want to hear any more about. It's a big legal thing. They call it deniability.

Lucky him, like I told him. You following me here, Finley? You were right when you said I should start worrying about my job. At least two of my people—Marchese and Rigas—were involved in this report stuff. I'd say Ray Black was a third. How's that for running a command efficiently?"

Sometimes five years were longer than five years. "I thought you needed a reality check. But first we're talking about your marriage and now your professional reputation. When do we get to Connie Marchese, Corpse?"

She glanced over to where the busboy was making a hash of tying up a garbage bag from the can near the door. She looked ready to jump up and help him to get away from me and whatever was on her mind. "I suppose I deserve that," she said.

"Shelton and IAB will think so."

She shook her head to herself. "That's why Roger said he wants me out of it. Good try, but we both know it's too late for that. It's all going to come out eventually. The only shot I've got, Finley—yes, for my marriage and my reputation and maybe even for my cholesterol count—is to stay out in front of it all, to nail down what really happened to Marchese."

She left out the trailer of *Do you think I'd be seen here with you otherwise?*, and maybe that enchanted me. Or maybe it was the fact that she seemed to use the same Secret deodorant Cynthia did. Another one of those road signs that I was getting on with my life, but only a centimeter a year? "Always back to the ABCs," I heard myself say. "Appointments Marchese had? Trips he was planning? An outing with his kid? Anything besides the tailor that said suicide definitely wasn't part of the immediate future?"

"Nothing."

"This because Ray Black said so?"

She nodded dubiously. "Okay, that's beginning to smell. But we've also talked to his ex-wife and daughter. Forget the ABCs. I've been through the whole goddamn alphabet. Nothing."

According to the manual, that left looking more closely at the suspected killer instead of at the victim. But that wasn't much help, either. The suspect didn't really scan as a suspect.

"What's the matter?"

"I was just thinking of what somebody told me about this guy Keenan. If he left his office or arrived home five minutes off his schedule, the steeple bells in his neighborhood would start ringing."

"So?"

"So if it is homicide we're talking about, there's somebody besides Keenan involved in this. Somebody who went out of his way to Marchese's place and didn't worry about his daily curfews back and forth."

"You're back to Black," she said skeptically.

"Am I? I'm not sure of that. But we're probably talking about somebody who had as much to lose as Keenan if too many people started prattling about those reports."

She stared at me until her skepticism faded from her eyes. I might not have recognized the new expression if the busboy didn't snap his head around at us as he was walking toward the back with his garbage bag. It had been how many years since I had heard Ellen Miles laugh? And how many years *before that* since it had been a full-throated laugh, nothing snide or snickering about it?

"I'm a goner, Finley," she said. "A real goner."

Not laughing with her suddenly felt like wearing a jacket and tie at a nudist camp. "What better company could you be in!"

The busboy whispered something to the counter girl, and both looked over at us like old churls about to call the cops.

CHAPTER 43

I still had Christman's reports in my glove compartment when I went home. I knew Ellen hadn't forgotten about them; they were my stake, my souvenir, my leash that kept her believing she wasn't alone while she spun around in smaller and smaller circles. I had been selective in what I had pressed her about, too. I hadn't pushed, for example, on hubby's denial of involvement in the Lewin-Cassidy death race. According to the Morantes, though, it had been Ware *and Marchese* who had steered them away from lawsuits. The odds were, Ware had been the first phone call the Morantes had made after I'd left their brownstone. And Roger being the tight-ass he was, would he really have put up with Marchese making a scene about venerable institutions like the Immigration Department, then just told Marchese to get lost and returned to his Dover sole? I didn't see it. Some people crossed their *t*'s and dotted their *i*'s, Roger Ware used a compass to make his *o*'s.

I suppose I did what I did next in the key of wanting to think of myself as the ultimate anti-Roger Ware. If he handled things one nervous-nelly step at a time, didn't it fall to me to do a little more of that trampling Marcello Fantone had said I was notorious for? What was the last thing someone in my spot should have done? Just asking the question gave me the answer, and the more I thought about it, the more I loved it. Cynthia wanted to see me being more than an inert receiver of phone calls and e-mails? Okay, then. She should have been ecstatic. I was already imagining the expression on her face when I told her what I had done.

CHAPTER 44

And so the next day, with the pretext of my infinite gratitude bulging out of my every pocket and pore, I went over to One Police Plaza in Manhattan to look up my bomb threat benefactor Patrick Keenan. What did I hope to accomplish? I just said it: Thank my bomb threat benefactor.

It took so long to get through the obstacle course in the 1PP lobby that I expected an El Al flight to the Golan Heights to be waiting on the other side of the last security booth. The elevator that brought me up to the sixth floor was one of those jobs that was noisier for not making a sound. I knew I was getting close when I had to explain the purpose of my visit to only one more receptionist and one hallway detective on soft duty. The plainclothes, a linebacker gone to seed who had too much white shirt at the cuffs and collar to go with his shiny blue suit, wasn't sure if I was making a fashion statement or a political protest when I showed him how my Visitor badge was cutting into the lapel of my only summer jacket. But he turned out to be a laugh riot on our walk down a long halogen-lighted corridor compared to the emaciated bird of prey waiting for me in front of the last office door. Carrington had called Keenan an ex-Marine with a petrified jaw and dead eyes; he had left out the glasses electrifying the eyes, the hawk nose, the graying of the buzz cut, and the bones that seemed close to collapsing under his tan summer suit. But who ever said IAB rats had to be romantic poets?

"Paul Finley?"

It might have been doubt that was my name, a warning I didn't have an appointment, or a signal for the linebacker to stay where he was for a second. I embraced every possibility as I extended my hand to him. "It's a real pleasure, Captain. I just wanted to thank you personally for your interest in that little bomb threat problem I had a few days ago."

He wasn't that easy; his arm stayed rigid at his side. You had to earn a handshake with Captain Patrick Keenan. "I'm not sure what you're referring to, Mr. Finley."

"Sergeant Silva at the 68 Precinct," I said, trusting I looked as serenely mystified as he did. "I know it's regulation and there would have been due diligence by the Department anyway, but I also know from experience that an extra phone call doesn't hurt."

He went for the only particular I cared about. "I don't know any Sergeant Silva at the 68."

"Oh. Well, he seemed to be in charge."

He could go on playing dumb or he could show me—and the linebacker standing at attention—how he had earned his promotions in his 175-year career. He wasn't comfortable playing dumb too long. "That bomb threat out in Bay Ridge? You're telling me a sergeant was in command of the response team sent to the scene?"

The linebacker cleared his throat; he heard trouble coming. "He was the one who asked all the questions. I can't say he was actually in charge."

"Then who was? We don't take bomb threats lightly around here. In case you missed it, we've been the target of terrorists in this city."

"What can I tell you? He said he was a sergeant."

Keenan was hardly satisfied, and wouldn't be until he got to a phone and barked a volley of questions across the East River. But in the meantime, he also found something amusing about me in his graveyard way. "It's okay, Phil. Mr. Finley has come this far to thank me. I have a few minutes."

Phil got away from us like he was tearing through a defensive line. Keenan gave me one last chance to pull a surprise on him, then worked up a grimace of a smile and led me through the door of his office. It was like walking into a 3-D movie: The Brooklyn Bridge was all but connected to his show window, and the pedestrians traipsing across the bridge seemed about to walk through the glass. "I've heard your name somewhere else, haven't I, Finley? Somewhere less drastic than a bomb threat?"

"It's possible. I used to be on the job in Nassau County."

He nodded emphatically: Oh, how could he have forgotten! "Yes, that could be. I live on the Island myself. But if I remember that report from the 68 correctly, you've gone private and our bad guy was one of your clients."

"Not a client. The nemesis of a client."

He pointed me to a plush leather chair in front of his neat mahogany desk. Ellen had said she had an office with a flag stand, but she would have stopped thinking of that as a status symbol if she got a look at the United Nations array of flags in Keenan's lair. The photos over the shelves and walls showed him with as many politicians and priests as NYPD brass. Some of them dating back years posed him in the same white shirt and wine tie he was wearing for me. "And what is it I can really do for you, Finley?"

He kept his eyes averted as he sat down. How could I not have told the truth to a man who was squeamish about watching others squirm in their lies? "Curiosity. I wanted to see what you looked like."

"I hope I don't disappoint you."

Actually, the Captain wasn't exactly the one-note deacon Carrington had described. Yes, he passed muster as the typical usher to be seen at Mass on Sundays: iffy posture from years of kneeling in pews, eyes darting behind his rimless glasses to ward off the next attack from wherever it might come, a hovering warning that coins wouldn't be tolerated in the collection basket. But that also left him close to being one of Johnny Yeager's fellow skels at the short arm of the Green Fox—the one that showed nothing but his talent for lifting a shot glass until he abruptly fell unconscious on the floor. "Walter was right on."

"Walter? That would be . . .?"

"Walter Rigas. We worked together at Major Cases. Back when."

He held on to the *back when* to test it for plausibility; he didn't find much. "Yes, Walter Rigas. He's no longer with us."

"Sorry to say."

"He was a member of an organization I belong to."

"The Faith Renewal Movement."

I seemed to have told him another faintly funny joke. "You're not going to tell me Walter tried to recruit you, are you? Something tells me you're not especially interested in renewing your faith."

"In the Church?"

"In anything."

I changed my mind about him fitting in with Johnny Yeager and the other Green Fox skels. They would have taken one look into his aluminum glaze and sworn off booze for life. And the odds were Patrick Keenan had given himself the same treatment at some point by staring into a mirror. If he wasn't AA, he was giving a good imitation of someone ever vigilant about dropping back into loathsome habits. "Well, I hope that's not true. Be kind of gloomy to think so."

"More than gloomy. Self-indulgent."

"I'm sure you're right, Captain."

The space between the zealot and the cop with years on the street allowed him to grin at the spectacle I was making of myself. I figured it was that space that also accounted for the bowling league pictures flanking all the priests and politicians. One of the others on the team was the linebacker from outside. Anybody willing to wear a yellow T-shirt with the words HOLY ROLLERS across it had his man-of-the-people moments, too. "We could sit here for the rest of day while I guess what you really came for," he said. "But wouldn't that back up all your appointments for the week?"

I didn't need the chill that Patrick Keenan had been looking into the thriving activities of Finley Investigations. "You must miss Connie Marchese, too. I heard he also belonged to your little thing out there."

"And why does he interest you?"

"The usual—a client."

He didn't buy it, but he was also simmering over something else. "That *little thing* you refer to happens to be what we believe in. It may not be fashionable in some quarters, but . . ."

"But you'd like to wipe out those quarters. And God bless, as my grandmother used to say. But in the meantime, we have the secular to deal with." His glance past me to the door said he was second-guessing himself for having sent Phil away. "As somebody who knew Connie Marchese, would you have taken him for a suicide? I ask for two reasons. One, because the Marchese I knew at Major Cases didn't tip in that direction. Two, because your organization seems to be uber-strict about interpreting Church doctrine and suicide is at the top of the no-no list."

"Why do you make yourself sound like an outsider? I'm sure you were brought up in that belief, as well."

"Brought up. Then I came across a couple of terminal cancer patients. They had other things to worry about than Church doctrine."

"A sentimental argument. Understandable but not worth destroying centuries of tradition and basic human principles for."

"I'm sure you're right, Captain. But we were talking about Connie Marchese as a suicide."

"Not everyone is strong enough to do what they espouse."

"So Connie wasn't one of the Movement's more militant members?"

"I would think your curiosity would be better directed to the people investigating Detective Marchese's death. That I know there's nobody like that in this building."

"But just as an acquaintance . . ."

His little wiggle to get more comfortable in his chair told me I still had a few grains of sand left in his egg timer. Why not? I could have gone on running my mouth and he could have found out all sorts of things. "As you may or may not be aware, Finley, the Movement has been growing for years. Once we had dozens of members, now we have thousands who believe you don't overcome degeneracy by ignoring it or shielding it with the pretense of being the law. That kind of law is on a shorter leash every day, and when it's finally wiped off the books, all the slime will respect the new rules or migrate to Canada. Who knows? We may even return to respect for the cop walking the beat. But all that said, we gather only for a weekly prayer meeting and as the social occasion demands. I can't claim a closer relationship to Detective Marchese than I can to others."

"Not even as fellow cops?"

"Meaning what? We have a special club? We didn't join the Movement as cops, Finley. We joined it as Catholics bent on renewing the commitment of the Church and its members to basic moral principles. I'm sure you'll remember what they are if you put your mind to it."

I recognized the priest in the biggest photo behind his head. It was the pope, and he looked delighted with Keenan and a dumpy middle-aged woman as they stood in the middle of some Vatican hall. "Was Marchese big on these weekly prayer meetings?"

"I didn't take attendance."

And that was a lie, of course: The Keenans always took attendance. It was also the kind of irritating lie that seemed to call for irritating him right back. "Were you aware that Marchese was looking into the death of your stepson Edward Cassidy?"

Finally, a bulls-eye. What was grayer than gray? Whatever it was, I zoomed right to the top of his Hate List. "I wasn't aware there were any open questions about Edward's accident," he got out.

"Connie seemed to think so. I'm not sure what, but my client would like to know what they were."

"Yes, the famous client."

"Him."

"And what's this client's interest?"

I thought about saying Truth, Justice, and the American Way, but was pretty sure Keenan was only a second thought away from opening a desk drawer and taking out his service weapon. "The privilege of a client. But the main thing is Marchese never approached you about anything like that."

We agreed it was better not to think of it as a question. "Wherever this client of yours is taking you, Finley," he said instead, "I hope it isn't anywhere that might upset Mrs. Keenan. It's taken her a long time to get over Edward's accident. In some ways she never will."

"Of course."

He leaned his bones forward like somebody who had been saving the worst for last. "And nobody should understand that better than you," he said, locking his fingers together on his desk blotter. "None of us need reminders of our failings, especially when other people pay with their lives for them. I'm sure in your own life you've had to reflect on that more than once."

CHAPTER 45

Without ever thinking about it much, I'd assumed I had about a dozen names on my own Hate List, starting with George Markovich who had torn up my drawing of the Statue of Liberty in kindergarten down to the Kim Il-Sung dynasty that had forced millions of Koreans to eat rocks. But leaving Police Plaza that day, my Hate List consisted of one and only one name—an NYPD captain of detectives called Patrick Keenan. A beer in a South Seaport café for calming down didn't produce any others from my memory banks. The creep had not only been delving into the booming activities of Finley Investigations, he had also been brushing up on when Finley himself had gone boom. No wonder Carrington had the guy in his craw.

On the bright side, as the weather forecasters said, my urge to put my hands around Keenan's throat got me back to a question I should have been giving more attention to: What exactly was Carrington's interest in him? I was a connecting door between New York City and Long Island jurisdictions for Chirpy Billy? Fine, but doors connected rooms and the only room furnished even by suspicions (about the Columbia Diner and Connie Marchese) was Long Island. And that was none of Carrington's business. So where had Mister Faith Renewal slammed into the penal code in the city?

The Professor was no help. When I got home and saw him coming out of my building, I praised the gods for their foresight: I was still in the mood to vent with someone, and who better than the old man? Just about anyone, as it turned out. As I dragged him back upstairs, he only wanted to talk about the thoughtless people who weren't home to answer their bells when he made surprise visits and about another cocktail party Belinda Massey had organized for him in the evening, this time at Brooklyn College. Then in the apartment, when I finally got in my doings since we had talked last, he gave me one frown after another. "You're out of your mind," he summed it up, punishing my couch cushions down to the floor. "You go over to this one and just let loose with some fiction about a new investigation into his son's death?"

"Stepson."

"Good. That makes it different."

"I wanted to kick him in the balls. He had it coming."

"Oh, okay, then. That makes it a brilliant move."

"I didn't say that. He was just irritating, Joe. Very irritating."

"And how did you expect him to be when you had this great idea to go visit him? Happy to see you?"

I hadn't needed much more of that, and was glad when he looked at his watch and grumbled that he had to go meet Belinda. It was only after he was gone and I was putting the finishing touches to my written report on Doctor Kim Dolittle that I gave myself a gold star for something—for never having mentioned to the old man the inclusion of the report on Jennifer and Susan in the Christman bundle. To put him through the mental gyrations I had gone through for no reason but Christman's notions of how to intrigue me would have been a little sadistic. In fact, when I thought about it, Jerry Christman had also earned a place on my Hate List, somewhere below Keenan but still there. Joe Carroll didn't realize what he had missed.

And maybe Ellen didn't, either.

The thought was there, then darted away between my pen cup and paperclip box on the desk. When it came back a second time, I snatched it before it escaped again. Forensics said Marchese had died somewhere around five or six, before he was due to go off for a night tour. But that was also the hour when most people in his building were coming home from work. So how many of the neighbors who said they had heard nothing unusual were talking about the entire span of time covered by the Forensics estimate? How many of them had come home in the middle of that period, heard somebody next door and just supposed it was Marchese? If there was ever an apartment house that was missing a Mrs. Chalian and an ear pressed constantly for all comings and goings, it was the Despondency Now building where Marchese had lived. Questions weren't asked, interest in a neighbor wasn't a virtue. A Ford would be parked in the vestibule before a baby carriage ever would be.

Could Ellen really have missed that, never suspected its importance? Of course, she could have. She didn't have my credentials. She wouldn't have spotted what was missing because she couldn't imagine anyone missing that much. She wouldn't have been a sucker for an extra police report.

CHAPTER 46

Here's the thing about bad ideas: If you play them out energetically enough, you might come off the worse for wear in the end but only after you've infected others with your idiocy. No matter how solemnly onlookers warn you that you're headed for a cliff edge, a few of them will also be tempted to run along with you on the million-to-one chance you're on to something. The temptation won't last more than a second or two before they return to their senses, but it will be there.

The Professor's temptation lasted more than a second or two. Maybe it was just sitting through a meal with Brooklyn College history teachers and Belinda Massey to hear again about what a great man he was. No, scratch that; he could never get antsy about that. More likely it was sitting through a meal with Brooklyn College history teachers and Belinda Massey to hear about what a great man he *had been*. Joe tended to get crusty about history as a synonym for the past, the what-we've-moved-beyond, the ancestral influence. It was bad enough when that conversation was about Henry the Eighth or Abraham Lincoln; when it was about him, tempers tended to get frayed. In any case, he was on the phone to me that night with the vision he'd had over "greasy burgers in some smelly sty off the campus." All his earlier disapproval about going to see Keenan had evaporated.

"I looked it up on the Internet," he said. "The next prayer meeting is tomorrow. In St. Brendan's Church in Rockville Centre."

"So what?"

"What do you mean so what? You get a look at who all these crusaders are. That's why you went to see this cop, isn't it?"

"Which you thought was a lunatic idea."

"It was. But you're in the quicksand now. What've you got to lose by flailing around a little more?"

"Lovely image, Joe."

"Screw the image. You're the one who started all this. You want to see it through or not?"

I gave him the whole next morning and afternoon to phone to say he had changed his mind. That also should have been time enough for me to get over the connection between Christman's telephone numbers and the St. Brendan's housekeeper who had answered my call about what I presumed was the whiskey priest, Bernard Tully. But every time I thought about the connection, a little gut stir told me not to be so hasty about wanting the Professor to get over the bad idea he had picked up from me. By six-thirty I was gassing up the car and watching the rolling pump numbers thinking how much nicer they would have been if I had been earning that much instead of spending it. The hot drive out to Rockville Centre at the tail end of rush hour might have been torture, but I had left my measuring rod home. Somewhere in my recent past, I could have sworn, I'd known what I was doing. Even when I'd been guessing that Christman had thrown Delaware Avenue into his packet just as catnip for me, I recalled being pretty balanced of mind. Now, though, I no longer had the alibi of Jennifer and Susan. At bottom, did I really care if Ellen worked out things with Roger, her investigation into Marchese's death, and the IABs from Nassau, New York City, and all the ships at sea? I was too groggy to trust my answer. I wasn't asleep exactly, but I was in some peculiar state of having just woken up and gotten a whiff of the bees.

It was in that jolly spirit that I parked across the street from the squat rock fortress of a church advertised as St. Brendan's. The signboard on the wall said FAITH RENEWAL MOVEMENT: Be More Than a Census Category. There were about 30 or 40 people lingering on the steps in front and what looked like another small mob crowding the vestibule inside the wide-open doors. I'd come with the idea that most of them would look like survivors of alien space ship probes, and a couple might have fit that part. But more of them reminded me of a neighborhood bake sale where homemade salvation was being offered instead of homemade peach cobbler.

The Professor was standing near the curb, like a twin to the chunky mailbox he was holding up. For once he was doing the listening—to a pair of teenagers apparently telling him about the Good News awaiting inside. The kids were heading up the front steps by the time I got across the street, but they had left their mark. "Just entered the History Department!" he said to me apoplectically. "*My* History Department! Jesus Christ, in a few years they'll be teaching the Blitzkrieg as a reaching out campaign!"

"What'd you expect—they'd all be returning to earth after being probed by aliens?"

Inside the church conviviality reigned. Everyone was happy to see everyone else as they slid into pews. There were all ages, even a pretty good sampling of the ethnic boxes they shouldn't have been satisfied checking off for the Census. There was a predictable majority of third generation donkeys, as my grandmother would have called her fellow immigrants, but also a few blacks, a few more Latinos, Filipinos, Chinese, and here and there maybe a Lithuanian born of an Italian and a Swede in Amsterdam during the last dam break. Evidently, they didn't think the Movement's ravings on immigration applied to them. Keenan was in a front bench, looking as raring to go as those around him. He had traded in his white shirt and wine tie for some green and yellow flowery job hanging outside his pants. I almost didn't point him out to the Professor from our back pew. *Hawaii Five-O* wasn't the picture I'd given him of Keenan. Naturally, the old man reminded me of that. "Him?" he asked in something like a whisper. "Maybe he wouldn't have irritated you so much if you'd given him a drink with an umbrella in it."

The master of ceremonies was a husky blond priest in his 30s who was standing up on the altar and beaming back to everyone greeting him. I guessed he was the Reverend DWI. Without his cassock he might have been a football coach getting ready for a pre-game pep rally. When he decided there was more talking than moving around for seats in front of him, he held up his hands in a call to order. "Glad to see you all here tonight," he said, sounding a little squeaky for his burly build. "For the first timers—and I'm happy to see we have a few this evening—I'm Bernie Tully and you'll have to put up with me for the next hour."

He was so confident of his laugh that he used it to drop his head to dig a sheet of paper out of his pants pocket. "He's one of them," I blurted to the old man, feeling as if I had tracked down the killer of *all* the Kennedys.

The Professor looked at me oddly. He was right. Of course, Tully was *one of them*; the whole church was *one of them*. I turned back to see who else was around. I didn't know who I expected to recognize outside of Keenan. I didn't see Ray Black or anyone else from my days at Major Cases. The woman in the front pew next to Keenan might have been the one in the photograph with the pope, but then again might not have been. Was the guy with the big head and mustache the Arthur Featherstone I couldn't make out on the Facebook photo? Tully seemed to be as good as it was going to get. I was just about to say something to Joe about his grand idea for a night out when there was a flickering of movement to my right. I turned into Roger Ware tiptoeing into the back pew across the aisle. He smiled at the elderly woman who looked back from the pew in front of him to say hello, but he could have done without the bother. He was so undiplomatic about lifting his eyes toward Tully that she got the message and went back to the altar.

Roger had aged better than some of us. Because I liked taking the low road when possible, I had kept a picture of him as a puffy little man with the anxious air of going for a job interview. The puffy part was right, but he wasn't all that short and he had grown a salt-and-pepper goatee that gave him a look of more cunning than I liked. Richard McCoy had said he had a broomstick up his ass, but then Richard McCoy hung around all day with people who thought nothing of having brake fluid dripping into their eyes. Even for my higher standards, Roger Ware acted unnervingly on top of things.

Tully didn't waste time setting up his targets, and I was swallowed up in a time warp. In my pre-teen years the Tully of the occasion had been named DiMarco, and he had used his Sunday pulpit to go after the United Nations, Jimmy Carter, and what he had been fixated on calling "the Arabians." The United Nations was a nest of vipers, Jimmy Carter was a liberal commie, the Arabians were dedicated to burning Bibles in favor of their Koran. I had never figured out where my immediate hostility to DiMarco had come from—certainly not from a 12-year-old's sophisticated command of the political issues involved and certainly not from the opinions expressed around the house by my mother or father. It hadn't been anything intellectual or philosophical at all. There had just been something too snickering about DiMarco's tone, a presumption that nobody at Mass would dare think otherwise than he did about anything. Of course, I'd also had my ultimate weapon for dealing with him. Every time he had finished one of his tirades about the lefties and the Arabians who were taking over the world and had thrown in a blessing for the congregation before sprinting back to the altar, I had, thanks to my grandmother, equaled him in good will. "God bless, DiMarco," I had liked mumbling.

Tully mentioned a few news events to remind people why they couldn't trust people who threw around the word *rights* too much, why terrorists were bad (at least now that the IRA was on the sidelines), and why Jesus had chased the tax collectors out of the temple. He got the appropriate muttering back. I thought of Samuel Chilumu's zonked out smile and suddenly felt affection for it compared to the lynch mob grunting around me. There were Jesus freaks and there were Jesus freaks. Some waited for the Rapture to take care of business, others wanted a replay of the Crucifixion with their pet enemies as stand-ins in the leading role. I was interrupted in this profound train of thought when Tully stumbled and had to refer to his sheet of paper. "Excuse me," he said. "Before we go on, we should also acknowledge some members of the Church Militant who have left us since we last met. In particular, I'd like to mention the tragic passing of Detective Ralph Marchese, which I'm sure you've all read about . . ."

The more he talked into the stiffer silence, the more it sounded like a commercial without a product. "We can't pretend to know how someone feels so bereft of hope that he sees no solution but taking his own life. All we can do is pray for his soul . . ."

For a blinding urge of a second I thought it was me standing up and calling out Tully. But when the heads started turning around, they were aimed not at me, but at Roger Ware, now on his feet across the aisle. "I think you may be jumping the gun there, Father," he said edgily. "There is an open police investigation into Detective Marchese's death and there has been no official conclusion yet about whether it was in fact suicide."

I didn't miss it. Tully's first dithering reaction was to shoot a look down at Keenan. But that didn't get him anywhere since, like everybody else, Keenan was halfway around in his seat looking back at Ware. Left on his own, the priest quickly nodded understanding. "Of course, of course. Roger is correct. We shouldn't get ahead of ourselves . . ."

Ware's goatee had annoyed me? I didn't know what annoyance was until I had to watch him retake his seat. Even then he showed no smugness to leap on. He had calmly but pointedly corrected the record, and that was all there was to it. If idiots like Paul Finley wanted to go on finding fault in him, he couldn't have cared less. And meanwhile, he had earned a badge of honor in a lingering glare from Keenan. Even as Tully was trying to cover up his fumble with an announcement that the evening's rosary would commemorate Marchese, Keenan was appraising Ware in a new, steely light. And the assistant prosecutor didn't seem to care about that, either, simply returning the stare until Keenan went back to the altar.

"What the hell's that all about?" the Professor half-whispered.

The question was too loud not to attract Ware's attention. If he was surprised to see me, it was between him and invisible face muscles. I might have been a stained-glass window he had never really looked at before and didn't spend much study on now, either.

"You see that?" the old man prodded.

"I'm not deaf, Joe."

"Nobody said anything. I mean . . ."

"I know what you mean."

And didn't, not a clue. The blandest explanation was that the domestic scene at the Ware house was having consequences. Or maybe it had been the Morantes alarming him that the past wasn't quite dead yet. But who was warning whom, and about what? Ware that he'd had enough of Keenan or Keenan that he'd had enough of Ware? I wasn't a credible witness even for what I had seen with my own eyes.

CHAPTER 47

I didn't know what I had come to see, but I had apparently seen it. As soon as Tully got down on his knees and headed for the Hail Marys, I tapped the Professor on the knee for us to move. But he was distracted by a sexton coming out of a door to the side of the altar. A pale, gnarled man in his 70s at least, he moped along so fraily he gave us a good look at the wine bottles and food platters on a trestle table in the room he was leaving before he managed to turn and shut the door behind him again.

"Looks like a party after," the Professor said.

"We don't have an invitation."

"You, no. Me, I'm invited everywhere." He nodded smugly over to the opposite aisle several pews down; it was the History majors he had been talking with outside. "Why don't you wait for me outside?"

"For what, for Christ sake?"

Suddenly, I was the one being loud, and the Filipino woman kneeling in front of me let me know it with her scowl. The old man thought I was funny. "Get to a certain age, you have to watch the volume."

Going outside to wait for him felt like the first steps toward dragged out aggravation. The rosary had a half-hour to go, who knew if Tully had more observations to make afterward about modern times, and then there was whatever the old man thought he was going to accomplish over Pinot Grigio and Ritz crackers. Call me lucky that I stepped back out into the twilight heat into a familiar voice: "Curious despite yourself?"

Carrington was sitting on the top step away from the main door, tie loosened and suit jacket over his shoulder. He was even more all-knees than he had been on my couch. "Maybe I should retire to the IAB instead of taking Social Security. You sure as hell have a lot of free time."

"Uh, oh," he said, unwrapping a piece of Dentyne and tossing it into his mouth. "Here comes the rat speech."

"Consider it delivered."

He nodded. "Received. But then I never told you I was with the 68 Precinct. You assumed that on your own."

"Stupid me."

"I've seen worse. Learn anything inside?"

The choice across the street for waiting for the Professor was between a pub called Grogan's and my car, and Grogan's was out because a bar would have been an opening for Carrington to be even more sociable. I'd already lost enough face with Roger Ware. It seemed important to get back home with at least one of my prejudices still intact. "One thing: I shouldn't be so quick to judge people."

"Yeah, you hear that all the time, like it's the eleventh commandment. But I've never had much of a problem with it. I bet you look it up and you'll find first impressions are usually right."

"Like you with Keenan?"

He didn't stand so much as uncoil from the top step. Some of the sweat beads on his forehead made perfect partners for his freckles. "I'd like to say so, but there was a lot of paper first."

I opted for my car, and not for just sitting in it. Since the History students, Tully, or even Keenan didn't figure to give the old man the third degree for asking impolite questions, I saw no reason not to go home and get his report in the morning.

"Worked it out yet what the paper might be about?" Carrington asked, dogging me down the steps.

"Nope. And guess what?"

"Right. Now that you know this has nothing to do with your wife and daughter, you're back to turning off lights and closing doors. And that's the twelfth commandment. 'I have attained awareness for my own spiritual well-being so what just affects others counts for shit.' That one pisses me off more than the eleventh. Me, me, me."

"Why you so sure it has nothing to do with my wife and daughter?"

"I hear things in the middle of the night. Some people hear ghosts, I hear bright people wising up."

There was no traffic coming down the street in either direction, which made it all the more irritating that I wasn't crossing to get away from him. Maybe it was because he seemed to have tried to look into what had happened at Delaware Avenue. I knew I had to ask. "What paper on Keenan you talking about?"

"Ah, that lingering curiosity again."

"Forget it. See you, Carrington."

"Okay, okay. Want a beer?"

"No."

"Then how about a ride?"

"Excuse me?"

"A ride," he shrugged, all innocence. "Only a few minutes away. You'll be back in plenty of time to pick up your father-in-law."

A bus chose that moment to come rolling down the street. There probably hadn't been one in an hour and the next one probably wouldn't be for another hour, but this one came jauntily toward us as if by prearranged signal. And every one of its passengers, I thought, knew every inch of my business. "He's got his own car."

"You'll still be back in 15-20 minutes tops," he said, starting across the street as soon as the bus passed. "I'll show you something a lot better than paper. In your place I wouldn't miss it."

It was what the Professor had said on the phone: I couldn't have come so far without wanting to see it through. Maybe I could have, maybe I couldn't have, but then and there my hesitation definitely felt only for show. And what else was it but dated instincts from Major Cases that made me look up and down the street before I got into the black Mazda parked two cars ahead of my Subaru? Finley seen hobnobbing with the IAB? Just one more thing that had crept up to lose its importance without me realizing it. I really had to sit down and straighten out my relationship with the past.

CHAPTER 48

Carrington might have been a great detective, but not because of his driving. Within five minutes he ignored a red light and almost took off a rear fender. "I don't see how you did it out here every day," he laughed. "Give me cabs in the big city."

"Big expense allowance?"

"Depends on the investigation," he said, more seriously than the question deserved. "You never *really* like hanging out the Department's dirty wash, but some bastards won't let you rest so you got to give them a full-court press. Including a cab chit here and there."

"Like Keenan?"

"Like Keenan."

"Who still hasn't broken any city law I've heard about."

"Keep listening."

Our destination was a still street of severely mowed lawns, white landscaping stones, and signs. Even without the markers that identified a cluster of private nursing homes and rehab centers, there was no mistaking the institutional purposes of the buildings. The lawn billboard across from where Carrington parked said ST. BRENDAN'S RESIDENCE. There was a light on in the lobby, but only a couple of others on the three upper floors. The hazy twilight was as good as seeing the rooms for knowing how bleak they were. "Where the parish priests come to die?"

He shook his head. "Where what they call special people come to live even when they don't realize that's what they're doing."

"Oh."

"Some of them were born lousy. Others had things happen to them. All of them had parents who couldn't or didn't want to handle them at home."

"And we're interested in this why?"

He made an especially loud crack of his gum and turned fully around to me to see my reaction when he said: "Because one of the residents in there is Edward Cassidy Keenan."

I heard it, reminded myself I had heard it, wondered what game my friend Chirpy was up to in making me hear it. I bounced it off the light on the second floor, then off the one on the third floor. And through it all I didn't have the slightest doubt I'd heard the truth. In fact, I'd been hearing it all along. That was what Marcello Fantone had been lying about and why he had avoided saying explicitly that Cassidy had been killed in the crackup with Lewin, and also why Keenan had kept referring to his stepson's *accident* rather than his death. Walter Rigas's report had declared Cassidy dead, so of course he wasn't.

"He came out of that collision with Lewin a vegetable," Carrington said, satisfied by my reaction and turning back to the residence. "If you're Patrick Keenan, you don't have defective parts like Edward around. He never liked Cassidy anyway. Not only not his blood, but into every bookie on the Island because the Pacers or the Packers couldn't make the spread. Not good for a Captain of Detectives who has another promotion or two in him. So you pull some strings and whisk him off to some place where everyone can think of him as dead. If his mother visits him every once in a while, that's her problem, Keenan doesn't want to hear about it. He's even got a headstone for the kid out in the cemetery. And I'll give you odds, Finley, from what I know of this creep, he really thinks Cassidy is dead when he goes out there to pray. Patrick Keenan insists his world is all reality, not some personal fantasy."

That much I could believe. But it still didn't seem to have much to do with anything else.

"I don't know who Keenan thought he was fooling with it," he added more pensively. "We found Edward pretty fast, and there's a whole staff in that building that can attest he's still alive. It's like none of that matters. What the Captain takes to be true, everybody has to. Keep the lie out there long enough, it becomes a fact."

"Why were you looking for Cassidy in the first place?"

He came out of his little trance with a laugh. "Would you believe the NYPD magazine? One of those idiot articles about the cop's family and where he went to school and favorite war stories. Then the editor realizes he's got the same son and daughter as the official personnel files say, but not the stepson. The editor calls him for a clarification, Keenan says his stepson's dead, and that's the way it goes into the magazine. That gets them wondering upstairs why he's never mentioned it before or got them invited to the funeral. Believe me, no one was eager to go anyway, not with Cassidy's reputation. The feeling was that if Patrick wants to keep it low key, let's breathe a sigh of relief and respect it."

"But?"

"But there was a funny odor to it."

"Why? Cassidy could have died in Montana. No funeral to invite anyone to that way, either."

"Let's say it all came up while we were scratching at something else."

"Ah! Billy Quixote's famous windmill!"

"If you want," he shrugged.

"Yeah, I want. After all this time, I want."

He nodded reluctantly. "The magazine article started the chatter just before his last promotion. Normal review. We knew about the beefs as he was working his way up through the ranks. He didn't hold the record for Civilian Review Board appearances, but he was no stranger to them, either. Usually an excessive force thing of some kind. So you think to yourself, what else is new in the wacky, wonderful world of blue? No need to single out Keenan on that score. Plus, it was all on the record, in the past, and it obviously hadn't bothered the archangels watching over him. That should've been the end of it. But then he started surrounding himself in the office of Chief of Detectives with the same kind of eels he'd been. Guys who always just slid away when you were about to net them for good. Some really bad cowboys only Keenan would call New York's Finest. Odd behavior for somebody who spends his every off-hour telling us what God wants. Just on a career level, why go out of your way to give the finger to the people who always need p.r. reasons for moving you along the line? We thought that deserved a second look, especially when a couple of these demos out here for his Faith Movement got a little rough. The business about Cassidy seemed like another warning fart."

"But nothing blocked his promotion."

"No. Flash forward a couple of years."

"*Years?*"

"I forgot! In Nassau County you get a situation, you always fix it in 24 hours. Anyway, it percolates up from one of the commands that a bookie is telling historical tales about one Max Katz . . ."

"The Columbia Diner."

"Upstairs—the real Upstairs—takes it away from the precinct and hands it to us to look into. They tend to get nervous when the brass gets mentioned in certain contexts."

"So how many phone calls you make? One? Two?"

He did something like smile. "One with our usual liaison that got us nowhere. Then another with somebody less official who had more answers than we had questions."

"It still wasn't your jurisdiction."

He popped his gum in wonder. "For somebody who doesn't care where his nose leads him, you worry a helluva lot about jurisdiction."

"So I'm a neatness freak."

"No, Finley," he said, the somberness back, "what you are is a walking target. You made sure of that by dropping down to 1PP yesterday to see our friend . . . What? You thought you got in and out like a cat burglar? There's a reason for all those cameras."

It sounded more definitive coming from Carrington than it had from the Professor, and that was without him knowing how I had salted Keenan's tail about the Marchese investigation and the Cassidy accident. As aces up the sleeve went, that didn't promise much as a pot winner.

"All right, this guy who knows about the Columbia Diner fire."

"Yeah, well, what he mainly turns out to know is that there was once a fire in a diner called the Columbia. Thank you very much. But it's a scent, so we revisit Max Katz, erstwhile owner. Your former colleagues were very protective about that part of it. You might have thought they were covering their asses for a job done too quick. We really had to twist their arms to persuade them we were all on the side of law and order. That and a call from their IAB. A lot of effort for nothing. The one conversation we got with Max Katz was two cups of watery tea, insinuations, and rumors, but no smoking luncheonette. Max might have heard of Edward Cassidy. 'Oh, yeah, that deadbeat!' 'Black hair, about six feet tall?' But more than that, zilch. Your people looked as happy as Max when we finally called for the check."

"And so?"

"And so," he said, shifting his body to focus on the home more comfortably, "we really had nothing to tell Upstairs except that we'd keep our eye on things, including Patrick's involvement with his God Firsters. And then you came along with your bomb threat and Keenan's call."

"*I* got your motor running again? You're joking!"

"Take credit where it's due. You and Bobby Sprowl. You made me wonder where I'd been sloppy. So I took out the case file and went over it again. The cordon drawn up around Max Katz was too obvious."

"After a few years."

"So some things take longer than others to become obvious. Be a drab world if we were all on the same timetable. Anyway, I knew there was something there, my boss knew there was something there. And I'll throw in that Inspector Joel Weiss is a member in good standing of his local synagogue, so no ex-altar boy syndrome with him. I started again out here."

"Why?"

"Why else? The living Edward Cassidy was the only concrete thing I had. And with a little help here and there I got a look at their staff and residence lists from the day he was warehoused. And that's when I came across a familiar name. How about Angela Fantone?"

"How about her?"

"Marcello's older sister. Went gaga before she died, so she was given a room up there on the top floor. Marcello visited when he could. Jimmy visited when he could. The whole family. And during one of those visits they came across Edward Cassidy Keenan."

It was my turn to be disappointed. A Patrick Keenan and a Marcello Fantone should not have come together through the accident of getting into a sanitarium elevator with an Edward Cassidy and his attendant. They should have met in some upstate New York restaurant and broken bread sticks over wicker bottles of Chianti and heavy-handed threats back and forth. And Marcello should have recommended the pineapple ice cream for dessert.

"My boss Weiss wasn't impressed, either," Carrington said. "A teeny, weeny bit, maybe. Enough to look to see if there were any possible connections between Keenan and Fantone family interests, some indication the Fantones were shaking him down over Cassidy. But that led to nothing, and Weiss didn't think there was enough to go on assigning the file full-time. If I wanted to log some off hours on it, fine. There was no denying Keenan was popping up in too many places you didn't want your brass popping up. But nothing official until I had come up with something more than the coincidence of St. Brendan's Residence."

"And you still haven't."

"But we're getting closer." He reached over my lap to his glove compartment and came out with a sheaf of papers. The logo across the top was the same faded stamp on the papers I'd had in my glove compartment going to see Ellen. "You could've saved me some time by showing me these."

I looked closer at what he was holding. There were too many reports, at least two or three times as many as Christman had sent me. And I could see the top one was Herb Levine's alleged stop of Aaron Garrett.

"Good, huh?" he nudged me. "My source says they're all phonies. And that includes the Cassidy collision. Now who's Cassidy's step-father? Hold on a second. His name is on the tip of my tongue. Wouldn't be a NYPD captain who might have thrown around his weight to get a false report written, would it?"

"I'd be surprised if they're all phony."

So much for his sense of humor. "Why?"

"Because that pile looks like somebody just reached into a file drawer and copied whatever he scooped up."

"Maybe Christman just sent you a sample."

"Consecutive dates all the way down?"

He didn't want to, but he looked away from me to thumb through several sheets on his lap. "So?"

"So they all come from the same drawer. That's the way they file things there—by date, alphabetically, and by file number on the computer, but only by date in the basement filing room."

"Awkward system."

"You should've been there when they were installing it."

"And this tells you?"

"What I said. Those files all came from the same drawer, probably the one where Rigas was seen fooling around."

"But we *know* this one about the gun runner is phony."

"I'm sure it is. It's what Rigas or Christman stuck in to make sure that somebody like me would realize I was looking at phonies. A backup in case I didn't get the message with the form on my wife and daughter. Everybody knew Levine would never make a bust like that form says he did. But if you go checking into every form under it, you're going to wish you could be back chasing down my bomber. Your 'unofficial' source was too anxious to please, Billy. He's given you a Jiffy bag, and you have to sort out the potato peels from the used condoms."

"You say."

"Yeah, and I also say your source had a special interest in sticking that one on top. Only two people knew the drawer Rigas was fiddling around in, and I don't think your dynamite source is Ellen Miles. I'm surprised old Herb didn't just feel flattered by that little piece of fiction."

He wasn't ready to admit anything except that his gum had lost its flavor. "In case you've missed the idea," he said, firing the wad out his window, "we're on the same side here."

It could have been the sight of the papers on his lap or it could have been the blonde teenager vamping down the street in her khaki shorts: One or the other made me think of Cynthia in bed saying how she and I had gotten used to our inertia. "What Herb Levine saw wasn't Rigas taking something out, but replacing what he'd taken out before."

He skipped the Levine part. "Why?"

"Because Rigas wanted somebody to—like you say—smell the funny odor. Outlandish things. Levine busting a gun-runner alone? Would never happen. It was a bullpen joke."

"Kind of inside as a joke, isn't it?"

"I fell for the one about my family, didn't I?"

"But there *was* a crackup between Lewin and Cassidy. Fantone *did* knife that hooker in Hempstead."

I didn't know why I hadn't worked it out before. I had been dancing around it ever since my first look at the reports in the Professor's kitchen. "Okay, now leave aside the red flags of my family and Levine. We're just tools. Who you're left with are the people Rigas was trying to get back at. He didn't have the biggest balls in the world, so he did it by changing this detail and that detail. But he always kept his targets prominent, vulnerable to any second look. Even the Fantones have figured that out . . . Never mind. It was your day off. Anyway, Rigas took a piss at the front door, then ran off before anyone inside came out to see what he'd done. That was Christman's way, too. Why they got along with each other."

Carrington's bafflement died on his face. "You guys must have a tough psych test to get through. Norman Bates work for Major Cases before going into the motel business?"

"As opposed to what? Captains in the NYPD?"

"Right. You and me, we're the only straight cops in the East."

"Except neither of us is a cop."

"Get on with it."

"The bottom line is Rigas was counting on second looks at the files by somebody who would see there was something wrong with them."

"When? When Tampa wins the World Series?"

"Exactly. When he's listening to Verdi in Milan or plucking his harp in the clouds. The Never Day that would complicate his own life if he was still around here living it. His version of a conscience was clear."

"And you're so sure of this how?"

"Something a friend said to me recently." It hadn't really hurt when Cynthia had said it, so I didn't think it would hurt when I did. "She was talking about making the mistake of staring at something to make it more comprehensible. Finally, it dawns on her she should be staring at something else altogether if it's sense she wants. I've been staring at those reports the same way. They're all false in whole or part. But it's not just about how they're phony. It's about *who* is phony in them. That's what I should've been concentrating on all along."

"Renewal Movement people."

"Rigas got uncomfortable about something. Probably to do with the original report on the Lewin-Cassidy collision and some chest pains reminding him he wasn't going to leave the world with a perfect clerical record. Somebody had talked him into fudging things when it first came down. From what some people have told me, it was Ware and Marchese on behalf of Keenan. The theme would have been how the Movement had bigger fish to fry than being quiet about an addicted gambler being concealed at St. Brendan's Residence. And it certainly didn't need bad publicity about one of its leaders washing his hands of a stepson he couldn't stand."

"You're so sure of this?"

"Who put up the roadblock when you asked to talk to Katz?"

"The investigating detectives . . . Oh, Jesus!"

"Marchese?"

"And his partner."

"Ray Black."

He nodded numbly. "You're really so sure of this?"

"Stop asking me that or I might not be."

"Are you, or aren't you?"

I was—and suddenly of something else. "I think all this is what got Marchese killed. He wasn't Rigas or Christman. When he got fidgety, he didn't know how to play sneaky games with files, that wasn't him. He did old-time cop things. Burst through the door, make splinters, and roust who's inside. Use an elephant gun in case the fly had a friend. When he heard about Christman sending me those files, he panicked and went after Christman's nurse. After that he bearded Ware in public. No way he didn't contact Keenan, too. And want to know something else?"

"Not really."

"I think Keenan got so involved in my bomb threat because he was afraid Marchese was behind it."

"But Marchese was already dead."

"Just the day before. But Patrick Keenan knew all about loose cannons and the kind of trouble they could make."

He thought about it as he took out his gum, unwrapped another stick, and stuck it in his mouth. "Last I heard, this Marchese was a suicide and your old friends in Mineola haven't found a thread proving otherwise," he said, rolling the gum wrapper into a paper pebble and sticking it in his shirt pocket. "And the way you talk about the weirdos he worked with, he might have just been playing Can You Top This?"

I didn't have to answer him. A thin woman around 60 with short gray hair and glasses slammed the door of a green Impala in front of the Residence and started up the walk to the entrance. There was a tired familiarity to her stride, like that of a night nurse not eager for the shift ahead of her.

"Cassidy's mother," Carrington said. "She seems to time her visits for when Keenan is over in the church being holy."

I watched her go through the front door. I didn't know if my grandmother would have been sincere if she wished the woman a God bless.

CHAPTER 49

There are dreams and nightmares and then visions that can't decide what they want to be. In bed the same night I had run into Carrington in Rockville Centre, I kept unreeling pictures of a dog race in Miami. That was novel since I had attended only one dog race in my life, during a trip to Florida that had seemed like a good idea at the time because a couple of other rookies in uniform had talked me into using my first Nassau County vacation down there with them. About the only thing I had taken away from that track was the ferocity of the gamblers. There had been no horse track façade about appreciating the beauty or bloodline of the animal; the dogs were out there to get to the finish line first and nothing else mattered. After that, they could have been shipped off to a canning factory without too many tears from the bettors.

My sleep remembered all of that, and there were some pretty sweaty, ugly faces to underline the memory. But it also added a few details especially for me. For instance, all the dogs stuck to clearly defined lanes as they tore after the mechanical rabbit. There was no bumping, no snapping at one another as they bunched in coming out of the gate. In that they seemed as mechanical as their quarry. And once that thought descended on me, another did: that I would keep going for as long as it took, that it was too late to go back or even just to stop mid-track and let the other dogs get to the finish line without me. I would stay inside my lane, I would finish first or tenth, but I would not be interrupted in the pursuit.

And that idea scared the hell out of me—even when I opened my eyes the next morning. It hadn't been a nightmare exactly, but it hadn't been just an innocuous dream, either. Sometimes being awake wasn't quite as bad as some people said it was.

CHAPTER 50

I started feeling more protected than the President of the United States. Carrington had meant it about me walking around with a bulls-eye on my back for Keenan. If he still didn't have enough hard facts to have me watched around the clock, I left him with the feeling that some back-channel calls were going to make my apartment house more visible to the 68 Precinct's patrols. He also wasn't kidding when he told me to get my .38 out of my dresser drawer for company, even around to Sal's for breakfast or down to the Green Fox for a dose of Johnny Yeager. That didn't say much for my acquaintances, but I didn't argue.

Carrington wasn't my only protection. To hear him on the phone the next morning, there was the Professor, too. "They put me off at first," he told me about his post-rosary social in the St. Brendan's sacristy. "Most of them seemed to have real senses of humor. You usually don't find that with the true believers. The Tully guy seemed to be trying out to be a standup comic. *I* was the one who felt like a dead twig."

"But you got over that."

"Would I be telling you this if I didn't? As soon as the jokes stopped, I asked him why he'd been so quick to think Marchese was a suicide. He didn't like the topic, but when you want somebody in the confessional to confess his sins, you have to keep prodding. So I kept prodding, suggesting the occasions of sin he'd been vulnerable to."

"Thanks, Joe."

"No thanks required. He mumbled something about what he'd read in the paper, and I repeated what you said to Keenan about suicide being the worst sin of all. That got Keenan into the conversation, and before you know it, guess what came tripping out of my mouth?"

"You and I are related?"

"On the money, son-in-law. Keenan looked like he was mixing all kinds of red and pink paints on his face. Clashed with his Hawaiian shirt."

"And this was in the interests of what exactly?"

"What the hell do you think? You put yourself on the subway tracks with your little visit to Police Plaza. But now a big gabber like me is also down there, and who knows how many other people I've been talking to? So what else can Keenan think than all of Brooklyn and Garden City suspects what you do. What's he going to do—raze New York to the ground?"

If the old man didn't think too hard about being only a second person, not a representative for a few million people, there was a logic to it; a bizarre logic, but a logic. But more than by the Professor, Carrington, and Smith & Wesson, what I was most protected by, it seemed to me, was what wasn't to be seen—evidence Marchese had been a homicide. As long as suicide remained the going theory, there was no reason for Keenan or anybody else to commit another rash act.

I told myself that every half-hour while I found one excuse after another for not going out. It was amazing how many *Cold Case* and *Without a Trace* reruns I hadn't seen the first time on the air.

Too bad that also left me at home for the doorbell and an enraged Gwendolyn Cutter. "You heard what I said!" the auburn apparition in my hallway fumed. "They eloped yesterday!"

My immediate instinct was to feel sorry for her, to sympathize with her for having come all the way back to my apartment because she was too exasperated to act more coherently. But she didn't give me time to extend my solidarity. Out from behind her rope bag her hand found my cheek perfectly. There was some caterwauling about showing up at Nina's track meet and being spotted by the coach and how that had driven them toward a justice of the peace. I was more bogged down in the details that her slap hurt and had landed on the same side of my face as Jimmy Fantone's punch. I didn't think that was good for my face's underlying structure. And then she was charging back down the hall choking back tears. I told myself she was already feeling empty for the futile gesture of her slap. I didn't believe it, but it seemed like the thing to say to myself. And by the time it occurred to me to shout after her that the elopement had at least saved her a wedding present she was already in the elevator and on her way back downstairs.

I lingered a second too long watching after her. Before I could get my door closed, Mrs. Chalian had hers open. For once, she wasn't coy about eavesdropping. "I told them a hundred times to get one of those cameras for the lobby," she scolded me in place of Gwendolyn Cutter. "Jeffrey says it's the easiest thing in the world to run a line up into all the apartments. Then you can see who's ringing and decide whether you want to buzz them in or not. But of course, that makes too much sense for them. If that one had had a gun, you could be dead right now, Mr. Finley. And *then* they'd regret not listening to me and Jeffrey."

I couldn't have agreed with her more—or faster. But nothing was waiting for me inside my closed door but a picture of the furious Gwendolyn Cutter, the suspicion that Jimmy Heyer would be dragging his feet even more when I asked for the next favor, and the nagging mantra of *You could have handled it better, Finley.* An awful lot of things seemed to have fallen into that category lately. There probably would have been still more if I had been carrying my normal case load. That turned out to be the only benefit of having the Christman follies trickle down to bury the insurance companies and law offices I kept on Speed Dial for regular work. None of *them* could have told me I could have handled things better for the simple reason that they hadn't been giving me any new cases to handle. Ever since Samuel Chilumu had handed me his envelope, I might as well have lost their phone numbers altogether. For sure, it wasn't a good sign when a receptionist you had been going through for years welcomed the sound of your voice on the phone as that of a traveler back from Pluto.

But I was grander than my travails, I reminded myself. I looked more closely at the eighth and last form Christman had sent me. It was a two-year-old case. The perp was a 19-year-old marvel named Darrell Buckley who had mugged an old lady in Bellmore. According to the form, the victim, Regina McManus, 67, had been hospitalized with two broken ribs, a severe concussion, and several broken fingers. Buckley had been arrested near the scene of the mugging but had been released on his own recognizance. There was no identification of the miracle worker of an attorney who had gotten him out so fast.

Or of the judge who had gone along with it.

Or of the prosecutor who hadn't been able to stop it.

Or of the above-and-beyond gene that had prompted Walter Rigas to go back to the form to add the night court disposition of the arraignment.

I went to the website for the Faith Renewal Movement. Buckley was hardly the rarest of Irish names, but if Sal Rini had been around, I would have given him odds that the Gerard Buckley listed as one of the organization's wise men had blood ties to bad Darrell. I got Regina McManus's Bellmore number from Christman's legal pad list. I intended asking for an appointment with the hope it wouldn't be necessary, that she would tell me what I wanted to know on the phone. She didn't. A daughter named Linda Conte informed me that Regina McManus hadn't been making things easier for anybody since she had died more than two years ago. I had spoken to Linda Conte before, on my first reconnaissance call. She didn't sound 67 now and she hadn't sounded 67 then. Somehow that didn't make me feel more awake than I had been on my first call.

She asked if she could be of any help. She asked it as any normal human being on guard against telemarketers would have, but also with a strong tone of curiosity. Telling her I was a private investigator working on another matter seemed to pass her test, especially when I mentioned the mugging of her mother. I could hear her sitting down on a chair with her phone. "If you think I could be useful . . ."

That was a little bit *too* trusting of potential telemarketers. I wondered what it meant that Mr. and Mrs. Conte had to live in her mother's home. "The attack on your mother was about two years ago, is that right, Mrs. Conte?"

"Almost two-and-a-half years now. She never recovered from it."

It sounded like a declaration made a hundred times—to other family members, to strangers on the telephone, to anybody at all. "But the report I've seen said her injuries . . ."

The dead laugh shut me up. "The physical injuries? Oh, they didn't help, Mr. Finley. She was always getting dizzy spells afterwards."

"But . . . ?"

"But it was more about how I'd misled her by insisting she come and live with me and my husband. 'It's a perfectly safe neighborhood, Mom,' I told her. 'You'll have your own room. We'll even give you a separate telephone so you can talk with your friends all the time without me or Larry picking up an extension.' I was so stupid. If I'd left her where she was, none of it would've happened. But after that night she wouldn't go out by herself. She was always afraid. Do you know what that bastard took from her?"

I didn't want to know. "What's that, Mrs. Conte?"

"My father died when I was eight years old. Mom did it all—raising me, going to work at Macy's every day. When I told her I was going to get married, she wouldn't hear of not paying for the wedding. I told her no, Larry and I would take care of it. Larry's family said the same thing. But you didn't tell Mom no when she had decided yes. She paid every penny of the wedding bill—the church, the photographer, the reception, everything. And she was so proud of it. She always carried the bill from the reception hall marked PAID in her wallet. That bastard Buckley took that from her, too. For what, Mr. Finley? To throw in some garbage can a few blocks away?"

"You can't blame yourself, Mrs. Conte."

She pitied my naivete. "Then who should I blame? I was also the one who also pushed for the settlement."

"You sued Darrell Buckley?"

Her sigh was directed against herself more than at me. "Even that would have been taking some initiative. No, the money was offered to us. And when the police told us they didn't have a solid enough case to prosecute, I couldn't see why we shouldn't take it. I thought it would help Mom forget the whole thing, let us all get on with our lives."

I pictured a cancelled check with the name of Buckley on it. It seemed like the first breadcrumb of a trail I had found through the forms. "The check was from Darrell Buckley's family?"

"No. It was a money order."

Of course, it had been; Hansel and Gretel Buckley didn't leave breadcrumbs for marking their trail. "When the police told you they didn't have enough evidence to prosecute, didn't you find that funny? They'd had enough to arraign Buckley."

She was off somewhere else—to whatever she was looking at but couldn't see from where she was sitting.

"Mrs. Conte?"

"You know how they say numbers are infinite?"

"Excuse me?"

"Numbers. You can do anything at all you want with them and they go on forever and ever."

"Yes, I guess that's true."

"I can't tell you how many ways I've broken down that settlement money compared to how much longer Mom had. The highest figure I ever came up with was $1.64 a day. I tried another formula just yesterday. If I keep going, I'm bound to come up with some figure that doesn't make it look so horrendous, don't you think?"

I had to cut through to her before I too started staring at things I couldn't see. "The cops who told you they didn't have enough of a case; do you remember their names?"

"Is that important? They were all coming and going in the hospital while Mom was there."

"No name stuck out?"

"Just Gerard Buckley. They told Mom how he was so sorry for her, regardless of his son's innocence."

"You yourself, did you ever talk to him?"

She found some dark humor in something. "Once. He called me here at home one afternoon. I thought that was very clever of him. He knew Larry would be at work. And Mom didn't want to hear a word. But he stayed on the phone a good 15 minutes telling me how he had once lived in the same parish I did and how that gave us a bond and how he felt a responsibility to at least help with the hospital bills. The guilt was so heavy in his voice I couldn't despise him the way I should have."

"So you agreed to take the money."

"Larry said we should have held out for more than the hospital bills, but I could barely talk Mom into accepting that much. My mother was her own woman, Mr. Finley. She didn't like needing help from anyone."

If she used the word *help* again, I was going to slam down the phone. "Does the name Marchese, Ralph Marchese, mean anything to you?"

Hesitation. "I think I know that name, yes. But I can't remember from where exactly. Was he one of the policemen?"

I stopped myself. I'd been part of more than one lineup where a story in the newspapers had told potential witnesses what I had wanted to hear. I didn't need any more of Linda Conte's help. "It's not important."

To her, either. "Is this Darrell Buckley in trouble again? Is that why you're calling, Mr. Finley?"

"No, no, nothing like that."

She had finally found her anger. "Well, I hope he is. And I hope this time he gets what he deserves . . . But."

"What's that, Mrs. Conte?"

"I know you can't make promises and I realize how ridiculous it is to ask after all this time. But if you should have the opportunity, could you please ask him what he did with that reception hall bill? It meant so much to Mom and it means so much to me."

CHAPTER 51

I didn't hang up fast enough. I felt worn out. Questions went to answers I already had and didn't know how to use anyway. I wasn't qualified. A fellow obsessive like Carrington might have credited me with revving him up again for going after Keenan, but look at the source of the compliment!

It was early in the afternoon, barely lunch hour, but I felt like going for the scotch bottle in the kitchen cabinet above the refrigerator. I had blown too many good excuses lately for tying one on; why blow another one?

It was as though I had sent out a vibe of my intentions across to Manhattan and Police Plaza. Carrington couldn't have been jollier on the phone. "What's it going to cost you—gas money? You'd pay twice as much going to your local multiplex."

"What movie are you talking about?"

"A surprise is a surprise. How about you meet me in the lobby at 1PP at three o'clock? I'll be there waiting for you. Save you some of the usual strip searches they put you through."

I already knew hanging up that I was being played, that Chirpy Carrington was bad enough but that Chirpiest Carrington was *very* serious trouble. But then what was a game without all the board pieces in place? And at least I would be playing it sober.

CHAPTER 52

Why do we walk into pitch black rooms when we know a monster lurks inside? It must be one of two things: some hangover ancient belief in the inevitability of Fate or copying Hollywood's dedication to giving us the biggest bang for our buck. The heroine who peeks into the dark room and just closes the door on it and walks away doesn't make for a good trailer today, and wouldn't have made for a good one back in the stone altar days. When we fight destiny and refuse to look Evil in its bloodshot eyes, what's left except enjoying the benefits of AARP membership?

Carrington hadn't been kidding when he promised to be waiting in the Police Plaza lobby for me: He had the attention of everybody passing through as he blared out some story and slapped the back of a guard behind the security barrier for punctuating his punch-line. When he spotted me, he turned up the volume even more. "Paul Finley! Over here! We've got a detector with your name on it!"

I wasn't *completely* brain dead: By the time I retrieved my keys and change on the other side of the security booth, I knew I was already in Freckles' little comedy. There were three more announcements of my full name to this one and that one before we hit the elevators.

"Okay," I said as we went up to the tenth floor. "Now everybody knows I'm here. Including Keenan?"

He was so satisfied with himself he winked and ironed his bright yellow tie with his index finger. "Let's hope so."

"So you now like the idea of a target on my back."

"I'm not fighting it."

Somewhere down deep inside I admired his unapologetic tone. But I wasn't up for going down deep inside so I mainly hated his unapologetic tone. "How about this? We press the button and go back downstairs?"

"Too late for you and too late for him. You already put yourself in his sights by dropping around to see him. I wouldn't have rec-ommended that move, but you have to work with what you have. And the gnats that fly around this building for him are already making their way up the air shaft to tell him about our *tête-à-tête*. That should give him some indigestion after lunch, don't you think?"

I knew it was too late to be a spoilsport by thinking.

The tenth floor had more of those halogen lights, an unoc-cupied desk for a receptionist in front of the elevators, and a slew of unopened paint cans on the scuffed floors, and that was about it. The only people were echoing voices walls away. "We're taking over this floor, but they're not in any hurry about it," he said, as we went down a corridor of loose wires and canvas coverings. "I think the union guys are related to cops, and the word has gone out to keep us homeless as long as possible."

He kept up the IAB chatter until we arrived at a plaster-smell-ing corner room that was all conference table, expensive looking leather chairs, and a television screen; some of the plaster was splattered on the table and the chairs. The view outside was a higher take on Keenan's angle over the Brooklyn Bridge. The traf-fic on the bridge looked more controllable.

"Take the chairman's seat up front here," he said, removing a DVD from his jacket pocket as he went up to the console. "I'd order in some popcorn, but the phones aren't working yet."

He was so chirpy he had to have found the smoking gun in Keenan's hand he had been looking for so long. What I couldn't figure out was why he wanted me in on it or what it had to do with a DVD.

"I didn't get this from Levine," he said, studying the VCR but-tons. "He seems to have scruples where ongoing investigations are concerned. Let's just say I got it. Your friend Miles won't be happy, but, hey, if making people happy was what we're here for, we'd all be Santa Claus, right?"

I woke up and smelled the bees. A fraction of a second before the dim, wavy black-and-white images came on, I knew I was looking at footage from the surveillance camera in the vestibule of Marchese's building. Gwendolyn Cutter—and Mrs. Chalian—had been the omen for the day.

"They ran it back to when Marchese went out earlier in the afternoon," Carrington said, "and didn't see anybody but tenants. But they missed one—exactly when he was going out."

The grainy footage showed Marchese coming through the lobby door out to the vestibule just as two people were coming in from the street. One was a giraffe of a woman with what looked like a Barnes & Noble tote bag, the other was a thick-necked wrestler with an attaché case.

"Recognize him?"

I thought I did, I thought I should have, then I didn't. Marchese greeted the woman and the wrestler politely, held the inner door for them as they proceeded inside, then continued out into the street. Inside the lobby door the woman went off to the left, the big guy pivoted to the right. Marchese disappeared from the camera's range altogether.

Carrington froze the vestibule image and looked back at me. "No? You're not trying, Finley."

"I *think* I've seen him before."

"Damn right you have. Unless you crawled through Keenan's window when you came calling the other day."

It was another proof I would have beaten Einstein to his theories if I'd been given more time. "The linebacker who escorted me to Keenan's office!"

"Phil McNair," Carrington beamed. "One of Keenan's cowboys. And guess what? He lives in Rockland County, doesn't belong to that Renewal gang, and has no reason for being in Marchese's building on Long Island. You saw it: Marchese doesn't know the guy. I'll run it again."

He didn't have to play it back, but he was having too much fun not to. The fuzzy images were what they were, but they were clear enough to show that Marchese didn't register a flicker of recognition of McNair. Ellen had missed it because she had assumed Marchese was nodding to fellow tenants he knew only by sight.

"Maybe he was visiting somebody else in the building."

He gave me the plastic smile I deserved. "Or maybe he moonlights as a gas man and is there to read the meters. You don't have to defend Miles. She doesn't know McNair. In her place I would've missed it, too."

"But you didn't because you're fixated."

"I'll take that as a compliment." He froze the picture again and, slapping the remote into his palm, sauntered over to the chair adjacent to mine and flopped down. "Back in the day, the Crooked Noses brought in people from Detroit or Las Vegas for their one-shot jobs. Nobody local knew them. In and out. Keenan didn't have to do that because he already had McNair on tap down here. It's like he was counting on needing him some day for a situation like this."

"That'll sound good in a courtroom."

"You're really pissed about running around Miles!"

He was right. Since she wasn't there, I had to be indignant for both of us that Shelton or somebody else from her IAB had been poaching her files for Carrington. "Shouldn't you be showing this to her instead of me?" His shrug of an answer was what I had warned her about in the Gibson parking lot. "You're taking it away from her."

"I'm not taking anything away from anybody. That's their business out there. All I'm interested in is the Keenan connection."

"So work on that instead of entertaining me."

"No need to alert Keenan just yet. I want him guessing, twisting his insides out trying to figure out what we're talking about this very second. A good cop like Miles would just pull in McNair, and Keenan would know everything too soon."

"She might also get McNair to roll over on Keenan."

He smiled dismissively. "You didn't pay much attention to the lug, did you? He saved his badge because Keenan asked for him. From what I hear around the water cooler, there's this loyalty thing some cops have about the people who save their jobs from too many brutality beefs. Then there's what any storefront lawyer will tell you: We don't have him in Marchese's apartment and we don't have physical evidence of homicide. All we've got is McNair walking in just as Marchese is walking out. How many explanations can you work up for that? Being the gas man is the only one that *wouldn't* get him an apology and go have a nice day. Right now, this movie is just a hole card, and we don't show that until the end of the game."

"That sounds right—*game.*"

He got instant sunburn. "Holy mother of Jesus, Finley! You score the run! You want pretty or effective?"

"And you're a bottom line guy."

He smiled himself back to calm. "'You got that right, Howie!' And so is Inspector Joel Weiss. Now you want to help or you want to go on building nests on the moral high ground?"

"I thought I already was helping by being here."

"There's that. But you can do a little more."

"I can't wait to hear."

Down to it, he had to convince himself he wasn't asking for too much. It took him half a second to succeed. "One call, one question—to Keenan. You told him you were looking into Marchese's death, right?"

"Telling you I did might've been a bigger mistake."

"Hey, nobody's forcing you to do anything."

"Get on with it. What's the question? 'Did you send Phil Mc-Nair to murder Connie Marchese?'"

"Simpler. 'Does Phil McNair belong to the Faith Renewal Movement?' Nothing more than that."

He had the grace or shame to divert his eyes to watch where he was thumping the remote into his hand. Thoughts of how freckles often turned into cancerous cells wanted my attention. But then I remembered I was bigger than that: I didn't like Keenan, either. "Something I'd ask because . . ."

"Because you came across McNair's name somewhere. You can't say where exactly since there's that client confidentiality thing you're big on, but you were just curious about it."

"In other words, it won't be just a bulls-eye on my back, but the whole barn *and* the bulls-eye."

The earnest Carrington, the one who in my apartment had sympathized with my pension rights, came back. "How long were you a cop? You know as well as I do half the people you chased after arrested themselves. They couldn't resist thinking and guilting and calculating themselves into it."

"I think that's an IAB experience."

"All right, maybe it is. One way or another, I'd like to get that ball rolling with Keenan. Being the loose flexible guy he is, it shouldn't take all that long for him to cuff himself."

"And you'll be on hand for that dramatic moment?"

"What do you think? I've been taken off the squad car guys sneaking free hot dogs in Coney Island. Weiss seems to think this is more important."

Every time he opened his mouth, there seemed to be another corner looming up ahead; not what was around the corner, just the corner itself. I didn't mind the thought carrying through the silence between us.

"Look, Finley," he sighed, aiming his zapper at the screen and erasing the picture of Marchese's lobby. "We both know you don't give a shit about Patrick Keenan or Phil McNair or even Connie Marchese. Christ knows you don't care about boosting me through the ranks and getting me another nice photograph with the Commissioner. You're the eighth car in a highway chain collision. You've got this small dent and you just want them to clear the traffic so you can get going again. I understand that, I even think you're right. But not giving a damn about things doesn't mean you can't be helpful. I'm not asking for your spiritual rebirth here, I just need a hand. Like it or not, you're the only one I know who can give it to me."

"Plain enough."

He wasn't all that positive. Unwrapping himself from his chair, he took the zapper back to the TV set. It occurred to me that the business about the *highway chain collision* might have been deliberately slimy. I didn't need the Professor for the reminder that there were a thousand other metaphors he could have used. "Know what I realized a little while back?" he asked, all innocence. "That I'm in Keenan's debt. I mean that. Without him I'm just crosschecking reports and complaints, records and codes, writing up interrogations and recommendations. Sure, it's nice nailing a bastard who needs nailing. The Department is embarrassed but relieved, the Republic is saved, and they owe it to me. But that's also just the job description. I make sure they deposit my salary in my account, I subtract the bills that have to be paid, and what's left is what I've accomplished." He folded his arms and spread his legs out to block the dark screen behind him. I didn't know if it was a serious lecture pose or he was afraid the dead screen was competition for my attention. "Keenan, though, that's different. He's what goes beyond the job description. He's the real hypocrisy in the job because he doesn't know it. Nature's perfect child. The badge didn't give him what he is, he gave it to the badge. They should have a security booth like downstairs for people like him when they first enter the Academy and it should go buzz, buzz, buzz as soon as he steps inside. Any cop can put his hand in the till or stun gun a suspect to say what he wants to hear. Guys like Keenan think they have a divine mission to do those things."

I remembered what Heyer had said about Carrington's father. On the phone, it had sounded like Paperback Psychology 101; in front of him, I wanted to read more paperbacks. "Got it. You don't like his politics, his religion, or his ties. I think we established that a while back."

"No, you don't get it," he said sharply. "I said I was in his debt. He's made me hate him as much as he hates most things that breathe. Maybe you're luckier. You love a woman, the sun in the sky, and the flowers in the field. I have to take hate as my second prize when I get up in the morning. And to me that means Captain Patrick Keenan."

"Never ask yourself why?"

The smile was more forced. "All the time. He's me 20 years from now. He's my old man 20 years ago. You want him to be anyone else? Or how about just this: He's bad for every image I have stock in? If he's touched it or been part of it, I'm less for having touched it or been part of it."

He was daring me to hear more than the overblown and the insulting, to read into personal hang-ups that were really none of my business and made me squirm. And that too felt like part of the game's rules. *Everything* was part of his game. "You're still missing a connecting dot, Billy. I don't have your altar boy nightmares."

"You sure?"

I thought of my old priest friend DiMarco. "I was awake when I had mine and that's when I told them to go fuck themselves. That saves you a lot of hangovers the morning after."

It took a moment, but he came back to shambling Billy. "Like I say, you're lucky," he said, going over to the window.

"I guess so."

He thought about it another second, then turned back with a wide smile. I was sure I could see more corners ahead atop the bridge stanchions behind him. "So how about doing it just to break Captain Keenan's balls? Tell me you wouldn't like to do that."

I didn't know why he hadn't appealed to me on that level before. And now it was too late. "No, thanks. I think I've gone as far as I'm going to go with Jerry Christman's legacy to the world."

"I don't believe you."

He didn't, either, and maybe the fact that I hadn't given him any reason to chilled me more than anything else he had been saying.

CHAPTER 53

I still felt a responsibility to Ellen. In a perfect world I would have brought her together with Carrington and they would have plotted a single strategy against McNair and Keenan. But it wasn't a perfect world, not with two separate police forces and two separate IABs inside them. It was still her case and she shouldn't have had to worry about sneaks swiping DVDs from her desk. But Chirpy Billy also had a point about her grabbing McNair as soon as she was told who he was. And that was without him knowing how anxious she was to make the score before her betters decided she was too compromised by hubby Roger to continue heading up the investigation.

"So you're the king maker, that what you're saying?" the Professor grumbled after I had phoned him with the problem.

"I don't think I said that."

"No, what you said is you can barely pay your rent but you're the Great Mediator between two police forces. I'd ask how you got yourself into a situation like that if I was sure you were really in it. Or are we talking the usual megalomaniac airs from Bay Ridge?"

He could really be irritating when he tried hard, but even more so when he didn't have to put much effort into it. "I told you how it's shaken out. I just think I owe her more than my silence with Carrington."

"Why you walked into all this bullshit in the first place is beyond me. You need something to do so much, get on that Craig's

List thing they have on the Internet and come up with a few more clients. I'm busier than you are and I'm retired, for Christ sake!"

Christman's accident report on Jennifer and Susan never came closer to my tongue. Instead, I grabbed for the old pack of Marlboro Lights on my desk. He heard that, too.

"Lovely, you're back on the butts. They'll help. Jesus Christ, Paul, will you please tell all these people—the dead ones and the living ones both—to go to hell?"

"You didn't seem to mind when you were pulling tails at the church."

"I was bored. Belinda's acquaintances put me in that mood. If you'd had any sense, you would've talked me out of that, too. But you're not just bored, are you? It's going on too long. What in god's name are you atoning for after all this time?"

The question was too close even for him. Suddenly there was some fictitious somebody calling him on the other line and he had to go. He hated these multiple lines to the same phone, but what could he do? The modern world was what it was. Call later when I had gotten a little more sense.

As it turned out, I didn't have to worry much more about plotting with Carrington to keep Ellen out of things.

CHAPTER 54

I was creating bats in the ceiling by turning on lamps in the living room when the bell rang. The door peephole made it unnecessary to walk around the house all day with my weapon in my belt, but I kept it on the bookshelf near the entrance just in case Keenan and McNair didn't approve of who dropped by Carrington's office. Only with its permission did I look through the peephole. I told myself I shouldn't have been surprised to see Ellen standing in the hallway, then wondered why I shouldn't have been.

She tried not to look as off guard as I was as she strode in past me with more of her orange blossom scent. She covered some of it by what had become a standard first reaction to the headquarters and brain center of Finley Investigations—inspecting the place for building code violations.

"Don't tell me you were just in the neighborhood."

"I came for what Christman gave you. As of tomorrow, you're better off not having those forms."

She had her back to me, and acted reluctant to take another step until I sounded ready to accept whatever excuse she had brought along for her visit. She had returned to the blue skirt with the white blouse and the sharp outline of the white bra under it. I was beginning to wonder if Ware's religious convictions included a fetish about his wife dressing like a student from a Catholic girls' academy. "What's tomorrow?"

"The DA is holding a press conference," she said, giving in to go for the couch. It was the darkest spot in the room, and the furthest from my office space desk. She appeared to unfold herself into separate legs, torso, and head when she sat down. Then all the separate pieces came together again as she craned forward and clenched her fingers prayerfully. I was supposed to say something.

"Press conference for what?"

There was a glaze in her eyes and her chin might have been a cocked weapon. "Lots of things. How the Marchese investigation is open and not necessarily a suicide. How one of his assistants, Roger Ware, will be recusing himself from the case because of personal relations with Marchese, especially in the Movement. And let it be clear that Roger Ware himself proposed that step to head off any perception of impropriety. Finally, how the DA's office has proposed that the investigation be taken away from Major Cases, where Marchese worked, and be assigned to the IAB. That's not really his call since IAB is going to take over anyway, but he'll still leave it up to the Alan Crosbys to point the arrows at me. Gallantry isn't completely dead."

Somewhere in there, in the part about the IAB taking the case away from her, there seemed to be at least a partial absolution for me watching the DVD with Carrington. But then again, I might have been getting ahead of myself. My penalty was dropping down into my one easy chair too carelessly; I had forgotten about the spring that liked to zap spines. "That certainly erases the blackboard, doesn't it?"

"Just like you predicted."

"It's not that I wanted to be right."

She didn't want to think about that one way or the other. "Roger knows what Christman sent you and he's passed that intel along," she said. "It's better I have that stuff. We can say you gave it to me that day at the Gibson station. Even if Black admits he followed me there and saw you, they shouldn't bother you more than once. Just be mystified Christman sent you the papers in the first place. You're mystified, right?"

The tactics were infallible; the tone and the body language weren't. She seemed to be performing for an Invisible Friend. "You talked this out with Roger? You're agreed it's the best way to go?"

I heard it before she responded. Five years had disappeared again: I was instinctively back to anticipating her habit of changing the subject when she was still trying to think of the best answer to a question. "There were no steeple bells in Keenan's neighborhood."

"What steeple bells?"

"The kind you said went off when he was behind on his commuting schedule. He got home right on time the day Marchese . . . died. He couldn't have been anywhere near Connie's apartment."

No, he couldn't have been and no, he hadn't been. "Where'd you find somebody to vouch for that?"

"His neighbors."

"I would've loved hearing how you put that question."

"So it gets back to him," she shrugged. "What can happen? He gets pissed we were thinking about him for Marchese? Well, he can be relieved. We have nothing on him. Or on anybody, for that matter. Whatever I thought about Marchese, I'm beginning to doubt anybody like that exists."

"Weird marriage dynamics you two have. Roger's agreeing with his boss Marchese might have been murdered and you're taking a big step back to leave suicide on the table."

"You should read UN reports. Suicide accounts for more deaths around the world than wars and homicides combined."

"And these reports cite Connie Marchese, do they?"

"I'm saying my mind is still open."

"Oh, good for that."

She slapped her bag so hard against the back cushion next to her I thought it too had begun springing springs. But she was just being angry and angry and angry again. "I want to blame you for a lot of things here, Finley," she said. "But you're not to blame for much of anything, are you?"

"Don't make me sound *too* insignificant."

She took a deep breath, then a second one. She had forgotten how trying it could be to deal with riffraff. "But it gives you a vantage point for telling me how I'm to blame," she said. "This shit's been going on under my nose for years. Do you get that?" I had my evasive maneuvers, too: I cleared my throat. "Did you

know Cassidy was alive and in a Rockville Centre sanitarium for
hopeless cases? . . . No, don't answer that. You seem to know a
lot more than you've told me. But as far as this is concerned, you
just heard it from me for the first time. Roger knew all about it,
of course. He was just being a humanitarian, helping Keenan, his
fellow warrior in Christ. And why not? The stepson woke up from
that crash condemned to a black hole for the rest of his life. Why
go on having all the Lewins searching for him to squeeze out the
last dollar he owed this bookie and that bookie? Roger was just
trying to do the right thing."

"I don't think that's so hard to believe."

Her laugh was a blurt. "Really."

"Really. In Roger's place I might have done the same thing. It's
after that it got complicated."

Even if I was being a clown, she wasn't all that amused when
she thought about it. "Things Roger said he knew nothing about,"
she reminded both of us. "But suddenly last night he remembers
it all. That diner fire. Cassidy ending up in the same place as a
Fantone relative."

"You said it yourself: Admitting things to somebody else can
be more humiliating than having them eat you up every day."

"Well, I don't want any more layers. I don't want to go home
tonight and hear how he's the one who killed Marchese."

"He didn't."

"Oh, okay. You say so."

"That's why you've gone back to the suicide version?"

"I'm not back with anything. I told you . . ."

"You have an open mind. Got it. Me, I don't see what you
should be afraid of. If Roger did do it, he's got an original way of
trying to hide it. Now it's publicly recusing himself and a press
conference. The other night it was getting up in front of Keenan
and dozens of other people . . ."

"He told me you were at the church. Thank you for that. I
thought I asked you not to be conspicuous."

"You're asking a lot of things, Ellen, but I'm not sure what
they are. Do you know?"

She did her face thing: One second brooding into an abyss, then all mocking cheer. "Getting laid. How would that be?"

The meteors from her first message on my machine started flying again in my chest. She had come visiting with her perfect bare legs just to provoke me. Even in the dim light I could see the blue where she had bumped her right shin. Lucky end table. I might not have been that insignificant, but I wasn't that mature, either. "Because I owe you?"

She didn't buckle. "That might do."

Smart answers died in my head. I wanted a living one from her—something not about bossa nova versions of *Chances Are* or umbrellas or self-delusions about the lower cost of sex after people got killed in accidents.

"But it wouldn't be the same," she broke the silence. "Or maybe I just want to hear us talking about it to get the whim out of my system. You mind?"

"Yes."

She looked quickly away to her nails. "Sorry."

"Everybody plays games. It's the kid in us."

"Too bad for the kid. I came here thinking about a very adult fuck."

"Then look at me when you say that."

I could have done without the concession: She was as embarrassed as I was when she lifted her eyes. "Now I need a little help even to say it."

I didn't know if I'd offended one or both of us, so I got up and went into the kitchen for a couple of beers. The refrigerator didn't clear up matters, not with Phil McNair sitting next to the tuna salad. When I returned to the living room, she had her head back on the couch cushion and her eyes closed. Raised, her chin was soft, not at all pointed. There was a tiny scar under the nub, maybe from a playground fall a few lives ago. She didn't open her eyes even with the crack of her beer top. "I didn't mean this kind of help," she said, a blind woman accepting the can I put in her hand. "You really should drop these high school standbys."

"They can work."

"But you should want them to, and right now you don't want them to. It's just your old partner. You know what she looks like without her clothes on anyway. Why waste your industry?"

"I didn't say that."

"Some silences are louder than others." She finally opened her eyes to the ceiling. She looked resigned to something. "Ever have a picture in your head for years and years and then suddenly one day you realize there's something wrong with it, it couldn't be that way?"

I could have done without talk of pictures. "Like?"

She moved her head off the cushion and sat up with her beer. I had a bad feeling she had arrived at the question she had rehearsed with her Invisible Friend. "You're still not over it, are you?"

She wasn't talking about us. There had never been an *us* in that way, in her imagination or mine. "We were talking about you."

She nodded and sipped some beer. "Right."

"And I don't know what you mean by *it*. What is it I'm not over yet?"

She toasted the ceiling. "And to hell with Connie Marchese!"

"One pope dies, another gets elected. What's this *it*?"

"You and Jennifer and your daughter."

I had been stupid enough to ask and to keep asking. "I didn't know there was a time limit on that kind of thing. Anyway, I don't need to be reminded of them right now."

"You have no trouble reminding everybody else of them."

It was basic interrogation box technique. I had seen her do it a hundred times with people she wanted to force into losing control. It should have been funny that she was trying it with me, but it wasn't. "Sorry to have bored you. But it's not like we've seen each other every day since then."

"No need to. We just need ourselves to think back on things. That picture we've always taken for granted as fact. Things we can't do anything about anymore. Billy Spilatro looking disappointed in fourth grade when I said I couldn't come to his birthday party. But how disappointed was he since Linda Martinez was there? Mrs. Stein saying I should have won the eighth-grade spelling bee instead of Mark Ryland. But she'd been saying things like that to losers for years, right? And she would have said the same thing to Mark Ryland if I'd won. Why did it take me until last year to wonder about that? And why do I also have that frozen picture of Jennifer on that road without you that Christmas night?"

She sipped her beer instead of looking at me. "Bulletin: I was drunk. I think they even made a TV series about it."

"Right. Your father-in-law took forever to baste a turkey."

"Let's stick to Marchese. Him you can still do something about."

"You don't listen very good. As of tomorrow, I can't."

"Then Roger. What're you going to do there?"

"You tell me. I'm asking you for your experience in blame. If Roger didn't feel free enough to tell me about all this crap before last night, he had a reason. He didn't trust me, maybe?"

"Ask him."

"Trust is probably near the top of the list, right? So come on, level with me. Share. Teach. How can I roll around content as a pig in pig shit for what I feel responsible? What should I be taking the blame for?"

"What you want to."

"Come on, Finley. You can do better than that. What can I get a head start on right now hiding from the world? Screw Roger for this and screw Roger for that. But what about me? I need more than him as a secretive bastard. You've always needed more than Jennifer just losing her temper and going home without you. I need to be clear about my part in all this so I can seal it away forever. You're the expert. Look at you. You're sitting there with a dozen things you're ashamed to admit to me. If Paul Finley doesn't understand what I'm asking, who the hell will?"

"Dead turkeys in an oven don't count *that* much."

It was out before I could pull it back. It should have been about McNair and barely visible vestibule camera footage, but it wasn't. And she was so surprised she let a second go by before looking blank and rolling the beer can across her cheek. But there was no way she hadn't heard me, so I suddenly had nothing more to lose. "He could've had the dinner waiting for us on the table when we walked in. It wouldn't have made a damn bit of difference. I just wanted to be home."

"Families," she muttered.

"What?"

"Families, I said. They're supposed to depress you on the holidays."

"For me it was a new experience that year."

"You're lucky."

It might have been a crack, it might not have been. The can she was rubbing across her cheek with her long fingers might have been cooling her or might have been getting her off. She was rattling me. She could have understood everything or she could have understood nothing—that too was infuriating interrogation box technique. The trick was to fill up the quiets before the wrong conclusions were drawn, and to fill them with a sense of control. "Know the one thing the old man did right that day? He didn't invite any of his disciples. It was just the four of us. None of the usual acolytes from the university. No outsiders. The family—here it was. The Finleys and the Carrolls, God bless. And I was beginning to suffocate from it. Not the individuals. I couldn't look at Susan without remembering how I'd melted in the hospital the first time I saw her. How I'd melted the day before because of something precocious she did or said. No matter how bad the argument with Jennifer, I had my bank deposit up here from when we had first been living together, from when she had simply walked into a room where the other cops' wives were, every bone and muscle announcing she wasn't there just to talk about the best kindergartens or donations to the Emerald Society. Smart, edgy, and sexy wasn't a fund drive. Jesus, even the old man was tolerable when he was just being the old man, yakking on about Garibaldi or Robespierre. But they weren't just individuals anymore. They'd all come together to add up to a . . . thing." I wasn't supposed to notice she was paying attention. "A thing that had already closed its doors on us and promised nothing more than a window here and there to see how the rest of humanity was getting by outside. Don't ask what I saw out there. Nothing I ever really dreamed about doing or being. The only time I ever wanted to be an architect or marine biologist was watching *Seinfeld* . . .

That's a joke. From that show. You're allowed to smile." She did; furtively. "I was a cop. I worked for Major Cases. I wasn't Mister Popularity for everybody, but I was damn good at what I did and I wasn't on anybody's pad. I had a wife and a daughter. I knew what fun was about. What was wrong with any of that? Who cared what was happening outside the window?"

"Who did?"

"Me. Who else? The outside was like what I had inside with the family, just in reverse—the individuals out there did nothing for me. There was no *femme fatale* luring me away from Jennifer, no gambling addiction that profited only Benny the Bookmaker, no bartender I couldn't get through the day without visiting. But there might as well have been. Together, they—and everybody else out there—were this world I was getting afraid of missing out on. There wasn't enough booze in Joe's house to blot out that dread. And it was no consolation to think he could restock his bar for the next har-har-har the next Christmas. That thought just made it more of a . . . thing."

"I guess there was no way of hiding that from Jennifer."

"Hide it? It was up there in neon, had been for months. That's what she and the old man were arguing about while I was sleeping. She'd had enough of it. He told her to grow up, it was a phase. History teachers are good about phases. Phases and eras and ages. Everything's marked off in some way. But she didn't want to grow up, she just wanted to take Susan home. She had read enough about husbands like me in the library books she stamped every day. She didn't want to be part of those books. That's why she lent them out to other people. So she left. The end of another phase, I suppose. And maybe the next one was going to start the next day—getting a separation."

"Carroll told you that's what they argued about?"

"And sometimes I even let myself remember it."

She took it in for a second, then nodded. She had been there all the time. Hide-and-seek. "Thank you."

I had no idea what she was pretending to understand. It couldn't have been anything I'd said because that blew back only a middle-aged juvenile with a growing drinking problem even to me. "You don't know what you're thanking me for."

"Yes, I do," she said without hesitation. "For getting rid of another one of those false pictures in my head. For telling me I wasn't just undermining your nobility that time. I was beginning to feel like my mission in life was to be somebody else's bad conscience. Thank you for telling me that wasn't always the case." She put her can on the coffee table. "I don't really want beer. Why don't you get me Christman's stuff and I'll get back to the next joust at home?"

I didn't want her moving. She was already too far away on the other side of the coffee table. Jan Rakosh occurred to me. "There was a guy I went to the Academy with. Hungarian. Spoke English perfectly. Except there were some idioms that foxed him. One of them was what you just said— 'Why don't you get me Christman's stuff?' If you said that to Jan, he would answer, 'Well, because I don't feel like it' or 'Well, because I don't want you to leave right now and I don't care how much Chinese Roger has to order in tonight for himself.' He took that *why don't you* literally, know what I mean?" She hadn't sat down with the beer, but the open palms on her skirt looked unnaturally unencumbered. I thought about counting off numbers to see if she would reach for her bag to fill her hands, then I didn't want to count anything. I didn't want to think of predictable numbers. Whatever Linda Conte had convinced herself of, they always turned out to be the same.

"I don't feel ironic, Finley," she said, looking ironic.

"Then don't be."

She nodded—plainly, simply, the way she would have if she had agreed to have a sandwich. Only her hard swallow was out of place. "Just don't make me the one to get up," she said.

I didn't. Every vein in my legs broke a clot as I went over to the couch. She didn't lift her head. I had to do that. I had kissed her before—not through such a heavy orange mist, but before. I could have sworn the grooves on her lips were familiar, that the mint of her breath was, too. And that, of course, was ridiculous because she preferred butter scotch to mint. And I certainly hadn't remembered the perspiration slick on her face. Or her long fingers covering both my ears. She didn't want me hearing any more truths than I wanted her to hear.

CHAPTER 55

Pirates had the right idea. You just threw the blanket off the bed and dared the sheet to slide up off the mattress corners, too. When you could grip fierce need under you, looking for your own face in the glint of deer eyes, feeling big plastic buttons pressing into your knees, you were free to betray, celebrate, whatever it was, one and all. Everything that hadn't already been taken was still for the taking. We had all asked for it. Carrington wanted to trust me to keep Ellen in the dark? His problem. Ellen wanted to trust me to help her in the investigation? Her problem. She wanted to trust Ware to be a husband honest about his activities? Her problem, again. He wanted to trust her to stay out of other people's beds? His problem. It was all very simple once everyone was ready to celebrate lies. You didn't even have to put up a Christmas tree and roast a turkey to mark the occasion.

I waited until she came out of the bathroom to tell her about McNair. She was hardly at home in my apartment, but she slowed down her hips and legs to move methodically, to make sure her nakedness claimed its space. She didn't give me points for bluntness (that was already beginning to feel quaint), but she sat down at the bottom of the bed and wrapped her forearms together below her knees instead of grabbing her underwear off the floor or running for the cellphone in her bag. Her small breasts and the one fold too many across her belly lent an oddly unphysical gravity to her concentration. If she hadn't kept flexing the toes of her right foot up and down, making a faint cracking sound, we could have been back in the box doing an interrogation. "So this press conference is for nothing," she said, not quite up to her smirk. "The case has already been taken away from me."

"Is that what's important?"

"You keep saying that like it's a minor thing. Marchese belonged to my unit. It's my job."

"So what do you want to do about it?"

"Aside from hoping this McNair blow your brains out?"

"Aside from that."

"That might be enough."

"Practically speaking."

"There is no practically speaking," she said, having already worked it out while she had me jabbering. "I'd need to look at the tape, go *voila!* at the sight of McNair, and then put off a lot of questions about how I knew who he was while I went into the city after him. Then the *real* problems would start. Or would your IAB friend be disappointed in you if I marched into Keenan's office to wish him an early Fourth of July and said, 'Oh, Patrick, by the way, that slug outside looks an awful lot like somebody on the Marchese video. You mind if I ask him a couple of questions?'"

"You want to do that, do that."

"No skin off your dick."

"None."

She nodded: I had reached wherever she had been waiting for me. "You've been tramping over so many other flower beds without me. Don't tell me you're suddenly out of an action plan."

"Punt."

"One of those sports metaphors I live for."

"Let it play out with the press conference. You don't have much choice anyway. See who covers whose ass. You still have the original of the tape, don't you? Then you move in."

"By which time Carrington will have all his scalps."

"No, he won't. He admits he has no physical evidence of McNair in Marchese's apartment. That's what you have to find. The rest is shitty NYPD politics. Some of it may get noisy, but it's still not evidence of homicide."

She shook her head in bafflement. "Said the enlightened politician. When did you start sitting around back rooms?"

"The company I keep, I suppose."

"I'm sure Marchese would be grateful."

"Let's not forget who we're talking about, Ellen. Connie Marchese wouldn't have been collecting a Nobel Peace Prize next year anyway. He sat on anything that would've brought up Cassidy and Lewin knocking traffic around the Sunrise Highway. Cost: One guy in a wheelchair for the rest of his life. He covered up the investigation into the Columbia Diner fire. Cost: A lot of ruined lemon meringue pies and an NYPD captain still on the job when he should at least be reporting to his parole officer. He covered up the still-living Cassidy. Cost: Whatever the Fantones have been able to use it for, starting with a stabbed hooker and including Christ knows what else. He didn't like Christman sending me envelopes. Cost: Seeing what it would take to get someone deported back to Ghana and probably his own life. There was nothing cheap about hanging around Connie Marchese."

"So why not just say fuck it, who cares how he died?"

"Okay. Fuck it. Who cares how he died?"

"Right."

"The field's all yours. Go to it. Forget about me and Roger and Carrington and press conferences. You still have until tomorrow. Go back and look at Marchese's apartment with the blinders off your eyes."

Wasps didn't react faster to a hand in their nest. "What blinders? I've never conducted this . . ."

"You've been doing everything with one hand tied behind your back, and you know it. You may not have wanted to be, you probably kept telling yourself you weren't, but you had to be with Roger hovering over everything. Sometimes I've wanted to think of you as the stuff the Grand Canyon is made of, Miles, but you're not. You're just a pain in the ass now and then while you worry about defending your turf. And that's included Roger lately."

"Then I *should* be taken off the case."

"I think I said something like that in Gibson. Diplomatically."

"So Roger comes out more honest than I am?"

"Suddenly Roger's being correct with all this recusing stuff and heart-to-hearts with his boss. Is that being honest? Maybe he just realized he had no choice and wanted to get to the pass before the Apaches got there."

She settled her chin on her knees; it had been about to drop there anyway. "I'm tired, Finley," she said. "I want to disappear in some steamy sauna where I can forget about all the things I should be able to do. Then I want to be pounded and kneaded and know it's being done for me, not to me. You're right. When nobody's listening, I don't give a damn about Connie Marchese. I know that's not the team spirit or the sense of duty from an office boss, but the only thing he ever said to me in 10 years I remember was during a stakeout in Huntington when he felt obligated to break a silence by asking, 'So you think you and Ware will ever have kids or is it too late for you?'"

"Then give the headaches to the people who want them."

"Like you are."

"That's different."

She blinked back another hurt to see me again. "Why? Because Christman was clever enough to mention Jennifer's holy name? Excuse the profanity, but this is my ass on your bed right now, not hers. I don't believe that's the reason. I don't think you do anymore, either."

"Like it or not, Christman put my name on this. More than the crap I call making a living."

"That's good. As good as my excuses to myself. I've got Roger, you've got Christman. We're both playing ourselves, but why bother about that when we can blame others for it? So what the hell? Let's get back to the serious stuff. I haven't come twice in the same night in a long time."

But she didn't move. She wasn't even looking at me, but at some spot on the wall behind me. I thought of my dogs in Miami. They were more of an excuse than Christman and Jennifer when it came down to it. But then they were all over the finish line, and I didn't have my separate lane anymore. There was nothing more to admire in my finicky neatness because the race was finished and some anonymous winner had already been declared. People were walking this way and that way over the track to get ready for the next race. I really had run out of excuses.

"Would you have to go to the office before going to Marchese's?"

She came back from my wall, rolling the thought around with my face. She didn't move her arms off her legs, but now she was aware that was an option. "No," she said. "I have my Visa card and Discovery card and all kinds of other hard plastic."

CHAPTER 56

I saw the light through the fourth-floor window as I was braking across the street. It had been years since I had been there, but I was sure it was Marchese's apartment. Ellen confirmed it. Getting out of her car a half-block down, she stopped herself at the last second from slamming her door and shoved it closed softly. As the flashlight continued roaming in the apartment, she unholstered her weapon inside her bag and cut a wider swath than normal crossing the street.

I waited behind the wheel as we had planned. She was supposed to let herself in without apologies to the vestibule camera for being an especially dedicated investigator, wait three minutes, and then open the inside door from the lobby while I simultaneously went through the motions of sticking a key into the lock. That was all fine and good except for what I knew would be her instinct to forget about the waiting-for-me part and get upstairs to see who had beaten us to the crime scene. It was a very long three minutes, and it didn't feel any shorter with my .38 pressing against my spine. Miracle of miracles, though, we all stuck to the script. The .38 didn't numb my spine, she let me through the inside door with what couldn't have been more than her hand visible to the edge of the camera's range, and I timed the opening perfectly with my key charade.

"Maybe it's not Marchese's place," I muttered for the hell of it.

She had her officially irritated face back on. "No, it's a tenant who prowls around his place with a flashlight instead of clicking a light switch."

I kept my mouth closed as I followed her up the fire stairs. It was an inappropriate thought so I wallowed in it as she took two steps at a time: Her blouse and skirt didn't look so Catholic girl schoolish anymore, they were on a 37-year-old police lieutenant who was much more exciting out of them now than she had been five years ago. Why couldn't she stop and get out of them on the stairs? We could bump back down to the lobby step by step inside one another and go *whee!* when we finally landed.

When we got to the fire door on the fourth floor, she checked her weapon again but kept it at the top of her bag in case we ran into somebody out on the floor. I felt like I was following the number one ranked cadet in our Academy class as I went after her through the door into the hallway's cloying mix of pasta sauce and lemon deodorant. I didn't recall Marchese's apartment as diagonally across from the fire stairs, but the torn crime scene tape said that was where it was. What sounded like Bob Dylan was playing from one of the apartments down the hall. Inside 303 there was some light scuffling, then mumbling. Without a cowboy marathon blasting on the TV, the acoustics were too clear through the thin walls for anyone to have missed Marchese being in a struggle. Too bad there *had* been a cowboy marathon blasting on the TV when any scuffling might have taken place.

I barely had my weapon out of my belt when she slipped her Visa card into the lock. A heads-up would have been nice, especially with her needing both hands to work the card and the knob, but maybe she was rusty after not working with me for so long. Or—more deflating thought—she assumed she was still working alone.

Even if procedure hadn't spelled out how unwise it was to stand tall in a doorway when walking in on a suspect, the flashlight's wobbly beam in our direction was clue enough. Ellen hit the ground while I clung to the hall wall and tried not thinking about how thin it was. She didn't care anymore about disturbing the neighbors: Her command for the intruder to freeze could have carried over the Sound to Connecticut. Still, he didn't seem to hear it, and I had a bad feeling. I pictured too much beef on McNair to get him down quickly and I couldn't believe the door directly across the hall wasn't going to open any second to put children and cute kittens in harm's way.

"Lieutenant?"

The voice wasn't McNair's. I peeked around the door frame and saw the silhouette wasn't his, either.

"Get that light out of my eyes!" she ordered.

There was a shaky second, but the light was lowered.

"It's me, Lieutenant. Ray Black."

And so, it was. I didn't believe it until he obeyed her order to turn on a table lamp next to the couch. And I still didn't know if that made any difference even after she ordered him to show his hands, then got to her feet and walked in keeping her gun cocked toward the floor. She had to show she at least half-trusted Ray Black, I didn't.

He had the same attitude. "What's he doing here?"

"You're not asking the questions, Detective," she reminded him.

He thought about another protest, but was saved by the sound of the elevator arriving at the floor. I closed the door before we were all answering questions. With the windows also shut, Ellen had found her sauna.

About a minute into Black's tale I relaxed. He was bitter about so many things involving Connie Marchese he had forgotten he was in trouble with his boss. Lucky for him she listened like somebody who had more on her mind than reporting crime scene violations. Except for one thing, the years hadn't been kind to Ray Black. He had the belly of somebody already in retirement, a hair piece that could have covered two heads, and the pasty coloring of somebody who needed a cardiologist on Speed Dial. There was nothing about him that wasn't the Before part of a TV ad for a revolutionary medicine. But as he went on repeating that he would never accept his partner as a suicide, there was also that one exception: I had found somebody who cared about Connie Marchese as more than a piece of a puzzle or a career.

"I'm telling you, there's no way," he said for the hundredth time. "We had to have missed something. That's why I had to come."

"So what revelations?" she finally cut him off.

Black's anger couldn't stop his helplessness from showing. "I've gone over it three times already," he said, "and nothing's showing up."

"Do it a fourth time."

It was what we would have done without Black on the scene, but she made it sound like he was just going to do something unimportant to get it out of the way of the more serious intentions we had brought to the party. He went over to a dining nook tucked into the end of the living room and sat down at the polished table where he had apparently found Marchese. Eating there looked like it must have been lonelier than eating off my kitchen counter after a bad day, and the bowl of plastic fruit left there for some reason by the CSU didn't make it any merrier. I didn't think I had anything to learn from that kind of pantomime, so I renewed my acquaintance with the apartment. It was all Levitt Cop Furnishings: a tan couch that looked threadbare even with bulging cushions, a couple of fake leather chairs, a TV set encased inside some phony oak thing, and a tinted glass Jungle Jim of shelves and compartments for CDs, books, and photos. If you didn't mind cracking your shins on the coffee table or tripping over a hassock, you could get to the radiator and a window over the building courtyard. Marchese's personal touch was in the bare wooden floor instead of the regulation carpet.

And in the rubbings, of course.

Ellen wanted to be in a sauna, I wouldn't have minded being in Pompeii. A sauna would have been me left alone with more thoughts I didn't want to dwell on. Pompeii, on the other hand, would have been flying off to other times and other civilizations. There probably wasn't a restaurant owner in Pompeii who had heard of Paul Finley, and what better recommendation was there than that lately?

And it was all wrong.

Even without Ellen blocking his sightline from where he was sitting, it would have been impossible for Black to have a clear view of either the rubbings or the photos of Marchese's daughter on the glass shelves. How suicidal could a suicide be? In Marchese's place in those last minutes I couldn't imagine not wanting to see Susan or something else that comforted me that it hadn't *all* been a waste. Or maybe Connie Marchese hadn't been as sentimental as I was?

"Black, how were Connie's relations with his daughter?"

"What business is that of yours?"

She didn't like being interrupted, but she was responsible for bringing me to the dance. "Answer the goddamn question, Detective."

"Marisa was the only thing he cared about. When he wasn't talking about her, he wasn't talking about much at all."

"What is it, Finley?"

I had to go for it. It was the only thing that made sense. "Whatever happened to Marchese, it didn't happen at that table."

"That's where we found him." The objection should have come from Black instead of Ellen, but he was distracted with the thought I might have been saying something he wanted to hear. "The brain matter was there. There's no sign of anything on the other chairs, nothing on the floor to say he was dragged over to the nook."

I flashed back to the linebacker who had escorted me down to Keenan's office and then to the physically slight Marchese whose muscles hadn't impressed Felipe Morante. "He wouldn't have had to be dragged," I said, taking another look at the floor in case contradiction was only a foot away. "He could have been carried over there."

"But why do it in the first place?" she asked. "Why carry him, drag him, or anything else to the table?"

Black was looking more hopeful with every passing second. "What are you saying? You see something that doesn't say suicide?"

I was beginning to feel the what, but still didn't have a clue about the where. "Probably because that's the furthest spot in the room from where it happened," I answered Ellen. "It couldn't have been on furniture. Forensics would have found something."

Black was making all kinds of animal sounds lifting himself out of his squeeze in the corner. "And they were all over the bathroom and the bedroom," she said. "Nothing whatsoever showed up."

"Kitchen, too?"

"Kitchen, too."

That didn't leave much except the small vestibule. I hit the switch next to the door. The dimmest of wall lights came on. There was just enough room for somebody, even a heavyweight like McNair, to stand in wait for Marchese to enter. As I studied the floor for anything at all, Black caught up. "Right! If there was somebody waiting for him, he wasn't going to let himself be seen, give Connie a chance to react. He would've had to get behind him as soon as he walked in!"

Black had the gist of it, but the only object on the floor was the blue doormat—one of those soft rubber needle jobs that cats liked to roll around on. The floor looked spotless. There was nothing under the tiny mail-and-keys table, no scuffmarks under the coat hooks that CSU probably hadn't already printed and taken away.

"You guys came here with an idea, didn't you?"

Ellen left him in his agony with a terse "maybe," then came over to study the floor with me. "If anything happened right here, we have to assume that TV western was blasting like hell for nobody to hear."

"Right."

"A silencer scrape would have shown up. The TV was the silencer."

"Right."

"But the TV would've also put Marchese on guard."

"Right."

"Unless he was used to leaving it on when he went out."

"Right."

I wanted her to keep talking; it was soothing background music. And the more she kept her music coming, the surer I was that the only possibility of a telltale sign was in the doormat.

"Tell me what you got, Lieutenant. Maybe I can help."

"Help by staying out of the light," she barked at him. "It's hard enough to see here. And then we're going to have a little talk about what passed for conversation between you and Marchese when the subject wasn't Marisa."

Black retreated sullenly to the couch as she committed herself to haunching down with me. After that buildup it was a good thing I spotted the scrap of blue plastic material—almost the same color as the mat—between two of the rubber needles. I handed it to her so she could be the first to say she didn't know what it was. She compromised: "Not likely you'd pick this up on your shoe," she said, holding it up to squint at it through the dull light. "It wouldn't stick. It's like tarpaulin."

"Or a mat. What the exercise fanatics lay on the floor."

"I don't recall Marchese being big on exercise. Was he, Detective?"

Black couldn't wait to contribute. "Connie? If he could have, he would have outlawed walking."

We were both reaching, but it was either the blue strip in her hand or nothing. "He put it on the floor to catch what came out of Marchese," she said, "but he would've had to shoot downward not to leave something on the walls or off the mat. Possible?"

"Possible. He's a good four or five inches taller than Marchese. And the mat was what was inside the attaché case he was carrying."

"You know who it is!"

She ignored him with a longer beat of silence. She had always had a hundred different kinds of those. "Then what?"

"He would've carried Marchese over to the table, to make sure your guys didn't focus too much on this area. Did they look here at all?" She pretended I was Black. "Anyway, he then carries the mat over to the table and empties out what's on it."

"But how would this come loose?"

"You've got two people trampling around here on a small space. Maybe this edge was already hanging off and somebody's heel did the rest."

She looked at the material between her fingers until she was sure it wasn't going to give her any more answers. "Maybe," she decided, making it sound like much less.

"But if you were to find a mat and see if a piece like that was torn off it, then you'd have what they used to call physical evidence. And by the way, this would also answer your question about the tailor's plastic covering. It had to have gotten splattered if Marchese was holding the jackets when he came in the door. So our friend got rid . . ."

She cut me off with a preemptory nod and stood up. Black was waiting to be finally taken into her confidence.

But that wasn't her agenda.

CHAPTER 57

"Sit down, Ray."

Black sagged down on the couch in bafflement; he looked like one more bulging cushion. "You got to tell me, Lieutenant. We owe it to Marisa so she'll know her father didn't kill himself."

She thought about one of the leather chairs, then chose the edge of the coffee table right in front of him. It was bad etiquette for a guest, and seemed like the official announcement Connie Marchese would never be coming back to the apartment. "We all owe a lot of things to a lot of people," she said drily, preserving the mat shred in a tissue and sticking it in her bag. "Let's start with what you owe me. And before you open your mouth, remember: Your badge is already on the table. Don't make it worse."

His best answer to that was to forget about what we had been doing in the vestibule and to go back to shooting me a resentful look. He wasn't up for being taken to the woodshed with an outsider around. I didn't blame him. On the other hand, I got to see how cruelly the table lamp was penetrating his hair piece to the scalp.

"You belong to this Revival Movement?" she asked.

He hadn't been expecting that one and breathed easier for the lob of a question. "No, I don't get involved in that stuff."

"But Marchese was enthusiastic about it?"

I took the leather chair she had passed on. She wasn't making notes, which made me think she had double-dipped in putting the mat shred in her bag, also using the move to turn on a tape recorder. I wondered if it had been running back in my apartment.

"Sometimes I thought so. He could sound like one of those holy rollers on cable when he got wound up. Immoral this, immoral that. What kind of a world was Marisa growing up in? What was she learning at school? That kind of thing. Other times I thought he was just with them because he wanted to rub shoulders with . . . well, with people with clout."

"You mean like my husband."

He nodded. He was starting to think he would ace his exam. Which was too bad for Ray Black. Aside from the small wrinkle on the back of her blouse collar that she hadn't caught in my bedroom, she had gotten even smoother in five years.

"Edward Cassidy. You helped cover that up?"

He was confused. "Me? Who didn't . . .?" I couldn't see her face from where I was sitting, but I didn't have to. "I mean, I thought you and everybody else were down for that . . ."

"Stop thinking, Ray, and just tell me."

The Professor would have called it the first flailing at the quicksand. "Somebody reached out to Connie. I'm pretty sure it was Cassidy's father."

"Here's what vague gets you, Detective: Nothing."

"Okay, okay. The step-father. Keenan. He's on the job in the city."

"Patrick Keenan. Chief of Detectives office."

He was guessing a tape recorder in her bag, too, but he didn't ask for a union rep. I didn't like it: Suddenly, I wasn't just an outsider, I was a witness. "Him. Connie said Keenan asked for his help and there was no reason not to give it to him. Cassidy was a skel with debts up to his ears and nobody was going to miss him but his creditors if he was declared dead."

"What was Connie's help, exactly?"

Black shrugged; he was lowering his happy expectations. "Talked to the hospital. He had to have found somebody on board there, too, right?"

"What else?"

Another shrug. "He said he went to talk to some people in an accident that night caused by Cassidy. Convinced them to forget about pressing any charges. This Keenan didn't want anybody drawing straight lines from them all the way back to his stepson."

"What about back at the house? Who covered there?"

"Rigas, I'd guess. He was one of them."

"And all this friendly talking by Marchese was okay with you."

"Hey, Lieutenant, I wasn't there! I was off for the holidays. What I know about it Connie told me when I got back after New Year's. Stories. You can't tell me your partners never told you stories."

I got my eyes up to one of the rubbings before he got over her shoulder to me. Marchese had been right: There was absolutely nothing erotic about the damn things. The Pompeiians or whatever they were called must have had very horny minds.

"But you *were* there for the fire at the Columbia Diner, right?"

"Connie and I caught it, yeah."

"Just that?"

"Just that. What are you saying?"

"I'm asking, Ray. You found nothing suspicious about it?"

"Damn right I did, and so did the Fireflies. No question it was arson. If you look at my report, you'll see I said that."

"That what Connie said, too?"

He could speak *a little* ill of the dead. "He didn't want to hear it at first. I didn't get it. It was pretty clear to me and Arson. I told him if he didn't want to go along, I'd take care of the paperwork. He said no problem."

"You never talked about it later?"

"Sure, we did. And he came around eventually. Talked about all the sore losers Max Katz, the guy who ran the diner, had probably piled up over the years. Who could argue? And the report was in. You look it up. You'll see I said suspected arson."

"But the case was never closed. It's still open."

"That's right."

"That's right what, Ray? You never connected Cassidy and Keenan to the diner? It never came up in conversation with Connie?"

Sitting back made his paunch look bigger. There was no way his BVDs weren't cutting into his balls. "There was a lot of scuttlebutt around that. You must've heard it yourself. Lewin, the guy Cassidy cracked up with, was no stranger to anybody. A collector for Katz and a lot of other bookies. It figured that was what he was out doing that night, right? I'm sure I said that to Connie at some point."

"And what did Connie say?"

"Nothing I remember. I mean we're talking about years ago!"

"All right, let's be more specific. Did you ever get the impression from Marchese he suspected Keenan had something to do with the fire? Let's not forget where your badge is, Detective."

I suppose he deserved some sympathy for all his squirming. But when the idiot once again passed up the chance to ask for his union rep, I wanted her to go after him all the way. "Nothing was ever said," he mumbled.

"But . . .?"

"Okay. It was in the air. Does that put it on Connie? If you don't mind me saying so, Lieutenant, it had to be in the air in your house, too. Does that make you and your husband conspirators?"

I wouldn't have minded asking her that myself at some point. Or had I? Maybe I was mixing her up with Gwendolyn Cutter getting to the elevator before I could shout out my crack about the wedding gift. Or maybe the goddamn apartment was just beginning to feel like a furnace and I wanted to be back on the street.

"You seem to think so."

"What?"

"Or do you just follow somebody different from Major Cases every day and that day at Gibson just happened to be my turn?"

I could have done without that question almost as much as Black. My mother had never liked me being a tattle-tale. But he had more to lose than my reputation as a Sphinx. "Okay," he said. "You all seemed ready to write Connie off as a suicide. I got to thinking that maybe it was your little group again, that you had a special interest in saying suicide. Don't ask me what. I was just knocked out about Connie. I wasn't thinking too clear."

"I don't belong to the Movement, Ray. My husband does, but I don't."

"Yeah, yeah, I understand that now. I'm sorry, Lieutenant. At the time it just seemed like something I had to be sure of."

She didn't bother granting him absolution. "The Fantones." Black closed his eyes with the agony of it all. "You're not going to tell me that was just Marchese, too."

"No."

"Excuse me?"

"It played out."

"*It played out*? What the hell does that mean?"

"We got a call from West Hempstead," he said, suddenly in the too-patient tone of a kindergarten teacher. "There was a beef about this hooker and Jimmy Fantone had dropped Connie's name, could we get out there? I told him, I said, go yourself, they're your friends."

"Where'd you get that idea? He'd done other favors for Jimmy?"

He had better reasons for feeling hot, but he preferred blaming it on the lamp. "I didn't mean that," he said, trying to push the thing to the far side of the end table. "I'm talking about this one call."

"Forget the lamp. Tell me about this one call."

"Like I said. Fantone mentioned his name so Connie thought he should go. When I said I wasn't interested in going with him, he pulled a card on me. Said if he went alone, it would look like he was a Fantone family retainer or something. At least if the two of us went, it would look more like procedure. Me, I don't say no to a partner when he puts it that way."

"And on the drive there, how did he explain himself?"

"He didn't say squat and I didn't ask him questions. I figured he'd get around to it when the time came. You ask some people too many questions, they never tell you what they intend telling you someday."

Her shoulder blades almost came through her blouse on that one. "And what happened when you got to Hempstead?"

He dropped another few inches in the quicksand. "Connie told the locals we were taking over. There was this sergeant there who didn't want to hear it, but Connie walked him away for a few minutes and when the guy came back, Fantone was in our custody."

"Let me guess: You didn't ask Marchese what he told this sergeant."

He thought about being proud of it, then took another look at her and changed his mind. "There was no hassle, that's all I was thinking about. And that wasn't easy because Fantone had a snootful."

"And in the middle of all this where was the victim?"

"The locals piled her into an EMS bus. She was just being taken away when we got there. There was a lot of blood on the sidewalk, but I didn't get a close look at her. I don't know how bad she was cut. You know how some wounds bleed worse than they are."

"Plus she was a whore?"

"I didn't say that, Lieutenant."

"But you questioned her in the hospital."

"Well, . . ."

"Well, what?"

"Connie handled that."

"Connie handled it and before you know it there's no more knifing assault in West Hempstead?"

"Something like that, I guess."

"And what was the county paying you for, Detective? Never mind. How many other Hempstead kind of calls did Marchese get?"

He needed a look around the room to remember he didn't owe much more to his partner. Who else but Connie Marchese was responsible for his misery? "There were a couple of things," he conceded.

"That just 'played out.'"

"I guess."

"Like what?"

"Traffic stuff, mostly. Tickets. The usual."

He didn't even try to sell that one. "And the Fantones are going to go out of their way to reach out to Marchese because of an illegal parking summons? I don't think so, Detective. What are we talking about here? What is it you were content seeing being played out?"

They could have heard the glug-glug down in the courtyard: First the badge and then the fatally squeamish Ray Black disappeared into the ooze. "Maybe there was this one time," he struggled to say. "An associate of Jimmy Fantone's, Ralph DeLozier, was picked up for crack dealing. What made it worse was that he specialized in kids."

"Yes, I guess that would make it worse, wouldn't it?"

"I told Connie to leave it alone. He said he couldn't, he was getting too much pressure to put his oar in."

"Pressure from who?"

"I was supposed to understand."

"What were you supposed to understand?"

"The people he met through this church group of his."

Either she shied up or her leg went to sleep, but she came close to rocking herself off the edge of the table. But then she reminded herself Roger Ware wasn't the only member of the Faith Renewal Movement. "What people are we talking about, Ray?"

"The one I was there for was this priest. He didn't like it any more than Connie, he kept saying, but it would really be a favor to a lot of people if the crack bust on DeLozier went away. I told Connie in the car, I said, 'Hell, isn't this priest supposed to be more worried about the kids than the dealers?' And Connie just sighs and says something like the world's more complicated than that. We both knew it was a bullshit answer."

"So he put his oar in."

Black nodded. The non-drug bust loomed as just one of a grocery list of items she was going to get out of him—what she would have called bookkeeping and what she didn't need me for. "Mind if I ask a question?"

"I do," he snapped immediately.

She might have been about to say the same thing, but she had to keep him reminded of where he stood with her. "Go ahead."

"There's this rest home where they have Cassidy and where Fantone's sister was. But you're talking about a lot of payback just for knowing a guy reduced to a vegetable isn't dead. There's something else, isn't there, Ray? Some other connection between the Fantones and Keenan?"

He surprised me. Maybe it was because the topic was Keenan and the Fantones instead of him and Marchese, but he skipped the sneers and settled for looking at her with his answer. "From what Connie said, they donate thousands to this Movement thing. Maybe Jimmy don't give a damn about it, but old Marcello and Jimmy's ditzy English wife do. They don't go to any of the meetings or demos or anything. The priests there don't want them in case it gets into the media. But they have a lot of juice money-wise."

"They can't be the only ones."

"Maybe not anymore. From what Connie says, they've gotten so much exposure on the tube lately they're getting donations from these pro-life types from all over the country. But once upon a time the Fantone money was a good part of their treasury. I guess all those signs aren't so cheap."

He deserved a smile for trying to make a joke from his tight box. I knew she wasn't going to give it to him, so I gave it to him for both of us. I also had a hunch he'd given me the *why* for the recent distance in relations with Keenan and the Movement Marcello Fantone had hinted at. They had become less dependent on the old thug's money.

When Ellen went on to her next item, I started to tune out. What I really wanted her to do was to continue her chat in her office the next day, but I knew better than to break her roll by standing up and saying I was going home. Besides, there was one question I still had, and if I had to wait until she was finished, that's what I would have to do.

I didn't have to. One gun run tale involving Marchese and the Fantones later, she was channeling me. "Marchese was acting pretty harried the last few days," she said. "As you must know, there was a scene in a restaurant with Assistant Prosecutor Ware. Then . . ."

Black considered taking a shot, but then changed his mind. "Yeah, I heard," he nodded. "He was acting crazy. I told him he needed a vacation. That got me far. Like I'm talking to a wall."

"He must have given you *some* idea of what was wrong."

He looked past her shoulder again. "Him. Finley."

I froze. It was even better than when Carrington had said I was the one who had gotten him back on Keenan's case. Should I have been honored? It was always nice when your peers acknowledged you.

"When Connie heard about reports Christman sent Finley, he really lost it. He knew what was in them."

"How did he know?"

"I saw him talking to Christman's nurse at Christman's funeral. After that he went into a free fall. Wouldn't spell it out for me, but I could guess."

"Guess what?"

"The ex-wife has been going at him . . . well, I mean she *was* going at him about custody things. Connie got it into his head he was going to lose Marisa if it came out he had been . . . doing some of the things I just told you. I never saw him so panicky. He was sure Finley here was going to fuck him over some way." He had saved his best glare of the night. "I guess he was right about that, huh, Paul?"

She didn't wait for me to answer. "Okay, Detective," she said, getting up from the table. "We'll continue this in my office tomorrow morning. Nine sharp. Don't be late."

He wasn't sure he was relieved or not as he pulled himself up off the couch. "You got to tell me, Lieutenant. No suicide, right?"

Reason said she was being smart merely repeating their appointment time in the morning. She still had only the mat scrap and she didn't need him making any premature announcements to Marchese's family or anyone else. But I couldn't help feeling a little sorry for the ape as he trudged out.

I was in the minority. "Idiot," she muttered. "'Gee, you mean I should've done something about it?'"

"That go on the tape, too?"

She offered no apology as she reached into her bag and clicked her machine off. "That I'll cut. And your question, too."

"What are you going to do?"

"What do you think? Give it to Shelton. The IAB can run whatever they want, but they won't be cutting me out."

"Because you can give them Black's head."

"Because I can give them Black's head."

"And that's what this is all about to you?"

She looked around the room as if to make sure everything had been locked down before going off to the Bahamas for a vacation. "Don't spoil it, Finley. I started out tonight wanting to blame you for everything. Now I'm grateful you talked me into coming here."

"You know the address where you can send the check."

She bristled, then thought of something that brought a skeptical smile. "That business about how he couldn't have shot himself at the table. How did you get there? The photos of his daughter?"

"Good, Lieutenant."

She wasn't so sure. "Yeah, but that's based on your premise that he'd want to remind himself in the last few minutes that not everything he did on earth was a disaster."

"Something like that."

She swung her bag up over her shoulder. It made her straighten out her blouse collar all around. "In your place I might not have made that leap," she said. "I could just as easily have imagined him hiding himself from those photos out of shame. But that's me, and if this piece of mat turns out to be useful, I'll be glad you didn't think like me."

CHAPTER 58

There was no press conference the next day by the county prosecutor or anybody else. Two days later, Alan Crosby reported in his political gossip column that Major Cases was taking a "hard look" at the death of Connie Marchese and had not ruled out homicide. Also, according to Crosby, in the same column and with no explicit reference to the Marchese investigation, there was a "big shakeup" going on at Major Cases supervised by Lieutenant Ellen Miles and other brass. Anybody not knowing better would have thought that Marchese's death had at most provided the excuse for a long-planned move to play musical desks.

I gave the lieutenant two cheers. She had apparently negotiated herself back into the good graces of the hierarchy with the head of Ray Black. She wasn't going to make the brass forget too many of her charges had been scrawling dirty things on the blackboard behind her back and she wasn't going to earn an entry in the encyclopedia of Classy People Doing Classy Things, but neither had she been running Major Cases when the Lewin-Cassidy accident had happened. Anybody for a history lesson? No, I didn't think so. As for Black, he sure as hell didn't deserve a solidarity banquet. At bottom he was just a surviving version of Christman and Rigas—see no evil and hear no evil until his conscience got caught. He should have regarded himself as lucky if he fell into a security job paying only $200,000.

So why was I uneasy anyway? Why had my ferrets been nibbling at me since leaving Ellen in front of Marchese's building?

It wasn't because of the bulls-eye still theoretically on my back. Whatever Ellen was cooking up with Shelton and his IAB friends had to involve the McNair tape, making me an extraneous factor for Keenan's scuffling. In the big picture I just wasn't important to him. But my ferrets wouldn't leave me alone. They weren't gnawing yet, only nibbling, but something still felt very wrong, and they didn't like how I was being so dense about seeing what it was.

I waited for the third day to call Carrington. He tried to sound like a good sport. He didn't make it. "You couldn't resist, could you? You really had to save her ass, didn't you?"

"The lady does pretty well by herself."

"Tell me about it. Know how I spent yesterday, Finley? Accompanying Lieutenant Ellen Miles and Detective Herb Levine to the home of Detective Phil McNair up in Stony Point while they executed a warrant to search for an exercise mat. There was a cast of thousands, and that's without counting McNair's wife and their two preschoolers. I even learned Stony Point was where Benedict Arnold turned over the plans to West Point to Major Andre. All kinds of history up there. But you know what wasn't there?"

"An exercise mat?"

"There you go!"

"So he got rid of it."

"You think?"

"Doesn't make it a bad lead."

"No, what it makes it is no lead at all. And of course, now we have the sixth-floor downstairs on full alert."

"It was bound to happen."

"You sound almost happy about it."

"A purer state than that—indifference."

The silence was so heavy I imagined traffic sounds from the Brooklyn Bridge behind him. "Yeah, they say that's Nirvana," he finally said. "I guess I'm just too Irish for it. See you in another life, Finley."

It wasn't that we had crossed through jungles and climbed mountains together, but I thought there should have been more than "See you in another life" and a dial tone. So much for Billy Carrington on my Christmas card list.

CHAPTER 59

My ferrets didn't go away. At times they didn't even bother nibbling, just shifted positions to let me know they hadn't abandoned me. I could have done without their concern. In the meantime, no news was no news. Alan Crosby said nothing in *Newsday*, the Long Island TV stations were preoccupied with Suffolk County budgets, and nobody came around to ask about the reports Christman had sent me. I tried thinking I knew what was going on. After a full-scale production (like descending on Phil McNair's house in Rockland County) with nothing to show for it but expense vouchers, there was usually a lull while the best minds worked out moves that risked less embarrassment. Every speck of dust was put back under the microscope for what had been missed the first dozen times and every new day brought endless skull sessions with the higher-ups for making sure the Fire Department or Sanitation Department shouldn't have been given the job for more effective results. There was nothing exceptional about it—a fact I pointed out to my ferrets whenever they began to shift again. The disadvantage to the slowed pace was the statistical one that the longer an investigation went on, the slimmer the chances of a happy ending.

But I wasn't being paid for analyzing statistical probabilities, and lacking calls from Mineola for my expert counsel, I had no choice but to get back to real work. The wrong teeth were still being pulled and the wrong legs were still being amputated, and it was up to me to remind the insurance firms on my Rolodex that Finley Investigations had contributed profitable facts to their settlements in the past and stood ready to contribute them again in the present. A couple of them took me up on it, and I let myself imagine they had heard I was through with the Christman Follies and was ready to put my shoulder to the wheel again. For a few days, things seemed to lapse back naturally into my rut.

Not that it was *all* ecstasy. Besides my ferrets, there was the need to go downtown to make a deposition in the Bobby Sprowl suit. Any doubts the goon was serious disappeared as soon as Martin Nesbitt raised his lizard head from the table in a conference room to give me his version of a hello. The khaki-colored summer suit he had wrapped around his scales seemed appropriate, but he never quite slithered out his tongue while I recited into a stenographer's machine. At that, Nesbitt wasn't the worst thought I carried away from the session. That belonged to the lawyers for the Buona Italia partners, who listened to me as though they had already worked out the legal tactics for separating me from their corporate clients in the lawsuit. Thy could barely get out hello *or* goodbye.

I stayed away from the Green Fox for a few days, not up to sending off vibes to Cynthia about my night with Ellen. It wasn't that we had signed a mutual fidelity pact; in fact, every time we were together, she seemed to bring up the subject of somebody else she might have been with and I managed to insert the topic of the wife I had been with. But Ellen Miles was neither an ideal nor a ghost, and that seemed to present complications for one party (me) who had a hard time disguising murky thoughts, especially from women, and another party (Cynthia) who had a doctorate in reading them from her years behind a bar. Upshot: I avoided the Green Fox's jet set crowd.

At least until the night I stopped avoiding it and the Professor might have gotten himself killed.

CHAPTER 60

The bar was a tomb. Johnny Yeager and Miles Harkleroad were holding up the short arm without help for their debate on whether FDR had or hadn't been a Communist, and the only other customer was a college student nursing a beer and reading a Stephen King paperback. I knew he was a college student because he was jotting down notes in the margins every few pages. "Who the hell makes notes in a Stephen King novel?" Cynthia asked under her breath.

She had been wiping a dish towel over the bar between us since I had sat down, making me feel a little like Lady Macbeth's candle. Any break in the stilted conversation was a break in the stilted conversation. "People learning how to train their Cujo."

Chortle, chortle, chortle. Two middle-aged people needing a bar for their elbows taking whimsical shots at a kid who could have been theirs if they had known each other 20 years earlier, if they had liked each other enough back then to skip birth control, if they had gotten through their son's measles and whooping cough and flu attacks, if they hadn't strangled him for blasting music in his room and drenching the apartment in pot smoke. In short, two smug middle-aged people wondering what might have been if they had been any other two smug middle-aged people.

I took it as a reprieve when Silva came through the door. He gave me a half-nod as he took a stool next to the Stephen King kid and Cynthia meandered down to him. In his place I would have held back even the half of a nod. The only thoughts the sergeant had been good for lately had been to use his name to get into Keenan's office and to decide he was merely a candle next to Carrington's neon when it came to handling bomb threats. The least that stupidity seemed to call for was a Stoli O. "Mine, Cynthia."

She looked more surprised than he did. She wasn't used to me even paying for my own drinks. There was a gloat in his smile. "What are we celebrating? Turn in your IAB papers?"

"I didn't know that's what he was."

"You've lost your nose, Finley."

"You could've given me a clue besides rolling your eyes."

He nodded agreeably. "Yeah, maybe so." She put his drink in front of him, and he saluted me with it before polishing off half the glass in one swallow. "They think they're the only ones that take the job seriously. All the rest of us come up short."

"He's working on being an idealist."

"Bullshit. Idealists go work for something like the Peace Corps, to help somebody. These guys need scalps to feel helpful."

"Sounds like a station house commercial."

He finished off the other half of his glass, making it look like he wanted to get rid of what I had bought for him to get down to his own spending. "So buy the other cereal instead," he laughed. "Another one here, Cynthia."

Instead, Cynthia made the mistake of answering the phone.

CHAPTER 61

In my rush out to Garden City, I told myself I would be prepared for anything. Since the Professor had been able to call the Green Fox, how bad could things have been?

Surprise, surprise.

The house gave off the only light in the sleeping street, making the old man's living room blaze out like some Ginza billboard. Then there was Belinda Massey. As I was putting my key in the lock, she swung open the door and wrapped her formidable arms around me in a Chanel hug. "He's really upset," she whispered urgently. "Please don't rattle him any more than he already is."

I let the implication that my mission in life was to agitate Joe Carroll go. For once anyway, the warning turned out to be not all that out of place. The Professor was sitting in his living room lounger staring off into space, looking unaware of the glass of ginger ale in his hand. He wore a robe over his pajamas and his ratty slippers, but what was left of his hair looked like it had come through a tornado. "Joe, Paul's here."

His big fish eyes came back reluctantly. "What, am I blind?" he fired at her thickly. "Bedroom window."

It was a direction, so I followed it, and not just to save my eyes from the standing lamps, table lamps, and ceiling light flooding the room. Any second he was going to come out of his stupor, and I didn't want to be there when it dawned on him how much he had given away—sitting around acting dumbfounded in front of his public, having Belinda going around the house barefoot and in the idiotic cowboy shirt I had bought him for one of his birthdays, and realizing he had to give up his airs of long-suffering because of all her attentions. As awakenings went, that one wasn't going to be pretty.

The bedroom window fronted on an alley shared with the adjoining house. The bullet was torso-high, and wouldn't have missed anyone standing near the bed or the bureau against the wall behind the bed. Lucky for the old man, he had been pressing his head down on one of the bed pillows. Just as lucky for Belinda, she had been doing the same thing on the other pillow.

I followed the trajectory to a hole in the middle of the dresser's top drawer. The bullet had kept going over clumps of rolled up socks through the rear board and then into the wall behind. I was pretty sure it was a nine-millimeter. What I wasn't at all sure about was what it was doing there. The shooter had gone to the trouble of getting out of a car and sneaking around to the side of the house, risking discovery by who knew how many people, starting with those in the house next door. But if there had been any sound at all from inside in the darkness, it would have come from the bed—much higher than his aim. Ergo? Ergo, he hadn't been looking to hit a target so much as scaring one? Ergo ergo? Ergo ergo, the shooter still hadn't gotten over a failing history grade 20 years ago, had always despised the Professor for it and had finally decided to act, but also hadn't wanted to ruin his life as a middle manager for an insurance company?

Or was it ergo ergo ergo—the Professor and Belinda Massey hadn't been the ones he had wanted to scare?

I sat down on the bed with a bad feeling that Keenan and McNair hadn't been so philosophical about my visit to Carrington and Ellen's visit to Stony Point. It was the only explanation that justified the boil rising under my skin. And the old man had probably given the bastards the idea with his little show in the St. Brendan's sacristy. He had been right the second time: I should have talked both of us out of going out to Rockville Centre that night. Once again, Finley could have done better.

"How long you going to be in there?"

Some strength had returned to his voice. I didn't know if that was good or bad. When I went back outside to the living room, he was handing his empty glass to Belinda. She gave me a look with another warning, then went off to the kitchen. I'd had enough of her pregnant looks.

"You call the cops?"

"For what? To do what you just did and clutter up the house in the bargain? No, I didn't call the cops."

"It might be an idea, Joe."

"Yours, not mine."

"What about your neighbors next door? How come they didn't hear anything and report it?"

He waved me away. "They're in Europe. Probably walking along the Seine and wondering what it's got the East River doesn't. You're avoiding the question. Are these your friends or not?"

I was calmer, so I sat down on the couch wishing Belinda would bring me a ginger ale, too. "To gain what? They're already in the sights of two police forces. How's giving you a bad night help them?"

"Because it'll make you think twice about saying something nasty about them." He found a smile; a surly one, but still a smile. "And you *are* thinking twice, right?"

"I'm out of it. It has nothing to do with me."

"That's been true since the start."

"Whatever. It's all Miles and Carrington now. You think somebody like Keenan would pull this just to be . . .?"

"*Gratuitous* is the word you're looking for. Maybe not Keenan, but maybe that other slug thought he was being clever."

The picture came easily: Lining up McNair against a wall and taking target practice, one limb at a time. "Possible, I guess."

"Screw the possible! That's a hole in my window in there! And I didn't have bullet holes in my window before I met you!"

It should have been a joke, an absurdity covering 12 or 13 years. But he couldn't get his beet face down to his lap fast enough. It was as if he had finally blurted something he had been holding back since we had met.

"Never mind. You know what I mean. Now I got to get a glazier over here. Know how much those crooks charge?"

Belinda did. She came back in with ginger ales for both of us, and with her experiences with glaziers and the name of one who should have been given the bedroom job. I stared at the old man until I convinced myself I couldn't see any more bitterness sliding off his face. He was right: I had finally succeeded in making the indifferent personal.

CHAPTER 62

Belinda saw me out behind an effusive endorsement to the old man that I would know the best way to handle things. He was so lost in what he knew he had given away that he wasn't up for a come-back. I had dug out the bullet from behind the sock drawer to take with me. As I slipped it into my shirt pocket and started the car, I figured I had three options—turn it over to Ellen with the story of where I had gotten it, make a keychain with it, or jam it through Phil McNair's front teeth. But official solutions were only official solutions, and I didn't need a keychain.

When I got home, I heard Jeffrey Chalian beating off the lat-est invasion through my bedroom wall. For once I was up for computer games in the wee hours, too, and it didn't take all that long to track down what I was after. I wanted Keenan and McNair together, but that wasn't so easy when they worked at the Police Plaza fortress during the day and then separated for Long Island and Rockland County after work. On the other hand, there were those photos in Keenan's office when both had posed as members of the Holy Rollers bowling team. Googling the NYPD with Holy Rollers brought me to the team's lopsided victory over the Fire Department six days earlier in the tournament at the Rand Lanes in Jackson Heights. Better than that, it got me the information that the Strikers from the Department of Motor Vehicles would be playing the Holy Rollers in the tournament final the next night in the same place.

I had 60 minutes of every hour the next day to come up with a smarter idea. But whenever one slithered out for approval, through my message machine or my own head, I was ready for it: I wasn't interested. I didn't care about Connie Marchese or Edward Cassidy or the Fantones. I didn't care, either, about all the hypocrisy Keenan paraded around in his little moral rearmament club. Hypocrisy was an occupational hazard for anyone born: You learned that in high school along with biology and driver's ed. What I cared about was all the time I had spent chasing down the wild geese Keenan had sent flying across my sky through the Rigases and Christmans and Blacks. When nobility wasn't being offered, the next best reward was not deluding yourself you had any.

CHAPTER 63

I brought along my weapon to intimidate—me, if not Keenan and Mc-Nair—and tried to time my arrival in Jackson Heights for near the end of the game. I didn't feel like standing around too long and I hadn't had an aesthetic appreciation of bowling since scoring a three-strike turkey back in community college. I was sweating in the evening heat before I got out of Brooklyn, and felt a little better blaming it on the radio announcer. She was one of those DJs who played back every word to her own ear, leaving an audible beat between what she said into her mike and her pleasure in it before moving on to the next word. Right: She reminded me too much of me. The only difference was that she was announcing the forgotten hits of Christopher Cross and I was announcing why taking a shot at what was left of my sour family was more outrageous than killing Connie Marchese or abetting the Fantone clan's social activities. But why get hung up on details?

Rand Lanes was on a tatty street down from the elevated #7 train and the rest of the commotion along Roosevelt Avenue. It had a narrow doorway and staircase up to a second floor where the thud of balls all day had to have charmed those in the check-cashing place and Dunkin' Donuts underneath at sidewalk level. The whole street smelled of fried B.O. I didn't know why municipal office teams couldn't have found lanes in Civil Serviceville closer to downtown Manhattan, but then again, I wasn't the cop, garbage man, or fireman who had a friend in a Queens bowling alley willing to throw me a few bucks for moonlighting as a broker.

Two County Donegal bruisers were catching smokes outside the place; the blond with a crewcut and the build of a high school shot-putter wore his badge on his belt. They followed the constant stream of Latinos and Asians passing by in wonder at being on such a great adventure for the night. I owed them thanks for being there, for replacing the gray matter I had lost after seeing the bullet holes at the Professor's. I couldn't go up against them *and* their teammates in addition to Keenan and McNair. Moods were moods, but stupidity was also stupidity. There could be no scenes in the bowling alley itself, not without getting my skull broken.

The garage at the end of the street helped me believe I was thinking again. Since there was nothing parked at either curb except car lot retreads that would have been stripped down to their frames before being allowed anywhere near Police Plaza, I told myself the Holy Rollers had to have held their noses and paid the garage's gouging parking fees. And that meant they would also have to return there after they had toppled their last pin.

Thinking 101, and I passed. The garage wasn't exactly doing Midtown business, but against the longest interior wall, street level, it had a monopoly on Mercurys and Dodges with NYPD and DMV stickers. There were so many of them clustered together the parking spaces might have been part of a package deal with the bowling alley. It would have been nice to know which drives belonged to Keenan and McNair, but I didn't press my luck with the attendant, a tall rail of a Latin identified by his name tag as Raul. Raul acted edgy I would knock down his wall parking. He was so relieved when I handed him my keys and started back out to the street I wondered if my personable Dr. Jekyll had grown Mr. Hyde's snarling face. I skipped the mirror near the garage entrance just in case I had.

The cops had finished their cigarettes and gone back up the splintery stairs. Every wooden step creaked and looked a century old, three or four Queens immigrations ago. For all I knew, the initials **PJ** in the middle of the top step had been carved by one of Woodrow Wilson's long decayed Irish voters. The alley itself couldn't decide if it was in the 1950s or the new millennium. The sound system was playing elevator music, but strictly for modern elevators that accommodated strings versions of hip-hop. The service counter, snack bar, and pigeonholes of gruesome shoes behind them were the stuff of old tabloid black-and-white photographs, but the 18 lanes had the spotless gleam of Fiberglass Now. The only ones being used for the sleepy weekday night were the first one, where a tense father was teaching his pre-teen son the game, a middle one, where two blondes and their boyfriends were having more fun mocking each other than actually bowling, and the last one, where a good 50 people had gathered for the tournament. The yellow shirts of the Holy Rollers and their fans were cheering a clatter of pins and the drone of the machine resetting things for the next roll, the blue shirts of the Strikers were moaning. Not many Holy Rollers had missed a meal since Great-Grandfather Rand had opened for business; as a group, they looked like fugitives from a fat farm.

Nobody was behind the snack bar, and the guy sitting on a stool behind the main counter, a chunky pit bull with black-rimmed glasses, was absorbed in the comic book he was scanning. He was diplomatic enough about his special trade for the evening to look up and pretend interest in the cheering, but he didn't let that take more than a second before he was back to his comic. He was appraising it more than reading it, and had covered his hands in plastic butcher's gloves to make sure he didn't mar the pages he was turning. When he noticed me out of the corner of his eye, it was only as another intrusion on his investment inspection, and he didn't bother asking if I wanted him to open another lane.

I saw McNair first. He was apparently the hero of the frame, getting slaps on the back from his rooting section for whatever he had just done. The linebacker didn't look any more svelte in his yellow T-shirt than he had in his blue suit: He might have stolen his breasts from a plastic surgeon and his gut from Pastrami Joe's. Just seeing him trying to look like a shy Gary Cooper accepting congratulations for hitting another Lou Gehrig home run blurred my eyes. I had too hot a picture of him squeezing himself up to the Professor's window and letting go with a round. Like the old man had said, it had all been gratuitous, and achieving nothing but whatever contempt I was able to muster up for the thug and his master. At least it was satisfying knowing I hadn't left my bile back at the apartment.

Keenan was in a curved plastic seat waiting his turn. His teammates and fan club might have been threatening the Department's weight guidelines, but not him; his T-shirt and pale arms made him look almost undernourished. His stoical gaze made me think of those bishops who sat at the side of the altar at the Christmas Midnight Mass televised from St. Patrick's Cathedral: They weren't needed right now, their expression said, but if they were, they would step in with more authority than those they were observing showed. I couldn't picture him sneaking into the Professor's alley at all; that was a job for his hirelings. But the bile was still in my throat.

"You with them?" The collector had torn himself away from his comic to admit I was there.

"Yeah. How far along are they?"

He had spent enough words; he jabbed a plastic-wrapped finger to the electronic board over the lane as he went back to his comic. The board showed the game to be in the ninth frame and the Holy Rollers in another rout. That posed what should have been a predictable complication—that somebody on the Holy Rollers, maybe McNair or Keenan, was going to have to stand the drinks for a Beer Frame when the team won its championship. That didn't promise much for being able to get them together in this life.

Neither did Keenan's glare at me through some arms and elbows. It was the same you're-a-frog-and-I'm-about-to-dissect-you look he had given me across his office desk. What else was there to do except nod and smile back, hoping he would burn in Hell? And then he was gone again, lost behind a woman with too much flab on her arms and too high-pitched a laugh.

A freckled carrot-top somewhere in her 30s came slopping out from the back in flip-flops cradling half a dozen cans of soda to her chest. Her tight lips and dulled eyes said she was thinking how the night would never end. Her faded green T-shirt declaring RAND LANES looked to be a promotion from the days when the place hadn't depended on under-the-table payments for business. I was about to ask for a ginger ale when Keenan jumped up for his roll. The subdued cheering said he might have been the senior member of the team and worthy of respect just for that, but not the best player. I felt as good as I'd felt in days when he left a 7-10 fence post on his first roll and then missed both pins on the second. He was deaf to the encouragement around him as he returned to his seat. I hoped he would blame me for his score, but he sat down without looking at me.

"Want something?" the redhead asked. She didn't like my choice of ginger ale. "No ginger ale. Pepsi, Coke, Fanta, Sprite, Mountain Dew, and maybe some cherry thing."

The collector sighed at her tone. Man and wife, living-together lovers, or just employer and employee, I could see them arguing about her manner with customers when not about how he was spending too much time on Batman and Superman; whatever they were to each other, they were an open-ended argument. I went for the cherry thing because it had a *maybe* in front of it. "No promises," she said, digging into the cooler.

"Why start counting on them now?"

There were no more obstacles between me and Keenan, but he wasn't looking in my direction anyway. For a second he was just the guy brooding on the bench for having let down his team. "You're in luck," the redhead said, pulling a cherry soda out and slamming it down hard enough to blow up the block when she yanked off the tab. "That's $1.50."

I hadn't had cherry soda for so long I didn't know if that was dear, average, or cheap. What I did know was that I really didn't want it, just wanted the Holy Rollers to get their damn game over with. "These teams usually hang around after the game?"

She took my singles briskly and instead of going to the register on the main counter, reached down over the hip bone in her jeans pocket to come up with two quarters. The tattoo head of some mythical creature peeked out of her pants. "Here? What for? We don't sell beer, and that's what they usually want. Original, huh?"

I left the quarters on the counter. One more word from her, and I would have been tempted to recommend her to Cynthia for the Green Fox. Maybe it was that thought that set off the fuzzy feeling that I wasn't alone—not because of the spirit of Cynthia or the presence of Keenan and his bowling friends, but because of *somebody else.* If I turned around fast enough in the right direction, I thought, I would see him—or her. Or was I just grasping for allies because I had realized too late that all my intentions on the day had been perfect in every way except for their practicality? The Holy Rollers celebrated in some bar or they didn't celebrate in some bar. Keenan begged off the celebration and went back to the garage by himself, or McNair did that. They both went to a beer fest and then returned to the garage, but with half a dozen of their beefcake friends with them. The possibilities were endless, and I had planned for none of them. I didn't need an Invisible Friend for an ally, I needed an Invisible God.

The Strikers went down without much of a fight. I showed more resistance taking a second and third sip of the soda that tasted like liquid sugar. Since it seemed too late to do anything else, I hung off my elbow at the snack bar as the teams shook hands, slapped one another's backs, changed shoes, packed up their duffel bags and ball carriers, and began drifting out. Except for a woman on the Strikers, the place hadn't done any business on shoes, so the collector had to interrupt his inspection only for one pair. The redhead took over the register for whatever else had to be paid, making me wonder what had been so special about the cherry soda change that had come out of her pocket.

"It's not much as a spectator sport, Finley."

I heard the crack a fraction too late, as I realized Keenan had cut around a few ends and was passing me in between two hulking palace guards—McNair and the blond shot-putter from downstairs somebody had called Robby. McNair looked back at me, gave me a crooked smile, then went back to his escort duty. Keenan seemed twice as shrunken from behind and sandwiched between the two towers. The .38 in my belt gave me another Bronx cheer by jabbing me in the back for standing up straight too abruptly.

I was still calling my mind to order about my next move when Keenan stopped short of the exit to watch the kid on the first lane.

The father acted jumpy for the outside attention, but the kid, no more than 10 or 11 and as slight for his age as Keenan was for his company, didn't notice. He was all fierce determination as his small hand let go of the oversized ball, then he was all bright-eyed hope as the ball wobbled down at the pins. "Go, go!" Keenan burst out, a big smile on his face. The kid turned back, almost missing how the ball took out two, three, four pins. But just in time he remembered his priorities and saw them go down.

"Great stuff, son," Keenan beamed. "Keep at it and you'll be better than me. In about a week, wouldn't you say, Phil?"

McNair kept his own counsel behind a sardonic smile, and nudged his charge forward. The father and son exchanged grins.

As the Professor had said about the little social in the St. Brendan's sacristy, zealots with senses of humor could catch you off guard. It took me until the kid had knocked down a couple of more pins with his next ball to get myself together and go downstairs to see if the murderers were still together.

CHAPTER 64

It was a split. McNair and Robby were meandering after the other yellow shirts and a couple of blue shirts toward a surviving neighborhood Irish bar directly across from the bowling alley. On my side of the street, Keenan was carrying his ball bag down to the garage, fishing in his pants pockets for something as he went.

"C'mon, Finley. If there's something you want to say, come and say it. I have to get home."

He didn't bother turning back; he acted more interested in finding the loose credit card in his pocket that he came out with than in me. I glanced across the street again. McNair and the other lummox were approaching the door of the pub. It didn't look like a feint for getting me in a squeeze play, but it wasn't supposed to, that was how squeeze plays worked. On the other hand, there was Captain Patrick Keenan's arrogance for all seasons. If you couldn't count on that, what could you count on?

"I have something to give back to you," I decided.

That stopped him, and without my voice carrying over to the bar to give McNair second thoughts about going inside. "And that would be?" he asked, as curious as he was suspicious as I caught up to him.

What was the opposite of nothing to lose? I held up the slug from the Professor's bedroom in the street lamp. Keenan raised his glasses into the light like a jeweler examining a precious stone. "Nine-millimeter? And it belongs to me, you say? I don't see my name on it anywhere."

"Okay, we'll play. From my father-in-law's bedroom."

"Father-in-law? I didn't know you had one . . . Oh, right. That would be that history guy Carroll. I suppose he still is your father-in-law. And somebody fired this at him?"

"News to you, I'm sure."

"Nassau doesn't copy me on things. Well, I'm sorry for his trouble, but I'm sure he's collected quite a few critics over the years for his rantings. One exposure to him was enough for me."

I bought his smirk the way he had hoped: Just standing there and steaming at his nerve, a thought for even giving him the benefit of the doubt he hadn't been the one behind the shot. Between that and worrying again about McNair coming back out of the saloon, I let him and his bowling bag continue down to the garage. I might have stayed hobbled where I was all night, racking up another deflated balloon to Finley Investigations, if two young, high-heeled Latinas hadn't scowled at me for blocking the sidewalk. Even they seemed to know how easy it was to play me. The opposite of nothing to lose, I should have figured out by then, was nothing to gain.

But nothing ventured, just more wasted gas.

Keenan was already paying at the garage booth when I got there. He ignored or didn't hear a goodbye from one of the Strikers driving past him and up into the street. "On to Connie Marchese, then."

The Indian or Pakistani toting up the charges behind the glass didn't have a name tag like Raul. What he did have was a distrust of both my tone and Keenan's icy smile. "Something else you keep tossing out like I should know what you're talking about."

"Listen to the footsteps behind you, Captain. Internal Affairs, Major Cases, they know how it was done. All it'll take now is McNair rolling over. And he's got a family to think about. You know how families come first, other loyalties be damned."

"You've got problems, Finley."

"Not yours or McNair's."

He snatched the credit card receipt out of the cashier's hand and scribbled his signature while the cashier sulked at his brusqueness. "I should have known your DTs had something to do with the stress the McNairs have been subject to the last few days. Or is it this famous client of yours?"

The cashier took his time about accepting the signature and then finding the right key on his hook board. He was ahead on points until he tapped his hotel desk bell for the parking attendant to come. Then Keenan snatched the key from him, too. "I'll get it myself."

"I am sorry. We do not . . ."

"I know where my car is."

"That is not allowed, sir."

The shield flew out of Keenan's back pocket and into the guy's pouchy face. "I'm allowing it. Okay?"

The cashier was grateful for the window between them, but he didn't quit altogether. "I have a witness here, sir. Any damages to your automobile or to others will be your responsibility."

"Wouldn't have it any other way."

Keenan headed down to the cars so fast I would have patted myself on the back for having gotten to him if I could have remembered how I had. I went after him before the guy in the booth asked me to sign a statement.

I hadn't imagined the captain's attack of jitters. He needed two stabs and his best clenched jaw to get the key into the lock of his black Lexus. "Moving right along to the Columbia Diner fire. You remember that. The place that was burned out after your stepson Edward had his accident? Around the time he was moved to St. Brendan's?"

I might have been just another Striker waving goodbye to him.

"McNair do the fire for you, too? He doesn't look . . . what? I don't know. Slinky enough. You think arson, you think somebody who can climb up and down fire escapes in a hurry, run away in sneakers before the first drapes go up. That doesn't sound like McNair. He'd light himself up. Maybe I'll ask Marcello Fantone. He'd know who it was."

That was a little closer. As he finally got his door open, he not only had marbles in his mouth, he seemed to be tasting them. It wasn't really the same thing as shoving the bullet through his teeth, but then I wasn't just stewing myself into getting even for the Professor anymore, either. And why should I have been? Just mentioning them reminded me the bastard *had been* behind all the other things.

"Why don't you and your client catch a couple of beers together?" he said, throwing his bag in the back seat. "He really exists, doesn't he?"

"Oh, yeah. That would be Ray Black."

The lie came out so spontaneously I was taken off guard as much as Keenan was. "Ray Black?"

"He feels bad about his part in everything."

There was really no life in the eyes behind his glasses; just some kind of seeing function. "Not sure I ever met the man."

"From what I hear, Black has told a few tales and they're reopening the investigation into that fire."

"From what you hear."

"From what I hear."

He gave an impatient drum to the car roof with his fingers, thought about saying something, forgot about saying it, then got in behind the wheel. I didn't want him leaving. The cherry soda alone entitled me to letting him know what I knew. "Black, by the way, says you were right to worry about Marchese going off the deep end, like with that bomb threat against me."

He couldn't have believed it, but he didn't pull his door closed behind him or strap himself in with his seat belt. I couldn't see more than his black pants legs from where I was standing near the rear of the car, but he seemed to be just sitting and staring at his dashboard. "That's nice."

I was on a roll. "He made it clear to Black he was coming after me. Told him he didn't care what you or anybody else in your Movement thought. You were the ones who jammed him up to begin with. One way or another, he was going to get those reports back."

It was nice playing somebody else for a change. I had forgotten the feeling. The red face that peered back out of the car wasn't the one that had left the 7-10 split back on Lane 18. Then he had let down his team; now he was the one who had been let down by the team. "If I didn't know better, I'd think you were wired for your friend Carrington, trying to get me to underwrite some fantasy in his rat mind. But not even he could be that naive."

I didn't have the chance to tell him he didn't have the slightest notion of how naïve Carrington could be. The raspy voice behind me asking "Everything okay, Captain?" cut me off.

It *had been* a squeeze play, but only McNair and Robby standing under the low ceiling beam appreciated it. Keenan was too busy thinking back on what had just been said and on charting what to do next as he stood up out of the car again. At the very least, I would have bet, he had given himself the idea to make sure I *wasn't* wired. One problem, though, was the gangling parking attendant Raul who came ambling up from the back of the garage. Raul was whistling a happy tune, and Keenan didn't like it. "Everything's fine, Phil. Finley's going to come with us for a coffee and tell you what was behind that visit to your house the other day."

McNair needed a moment to look okay with the announcement. I needed a fraction less not to be. We did a two-step: McNair started toward me, I moved around the car—close to Keenan and away from the pair who seemed to represent the more pressing obstacle. Keenan's false laugh ricocheted off the cavernous walls. "God, look at you! Like we're going to take you for one of those gangster rides! You're a cartoon, Finley!"

"Right. And that's all, folks!"

No laughs. For a second everybody, including Raul, just stood there. I should have left it at that. My first mistake was not hanging with Keenan. Leaving his side again to start back for the entrance was also a move toward McNair and Robby, and they immediately straightened up their blubber and grew inches of width across their shoulders. The hot beats in my chest told me I had serious trouble. "You know what dumb is, right, Keenan?"

My second mistake was apparently taking the captain's name in vain. McNair was still flexible enough in his putty face to narrow his eyes to show offense. The Captain was the Captain, not somebody named Keenan. I saw he had also used his feint across the street to the pub to hitch his weapon back to his belt under his yellow shirt.

"It's okay, friend," Keenan called out behind me to Raul. "We're police. Go on with your business."

Raul wasn't sure. He sensed enough to stop his whistling, but not to work out anything else. To keep him uncertain, I sent him a nuclear vibe that I wasn't Mr. Hyde, that I had truly appreciated his concern for the garage while I had been parking, that I really liked him and would give him a big tip if he would just hang where he was for another few minutes.

"You hear me, friend?"

So much for vibes: Despite all the love I was communicating, Raul went for Keenan's unfriendly *friend* instead and started up the incline toward the booth. He had forgotten about us before he had taken three steps.

"The Captain invited you for a coffee," McNair said, lifting his size 15s toward me.

I told myself I had another warning -- or maybe a hundred more—in me before I had to reach for my .38. "And I'm passing. Move."

The third mistake was Keenan's. Maybe he just wanted to be fatherly, to cool tempers on the hot night, by coming up behind me and laying his hand on my elbow. I didn't give him the opportunity to say. What I knew right away was that a lot of things felt already too late as I threw his hand off. Was there still another second even after that when I could have frozen everything? Later, I thought there might have been, but later wasn't then. For that matter, I might have persuaded myself later that Robby had been reaching down for a scrap of paper the garage's maintenance crew had missed. What I saw him reaching down for then was his ankle piece, and that seemed like reason to head him off by pulling my own weapon.

It was ridiculous. Everybody was just not seeing things or blowing things out of proportion. McNair hadn't seen Robby's move to his ankle behind him, so couldn't know why I had gone for my weapon. Robby had had a brain cramp by threatening me with a move that could have never been explained away, not in some public garage where all the DMV stickers were still against the wall and when any one of the Strikers could have tired at any second of being a good loser in the pub and come across for his car.

"This isn't necessary, Finley," Keenan said behind me.

"What I'm thinking."

"I assume you have a license for that?"

I would have laughed if it was funny—and if McNair and Robby weren't waiting for me to loosen my guard and do something idiotic like that. "Oh, now you're a cop again?"

There was no retreat in his voice. "Three police officers are ready to say you drew down on them. There's no license for that. I could take you down right now."

That was the trouble with eyes that couldn't see behind them, car roofs that blocked out people sitting behind the wheel, and imbeciles who hadn't done half the thinking they should have. Keenan could have picked up a howitzer in the time I had lost sight of him inside his car.

"We bust him, Captain?"

McNair shouldn't have sounded so confident, not with my weapon out and his still holstered. I had a bad picture of the brute who had been waiting behind Connie Marchese's apartment door.

"No need, Phil. I think Finley's just going to put that back in his pocket and we'll all go have that coffee. Right, Finley?"

When somebody was right, he was right. But when someone was vain, there was also the question of not falling for a bluff. "Cock it. Then I'll know we're all being honest with each other."

That stumped the lummoxes, but Keenan thought it was funny. "Jesus, Finley! Forget about pride and the Fall?"

"If there's something really in your hand, let me hear it."

"He's armed, Finley. Really."

McNair looked almost sympathetic. Robby nodded, too. I should have called back Raul to make it unanimous.

"Put your weapon on my roof, Finley," the more impatient voice said. "We don't want any accidents dropping it on the ground."

There should have been more options, but there weren't. I had blown them out on the sidewalk when the Latinas had growled I was blocking traffic. Choices had moved on, and without me. Now the *chicas* were with their boyfriends somewhere while I had to bet Keenan wasn't bluffing and had to lay my .38 on the roof of the Lexus.

But sometimes luck threw in compensations. How shrewd would I have had to have been to put my weapon on the roof of the car so that it would instantly slide off and send everybody scrambling? Too shrewd. The fact was, I just didn't put the damn thing far enough away from the edge, then made it worse by dragging my finger on the trigger too long as I pulled back my hand. Why it didn't go off when it grazed the recessed car handle on the way down I had no idea. And then it missed its chance a second time when it landed on the garage's concrete floor without firing.

McNair and Robby were moving their arms like windmills. But Keenan, a Glock in fact in his hand, was the first problem. He turned white before the clatter of the gun on the ground. His orders hadn't been carried out to the letter, and nothing was more critical than that! I hit him hard with my right arm, smashing parts of hand, gun, stomach, and belt buckle. None of them satisfied, a couple hurt, and all stayed in my way as I yanked him around to put something between me and the other two. He was bony and wiry, no fat, but he was also 60, and I got the Glock with my second grab. "Don't, Phil!" the winded voice said.

McNair needed the order. For somebody who had done a pretty snug job on Marchese, he looked too approximate about where he was aiming his .22. Again, he should have paid attention to Robby, who was maneuvering around to line me up from the far side of the Lexus.

"We have witnesses, boys!" But no, we didn't. As soon as I let the words go, there was a slam of the booth door and Raul and the Pakistani hotfooted it up to the street. The Pakistani was limping. I had never seen a limping Pakistani before. Or even a limping Indian.

The first shot should have come from one of us, but it didn't. It cracked through the garage from a distance, sounding as if a wall was coming down. Robby spun around 90 degrees. He looked astonished that something as small as a bullet could have moved him like that.

I hadn't imagined the *somebody else.*

CHAPTER 65

Being helped doesn't always play out as that. On paper, reducing the odds from 3-1 against to an even 2-2 might have looked like the last step before the victory parade. But the 2-2 was overconfident advertising. Robby might have been astounded by the physical law of projectiles, but he hadn't lost his survival instincts. If he couldn't see who had hit him in the side he was clutching and cursing, he could still see me as a closer target he could hit. And I might have still worried about him less as he dropped down to a knee to refocus if Keenan hadn't seized on my slackened grip to go for my hand holding his Glock. He might have been 60, but they were in Rottweiler years. Not only was my grip going, but having to scuffle with him was leaving me directly open to both McNair in front and Robby from the side.

I did what I could to tighten my hold across his chest and drag him toward the front of the car, toward the crawl space between the wall and front bumper; it wasn't much as cover, but there was nothing better within reach. What was supposed to happen after I got there I had no idea. Whoever had fired the shot from near the entrance sounded like he was making a zigzag advance into the garage, and he was squandering my goodwill by not hurrying up. A Galahad to the rescue had to be a Galahad who understood double time.

But then everybody's timing was off; just by a tiny fraction, but off, making the bad news not quite as bad as it could have been. I was so fixed on keeping my head below the car roof and

Robby's aim and on crouching down in front of the Lexus's left headlight that Keenan managed to wrench himself free of my hold with a violent forward thrust. He was clear of me, and diving for the .38 I had dropped off the car, but by then McNair had lost his shot. When Robby fired over the car, flunking me for my next hearing test, he couldn't have done it for more than to tell McNair he was still in the game because I was out of his line of fire again. Everybody was a second too late.

Galahad might or might not have saved my life by hitting Robby, but his accurate shot had given Robby a reason to put me on his shit list. For my rescuer I thought Carrington, I thought Miles, I thought Black, I even thought Jimmy Fantone for whatever low-life, oddball reasons he might have, before snapping out of my delirium and paying attention. I had a shot at Keenan's back as he was scrambling for my gun, but that wasn't why I had come to Jackson Heights, was it? Even if I hadn't had to concentrate on making sure the safety was off the Glock, I would have let him crawl up to where McNair was. Maybe I couldn't have sworn to what my style was, but shooting somebody in the back definitely wasn't it. What had happened to that simple idea of just jamming the slug from Garden City between McNair's teeth? "You're calling it, Keenan! Tell them to end it!"

Another example of being a fraction late. Instead of accepting my tardy deference to his rabbi, McNair took it as a reason to use his .22, chipping the floor next to me with his first shot and skimming the second one off the fender of the Lexus and into what made a loud squish behind me. It was some kind of inflatable tube hanging on the wall and the noise it made said it didn't have a high opinion of my chances. Even then I wanted to believe Keenan was going to call off his ape.

I was wrong. "Assault on a police officer, Finley! Give it up now or you don't leave here!"

The cry was definitely Keenan's, but not the Patrick Keenan I had been grappling with only seconds before. There was a scary tremor in his voice, and it wasn't just due to his exertion in getting away from me and crawling over to McNair. He might have been some demented block boss who had been disrespected in front of his crew and couldn't get over the insult. A new adage to be added to those Benjamin Franklin sayings around the classroom: The tighter they were, the messier they came apart.

Then McNair made the mistake of being McNair, raising his bulk to the rear of the car to take another shot at me. Later, it occurred to me that he might have exposed himself because Keenan had told him to and he had never gotten much practice in saying no to Patrick Keenan. Whether that was true or not, he was so indifferent to Galahad behind him that I had a hot flash he knew something I had missed, that Galahad was either down or gone. Otherwise, why stand up so vulnerably?

There was no otherwise. McNair just wasn't what they might have called processing his situation. One second the lug was standing and peering out for a better shot at me, the next he was going down from another crack from near the booth. He was a mountain anyway, but it wasn't just because of his build that the .22 toppled from his hand and hit the back of the car first before he followed it down. His thick-lidded eyes were closing as he disappeared. I wondered if Connie Marchese had looked the same way when he had slumped to the floor inside his apartment door.

The horse syringe plunging into my left elbow stopped me wondering. Skin that had never bothered anyone flew away and blood rushed up to replace it. The blood was immaculately red, all but sparkling in the ceiling lights, and it wasn't stopping. The wound didn't hurt, then it did hurt—a tingling heat that felt like it was determined not to be outdone by the blood and to prove it was going to swarm out over all the veins I had. Robby thought I was the kind who got self-absorbed about things like that because he suddenly popped up from the other side of the car and took steadier aim at me. Sweat matted his forehead and the watery thing swimming in his blue eyes looked a lot like hatred. Maybe I should have sympathized for the pain he had to be feeling from his wound, but he hadn't shown nearly as much sympathy as McNair in warning me Keenan hadn't been lying about having a weapon in his hand. I forgot I had Keenan's Glock and not my .38. By the time I stopped squeezing, Robby seemed to have spun around three full turns before subsiding against the green Corolla two parking spaces away. I had hit him about half the times I had fired, and that was too many.

Then my left arm *really* started hurting, the blood was dripping to the floor, and I could see slivers of body things under the blood I shouldn't have been able to see. I had to make do with a handful of Kleenex I had shoved into my pocket on the way out my door. McNair and Robby were both down, but it felt more like two of me were gone.

Keenan shouted out for Robby to say something. The cracked agony in his voice was creepier than the rage of the raving block boss, and it felt worse when Robby didn't answer. I had a pang I didn't need: *Suppose I had been wrong, suppose Keenan **hadn't** ordered McNair to kill Connie Marchese? Carrington, Miles, Black, Edward Cassidy, the Fantones—there wouldn't be enough people in the world to blame **that** on!*

"Robinson!"

This time he got an answer—from the siren of a patrol car up the block that sounded like it was doing the Indy 500 toward the garage.

"Give it up, Captain!"

It was Carrington, and he was closer than the booth, near the first row of parked cars. But if it was Carrington, why hadn't he warned Robby before the first shot? He had called me a stickler for jurisdiction questions, but there was also the one about a cop identifying himself before blazing away.

"Your troubles are just beginning, Carrington!"

"Stand up and come out with your hands raised, Captain!"

Heavier left arm or not, I had been pushed back into the grandstand as a spectator to Team Keenan versus Team Carrington. I should have been content to watch the two of them blow each other's brains out. But my arm was beginning to throb all the way up to my throat and I had probably killed a man, and that entitled me to more.

"You've shot two officers doing their duty! How do they get you out of that on the tenth floor?"

"Be smart, Pat!"

I unwedged myself from the headlight as quietly as I could. There was no sound from where Keenan had to be crouching, and I had to think he was listening for me the way I was for him. Then I saw the black rubber soles of his shoes sticking out from behind McNair's motionless head. They rubbed up and then down against one another the way a house fly rubbed its paws or tentacles or whatever they hell they were. But whatever he was doing was up where his hands were, and those I couldn't see. I had already made that mistake when he had been sitting behind his wheel.

"Finley has my weapon!"

As half-truths went, that one was pretty good. But before Carrington could fall for whatever Keenan had in mind, the whole building shuddered as the patrol car and its wail of a siren rocked the mouth of the garage. Carrington yelled back at the cops. Hearing him felt like the same thing as talking and giving away my movement to Keenan, so I tuned him out and inched another bit toward the back of the car. Whatever Carrington yelled had the cops slamming their doors and echoing more feet on the ground.

"We have other officers here, Captain. Don't do anything stupid."

But I knew Keenan was going to do something stupid. He wasn't the steel-eyed embalmer from his office and he wasn't the self-righteous zealot from his protest marches. He was a colossal ego in pieces, and the pieces were all over the bodies of Robby and McNair. He hadn't shot them, but he had lost them as finally as if he had.

I heard a click. I had heard it often enough when I had checked the chambers of my .38. The soles of his shoes drew up out of my line of vision.

"Keep your eyes on Carrington, officers! He's IAB! You know what rats are! They want their trophies!"

I couldn't see the cops, but I could feel their hesitation with Keenan's cry. In their place I would have hesitated, too. Captains were captains, rats were rats, and the twain wasn't supposed to meet.

"There's another gun back here, guys! Right behind me! Keep your eyes open when I stand up!"

Who needed another decision crisis? I didn't. But I also couldn't go on being a question mark for the two patrolmen. Not even Carrington talked faster than a bullet, and I wouldn't have been around to reassure Officer Whozit that, given the circumstances, it had been a good shooting so he didn't have to worry about a blotch on his record.

"Who else is back there?"

The cop sounded like he was 15, and that wasn't in the plus column. But Carrington tried. "It's all right! He's with me! Stop worrying about him and pay attention to Captain Keenan!"

"I need more than that, sir. I need everybody to walk into the center of the garage with their hands raised."

"Don't screw it up, kid. I have a warrant for Keenan's arrest."

That was news to me, and probably to Keenan. It might have even been true. But the bulletin didn't figure to make Keenan more reasonable.

"The person behind the Lexus—call out!"

The second cop sounded like he was 12. I would have loved to do what he said, but I still hadn't heard Keenan dropping my .38 and I was too close to him to tempt him to make me the object of his stupidity. It wasn't a good sign that I chose that moment to remember something my father had always said when told bad news. "What a revoltin' development this is!" he had said, mimicking William Bendix from the old TV show *The Life of Riley*. I could have picked a better time for feeling so ancestral.

"You better listen, Finley."

Keenan's voice came from the far side of the Lexus. At least that gave me ducking room if he swung around on me when I stood up. What it didn't solve was what to do with his Glock. Just lay it on the ground? Did I trust Carrington and the cops to protect me from being killed by my own gun? There was an odor to that I didn't like.

"It's all right, Finley," Carrington called. "I have my eye on Keenan. Stand up and show the officers where you are."

It wasn't the moment to be thinking about my father's favorite TV shows and it wasn't the moment, either, to be second-guessing Carrington's commitment to truth, justice, and Paul Finley. But there it was anyway. His greatest inspiration since we had met had been to have me walk around with a target on my back. That wasn't exactly a qualification for full trust.

"You're right, Finley," Keenan snickered. "I'd think twice about it, too. He's got to get me for something. It may as well be you."

Who was the ventriloquist—me for putting into Keenan's mouth what had been rolling around in the back of my mind or Keenan for putting the idea into my sawdust of a brain?

"We're waiting," the 15-year-old called.

Down to it, there was only one choice: telling Keenan my position. "You first, Captain."

I used what was left of my left arm to brace the Glock toward the spot where Keenan would have to show himself if he was more interested in me than in Carrington. I had always thought Glocks were a bad idea for the NYPD, and now I had another reason to write my city councilman: The damn thing swayed too much, wasn't made for one-hand control.

"Your funeral, Finley."

"Maybe. But you stand up first."

I heard a shoe scrape. Then I saw the back of a shoulder and a right arm raised. "I'm standing up, officers! Get Carrington and this one behind me to do the same!"

There was a silence, then the 15-year-old: "You in the back, do what he says. And you too, sir."

Give the kids credit: They weren't just doing it by the book, they had mastered the supplement insert updates. And as long as I had Keenan's back to me, there was no reason not to obey. I started to put the Glock on the ground when the 12-year-old apparently saw something he didn't like about how Carrington emerged from his hiding place. "Please holster that weapon, Detective. And now."

I held on to the Glock for a second, then two seconds, then three seconds. Finally, the 12-year-old was satisfied with Carrington. "Thank you, sir. Now please go out there on the floor."

There was a ceiling mirror halfway over to the other lateral wall. My eyes weren't good enough anymore for reading all the copyright seal lettering at the end of movies, but they were good enough to see that Keenan did have both his hands raised and that he was watching Carrington walking slowly toward him. Carrington's hands were at his side, but the patrolmen didn't appear to mind. One of them was a fat kid near a garage post. I couldn't see the other one, but assumed he was closer to the booth.

"You behind the car—you too, sir."

I told myself that made for a wash: shot in the arm, but a respectful *sir* in exchange. "Coming! I'm leaving my weapon on the ground here."

I had the purest of intentions as I watched Carrington in the mirror advancing slowly to within 10 feet of Keenan and then stopping. For somebody with two police guns trained on his back, he looked almost blissful. Lions couldn't have approached antelopes more hungrily.

"You behind the Lexus—hurry it up!"

"Gun!"

The shout came from all the wrong people. It was too close to have come from the patrolmen. Carrington hadn't moved his arms an inch from his sides. The only movement was from the worst place—Keenan suddenly dropping his right arm and reaching around to his belt in the back. He hadn't been checking the chambers of the .38 for nothing.

"Keenan, don't!"

But I didn't exist for him, only Carrington did. Their obsession with one another was a two-way street. I told myself to leave it at that, to let the cops handle it. But the Glock was already in my hand, and I was the only one with a clear shot, without Carrington in the way. I fired once, but the goddamn trigger didn't like going off only once. Keenan's yellow shirt burst into red splotches. He almost managed to complete a turn back to me before he ended his jig and dropped my gun. Almost, but not quite. Whatever my style was, it *did* include shooting people in the back.

CHAPTER 66

From what sank in, Carrington had saved me from joining Keenan in the hereafter by jumping between the cops and the Lexus. I wasn't awake for the negotiations. When I opened my eyes again, I was sitting on the garage floor against the car wheel. The dull ringing in my ears made me glad I wasn't on my feet. Carrington was tying off a handkerchief around my arm. One of the cops—the fat 15-year-old without a hat—was down on one knee examining McNair; he had a collection of weapons, including mine and Keenan's, on the ground around him. McNair was moaning. Behind the 15-year-old Keenan's shoes lay still. The other cop was at the garage entrance shouting for people to keep back. There was a background buzz in the street, and a woman was yelling to an Ernesto to come see what there was for seeing. Someone was playing salsa on a boom box. We had apparently drawn more of a crowd than the Holy Rollers and the Strikers had.

"I conk out?"

"For almost five minutes," Carrington said, looking satisfied with his tourniquet. "You lost some blood."

My pants and the floor around me said the *some* could have supplied the Red Cross for months. Which brought back firing Keenan's Glock and watching him go down. Who would have imagined Mrs. Finley's little boy ever capable of shooting somebody in the back? Obviously, I still had plenty to learn about the Paul Finley style.

"I owe you one, Finley. He didn't care how many guns were on him. He was past it."

"Suicide by cop?"

"More along the lines of murder-suicide. And you not being a cop, that doesn't exactly fit, either."

It was supposed to be witty. I wasn't up for witty. There were more sirens coming. I hoped one of them was the EMS. The hand-kerchief might have helped against the bleeding, but my arm felt petrified into a hard island of pain. "But you got what you wanted."

"I didn't want this." He looked earnest, but also seemed to have popped a few more bright freckles. "Robinson was about to blow. I didn't think I had much choice."

I thought I saw a skeptical look from the cop over McNair, but he hadn't been there when Carrington had shot Robinson, so how would he have known one way or the other? I was the only one still alive who would have known, and I didn't know what I knew. "But why are you here at all, Billy?" it occurred to me. "You a big bowling guy?"

He glanced over at the cop. "I think he'll be all right. He's got his personality back, anyway."

The cop didn't know what he was talking about, and didn't pretend to. Like 99.99999 percent of the NYPD, he wasn't used to seeing two dead cops and a third one in bad shape stretched out on the ground. "You're not answering me, Billy."

"I figured you might be attracted by the chance to get them together out in public," he shrugged. "I guess it's a good thing I did, huh?"

I had an uneasy memory—of being back in the Green Fox with Cynthia and Sergeant Silva. I had made my peace with Jerry Christman's envelope and my part in it, hadn't intended doing much more about it except to rack it up to an ugly learning expe-rience that had done nothing for my self-esteem, self-regard, and all the other selfs. But then Belinda had called to report the shot through the Professor's window. That telephone call had been the start of the overtime that had broken the Carrington-Keenan tie.

"So what you're saying is, all that stuff about getting me to call Keenan to yank his tail wasn't really the agenda. You weren't counting on them coming after me, you were counting on me going after them."

Were liars capable of grace? They might have been, but Carrington wasn't in that section of the club. "Does that matter now?"

"Oh, yeah. Those bodies say it does."

Another shrug. But he didn't move out of his squat in front of me because he didn't want to have our conversation picked up by the cop. "I thought we had a real shot when you came up with that exercise mat thing. But how many times can you bang your head against a wall?"

"I don't know, Officer. How many?"

"You know what I mean. And you know we are what we are. Some of us have short fuses, some of us have longer ones. What counts in the end is the rubble we clear out."

Rubble didn't sound right. Shitheads and scum, maybe, but not rubble. It seemed like an important difference. "But how could you be sure of me, Billy? How could you be sure I'd be the short fuse you needed?"

He sighed into the floor space between his thighs. Just another catcher of life having to deal with his daily foul tips. "Let's not pretend you don't have a reputation."

The same boil that had risen under my skin in the Professor's bedroom started cresting. "Yeah, let's pretend." He didn't want to. "By shooting through the window of somebody I know—that what made you sure?"

"You feel played. I know. I appreciate that."

"Another question you're not answering. That's the way it's done, Billy. One guy wants to know what the second one can tell him. And the second guy doesn't bullshit, he just says what he knows. Were you the one who shot into my father-in-law's bedroom?"

I'd done it myself a million times: that grow-up-it's-an-adult-world smile, no need for anyone to be surprised, let alone excited. But there was a reason to get excited. More than one. Three of them were spread around the floor of a Jackson Heights garage, a fourth one was tied around my arm with a handkerchief, a fifth one was probably pulling at the balloons of an old man's heart out in Garden City. And all of that was supposed to be explained by the sophisticated weariness crouched in front of me. It was the final score that counted, not how it was gotten, right?

Wrong.

Even my left arm was up for delegating the little it had left to my right hand. I hit him so square in the mouth that he toppled backwards off his haunches like a hundred Phil McNairs having a slug jammed between their front teeth. My penalty was not enjoying it for more than a second before all the anger retreated from my hand and went back into my left arm. I was already blinking out again from the hot throbbing as the cop jumped up from where he was to come toward us. I wished I could see Carrington's face before my eyes closed. Jimmy Fantone had seen mine when he had knocked me down. Gwendolyn Cutter had seen it before she had hurried off to the elevator. Wasn't I entitled to as good a look at my handiwork as they had been? It was unfair I wasn't.

CHAPTER 67

I borrowed my body over the next few days. It was there for the aching and stiffness in my arm when I needed it, but otherwise felt extra, like a loan I hadn't asked for but was reluctant to return just in case. My mind might as well have been a rental, too. After the parade of detectives from the Jackson Heights 115 Pct., the Commissioner's office, and the IAB, the questions lost any chance of surprising me and my answers slipped into auto-pilot. When the second wave headed by an assistant district attorney splashed ashore, I couldn't disagree with her that I wasn't taking my situation as seriously as I should have, if only because I wasn't sure what my situation was. She wasn't big on explanations, and I didn't miss them all that much. Besides, McNair had survived long enough to tell her and all the cops before her what they hadn't wanted to hear.

Although they overlooked Edward Cassidy and the Columbia Diner, and didn't always serve up what they had in the right contexts, the media brought home most of the details. IAB and Carrington came out as the stars for their investigation into the circumstances around the death of Connie Marchese and its relationship to years-long links between Keenan and the Fantones. Ellen and Major Cases drew second place as crucial partners in the investigation, this supposedly illustrating how separate police forces could work together without turf jealousies. The Commissioner admitted what he called "a black eye" for the NYPD, but hoped he didn't have to stress that the Keenans and their breed remained the exception rather than rule to city policing. Marcello Fantone was indicted for a data bank's worth of extortion felonies, but nobody was expecting him to last to a trial. Jimmy Fantone was named as a co-conspirator, to be tried at some future date after his lawyers had run out of delaying motions and his father out of dates; in the meantime, Junior was also booked on various dealing and facilitation counts that had gone officially unnoticed for years.

There were a couple of glancing blows to the Faith Revival Movement, but aside from the transfer of the Reverend Bernard Tully to a Vermont parish, they didn't amount to much, and certainly didn't prevent more demonstrations in front of medical buildings and the usual letters to *Newsday* warning that Jesus and George Washington were running out of patience. Radio demagogues and other right-wing icons appeared at rallies to de-nounce those who wanted to identify the Movement and its goals strictly with Patrick Keenan and Marcello Fantone, this repre-senting the latest evidence that secular, liberal evil would stop at nothing to fulfill its designs. Roger Ware ducked his head within both the Movement and the prosecutor's office and began to spe-cialize in cases that were reported in the press only after a verdict had been reached. About the only one putting up a sustained objection to all the political accommodations was Alan Crosby, at least until he was detoured by a bigger scandal involving the county supervisor's office and the governor's mansion in Albany.

Me? I was the ex-Major Cases cop who had lost my good buddy Connie Marchese, had never believed he was a suicide, and while conducting my own *pro bono* investigation, had ended up in the wrong place at the wrong time. At least the *pro bono* part was right. For a while, Crosby dedicated himself to analyzing the chinks in that version of things, but I kept him at wincing arm's distance until he was called away to his upstate priorities. I have little reason to think that's the end of it. Knowing Crosby, I wouldn't be surprised to open *Newsday* three years from now to see that he had painstakingly assembled the evidence to put the lie to the little story concocted by the powers-that-be about me. Too many people knew exactly how I had been involved, and that was without counting the friends of friends of the various stenographers in front of whom I had to relate the story. (Of course, for those never losing faith in deception, there were the scores of people who had known about Edward Cassidy's survival for years, and that had never reached public ears.)

One benefit from my haze was that it pretty much numbed me against other unpleasant events. When one of the Buona Italia partners called to say the restaurant was severing its defense from me in the Bobby Sprowl lawsuit and working out a separate settlement "in light of what happened this week," I barely worked up a laugh for my assumption that things had been heading that way anyway, garage shooting or no garage shooting. On the contrary, I could see the man's point. Why be coupled with a violence-prone private eye in front of a jury that couldn't wait to dispense millions to worthies like Bobby Sprowl and Martin Nesbitt? In Buona Italia's place, I would have severed ties with me, too. It also made sense for two of my insurance company clients to suggest I lower my profile before we discussed further assignments. I hadn't realized my profile was that high, but you could never get overconfident that a housewife dragging her bundles home from the supermarket wouldn't recognize you sitting behind the wheel on a stakeout of a Brownsville slumlord. Besides, there were compensations. The first time back in Sal Rini's luncheonette after the shooting, he broke with custom to nod to me as I passed him at the register. Then when I went up to pay for my French toast and coffee, he crumpled up my check with a muttered "someone had to get those scumbags, might as well have been you."

I wasn't at all sure of that. The fact that it had been me seemed like the maneuvered within the random within the maneuvered. It wasn't just that I had been played by Carrington, it was the nagging thought that if not by Carrington in the Patrick Keenan mess, it would have been by somebody else in another mess. Before Carrington, there had been Jerry Christman and the report on Jennifer and Susan. The call from Buona Italia said the same thing, and maybe even the marriage affairs in the Gwendolyn Cutter family did, too. Cynthia could complain about having to stand behind her bar too long for too little satisfaction, but nobody was suing her or shooting at her or thinking so little of her that she was accused of watering down the drinks. There was only one possible ergo from that big difference: Finley Investigations had become a dead end of a saloon.

CHAPTER 68

The Professor liked himself for showing up at my front door toting groceries from Grand Union. For a change, I was the infirmed party and he was the Good Samaritan. He was so delighted with himself that he insisted on lighting the kettle for tea and sticking the cheese and yogurt he had brought into the refrigerator. You might have thought being shot at had restored the spring to his step.

"Maybe," he said, finally stopping all his bustling and sagging down at the kitchen table. "Sure as hell simpler than eating cinnamon buns to death. You were right about that. I promise—no more suicide by bakery."

"Good for Belinda."

"Whatever. And you? What lethal things you swearing off these days?"

"Garages in Queens."

"Good idea."

"And maybe this shit I call making a living.'

"Yeah, there's always a call for nuclear physicists."

"I'm serious, Joe."

"Sure you are. Know how many times I thought of quitting teaching because of all the political crap at the university?"

"Never."

He smiled. "Okay. Bad example."

I hated blunting his good humor; it had been so rare lately. But it was either talking to him or to Jeffrey Chalian. "I got used to having a glass jaw. But walking around begging somebody to punch it is something else."

"Jennifer and Susan." He said it so decisively it wasn't a point of discussion. "What, I'm suddenly an amoeba? Soon as you told me about all those Major Cases people coming back into your life, I knew you were going back down more than one old trail. The least I could expect was that you hadn't forgotten my daughter and granddaughter."

"I used them as an excuse."

The admission was supposed to have been worth more than one of his grunts. "And for the very first time, I'm sure. I'm old, Finley, I'm not senile. At least so Belinda says."

It was my cue to laugh or wink or just be nudged. But I was too off guard from his light tone even talking about Jennifer and Susan. If he was ever going to be ready to hear about the oldest report in Jerry Christman's pile, it was then. "It was more than that. I thought for a while there were questions about how Jenny and Susan died."

"What questions?"

"The accident report was thrown in with the rest of the stuff Christman sent me. It turned out just to be a red flag he was waving in my eyes."

He took in what I said with a gape over to the pots on the stove. He wasn't sure which one to drop it in. "You've got nice friends."

"I didn't see any reason to bother you with it."

"But you're bothering me with it now," he reared up. "Why? Another excuse for your professional blues?"

"Forget it."

"All I'm saying is thank you for not telling me before and no thank you for telling me now."

"Got it."

"I hope so."

"What the hell's that supposed to mean?"

So much for his good cheer, especially when he wasn't even up to crossing his right leg across his left knee. "Let me think. Oh, here's a possibility! How about you didn't tell me about this phony report because you really liked the idea of me stewing about being responsible for the accident? Could that be it? No, couldn't be! You're not that much of a *schmuk*."

"That wasn't in my mind."

"In, under, on top of. Wherever."

"One of these days we're going to have a conversation and finish it."

I was as disappointed as he was that the kettle wasn't blowing steam so one of us could go get it. "Why? So you can go on picking at the edges of your guilt and trying to get me to do the same? I don't need that anymore, Finley. Either do you. The teller's window is closed. We wrote bum checks, and it's too late to make a deposit to cover them. I guess we're just going to have to make the best of it."

"That has nothing to do with . . ."

"The lousy world of Finley Investigations? You're right. It doesn't. So don't try to connect them. Jenny didn't even know you were going to do what you've been doing. So don't blame her."

"Anybody ever tell you you have a bad superiority complex?"

He considered it seriously for a second. "You probably, but who listens to you? But better that than the alternative."

"You say so."

"I do," he said, staring through me and the sun coming through the kitchen window. "One thing these books on Iraq have had me thinking about is how we should never underestimate our national inferiority complex."

"I guess I've missed that."

"You just think you have. But look at all these certified imbeciles we elect to office, we listen to on the radio and television. Half of them don't know the world is round and are proud of it, but we put them up there on our marquees because we hope they'll cover up our own insecurities. Who needs reason or serious thought when all you have to do is keep lying and denying if you get squeezed into a corner? 'Hey, if they're our leaders, our cultural giants, how bad can *we* be?' The morons and the ravers let us feel better about ourselves." He remembered he was talking to me. "I use *we* in the papal sense, of course."

The kettle started to whistle. God bless.